MURDER

AT THE WHITE

PALACE

Also by Allison Montclair

The Right Sort of Man
A Royal Affair
A Rogue's Company
The Unkept Woman
The Lady from Burma

MURDER
AT THE WHITE
PALACE

ALLISON MONTCLAIR

MINOTAUR BOOKS
NEW YORK

First published in the United States by Minotaur Books, an imprint of St. Martin's Publishing Group

MURDER AT THE WHITE PALACE. Copyright © 2024 by Allison Montclair. All rights reserved. Printed in the United States of America. For information, address St. Martin's Publishing Group, 120 Broadway, New York, NY 10271.

www.minotaurbooks.com

Designed by Devan Norman

The Library of Congress Cataloging-in-Publication Data is available upon request.

ISBN 978-1-250-85421-6 (hardcover)
ISBN 978-1-250-85422-3 (ebook)

Our books may be purchased in bulk for promotional, educational, or business use. Please contact your local bookseller or the Macmillan Corporate and Premium Sales Department at 1-800-221-7945, extension 5442, or by email at MacmillanSpecialMarkets@macmillan.com.

First Edition: 2024

10 9 8 7 6 5 4 3 2 1

TO NAOMI BOTKIN AND ED HAZELL,

IN-LAWS ON EACH SIDE,

TWO LOVELY PEOPLE WHO WERE BRAVE ENOUGH

TO MARRY INTO OUR FAMILY

Excuse me laughing, but I know what's coming.

—ARTHUR ASKEY, 1937

MURDER

AT THE **WHITE**

PALACE

CHAPTER 1

"I've just had the most wonderful idea!" said Gwen.

"Have you?" replied Iris, who was looking back and forth between two index cards of possible candidates for Deirdre Currier, one of their more problematic ladies.

"We should throw a party!"

"What?"

"No, better yet—a ball! A New Year's Eve dance!"

Iris swivelled in her chair to face her partner.

"Are you mad?" she asked.

"Not since mid-November," said Gwen. "So sayeth the Court of Lunacy. I have an official judicial order to that effect, so I expect all of my ideas to be taken seriously from now on."

Mrs. Gwendolyn Bainbridge was indeed in possession of a court order from Assistant Master Cumber of the London Court of Lunacy declaring her to be no longer in need of supervision by the Crown, freeing her from the tethers of her legal guardians and her court-appointed committee and allowing her imagination to run free in promoting The Right Sort Marriage Bureau. Miss Iris Sparks, her co-proprietor, on the other hand, still had occasional misgivings over the quality of Gwen's inspirations since she had become untethered, although if being honest with herself (which

Iris rarely was), she might admit that her own stability might not necessarily pass muster if challenged in that selfsame court.

"A New Year's Eve dance?" repeated Iris. "Do you mean like a lonely hearts ball?"

"Oh, that sounds so negative," said Gwen. "We know they're lonely, they know they're lonely. That's why they've come to us. There's no need to rub salt in the wounds. Let's call it a hopeful hearts ball."

"For New Year's Eve, though? It's early December, and that doesn't leave us much time," Iris pointed out. "Have you any notion how to organise something like this?"

"I threw some smashing birthday parties back when I was in finishing school," said Gwen.

"When you were sixteen and there were maybe a couple of dozen other girls to deal with," said Iris. "We're talking about our entire clientele. That's nearly two hundred people if they all show up. We would have to locate a hall, order refreshments, line up a band, send out invitations—I don't think we could even get invitations with the current paper shortages."

"So we will call our clients," said Gwen. "One by one."

"You mean Mrs. Billington will call them," said Iris. "She'll be thrilled with the prospect. What will we charge them for this extravaganza?"

"We'll have to figure that out," said Gwen. "The first step is to find a suitable venue."

"There won't be any available this late," said Iris. "They'll all be booked."

"Hopeful heart, dear," said Gwen. "Pass me the telephone, would you?"

But Gwen's optimism proved to be unfounded. Call after fruitless call was made interspersed between interviews of new clients and the hard work of trying to match the hitherto unmatchable, many of whom were matchless for very good reasons.

Meanwhile, the rest of London was gearing up for the 1946 Christmas season, its first after a full year of peace. Throughout the world, the remaining postwar issues were limping towards conclusion. Borders, amorphous as ever, were negotiated and fixed by the victors over the defeated and the liberated. Terms of truces were settled and signed. The Americans and British combined their occupied zones in Germany while the Soviets held tightly on to theirs and the French straddled the invisible diplomatic fence between them. A delegation of leaders from the subcontinent flew via a series of hops to London to meet with British leaders, then flew back without accomplishing much. The Persians invaded Azerbaijan to the bewilderment of the Allied powers, which hadn't been paying close attention to that region. American coal miners decided not to go on strike before the New Year, enabling much-needed transportation of supplies to continue, and the steamer *Saxon Star* sailed into the Mersey from Canada with a shipment of more than forty-five million eggs—enough to provide one for everyone in the United Kingdom, assuming such scrupulously fair distribution could be accomplished.

But no clubs, church social halls, school gymnasiums, or other spaces of the right size were available, because of either prior booking, exorbitant price, or general unsuitability. The one possibility Gwen found was immediately vetoed by Iris.

"But why?" asked Gwen.

"It's going to be closed down," said Iris. "The police raided it for gambling recently, and they're going to have their license taken away any day now."

"They didn't mention that when I spoke with them," said Gwen.

"They were probably waiting for you to put down a nonrefundable deposit."

"How did you know about that, anyway?"

"I was dashing out the rear door with Archie when the police were coming through the front. Quite exciting, I must say."

"Why does this have to be so difficult?" complained Gwen in frustration. "I must have made fifty calls, and there is not one legitimate hall available."

"Legitimate," Iris repeated thoughtfully.

Gwen looked at her partner suspiciously.

"What are you thinking?" she asked.

"What if we found a place that wasn't specifically a hall designed for this purpose?" asked Iris.

"Like what?"

"Remember the warehouse we used where we gathered all the parties incognito for our presentation of our investigation for the royals?"

"Of course," said Gwen. "But you can't possibly be suggesting we use that. It was dirty, it had broken windows, no decent lighting, and I doubt that the lavs were in any state of working order, much less cleanliness, although I couldn't screw up my courage to try them. And we found it through Archie, which means it may be a storage house for who knows what contraband."

"But that might add to the fun, don't you think?" Iris persisted. "The very illicit nature of it, the sense of danger. Dancing close to someone you've just met in the dim light, waiting for the clock to tick down to midnight. Think how many couples we'll match!"

"I should like to see the place again to determine if it's feasible," said Gwen. "Especially the lavatory situation. That would be crucial on New Year's Eve if we get enough liquor supplied. Which, come to think of it, also may have to come through Archie. I never thought I'd say this, but you having a gangster for a boyfriend has been quite useful, hasn't it?"

"And we've barely scratched the surface of what he can do," said Iris.

"I don't think we'd want to dig any deeper than we already have," said Gwen.

"Be fair. We've dragged him into more shady situations than he has us," said Iris. "In any case, unless you have a better idea, I'm going to call him."

"I don't," said Gwen, passing her the telephone.

Iris dialled a number. It rang twice, then was answered.

"Eggy, is that you?" she asked. "It's Sparks. Congratulations on your sterling victory over Callahan. I told you he was slower going to the right. Is Archie about? Yes, I would, please. Thank you, Eggy."

"You must tell me how he got that name someday," said Gwen.

"It's a good story," said Iris. "He was once caught— Oh, Archie, hello! I hope I didn't interrupt anything important. Are you available for a consultation? How lovely! Mind if we come to the office? Yes, I'm bringing Gwen. See you soon."

She hung up.

"Right, let's tell Mrs. Billington," she said.

They fetched their coats, hats, and scarves, then turned off the lights and locked up the office. Mrs. Billington, their secretary and de facto receptionist, had the office next door, which had been theirs when the two of them started up The Right Sort six months before on a bob and a notion; but as the business grew, they found they both needed and, more importantly, could afford a staffer.

"Are you going out for the afternoon?" she asked as they appeared, pulling on their gloves.

"We are," said Gwen. "We might have a lead on a spot for the New Year's Eve party."

"Oh, good," said Mrs. Billington. "Where?"

"Can't tell you yet," said Iris. "We're off to see Mr. Spelling about it."

"Oh, dear," said Mrs. Billington. "Are you sure you want to get him involved in this? There are reputations to consider."

"Whatever reputation I had was torn to shreds years ago," said Iris.

"I was thinking of the firm's," said Mrs. Billington. "You always say you want to avoid scandal, yet somehow you keep finding your way into the newspapers."

"Those incidents were out of our control," said Gwen. "But at least the publicity proved favourable. We ended up getting more clients each time. Don't worry, Saundra. Visiting Archie is strictly about finding a party venue. We aren't joining the gang."

"But if we do, we'll put in a good word for you," Iris added mischievously. "Their recordkeeping is atrocious."

"I don't suppose they like things written down," said Mrs. Billington. "Some of the coppers can actually read, I hear. All right, get on with you. I'll close the shop at five. Have fun gangstering."

The two women walked down from the fourth storey, then turned left towards Oxford Street. The shops were cautiously festive this year, having retrieved from their cellars whatever Christmas decorations had survived the Blitz and years of storage. The previous Christmas had been one of relief, coming only three months after the end of the war, when the tolls of the dead and wounded were still being added up and the full extent of the horrors perpetuated by the Axis was being revealed. The winter and spring clothes currently displayed in the shop windows were still limited by rationing, but Gwen thought she detected a splash more colour now, a little more variety, even some daring, in the cut of the women's dresses.

A hopeful heart needs a nice new frock, she thought, mentally adding up her current stock of coupons.

Iris, who was a devout atheist, glumly attempted to ignore the annual holiday onslaught, and felt an actual sense of relief as they left the surface of the city and descended into the chaos of the Oxford Circus Underground.

It was a slow, arduous journey to Wapping, requiring several changes, the last being to the East London Railway, and it gave them time to talk.

"I never thought when we began this mad venture that we

would end up spending so much time with the criminal element," said Gwen.

"Much less dating them," said Iris with a grin.

"Speak for yourself," said Gwen. "Apart from the night we all went out dancing, I've kept my contacts with Archie and company strictly business. And even that's astonishing when I step back and look at it. I wonder how many women from my social circle have had similar experiences."

"I'm sure most of them have someone they go to on the black market," said Iris. "It's the way life is nowadays. It will eventually settle down into something less desperate."

"I hope so," said Gwen. "But look at us, Iris. It's the season of comfort and joy, we're on a mission to bring love to people, and we are once again resorting to paths many would consider immoral."

"Think of it as offering our immoral friends an opportunity to use their powers for good," suggested Iris.

"Ends justifying the means," said Gwen with a sigh. "Maybe we should join Archie's gang. We could get an employee discount on whatever he's going to charge us for the evening rental."

"If there is such a discount, I should be able to get one," said Iris.

"You don't belong to the gang," said Gwen. "You're merely dating the gang leader."

"Then I should get the moll's discount."

"Don't call yourself that."

"Why not?" asked Iris.

"It's demeaning."

"I am dating Archie Spelling, head of the Spelling gang," said Iris, "and it has never felt demeaning, not once. I would even go so far as to say it's been the best relationship I have ever had, and that covers a largish sample size."

"So he's finally moved ahead of Mike Kinsey in the rankings?"

Iris grimaced at the mention of her second ex-fiancé, now

married and a detective with the Homicide and Serious Crime Command.

"Archie doesn't judge me," she said. "He accepts me for who I am."

"He accepted you for who you were when you were pretending to be someone else," said Gwen.

"But he didn't shy away when he met the real me, and he's the only man ever to do that. Mike judged me and then moved on. He was right to do it—"

"You still haven't told me the full story about that."

"No, and I never will," said Iris. "I can't."

"One of those," said Gwen.

"Exactly," said Iris. "I loved Mike, and I will always care for him, but it wasn't meant to be. As long as we don't bump into each other on any more murder investigations, we should be able to live our separate lives just fine."

"Sounds like you've been working this out with Dr. Milford," said Gwen.

"The number one hit on the psychotherapy charts," said Iris. "How have you been doing with him?"

"Today marks my first full week without Veronal," said Gwen.

"Well done! How do you feel?"

"Like I want Veronal," said Gwen. "But I'm holding on, gradually unclenching my teeth."

"Call me whenever you feel the pangs getting strong."

"Thanks, I appreciate that," said Gwen.

"Was that what's been troubling you lately? You've seemed more on edge than normal."

"I don't think you've ever seen me normal," said Gwen. "But that wasn't it."

"What then?"

Gwen hesitated, then reached into her bag and pulled out an

envelope. In it was a short note. She handed it to Iris, who read it quickly, then glanced up at Gwen, eyebrows raised.

"Mr. Walter Prendergast has requested the signal honour of having you join him for dinner," she said.

"He has."

"Have you replied to his request?"

"I have. The terms of our first date have been negotiated and agreed upon."

"One of the more ominous descriptions I've ever heard," said Iris. "You knew this would happen, Gwen. He said after your hearing that he would wait a decent interval, then resume his— What was the word he used?"

"His quest," said Gwen. "It made me feel like I had been locked away in a high tower by an evil stepmother so he could gallop up on his gallant steed to rescue me."

"He did step up to help you in Lunacy Court," Iris pointed out.

"I know, I know," said Gwen. "And he's been kind and patient and understanding, even while knowing I had gone out with Sally despite my saying I wouldn't date while my court hearing was pending, and that says a lot. I have no precedent for what constitutes a decent interval after the object of your desire has been ruled sane, or at least sane enough to re-enter the market. I suppose a few weeks is enough time. In any case, I've already agreed, so that's that. Yet I'm nervous about him."

"May I offer a suggestion?"

"Of course."

"Your ability to read people could be ruinous now that you're dating again. Give Mr. Prendergast a chance or three. Men, at least the more worthwhile men, have more to them than what appears on a first date."

"I have met him four or five times before," Gwen pointed out.

"Yes, but not on a date," said Iris. "Men present themselves differently on a date. Allow yourself to get to know him better than you would if you went solely on your initial impression."

"I'll try," said Gwen. "Would it be all right with you if I reject him after the second date?"

"Open mind, darling," said Iris.

"Very well," said Gwen. "Oh, God, I'm going out to dinner with Walter Prendergast."

"And you will call the moment you get home and I'll debrief you and talk you out of the Veronal," said Iris. "And here's Wapping."

They got off the train and emerged back to the surface, blinking momentarily in the daylight.

"From the Underground to the underworld!" said Iris. "Let's go find some spivs!"

"Here we come a-gangstering, among the thieves so mean," Gwen sang.

"They aren't mean," Iris protested. "They've been nothing but decent to us."

"It was the only rhyme for 'green' I could come up with," said Gwen.

They walked past Merle's, the pub where they had first encountered the Spelling gang. Gwen glanced quickly at it, then away, her eyes growing misty for a moment.

"You still haven't called Des?" asked Iris, noticing her partner's expression.

"No point, is there?" replied Gwen. "There was never anything real there, and he's moved on."

"He could move back," said Iris.

"I've moved on," said Gwen.

"Of course," said Iris, unconvinced.

They took the dogleg on Garnet to Wapping Wall. Their destination was the third warehouse on the left past Monza Street. Iris walked up to a door marked "Office" and rang the bell. It opened a few seconds later, and a man peered out.

"Hello, Tony," said Iris.

"'Allo, Sparks," he replied. "I see you brought the Duchess today. 'Allo, Duchess."

"Hello, Tony," said Gwen. "It's good to see you again."

"We're expected," said Iris.

"You are," said Tony, opening the door with his left hand, the right sliding behind his back to secrete something the ladies preferred not to know about.

Both had been there before—Iris when she had first tried to infiltrate the gang and many times since, and Gwen when some kidnappers had left her bound and blindfolded in an alleyway for the gang to find her. Iris reached inside her bag, but Tony held his hand up.

"You don't need me to surrender my weapons?" she asked. "You always have before."

"You've been elevated to trusted status," said Tony, taking his seat behind his desk.

"Congratulations," said Gwen to her partner. "Is there some formal ceremony for this?"

"It just 'appened," said Tony, picking up his racing guide. "You know the way."

They walked through the warehouse—dodging forklifts and handcarts maneuvered by young men working their way up the black market hierarchy—until they reached the steel door that guarded Archie's headquarters. Archie himself opened it.

"Good afternoon, ladies," he said. "Welcome to my 'umble establishment."

The room was set up as a private club, with tables for drinks and cards and a small bar at the other end where a redhead named Peggy presided. Archie's associates, a collection of larcenous gents with a variety of shady skills, called out greetings as they saw the ladies. Several were gathered around a snooker table, where the current match was down to the last four colours. The players were

Reg, a fellow in his early fifties who was Archie's right hand, and a younger man whom Iris and Gwen didn't recognise. The younger man wore the spivviest outfit in the room, the chalk stripes on his charcoal-grey suit a quarter inch across, with a bright green tie wide enough to picnic on.

Reg was studying the table intently, pacing around it, bending frequently to put his line of sight just above the baize.

The young man yawned dramatically, drawing snickers from his mates.

"Listen, Gramps, I'm gonna nip out and run a few errands while you're thinking about life," he said. "I should be back before you've taken your shot."

"I'll take my shot when I'm good and ready," said Reg irritably.

"It's just that there's other fellas who'd like a game," continued the other. "Take your shot, then I'll get on with the process of relieving you of your money before I get on to theirs."

"Youth is wasted," muttered Reg. "Right."

He struck the cue ball, sending it into the brown ball across the table. It rolled across towards the side pocket, only to miss slightly to the left, causing it to bounce back and forth between the jaws before settling on the edge.

"All that time for that?" scoffed his opponent. "Let me take care of it for you."

Without hesitating, he potted the brown, drawing the cue ball back towards the blue. Then, swaggering around the table like a young cheetah, he quickly potted the remaining three balls.

"Pay up, old man," he said to Reg.

"Old!" said Reg, bristling. "Just because you beat a man at snooker don't give you the right to insult 'im."

"Reg, pay the bloke before you embarrass yourself any more," said Archie. "I need you in my office for a few minutes."

"Here," said Reg, handing the winner a fiver. "But there will be a rematch, mark my words."

"Yeah, looking forward to that, I'm sure," said his opponent. He spotted Gwen and Iris watching and his smile broadened. "Looking forward to a lot of things."

Archie's windowless office was in back of the bar. It contained a desk with a telephone, two chairs in front, a pair of green filing cabinets, and some folding chairs leaning against a wall. There was also a stack of wooden crates with Cyrillic letters stencilled on them by the opposite wall.

Iris and Gwen knew better than to ask about the crates. They sat on the chairs in front of the desk while Reg grabbed one of the folding chairs and set it up to the side.

"Sorry about the game," Gwen said to him. "Rather an obnoxious young man. One shouldn't make winning unpleasant."

Reg and Archie both chuckled.

"Don't you worry about me," said Reg. "I've got 'im right where I want 'im."

"Reg plays the long game," explained Archie. "Next time, 'e'll come at the lad all full of fury and wounded pride, and the bet will get very large."

"And I shall win," said Reg. "Quite 'andily."

"You were setting him up," marvelled Gwen. "I love it!"

"Glad to 'ear it," said Reg. "We'd 'ate to think you disapproved of our little shenanigans."

"One may disapprove while still enjoying them," said Gwen.

"Which is why you are allowed admittance to our gentlemen's club," said Archie. "Now, Sparks, what brings you 'ere in person? You mentioned a consultation. My areas of expertise don't extend to matchmaking."

"Ah, but even Cupid needs assistance once in a while," said Iris.

"What manner of assistance?"

"We want to throw a party," said Gwen. "A largish party with drinks and dancing on New Year's Eve. And we've been having trouble finding a suitable space."

"We were wondering if that warehouse we commandeered on that business with the royals was available," said Iris. "You were able to get it on very short notice before."

Archie and Reg glanced at each other. Reg shook his head slightly.

"That one ain't available," said Archie.

"Oh, no," said Gwen. "Why not?"

"Well, first, it's in use," said Reg. "For other things."

"Ah," said Iris. "And second?"

"It ain't exactly ours," said Archie.

"It isn't?" exclaimed Gwen. "But you rented it to us for that evening."

"We charged you for it," said Archie. "Not quite the same thing."

"We were already paying you and your men," protested Gwen. "You mean we could have had the space for free?"

"You weren't paying with your own money," said Archie. "Why are you getting upset now?"

"That's quite illegal," said Gwen.

"The two of you were breaking laws right and left that week," said Reg. "What's one more among friends? Your Scotland Yard mate din't squawk about it."

"Well, in any case, that rules out that possibility," said Iris. "Do you know of any others?"

"As it 'appens, I might 'ave one available," said Archie. "A legitimate one, for a change."

"Really? Tell us."

"I own a couple of clubs," he said. "I've been looking to acquire a few more. They're doing good business now that the British lads are coming 'ome with cash in their pockets and the Americans and Canadians are 'aving their last flings with more cash in theirs. So I recently bought a place that got shuttered years ago after taking some bomb damage. The old owner died, and 'is widow didn't want to be bothered with fixing it up."

"Have you fixed it up?" asked Gwen.

"It's 'appening as we speak," said Archie.

"Will it be usable by New Year's Eve?"

"Don't know if it will be ready for inspection for public use by then," said Archie, "but this is a private party we're talking about, innit?"

"Sounds like one to me, Arch," said Reg.

"And it's my own private property, ain't it?"

"It sure is, Arch."

"So if I choose to 'ost a private party in my own private property, don't see that anyone 'as cause to squawk. Do you?"

"No squawking from this corner," said Reg.

"Could we see it?" asked Iris eagerly.

"I was planning on going over this afternoon to see 'ow things were coming along," said Archie. "If you got time, you can join me."

"We have time," said Gwen.

"I'll send Benny for a car," offered Reg.

"Then let's go 'ave a drink while we're waiting," said Archie.

"I'd love one," said Iris.

"Yes, please," said Gwen.

They adjourned to the bar while Reg went in search of Benny, Archie's preferred driver. The young sharp was racking the red balls and looking around for a match. He caught sight of them and grinned.

"Hey, beautiful," he called. "Fancy a game?"

Iris and Gwen glanced at each other.

"As one beauty to another, I'm not sure which one of us he's addressing," Gwen commented to Iris.

"He could mean Peggy," said Iris, as the barmaid handed them each a tumbler of whisky and soda.

"She is lovely," agreed Gwen.

"Let me narrow it down for you," said the sharp. "I'm speaking to Blondie."

"That would be you," said Iris.

"That isn't what I prefer to be called," said Gwen.

"Then tell me your name," said the sharp. "I know she's Sparks and she goes with the boss, so she's off-limits."

"Accurate," said Iris.

"But you got no ring," he continued. "So I figure you're available."

Iris glanced down at her partner's hand, concealing her surprise. She's taken it off, she thought. That's new.

"My name is Gwen," said her partner. "What do they call you?"

"They call me Mr. Sticks," he said, giving his cue a twirl. "On account of my prowess."

"We don't," said one of the other spivs.

"But you can call me River," he continued, ignoring him. "It's a nickname. You see, it's a play on—"

"The River Styx," said Gwen. "Yes, I get it. But a game between you and me would hardly be sporting, would it? I saw what you did to poor old Reg. And I don't have much time."

"A quick game, then," he proposed. "Ten minutes, and whoever's ahead wins. And I'll spot you ten points and the break."

"Is ten points a lot?" Gwen asked, looking around the room.

"I'd take it," offered a card player. "But I know what I'm doing with a cue stick."

"What would we be playing for?" she asked.

"I win, you go out with me," said River.

The chatter in the room ceased. Half the men looked at her for her reaction. The other half looked at Archie, who merely sipped his drink, watching.

"I suspected that might be what you were after," she said. "And if I win?"

"Won't happen," he said. "Bit of fun now gets you a date with me later, which will be more fun, I guarantee it."

"But if there's no bet from you, where's my incentive to play?" asked Gwen.

"All right," he said, considering. "Just for giggles, two pounds if I lose."

Gwen looked at him, her expression darkening.

"Do you mean to say that you consider a date with me to be the equivalent of two pounds?" she asked. "I'm insulted. You may be a wizard with a stick, River, but you don't play in my league when it comes to dating."

"I suppose you got some millionaire waiting in a Rolls outside," he said.

"The millionaire is taking me to dinner Friday," she said. "Tell you what—that diamond stickpin keeping your tie out of your soup. We'll play for that."

"This?" he said, his hand going to it. "This is my lucky tiepin."

"Perfect," she said. "Your luck against a date with me. And I get ten points and the break."

He hesitated. She could see it. Then quick as a flash, he grinned and pointed to the cue sticks in their holder on the wall.

"Lady's choice," he said, making a sweeping gesture with his free arm.

She selected one, examined it, then replaced it and took another.

"This likes me well," she said, moving to the table.

She looked at the cue ball, then down the length of the table to the triangle of red balls.

"So if I pot one on the break, I have to go for one of the coloured balls?" she asked uncertainly.

"Right," he said.

"I should aim for the centre," she muttered to herself, sighting over the cue ball. "Bang away, Gwen."

But when she struck, the ball went on a diagonal, barely touching the right corner red, then ricocheting off four cushions in an angular figure eight, coming to a halt just behind the brown ball on the baulk line.

"Blast, I missed it rather badly, didn't I?" she said in chagrin.

"Actually, that ended up being a good shot," said River, looking at her curiously.

"Did it?" she replied in surprise. "Well, beginner's luck. All right, your turn."

He looked at the table, then sent the cue ball careening around the table until it softly struck the pack from the bottom, barely causing the balls to shift before bouncing back an inch. The spivs in the room shifted their focus to Gwen as she stared at the table. The corner ball she had struck on the break was separated from its fellows.

"It's all about geometry, isn't it?" she said brightly. "Let's see if this works."

She struck the cue ball soundly. It collided with the corner ball that bounced off the side cushion and made a beeline for the opposite corner pocket. It disappeared, while the cue ball came back at an angle, rolling past the black ball below the pack.

"Oh, good—it did work," she said. "So I get to knock in a colour now?"

"You do," said River.

She sent the black into the other corner pocket, then slid the counters across the string as the cue ball bounced into the pack, dislodging a few more of the reds.

"That's eight for me," she said, replacing the black on its spot. "And this will be nine."

Another red ball slowly made its way to the right corner, paused as if considering its fate, then slowly toppled in. She picked off the pink, and the cue ball rocketed into the remainder of the pack, scattering it.

"Nice break," commented River, replacing the pink for her.

"Thank you," said Gwen.

She sent the cue ball into a small cluster of reds. One bounced off the side of another and dropped into the corner pocket.

"And you got a fluke into the bargain," said River.

"That was no fluke," Archie said to Iris.

"No, it wasn't," agreed Gwen, chalking her cue. "Neither is this. Pink in the right side."

She knocked it in.

"You've done this before," said River.

"We had a snooker table in our game room," she said, pocketing another red. "I was quite obsessed with it growing up. Black, corner pocket."

"No way you make it to fifty on one break."

"Care to make a side bet on that?" she asked. "Say, a second date against whatever you have in your wallet right now?"

She used the bridge to send the cue ball down to the corner to pot another red.

"No, I don't think I will," he said, bemused.

"One year, for Christmas, Daddy gave me lessons with a private tutor," she continued. "Have I done the blue yet? Let's try the side pocket. He was very good. He would take the train out from London to our estate every Wednesday. I learned a lot from him."

"And what might his name be?" asked River as she kept the break going with a red and the black for eight more points.

"I used to call him Uncle Joe," she said.

She potted one more red, putting enough English on the cue ball to send it spinning back to the black.

"You would know him as Joe Davis," she said, punctuating the finish of the story by knocking it into a corner pocket. "And that's ten minutes. Sorry you didn't get a turn, Mr. Sticks, but I have errands to run."

He looked down at his stickpin, then detached it from his tie.

"Well played, Gwen," he said mournfully, handing it to her. "Both the game and me."

She held it up to her eyes and twirled it around, watching it sparkle, then put it to her lips and gave it a quick kiss.

"Here," she said, handing it back to him. "I would never dream of taking a man's luck from him."

"The car's here, boss," said Reg from the door.

"Besides, I don't even own a tie," said Gwen. "Thanks for the game, Mr. Sticks. Good seeing you, gentlemen. Have a lovely day."

Benny was waiting outside with the car, a dark green Sunbeam-Talbot Ten sports saloon. He held the door open for Iris and Gwen, then went around to the other side to let Archie sit in back next to Iris. Reg got in the front passenger seat, and off they went.

"Just out of curiosity, what would you have done if you lost?" Archie asked Gwen.

"I would have gone out with him, of course," said Gwen. "A bet's a bet. I hope I didn't queer your game, Reg."

"Naw, you made it better," said Reg. "'E's gonna want to get back at someone now, and since it ain't likely to be a repeat performance with you, I'll do very nicely for 'im."

"Where are we going?" asked Iris.

"Mile End," said Archie. "That area's gonna be doing all right. They finished expanding the Tube station last week. The club's only two minutes' walk from the station, so it's easy to get to."

Benny took them north until he hit Mile End Road, then took a right.

"I wanted to ask you, Sparks," said Archie, "what I should bring for dinner with your mum? A good bottle of wine?"

"She's a teetotaller," said Iris. "She felt she needed to balance out my father's alcohol consumption."

"Candy, maybe?"

"That depends," said Iris. "Is this a bribe or a peace offering?"

"Your boyfriend is meeting your mum for the first time. It's both. You know 'er, I don't. What's 'er secret craving that I could indulge?"

"Ah, that I can answer," said Iris. "Cheese. Really good cheese."

"Reg, we got a cheese guy?" asked Archie.

"We got two," said Reg from the front. "French or English?"

"French?" asked Archie.

Iris nodded.

"Tell 'im to pick out a slab of something to make someone's mum 'appy," said Archie.

"Got it, boss," said Reg.

"Dinner with Iris's mum, then showing up together at Archie's nephew's wedding," commented Gwen. "It's wonderful seeing you transform into a respectable couple."

"I doubt anyone will ever call us that," said Iris, snuggling into Archie as he put his arm around her. "But I agree. Dropping the secrecy has been a weight off my shoulders. Or will be once I survive dinner with Mum. If I survive dinner with Mum."

"Does she know who Archie is and what he does?"

"She already knew who he was and that I was dating him when I suggested dinner," said Iris.

"Did she?" said Archie in surprise. "I din't know that."

"Mother knows all, Mother sees all," intoned Iris.

"And 'ow did she take to the idea of us?"

"Have you ever seen frost come through a telephone?"

"Doesn't sound too promising, Arch," said Reg.

"Yeah," said Archie. "Better make it two slabs of cheese."

They crossed the canal, passing through an industrial area, mostly ruins from the bombing.

"I thought you said this area was all right," said Gwen, looking at it sorrowfully.

"I said it was gonna be all right," said Archie. "Fixing up the station's the first step. Everything else will follow."

"They're going to rebuild the factories?" asked Iris.

"Dunno," said Archie. "Hope not. They were grinding people

down before the war. I'd like to see them put a park in 'ere. Kids need a place to run around."

Benny turned right on Burdett Road, then left on Hamlets Way.

"This seems a little out of the way," commented Gwen.

"Nah, it's right off Mile End," said Benny as he made a series of turns. "But we're coming up the back way because of all the one-way streets. It's right behind the Three Wise Men."

"I take it that's a pub," she said.

"Right," said Archie. "Useter be one of me dad's regular watering 'oles, wasn't it, Reg?"

"Oh, yeah," said Reg, laughing. "Your dad would 'old forth long past closing, 'im and 'is mates, and if anyone said otherwise, 'e'd counter with 'is fists. Saw some beauties of a brawl back then."

"And 'e'd come 'ome and tell us all about 'em," said Archie. "Showed me what 'e did, and taught me 'ow to do the same."

"Your dad never lost a fight," said Reg.

"Until that last one," said Archie. "Right, park the car in back of that lorry."

They got out on Maplin Street. The club had seen better days, and the south end showed the damage left from a heavy explosive hitting a few buildings down. A group of workmen were busy tearing down the damaged wall, while a young man trundled a wheelbarrow filled with broken masonry out of the front entrance.

"Hey, boss!" he shouted to them, waving. "You bringing us some birds for tea?"

"Potential customers," said Archie. "Everyone better be on 'is best behaviour."

"How long will that take to complete?" asked Iris, examining the repair work critically.

"End of next week for that bit," said Archie. "The holdup was getting in the lumber."

"But we got a lumber guy," added Reg.

"Where would people park if they're driving?" asked Gwen.

"There's a couple of garages by Tredegar Square on the other side of Mile End," said Reg. "They're safe. We own 'em. We use 'em for—anyway, we own 'em."

They paused in front of the entrance. A sign overhead, badly cracked and in need of fresh paint, proclaimed it as the "White Palace." Underneath in smaller letters, it read: "Dancing, drinking, and fine dining."

"It wasn't such fine dining," said Archie.

"But the dancing was good," remembered Benny. "They 'ad Teddy Foster and 'is Kings of Swing for a month back in thirty-six. I was twenty-two and came 'ere with a different girl every night. Best month of my life."

"I remember you being quite the dancer, Benny," said Gwen.

"You shoulda seen me then," said Benny. "You ever come 'ere, Reg?"

"Nah, I was usually playing snooker over at Brooke's, or at the Regal when it started up," said Reg. "Then I'd come to the Three Wise Men to get some liquid wisdom after, and that was as close as I got."

Archie held the door open.

"Watch where you step," he advised. "There's apt to be some loose boards and nails about."

They walked into the foyer.

"So the coat and 'at check is over there," said Archie, pointing. "You check in with the maître d' and 'e takes you through the curtains, only there ain't any curtains yet. And 'ere it is."

They went through and looked around. They were at the centre of a vast room, spreading some sixty feet to either side and forty feet deep. Even though it had been shuttered for six years and was lit only by work lights plugged into the baseboards, they could sense the grandness that had once existed there. There was a small stage across from them that could accommodate a decent-sized band, with an old rosewood Chappell baby grand piano on the left. There was a parquet dance floor directly in front of the stage, a few of the tiles pitted from shrapnel. Workmen were busy stripping the dark green wallpaper, which was streaked and torn.

"We're gonna paint when that's done," explained Archie. "Can't get new wallpaper right now with the rationing."

"You don't have a wallpaper guy?" asked Iris.

"No, but we got a paint guy," said Reg.

Gwen ascended the four steps to the stage and ran her fingers across the piano keys. The sounds that came forth were strong, albeit badly in need of tuning.

"Play something," said Benny.

She hesitated, then slowly began to play Chopin's Nocturne in E Minor, bringing quick howls of displeasure from the trio of spivs.

"Christ, that's lugubrious," said Archie. "Give us something we can dance to."

She thought for a moment, then started playing "When I'm With You," a foxtrot she had danced to with Ronnie when they had started dating.

"Care to take a turn around the floor?" Archie asked Iris.

"Only if you give Benny and Reg a chance, too," she said.

"Done," he said, taking her into his arms.

Despite his rough manners, Archie was an excellent dancer. He took her expertly through one circuit around the perimeter, then passed her to Reg, who was more careful and stiff in his approach. Then Benny swept in and whirled her through some combinations that would have been competitive at Blackpool. By the time he was done, she was laughing and out of breath. Gwen brought the tune home with a flourish.

"She plays snooker and the piano," said Reg as they applauded. "She's the perfect woman, as far as I'm concerned."

"Thank you, kind people," said Gwen as she came back down to the floor. "That piano will need to be tuned, maybe more than once. Now, the acid test. Where are the lavatories?"

"Downstairs," said Archie, pointing. "There's work going on, so it's lit well enough."

"I'm going to check out the kitchen," said Iris.

"Right, I'll meet you back here," said Gwen, heading for the door.

Downstairs, she found a long hallway with storage lockers and dressing rooms on either side. One held a long counter below what must have been a mirror, based on the shards still clinging to the edges of the splintered wooden frame.

They must have had dancers, she thought, as she wandered through. Where are the showgirls of yesteryear?

She found the ladies' lavatory and went in with trepidation. It was old, but it had been cleaned up recently, she was happy to see. She ran the taps. They creaked from long disuse, and the water that came through was rusty at first, but it eventually ran clear. The hot water hadn't been hooked up yet, she noticed. She added that to her list. The toilets all flushed, at least.

She assumed that the men's lavatory would be in better shape, given the needs of the workmen, and she was loathe to inspect it unaccompanied.

She heard a loud, heavy thudding noise from farther off. It was from the end of the basement under the side that had received the bomb damage. Curious, she wandered in that direction.

There was a section of wall there that had more recent brick-work than the rest of the cellar. Whatever explosions had levelled the houses farther down the street had caused a partial collapse of the wall, and a man was attacking the rest of it with a sledgeham-mer. She saw him from the rear, his shirt thrown over a nearby sawhorse, sweat pouring down his back as he repeatedly swung, his muscles rippling.

He heard her footsteps and stopped, turning towards her. Then he froze, an expression of surprise on his face.

Which matched the one on hers as her mind immediately summoned up the last time they were together, standing on the banks of the Thames as the sun set past the Tower Bridge.

If it wasn't for Ronnie, I would be saying yes to the next date, Des.

You almost sound like you mean it.

If you knew me better, you would have no doubt of it.

"Des," she said, trying not to stammer. "Des Burton. I didn't know you were working here."

"You din't?" he said. "Then what are you doing 'ere?"

"Iris and I were checking the place out," she said. "For a party."

"Was I invited?" he asked, grabbing a cloth and wiping himself off. "Sorry I wasn't dressed for it."

He grabbed his shirt and threw it on.

"Forgive me," he said, buttoning it hastily. "I wasn't expecting company. Shall I serve tea, milady?"

"I thought you'd never work for Archie," she said.

"Work's been slow at the shop," he said. "So when I 'ad a chance to pick up a little extra, I grabbed it. The work 'ere is 'onest compared to most. I'm saving up for—"

He stopped abruptly.

"For your wedding," she finished. "I heard you got engaged. Congratulations. I'm happy for you."

"Are you?" he asked. "Then I'm glad I did it. 'Ow'd you know?"

"Archie," she said. "He mentioned it somewhere along the line."

"So you're in tight with 'im now," said Des.

"Iris, my partner, is his girlfriend," said Gwen.

"Is that right? That's an odd coupling."

"On the surface," said Gwen. "But it seems to be working, despite their differences. You never know with people."

And who are you really talking about, Gwen? she thought.

"So what will this section be when you're done destroying it?" she asked, trying to change the subject.

"Dunno yet," he said. "Right now, I'm just clearing out the old wall and the rubble and seeing 'ow bad the damage is below the surface. Then I'll shore it up, maybe turn it into storage. 'E likes to have storage, does Arch. Never know what 'e's stashing away. I remember when we were in school as kids—"

"You knew each other as boys? I never knew that."

"Yeah, we were mates back then," said Des. "Until 'e lost his mum and dad. It was 'is uncle taking 'im in that got 'im into the game."

"But you didn't go that route."

"Nah, my uncle 'ad the carpentry shop, so I 'ad a trade waiting," said Des. "The ones around you when you're a kid make all the difference, don't they? But you know that better than me, I suppose."

"It's hard to escape your family," said Gwen.

"Why would someone like you even want to?" he said, picking up the sledgehammer.

"You'd be surprised," she said, coming over to peer at the half-destroyed wall. "Looks like there was a storage room in there before. No door to it?"

"It must have been destroyed in the wreckage," he said. "Maybe—look out!"

Before she knew it, the wall started to crumble and fall towards her. Des threw himself at her, wrapping an arm around her and yanking her away. They both fell to the ground as the bricks collapsed, bringing down plaster from the ceiling above, dust and debris shooting into the air all around them.

She lay on the ground, coughing violently, rubbing her eyes

with her sleeve. It was only when the fit of coughing eased that she realised he had his body pressed against hers, his arm still around her.

It might have been a pleasant distraction had she not seen the desiccated hand protruding from the pile of bricks that had just missed killing her.

CHAPTER 2

"A re you all right?" asked Des, getting to his feet, then helping her up.

"I am," said Gwen. "He's not."

He turned and looked where she was pointing.

"Jesus," he said, kneeling by it.

He felt the hand, then removed a few of the bricks covering it. The fraying shreds of a jacket cuff, possibly black once, extended over a bony wrist. The hand itself was discoloured, the skin torn, though whether that happened before or after death, Gwen couldn't say. There was a ring on the fourth finger, engraved with some military insignia she didn't recognise.

"Looks like 'e's been 'ere awhile," said Des. "Must've got buried in the bombing, and no one bothered to dig this place out until now."

"How terrible," said Gwen. "I hope he died immediately, for his sake."

"Yeah," said Des.

He looked at Gwen.

"You look a right mess," he said. "You should get yourself cleaned up before the coppers come in."

"The police? Do you think he was—"

"Oi!" shouted Archie from somewhere down the other end of the hallway. "What was all that noise about?"

"You'd better come take a butcher's, Arch," Des called. "You're not gonna like it."

Archie, with Iris, Reg, and Benny in tow, came up, then stopped short, seeing the two of them still covered in dust and plaster.

"What the 'ell were you two doing?" he asked. "Gwen decide she wanted to take a swing with the 'ammer?"

"We found a body, Arch," said Des, pointing at the hand. "An old one, by the looks of it."

Archie squatted down to get a better look at it.

"Take a look, Reg," he said. "'Ow long do you think it's been there?"

"I dunno," said Reg, coming over to look. "I don't 'ang around people after they've kicked it."

"Let me see," said Iris eagerly.

"Sparks, you shouldn't," said Archie, but she moved quickly around him and bent down to feel the hand.

"Iris!" exclaimed Gwen in horror.

"Skin's dry," said Iris. "He's been down here long enough to be mummified. When did you say you bought this place?"

"About three months ago," said Archie.

"Then I'd say you're well in the clear," she said, straightening up.

"I guess we'd better call the police," he said.

"Are you sure, Archie?" asked Benny worriedly. "Do we really want them poking around our business?"

"What do you think we should do?"

"Dump it somewhere where no one will trace it back to us," said Benny.

"If we get caught doing that, we'll be in more trouble than if we do what's legal," said Archie.

And there are too many witnesses here, thought Gwen, glancing at Des.

"Are we sure it's a body?" asked Benny.

"Are you barmy?" asked Archie. "Look at it!"

"I mean, maybe it's just an arm," suggested Benny. "An arm's easy enough to get rid of."

"You want to give it a tug to see if it's attached to anyone?" asked Archie.

"Erm, no, I don't, actually," said Benny.

"Take the ladies upstairs, then go to the Three Wise Men and call the coppers from there," said Archie. "We'll remain with the remains."

"Shouldn't I take the ladies 'ome?" asked Benny.

"Nah, the coppers will probably want to ask Gwen some questions, given 'ow she's the one who found the bloke," said Archie. "Sorry, Gwen."

"It can't be helped," said Gwen. "Of course I'll stay."

"Look at the bright side," said Archie. "They'll 'ave to clear up those bricks for us. That'll save us some work."

"Save me some, you mean," said Des. "But I'm still getting paid."

"Sure you are," said Archie. "Even as we speak. So stick around to tell your story. Benny, get going."

"Come on, ladies," said Benny.

He took them upstairs to the main room, then left.

"Let me dust you off," said Iris, pulling out her handkerchief.

"Please," said Gwen, looking down at her suit. "This is not how I wish to present myself to the police."

"They've seen you looking worse," said Iris as she began removing what dust could come off easily.

"Poor fellow," said Gwen. "He must have been caught in the bombing, and no one ever knew what happened to him. His family will have been wondering all this time. I hope they can figure out who he is so they can get some closure. I had that with Ronnie, at least. As terrible as it was to lose him, it would have been much worse never to have known what had happened."

"That's as much as I can do with a handkerchief," said Iris. "Millie will have her work cut out for her. Let's have a seat until the policemen come."

There was nowhere to sit except for the piano bench, so they shared that while they waited. Iris idly plinked a few notes. The workmen, unaware of what was happening below, continued stripping the wallpaper.

"Did I tell you that Millie will be coming with me?" said Gwen. "When I get my own place?"

"No! That's wonderful. As a maid, or are you making her the housekeeper?"

"As housekeeper," said Gwen. "As soon as I find a house to keep. There's one in Maida Vale I'm going to look at on Saturday morning. Would you like to come with me?"

"All right," said Iris. "Why Maida Vale?"

"It's pretty," said Gwen. "It's within walking distance of Little Ronnie's school, and there's a Tube station there that can get me to work well enough. Or an hour on foot if the weather's suitable."

"You're finally escaping the Bainbridge house," marvelled Iris.

"The house, yes," said Gwen. "The Bainbridges will be with me always. Little Ronnie is their heir. But he'll be mine again for the rest of his childhood once custody is restored, and that should be shortly, now that I'm done with Lunacy Court. I'm actually getting on with my life, Iris."

"You are," said Iris. "Speaking of getting on."

"Yes?"

"That was Des Burton down there, wasn't it? I mean, I only saw him briefly, and he was covered with dust, but that was actually him."

"It was," said Gwen. "Imagine my surprise."

"I'm imagining any number of things," said Iris with a grin. "It must have been quite the reunion."

"It was awkward, but nothing actually happened," said Gwen.

"Enough happened to shatter brick walls and raise the dead," said Iris.

"The fellow is still dead," said Gwen. "Nothing miraculous occurred. Quite the opposite, in fact."

"Still, the chances of a man you've fancied appearing in the unlikeliest of circumstances suggests the intervention of Cupid. Or Eros, to invoke his more interesting incarnation. Why, it would be like Mike Kinsey walking through the door—"

Then Mike Kinsey walked through the door, another policeman trailing him. He stopped short as he caught sight of them.

"Hello, Mike!" called Iris, waving from the bench. "We were just talking about you."

"Good afternoon, Detective Sergeant Kinsey," said Gwen. "And is that Police Constable Larkin with you? Hello, Constable. It's been a while."

"You have got to be joking," said Kinsey, coming up to them. "How did the two of you get involved in another dead man?"

"Her fault," said Iris, pointing at Gwen.

"Quite accidentally, I assure you," said Gwen. "We were looking at this place for a possible event. I was downstairs speaking to one of the workmen, and there was a cave-in. When the dust settled, I saw a man's hand sticking up."

"He's been there for years, I'd guess, based on the condition of his skin," added Iris.

"I see you've added medical examiner to your list of amateur titles, Sparks," said Kinsey.

"Everything I know about dead people, I learned from you, Mike," she said.

"Are you planning to take over the investigation?"

"Coax me a little bit, Edmundo," she said. "No, not this time, Mike. We'll let you have this one. It has nothing to do with us."

"Big of you," he said. "Who's with the body now?"

"The workman, the owner of the club, and the owner's assistant," said Gwen.

"You know their names?"

"The workman's name is Des Burton," said Gwen.

"And the owner is Archie Spelling," added Iris, watching closely for his reaction.

She was rewarded by him closing his eyes for a moment, then taking a deep breath.

"Of course," he muttered. "Why wouldn't it be him? And Reginald Townley will be the assistant, correct?"

"Do you know, I've never known Reg's last name before? And we've known him for, what, five months now," Iris said to Gwen.

"I suppose he's been reluctant to give it out," said Kinsey. "Right, that's all I need from the two of you for now. You're free to leave. So leave."

"You know where to find us if you have any questions," said Iris. "Have fun, Mike."

They watched as he and Larkin went to the door to the stairs and disappeared.

"See how well I handled that?" chirped Iris. "Dr. Milford will be so impressed."

"I got the car pulled up front," called Benny from the entrance. "I'll take you back to Mayfair."

He held the door for them, then got behind the wheel. He turned left on Mile End Road. It wasn't until they crossed the canal that Iris broke the silence.

"Apart from the dead body, how did you like the place?" she asked.

"It's rather difficult to separate the two at the moment," said Gwen.

"Well, we won't mention it to our clients when we invite them," said Iris.

"You're still seriously considering using it?"

"Why not?"

"Because there's a body in the basement."

"Which will be gone by the end of the day. Come on, Gwen, every club worth going to has had a body or six in its history. Assuming the place will be ready by New Year's—Benny, you'd have a better idea about that than we would. Think it will be fixed up in time?"

"I think, Sparks, that if it's you 'oo needs it done, then Arch will move 'Eaven and earth to make it 'appen," said Benny.

"Oh," said Iris, taken aback. "Oh, I didn't mean to make this into anything quite so—momentous."

"I guess we'll be holding our dance there, if that's the case," said Gwen. "Let's hope there'll be no ghosts as guests."

"I don't believe in ghosts," said Iris.

"There's always ghosts," said Benny. "The trick is keeping 'em 'appy."

"Do you have a ghost guy?" asked Gwen.

"Yeah, we do," said Benny. "Only, it's a woman. Spooky old dame, always muttering stuff you'd rather not be 'earing. We'll ring 'er up before we open, 'ave 'er give the place a good sweeping."

"That's nonsense," said Iris.

"Couldn't hurt," said Gwen.

"Fine," said Iris. "On to more important topics. Now that Des is back in your life—"

"He isn't," said Gwen. "Besides, he's engaged."

"But not married yet," said Iris. "Engagements never stop anyone from having some fun. Hell, I was engaged twice as far as I can remember. Possibly more. So carpe diem! Think of him as a rosebud to gather while ye may."

"The rosebud's fiancée might have objections to the gathering. Anyhow, nothing happened, and nothing is going to happen."

"If nothing happened when you were down there alone with him, how do you explain the dust on your clothes?"

"The wall collapsed," said Gwen in exasperation. "There was dust. Tons of it."

"And you were facing the wall when it happened," said Iris. "But the dust on the back of your suit was from the floor, and the pattern it made suggests you ended up lying on your back. If I hadn't recently cleaned up the evidence, I could show you."

"Good Lord, you're turning me into a crime scene!"

"Well? Who done it?"

"No one done anything. I landed on my back when Des pulled me away from the wall. It all happened very fast."

"Where did he land?"

"By me."

"Side by side, in Love's dusty embrace," said Iris. "Too bad we all came running down to interrupt."

"Yeah, sorry about that," said Benny from behind the wheel.

"I had already shifted my attentions to the dead man," said Gwen.

"Flighty, ain't she?" said Iris. "Stick with the living, I say. They're more fun."

"If you persist in tormenting me like this, I shall have no other choice but to bring up Mike Kinsey," said Gwen.

"Poor Mike," said Iris. "I wish I could have been there when he and Archie saw each other."

Archie looked at the detective closely as he walked towards them, then smiled broadly.

"It's 'imself, innit?" he said. "Detective Sergeant Michael Kinsey. 'Ow's married life?"

"I'll trouble you not to say another word about that, Spelling," said Kinsey. "Mind if I have a look at your dead man?"

"'E ain't mine," said Archie, stepping to the side. "'E came with the place. Be my guest."

Kinsey looked at the hand, then stood and looked at the bricks around it, particularly the sections of the wall still intact and clinging to the original structure.

"What was this?" he asked. "A storeroom?"

"Dunno," said Archie. "The part on the right was down when I bought the club."

"Which was when?"

"About three months ago, wasn't it, Reg?"

"Yeah, early September when we signed the papers," said Reg.

"This brickwork looks more recent than the original walls," observed Kinsey. "Any idea when it was done?"

"None," said Archie. "We knew we were gonna 'ave to do some work on this end of the club, including down 'ere, but we didn't look too closely at the time."

"You didn't have an inspector check it out before you bought the place?"

"Yeah, we did," said Archie. "And 'e told us what wasn't damaged would 'old up all right, so we only 'ad to fix up this end of it."

"Remember his name?"

"It's in the paperwork," said Reg. "I'll look it up and get it to you later."

"Thanks," said Kinsey.

He squatted by the hand and carefully removed some of the bricks and debris covering it, revealing more of the arm, then the first glimpse of the rest of the body. He straightened up, wiping the dust from his hands.

"We're going to need a team," he said. "I'll call it in, Larkin. You stay here with the body until I get back. Spelling, walk with me. Alone."

"Boss, maybe we should call the beagle," said Reg worriedly.

"No need," said Archie grandly. "I'm just an ordinary, 'elpful citizen assisting Scotland Yard in their enquiries. I don't need a lawyer by my side. Right, Detective Sergeant?"

"Assist while walking," said Kinsey.

He didn't speak until they reached the stairwell, then he stopped and faced Archie.

"Let's get this out of the way now, Spelling," said Kinsey. "I don't like you, and I don't like you being with Sparks. She's far too good for you."

"She's free to do whatever she wants," said Archie. "If you wanted some say over 'oo she's with, then you shouldn't 'ave dumped 'er and married someone else. As far as 'er being too good for me, I 'appen to agree with you, but if she ain't kicking up a fuss about it, then I'm gonna accept my good fortune, and there ain't a man alive 'oo can say anything against it."

"If anything ever happens to her, I will come down on you like—well, I was going to say a ton of bricks, but that seems callous under the present circumstances."

"You take care of your woman, I'll take care of mine," said Archie. "Anyway, she takes care of 'erself more than anything."

"That I know," said Kinsey, continuing up the stairs. "All right. Any idea who this dead man might be?"

"None. Like I said, I only bought the club three months ago, and never 'ad the occasion to be down there poking through the rubble."

"Who did you buy it from?"

"Vanessa Reese. She's Frankie Reese's widow. He ran the place until 1939, then closed it down when the war got going."

"How did he die?"

"Dunno, exactly. Natural causes, maybe a year or two later."

"And the bomb damage?"

"End of 1940, I 'eard, but I wasn't keeping track of where they were landing at the time."

They came out the front.

"There's a call box on Mile End," said Spelling. "By the Three Wise Men."

"Thanks," said Kinsey. "This is near the end of your territory, isn't it?"

"I'm a legitimate businessman," said Archie. "I own warehouses and nightclubs. I got no idea what you mean."

"Of course not," said Kinsey. "Was this part of the territory when your uncle was running things?"

"What's that got to do with anything?" asked Archie. "You got a dead man from the Blitz. Nothing funny 'appened."

"Anything connected to you is treated as criminal until we know otherwise," said Kinsey.

"Seems the opposite of the way things oughter be," said Archie.

"And whose fault is that?" asked Kinsey. "Wait here. I'll be back shortly."

"I wonder where Mr. Sticks would have taken you on the date," mused Iris.

"We'll never know, will we?" replied Gwen.

"Unless he asks you out straight up."

"I doubt he'd do that. He strikes me as a man who only wants to get things by winning them. And I am not a woman who wants to be won."

"But you flirted with him. Quite shamelessly."

"I was teaching him a lesson."

"You kissed his stickpin, which sounds grossly Freudian now that I've said it aloud. What lesson was in that?"

"That was only a momentary—flourish or something, I don't know what. It wasn't flirting."

"It certainly was," said Iris. "You may as well have dropped your fan at his feet."

"You do know that it's not the eighteenth century. More's the pity."

"Benny, what's your opinion?" asked Iris. "Was she flirting?"

"I was out fetching the car," said Benny. "I missed all of this. 'Oo was she flirting with?"

"The young man playing snooker with Reg. Called himself Mr. Sticks."

"Oh, River? 'E's a decent lad when 'e's not at the table."

"How often is that?" asked Gwen.

"Not often. So what'd I miss?"

"He challenged our Gwendolyn to a frame," said Iris.

"'Ow'd you do?" Benny asked Gwen.

"I emerged victorious," said Gwen.

"She took him to the proverbial cleaners," said Iris. "He had bet his stickpin against a date with her."

"Blimey! He 'ad to give that up? That was given to 'im by his dad. That must've 'urt."

"Not for long. She returned it with a kiss."

"You kissed 'im?" exclaimed Benny, looking at Gwen through the rearview mirror.

"Only the stickpin," said Gwen.

"Which I submit is flirting," said Iris. "What do you think?"

"Sounds like flirting to me," said Benny.

"All right, say I was flirting," said Gwen. "Was any harm done?"

Iris took Gwen's left hand and held it up, the unadorned ring finger on display.

"Welcome back," said Iris.

"I was wondering when you'd notice," said Gwen. "Yes, I have stumbled into the present with neither ring nor drugs to shield me. The last time I was unattached, I was in my teens, newly presented and out, with my parents hovering nearby, ready to shove me into the arms of the nearest suitable suitor. This time, I'm doing it on my own, and all the rules have changed in the interim."

"Not all of them," said Iris. "And this time, you have me as your grand vizier to advise you."

"And me," said Benny.

"I'm grateful for you both," said Gwen. "I'll muddle through as best I can. Benny, it's going to be past five by the time we get to Mayfair. Could we impose upon you to drop us off directly at our homes instead?"

"Sure," said Benny. "Sparks in Marylebone, then you in Kensington."

He darted through the London traffic in bursts of controlled mayhem, arriving in front of 51 Welbeck Street.

"Any luck on finding new digs?" asked Gwen as they arrived.

"None," said Iris.

"Maybe if you spoke to the landlord about extending the lease?"

"He wants me gone," said Iris. "I can't blame him. The lease wasn't in my name, the name that was on the lease was false, I've been carrying on there first with a married man, then a gang leader, and there was a murder in my front hallway. Apparently, he thinks these things make me a less than suitable prospect for renewal."

"The murder wasn't your fault."

"No, but even I would have to concede that I've been a most tumultuous tenant. I can't exactly go to the local rent tribunal and expect sympathy under these circumstances."

"Your landlord is much too picky," said Gwen. "Any flat worth taking has had a body or six in its history. See you in the morning, partner."

"See you, Gwen," said Iris, as Benny came around and opened the door. "Thanks for the lift, Benny. Tell Archie I'll meet him at my mum's tomorrow night."

"Will do, Sparks," said Benny.

She waved and went into her building. Benny got back behind the wheel.

"Benny, my address is—"

"I know where you live, Duchess," said Benny, putting the Sunbeam-Talbot in gear.

"Really? You've never been there."

"I know where everyone we know lives," said Benny. "It's me job."

The drive from Marylebone to Kensington was quick. Benny gave a whistle of appreciation when he saw the Bainbridge house.

"You did all right, Duchess," he said when he opened the door.

"It's only a house," she said. "I still have to cope with my in-laws once I'm inside."

"Yeah, we all gotta deal with our families at 'ome," he said. "But at least you got enough room to 'ide from them when you want 'er. Good seeing you again, Duchess."

"You, too, Benny," she said. "Thanks for getting me home safely."

The car roared off as she walked up to the house and let herself in.

Ronnie came running as he generally did when she came home, but pulled up short as he took in her less than immaculate appearance.

"You always tell me to wear my playclothes if I'm going to get dirty," he said accusingly.

"It would have been a very good idea if Mummy had put hers on today," said Gwen. "Unfortunately, I fell down accidentally."

"Are you all right?" asked Ronnie, shifting immediately into worry.

"I'm fine, just dusty," said Gwen. "I'm going to change before dinner. How was school today?"

"We drew Christmas cards for our families," he said. "I put Sir Oswald on mine. He's helping Father Christmas bring presents to everyone. Miss Ellingsworth never heard of a Christmas narwhal before, but she said there probably was one."

"I think Sir Oswald would make a wonderful Christmas narwhal," said Gwen. "I can't wait to see the cards."

"And did you hear? Uncle Simon is going to spend the holidays with us!"

"I did hear that," said Gwen. "In fact, your grandmother, he, and I are going to take you and John to a play."

"All of us? Wizard! Which one?"

"It's a surprise. Now, let Mummy go and change, or your grandmother will never let me hear the end of it."

"All right."

He dashed off.

Gwen managed to make it up the stairs and to her room without encountering her in-laws, much to her relief. She rang for Millie, who came within a minute and looked at her dusty suit in dismay.

"What happened?" she asked as Gwen removed it and handed it to her.

"A construction accident just missed me," said Gwen. "I emerged unscathed but dusty."

"I'll have this back to presentable in two days," said Millie.

"That will be fine," said Gwen. "Is it just family for dinner tonight?"

"It is."

"Then I'll wear the burgundy," said Gwen. "Could you rid my hair of any remaining dust and plaster? I don't want to be prematurely grey."

"Sit," commanded Millie as she picked up a hairbrush. "I will restore your youth."

Gwen sat at her dressing table while Millie unpinned her hair and carefully brushed it until its blond lustre shone again. It was relaxing as always, and Gwen's eyes closed for a moment. Immediately, Des's image appeared, his grey-green eyes widening in surprise and maybe—expectation?

She opened her eyes immediately, banishing the image.

"There, I think that should do for dinner," pronounced Millie as she reinserted the hairpins. "I'll take your suit down to the laundry and get to work on it."

"Thank you, Millie," said Gwen.

On the dressing table Ronnie, her late husband, smiled at her from inside a silver frame. Her engagement and wedding rings dangled from one corner on a silver chain. She picked them up and touched them to her lips.

"Forgive me," she whispered. "I miss you."

She arrived at work the next morning ahead of Iris and Mrs. Billington, as usual. She collected the day's letters from the box in the foyer, then jogged up the stairs until she reached their floor. After she sorted out what needed to be dealt with by their secretary and left it on her desk, she took the remaining letters next door into the office she shared with Iris. She tossed them onto the blotter on her enormous Gillows partners desk—one of two that had come with the office—hung up her hat and coat, then pulled out a feather duster from the bottom drawer and gave the desks and windowsills a quick going-over, opening the window on her side to shake the dust into the alley. A burst of frigid December air surged into the office, and she quickly shut the window, shivering.

Too much dust in my life lately, she thought.

The phrase *And your quaint honour turn to dust* popped into her head. Where was that from? Ah, yes. The Andrew Marvell poem about the coy mistress. What was the following line again? *And into ashes* something something.

And into ashes all my lust.

Lovely, she thought moodily. Make love to me or die unfulfilled. No pressure there.

She heard Iris clattering up the stairs, then saw her come

through the doorway. Her partner stopped immediately upon seeing Gwen's expression.

"I was going to say 'Good morning,'" said Iris as she hung up her coat and hat. "But it doesn't look like you're having one."

"Oh, seeing that poor bomb victim yesterday has made me gloomy," said Gwen.

"It was unfortunate," said Iris, "but not anything for us to worry about. Let me have half of those letters."

"Here you go," said Gwen. "Hmm, those are not Mrs. Billington's footsteps I hear. We don't have any early appointments, do we?"

"None," said Iris, glancing at her calendar. "Sounds like a man's shoes. A walk-in, I hope. Oh!"

Detective Sergeant Michael Kinsey appeared at the door.

"Good," he said. "You're both here. I need to talk to you."

"About the man from yesterday?" asked Gwen.

"Yes," said Kinsey. "Turns out he wasn't a bomb victim. The medical examiner found stab wounds. He was murdered."

CHAPTER 3

W e didn't do it," Iris said immediately.

"Don't be deliberately stupid this early in the morning," said Kinsey irritably. "It's bad enough to have you back in my life even for the brief amount of time I hope it's going to take."

"Sorry," said Iris. "Force of habit when I run into you nowadays. I'll try to be nicer."

"You suddenly turning nice would catapult you to the top of my suspect list," said Kinsey. "I wanted to know more about what Spelling told the two of you about this nightclub."

"Well," began Iris, but Kinsey shook his head.

"I'll hear Mrs. Bainbridge first," he said. "She's not sleeping with Spelling as far as I know."

Iris rose to her feet, her face turning red, her fists clenched.

"Iris," said Gwen softly.

Iris took a deep breath, then another, letting her hands go limp.

"Right," she said. "I'll go wait in the other office until you need me."

She brushed past him, bumping him into the side of the door as she did. They heard the reception door slam a second later.

"Didn't know she played rugby," he commented as he came into the office and sat across from Gwen.

"Whatever happened between the two of you in the past was no cause for you to be rude," said Gwen. "Ask your questions, keep your tone civilised and professional, then leave. Am I clear?"

He looked at her as if he were going to say something snappish, then stopped himself and pulled out a notebook and pen.

"When did you first learn about the club from Spelling?" he asked.

"Yesterday afternoon," said Gwen. "We've been searching for a venue for holding a dance for our clients. We thought Mr. Spelling might know of one. He did, as it turned out."

"What did he tell you about it?"

"That he had purchased it from the owner's family recently, that it had been closed after receiving bomb damage during the Blitz, and that he was having it renovated."

"Did he or the others say anything about any prior experience with the club?"

"Mr. Spelling mentioned that he had been there before the war when it was still a going concern, as did Benny."

"That would be Benny Fineman?"

"I don't know Benny's last name."

"Spelling's getaway driver."

"You mean driver."

"I mean getaway driver," said Kinsey. "He's a suspect in a number of unsolved robberies."

"He is an excellent driver," said Gwen. "We owe my father-in-law's life to Benny's getting him to a hospital quickly after his heart attack."

"Your loyalty to this pack of criminals defies all common sense," said Kinsey.

"They have earned my loyalty and friendship," said Gwen. "I don't condone their other activities, but I have not been privy to them, either."

Except for when I hired them to commit some, she thought. But there's no need to bring that up, is there?

"How did your friends react to discovering the body?" asked Kinsey.

"They didn't discover the body. I did."

"How did that happen again?"

"I was exploring the cellar, making sure the lavatories were in working order. I came across Des—Mr. Burton, rather—while he was demolishing a wall that was partially collapsed. While we were speaking, more of the wall came down, and that's when I saw the hand sticking out. Mr. Spelling and the others came to the cellar when they heard the crash."

"What was their reaction? Particularly Spelling's."

"He wanted to call the police straightaway."

"And the others?"

"Benny expressed some concerns, but Mr. Spelling overruled him immediately."

"Do you think Fineman knew something he didn't want us to know?"

"You'll have to ask him," said Gwen.

"I will, and he'll tell me nothing useful," said Kinsey. "You have a reputation for reading people, Mrs. Bainbridge, and we at the Yard have learned to take it seriously. Do you think Fineman had something to hide?"

"No," said Gwen, thinking back. "No, I don't. I think it was an expression of general policy of mistrusting the police more than any specific fear concerning the deceased."

"How about Spelling?"

"As I said, he wanted to call you in immediately."

"And what is Mr. Burton's role in the gang?"

"He isn't part of the gang," said Gwen. "He would never join up with Archie."

"How would you know?" asked Kinsey. "I thought you weren't privy to their inner workings."

"No, but Des—"

"You're on a first-name basis with him?"

"We met on a prior occasion," Gwen said reluctantly. "He was quite emphatic then about his dislike of Mr. Spelling and his— activities."

"How on earth would a woman of your standing meet a construction worker from the East End?"

"Des Burton is Tillie La Salle's cousin," said Gwen. "I met him when Iris and I were looking into her murder."

"Her cousin," said Kinsey. "Small world."

"Yes," said Gwen.

"What did he have to do with your investigation then?"

"Very little," said Gwen. "He was someone I spoke with about her, mostly for background information. She was involved with some of Mr. Spelling's activities, as you may remember, so Des's—Mr. Burton's—dislike of Spelling came up then."

"Why are you blushing, Mrs. Bainbridge?" asked Kinsey, looking at her curiously.

"Am I?" she replied, inwardly cursing herself. "I didn't realise I was."

"Is there anything else about Mr. Burton I should know?" he asked. "Like why you keep referring to him by his first name?"

"Nothing that I can think of," said Gwen. "Nothing that would concern the police, certainly."

"If Burton disliked Spelling so much, why is he working for him now?"

"He said things were slow and he needed the money," replied Gwen.

"Did he say whether he had been in the club before?"

"The topic never came up," said Gwen. "We only spoke for a minute before the wall fell."

"Any idea if he knew the deceased?"

"None. Although all we could see was the hand, so I don't see how anyone could have known. Have you figured out who he was?"

"We don't know yet," said Kinsey. "He had no identification on him. We're working on tracing his suit."

"What about the ring?" asked Gwen.

"What ring?"

"There was a signet ring on his hand," said Gwen. "It had some sort of military insignia. That should help."

"There was no ring when I saw him, Mrs. Bainbridge," he said, puzzled. "Are you certain you saw one?"

"I'm certain," she said. "Wait, I think I can sketch the design."

She took a notepad and pencil, then drew a large circle.

"It was pewter or some other cheap metal," she said, frowning in concentration. "There were oak-leaf clusters on the sides, like so. A pair of cannons facing out on the diagonals, and some kind of bird—no, a double bird, one of those symmetrical two-headed thingies the army likes to put on their accoutrements."

"Eagles, probably," said Kinsey. "It's usually an eagle."

"But they weren't," said Gwen, remembering. "They were sparrows. They had the usual bunch of arrows clutched in their talons, but they were sparrows."

She added them on top of the cannon.

"I think there may have been some letters and numbers on it as well," she said, tearing the page off and handing it to him. "But for the life of me, I can't remember what they were."

"This is very helpful," said Kinsey. "What's even more interesting is that one of those men decided to remove the ring before we got there."

"You think one of them knew something about the dead man."

"I do now. Mrs. Bainbridge, I want to say something to you while Sparks—Miss Sparks—isn't present."

"What is that, Detective Sergeant?"

"This connection to Archie Spelling—it won't end well. Sooner or later, we're going to bring him down."

"In other words, you're telling me that you are going to do your job," said Gwen. "I expect nothing less. Why are you telling me this?"

"Because I would like her—both of you, I should say—to be safely clear of him when we do."

"That sounds like a threat, Detective Sergeant."

"Call it a helpful warning," he said. "Now, may I trouble you to fetch Miss Sparks and let me speak with her?"

"Would you like me to remain as a chaperone?"

"That won't be necessary."

"How about as a bodyguard?"

"Miss Sparks has nothing to fear from me," said Kinsey.

"She's not the one who needs one," said Gwen. "I shall be right back."

She went into the reception room. Mrs. Billington had arrived and was going through the letters on her desk, studiously not looking at Iris, who was fuming on the couch, her knees drawn up to her chest, her arms wrapped tightly around them.

"He'd like to speak to you," said Gwen. "Think you can handle it, or shall I tell him something I've never said out loud to anyone in my life? I'd be more than willing right now."

"I can't have you jumping into the pits of sin on my behalf," said Iris, uncoiling from the couch. "Let me at him."

"Don't get yourself arrested," warned Gwen. "You still have your half of the letters to go through."

Iris stormed out of the reception room and into her office. Kinsey started to rise from his chair, but she put her hand on his shoulder and shoved him back into it. She walked around her desk and took her seat.

"As you may recall, the last time I saw you was when I was wrapped up in a situation involving my last ex," she said. "A situation which nearly got me killed."

"I remember," he said.

"And nevertheless, in the midst of all that chaos, knowing my life was on the line, I still took the time to apologise to you for all I had done," she continued. "Do you remember that?"

"It took you all of ten seconds," he said. "Rather a brief apology for such a large offense, if you ask me."

"If I had died that day, it would have amounted to a substantial portion of the rest of my existence," she said. "But I couldn't have what I did to you on my conscience. And after it was all over, and I found myself in the unexpected position of having to go on with my life, I worked very hard on staying out of yours, and on finding out if I could still live with myself after what I did to you. To myself. To us."

"We haven't been an 'us' for several years, Sparks," he said. "We never will be again."

"No, we won't," she said. "Which is why you had no cause to humiliate me like that. In front of Gwen, no less. We can't change what happened, Mike, but we can forgive and move on. I'm saying that for your sake as much as mine. If you let this fester, it will destroy your marriage, and Beryl doesn't deserve that."

"You never liked Beryl," he said.

"I still don't," she said. "But there's no reason for her and me to cross paths, so I can put her out of my mind."

"Unfortunately, your path and mine do cross occasionally," he said. "And when they do, there are generally dead men and gangsters involved."

"So let's talk about them instead," said Iris. "Much safer topics than love and regret, don't you think?"

"Very well," he said. "I apologise for my comment earlier. Will that suffice?"

"It will," she said. "Ask me your questions."

He took her through the events at the White Palace, taking notes as he did so.

"When you felt his hand, did you notice a ring on his finger?" he asked.

"I did," said Iris. "I don't remember any details about it. I was trying to figure out how long he had been there."

He pulled out the sketch Gwen had made.

"Military," she said, perusing it. "From the Great War, at a guess. I don't recognise the unit. The sparrows are a strange choice. Sparrows with arrows. That is curious. Do you know where it came from?"

"No," he said. "I only found out about it from Mrs. Bainbridge a few minutes ago."

"Why?" asked Iris.

"Because the ring wasn't on the body when I arrived," said Kinsey. "Any ideas how that happened?"

"Hmm, that's odd," said Iris. "Who was down there? Gwen and me, of course. Then there was Archie, Reg, Benny, and that workman. The ring was still on the hand when Gwen and I went back upstairs."

"Did any of the others go with you?"

"Benny. He had to go outside to call the police."

"And did you see anyone else go down there while you waited by that piano?"

"No," said Iris. "But there could have been others working down there that we didn't see."

"Good point," said Kinsey. "So, of Spelling, Townley, and Burton, who's your favourite for stealing that ring?"

"Couldn't say," said Iris.

"Say it was Spelling," said Kinsey. "If you found out he had something to do with it, would you tell me?"

"Of course," said Iris, her expression wide-eyed and innocent. "My first duty is to the law, boyfriend or no boyfriend."

"Loyalty to boyfriends has never been a strong suit of yours," said Kinsey.

"Careful, Mike," said Iris.

"Sorry, crossed that line again, didn't I?" he said, closing his notebook and getting to his feet. "Keep your ears open, Sparks. You may be dating a murderer."

"According to you, he may be dating one, too," said Iris.

"Still hope to close that case someday," said Kinsey. "One more thing, Sparks."

"Yes, Mike?"

"Why did Mrs. Bainbridge blush when she talked about Des Burton?"

"Did she? Interesting. But it has nothing to do with this case, so let it go."

"You don't blush when you talk about Spelling," he pointed out.

"Maybe I'm better at controlling my emotions," she said.

He smiled.

"You used to blush all the time with me," he said.

Then he left.

"Bastard," she muttered.

Gwen cautiously poked her head around the doorway a moment later. Then, seeing Kinsey was gone, she re-entered the office.

"Are you all right?" she asked as she sat.

"I am in the foulest of foul moods," said Iris. "I thought I had been making progress on the Kinsey front, but in one conversation after not seeing him for a month and a half he managed to poke nerves I didn't know were still there."

"Sorry," said Gwen. "At least that will be the end of it, as far as we're concerned."

"What makes you think that?"

"This one has nothing to do with us," said Gwen. "The police are handling it. We can get back to the more complex task of or-ganising our New Year's dance."

"Right," said Iris, reaching for her letter opener and stabbing viciously at an innocent envelope.

"Good," said Gwen, opening the first on her stack more gently.

They worked in silence for a few minutes.

"Only—" Gwen began hesitantly.

"I knew it!" Iris burst out, pinioning her letter onto her blotter with the opener. "Only what?"

"Are you going to tell Archie?" asked Gwen.

"Tell him what?"

"About the ring."

"Warn him, you mean."

"Yes," said Gwen. "I assume Mike's heading his way as we speak to question him about it."

"That wouldn't be fair to the investigation if I tipped off a suspect," said Iris.

Gwen looked at her, sorting out her thoughts before she spoke.

"You mean to say it wouldn't be fair to Mike?" she asked slowly. "After how he treated you? After how he just made you feel?"

Iris didn't answer.

"Would keeping mum be fair to Archie?" continued Gwen.

"No, it wouldn't," said Iris reluctantly. "It's just that—"

"What?" asked Gwen.

"What if he did it?" asked Iris.

"Killed the man?"

"No," said Iris. "Took the ring. Oh, hell, what if he killed the man?"

"Then he should tell you why he did," said Gwen. "You can't bury your head in the sand about everything he does. For God's sake, Iris, he's meeting your mother tonight! You can't go into that wondering what's going on."

"Give me the phone, damn you," said Iris.

Gwen passed it over to her. Iris dialled, stabbing furiously at each number.

"Eggy, it's me," she said. "Is Archie about? It's urgent. Yes, I heard about what happened yesterday. Because I was there when it happened! Look, put him on, will you?"

She covered the mouthpiece for a second.

"Eggy's a dear, but he's not much use out of the ring," she whispered.

She waited, tapping her foot impatiently.

"Sparks?" came Archie's voice. "Everything all right? Your mum getting cold feet?"

"No, that's still terrifyingly on schedule," said Iris. "Listen, Archie, Detective Ex came by the office this morning."

"Did 'e? Was it professional or personal?"

"Professional, of course. He's on his way to see you now."

"I figured 'e'd 'ave more questions."

"There is one in particular you should know about," said Iris. "Did you notice the signet ring on the dead man's hand when we came downstairs?"

"I remember some kind of ring," said Archie. "Didn't look at it too closely at the time. What about it?"

"It went missing," said Iris. "Sometime after Gwen and I went upstairs with Benny and before the police got there."

There was a long pause on the other end of the line.

"Are you telling me this because you think I took it?" he asked.

"I'm telling you this because you're going to be questioned about it," she said. "But did you take it?"

"No," he said. "Why would I?"

"Why would any of you?" she said. "But the simple fact is the ring is gone. If you say you didn't take it, that's good enough for me."

"I'm glad to 'ear you say that, Sparks," said Archie. "I appreciate the advance notice. I 'ope the ex is as accepting of my denials as you are."

"He'll be coming in with suspicions blazing," said Iris. "Professional and personal."

"Yeah, 'e gave me an inkling about that yesterday," said Archie. "I guess 'e 'asn't let go of you yet. Can't blame 'im."

"I can," said Iris. "But I've let him go, so no point in that."

"None," said Archie. "Right, I'll let Reg know, too. I'll tell you about it later."

"Okay," said Iris.

"And we've finally 'ad a conversation about a ring," said Archie with a laugh. "Din't think this would be 'ow it would go. See you tonight, Sparks."

He hung up. Iris stared at the phone.

"That conversation took a peculiar turn," she said. "All right. I've done it. You're up now."

"What do you mean?" asked Gwen.

"I've alerted Archie. Aren't you going to warn Des?"

"Des? Why should I do that?"

Gwen was blushing, observed Iris.

"Do you think Des took the ring?" she asked.

"Why would he?" replied Gwen. "If anything, he's the least likely of the three."

"Your reasons?"

"Because he's a hired workman, not a member of the gang."

"So we warn the spivs, and leave the innocent man to face the music unprepared? That's your idea of fairness?"

"Why are you doing this to me?" Gwen asked plaintively.

"Because you did it to me," said Iris, plunking the telephone in front of Gwen. "Your turn."

"I don't know his number," said Gwen.

"Liar. You called him in June after we solved Tillie La Salle's case. I'll bet you a tuppence it's in your address book right now. Shall I check for you?"

Gwen looked at the telephone, then reached into her bag and removed a small black address book. She opened it to "D," Iris noticed. Then she dialled a number.

She let it ring ten times, then hung up.

"No answer," she said. "He's probably back working at the club. Satisfied?"

"Let's hope he doesn't turn up any more bodies," said Iris. "All right, points for the effort. Let's get back to work."

Mrs. Florence Sparks, Labour member of Parliament for Hackney and surroundings, lived in a modest home on Hackney Road, some ten minutes' walk from the Overground railway station. The house was a brick cube, two storeys high, three rooms wide, with recessed arched windows on each side of a dark blue single front door. Gardens on either side of the front walk were devoted to vegetables, apart from one four-foot-square section given over to freesias, which must have looked nice back in the spring.

She had moved there, a moody, resentful adolescent daughter in tow, after her divorce was finalised. Her political work, first as a young suffragist, then as a crusading birth-control pamphleteer throughout the East End, as well as her rise through the ranks of the National Union of Teachers, had ultimately led to her being put forth as a candidate for the House of Commons in 1938, more as a token presence in the race than as someone who might actually win. Mrs. Sparks, as usual, defied expectations and ran a fierce and energetic race that put her over. Her subsequent efforts in support of the more progressive positions of the party, while stopping short of the Communists, sufficiently endeared her to her district to keep her solidly ensconced.

The plan was for Iris to meet Archie there at six thirty. She spotted his car parked by the house with him seated behind the wheel. He rolled down the window as she sidled up to it, looking conspicuously suspicious.

"You brought the stuff?" she muttered.

He held up a white paper bag.

"Two slabs, just like we agreed," he said. "Let's hope they do the trick."

"Right," she said. "Gird your loins. Follow my lead. Here we go."

He got out of the car, and they walked through the gate to the front door and rang the bell. A moment later, Iris's mother opened it and surveyed the two of them—her daughter critically and the proposed suitor skeptically.

"He's tall," were the first words out of her mouth.

"Most men are when they stand next to me," said Iris, "but he should be able to fit through the door without difficulty, assuming you are going to stop blocking it."

"Please, do come in," said Mrs. Sparks, stepping back. "Welcome, Mr. Spelling."

The apple didn't fall far, he thought as he crossed the threshold. Maybe an inch taller than her daughter, although Iris made up for it with higher heels. Hair the same brunette, but the eyes were grey to Iris's brown, and were magnified to an almost alarming point by the thick lenses in her glasses.

"It's a pleasure to meetcher, Mrs. Sparks," he said, removing his trilby. "I've heard a lot about you."

"And I've heard so much about you," said Mrs. Sparks. "None of it from my daughter, unfortunately."

"Well, I'm sure much of what you 'eard is an exaggeration," said Archie. "But in case it wasn't, I've brought you a little gift."

He held up the white bag. She accepted it with trepidation, then her nostrils flared suddenly.

"Is that—" she began as she opened the bag.

She took a cautious sniff, and her eyes grew wide.

"Roquefort!" she exclaimed. "And there's another one. No, it can't be! Chevrotin? How did you get hold of chevrotin?"

"Fresh off the boat, straight from the goat," said Archie. "I 'ope you like it."

"Are these from the black market?" she asked accusingly.

"This one was more greyish," said Archie. "Coupons actually changed 'ands."

"Whose coupons, whose hands?" she demanded.

"Greyish," he repeated. "Shall I take it back?"

"No need," she said hastily. "Let me bring it back to Patricia so she can find a proper board for it. Iris, bring our guest to the dining room."

She turned and walked to the rear of the house, veering into the kitchen.

"So far, so good," whispered Iris. "This way."

The dining room was small, with a square oak table in the middle. Dishes and glassware were stacked in a cabinet, and a secretary desk stood by the window, official-looking documents apparently gathered in haste and thrown into it.

The table was covered by a simple, cream-coloured cotton cloth and was set for three. Iris picked up a knife.

"She's using the silver she saves for company," she observed. "That's encouraging."

She flipped it into the air and caught it easily.

"How many times must I tell you not to do that in the house?" said her mother as she returned with the cheeses laid out on a wooden cutting board next to a pile of water biscuits. "Sit, please."

"Allow me," said Archie, pulling out Mrs. Sparks's chair.

She sat hesitantly, as if suspecting for a moment he might pull it out from under her. He pulled out the chair opposite for Iris, then took the one between them.

"Potato soup, a whitefish salad, and canned peas," said Mrs. Sparks. "I hope that will do. And now we have these lovely cheeses to supplement them. Please help yourself, Mr. Spelling."

"You don't want to say grace first?" asked Archie.

"We don't do that," said Mrs. Sparks. "But feel free if you like."

"No, I'll play by the 'ouse rules," said Archie, taking thin slices of each cheese.

The ladies followed suit. Mrs. Sparks bit into the chevrotin and sighed contentedly.

"Of the bribe attempts I have received, this is one of the most appreciated," she said.

"It's not a bribe," said Iris.

"It's sort of a bribe," said Archie. "Not in the grander scheme of things, but we're always trying to get on people's good sides, ain't we?"

"Especially on first encounter," said Mrs. Sparks.

"It ain't, you know," said Archie. "We met before."

"Have we?" asked Mrs. Sparks. "When was that?"

"You came by a ladies' meeting in Wapping when I was ten," he said. "My mum couldn't get anyone to watch me, so she brought me along. You gave a lecture on birth control. Since I din't know anything about any of that back then, it was quite the eye-opener. Afterwards, when Mum and I went up, you patted me on the 'ead and said, 'Good for you, young man. You know more than any boy your age now. Take it to 'eart.'"

"And did you?"

"There are no little Archies running around the East End, so, yeah, I did."

"I'm glad," said Mrs. Sparks. "So, to use the standard cliché, what did you do in the war, Mr. Spelling?"

"Supplies," he said. "I run a string of warehouses by the docks. We went straight into working with the Royal Army Service Corps."

"So you didn't go over to fight."

"I was a civilian the 'ole time," said Archie. "But we were needed and we did our part. And we took our losses from the bombs, along with everyone else in the East End."

"I suppose if a crate or two fell off a truck, you were not averse to diverting it into the community," said Mrs. Sparks.

"Every single crate we got went where it was supposed to go," said Archie evenly. "There was a war on. We 'ad to win it. And we did."

Patricia, a woman in her sixties, came out with a tureen.

"Patricia, it's good to see you again," said Iris. "This is Archie Spelling, my boyfriend."

"I know who he is," said Patricia, ladling soup into each bowl. "I'll be back in to collect when you're done, Mrs. Sparks."

"Thank you, Patricia," said Mrs. Sparks.

Archie glanced after her, then took a spoonful of the soup.

"Cold," he said. "I can see why. Good, though."

"It is," said Iris. "So how was work today, Mum?"

"The three 'C's. Committees, constituents, complaints. But I don't wish to bore our guest."

"I won't be bored," said Archie. "I like knowing what our government is doing to us."

"Doing *for* you, I should think," said Mrs. Sparks.

"Well, I suppose it depends on what's being done," said Archie. "Just to give you a for instance, what's going on with the Wanstead Flats?"

"What about them?" asked Mrs. Sparks.

"They're talking about putting up 'ouses there, and a bleedin' college," said Archie. "That's a park. It's where we'd go to kick a ball around when I was a kid, get some fresh air. And there ain't many of those available to us East Enders."

"I appreciate that," said Mrs. Sparks. "But surely you can appreciate the need for housing. West Ham alone lost fourteen thousand houses to the Blitz. People have to live somewhere."

"Then let West 'am put the 'ouses in their parks, not ours," said Archie. "They want to take a big chunk out of it, and once they get a foot'old, they'll keep wanting more."

"It's not that big a chunk," she said.

"An 'undred and eighty-two acres," he said. "That's almost 'alf the park. And your government, especially that Bevan bloke, is supporting it. There'll be kids living in new concrete blocks with nowhere to play, and what's the use of that?"

"It's an interesting viewpoint, Mr. Spelling," she said. "But my constituents—"

"I am one of your constituents," he said. "I voted for you in three elections now."

"Did you?" she asked. "I had no idea you had a, let's say, legal residence here. Did you know about this, Iris?"

"I can't say I did," said Iris, looking at him in surprise. "I've never been to his home."

"Surprise, we're neighbours," said Archie. "And I am not without influence around 'ere. I 'aven't used it, but you'd be amazed by 'ow many votes I could send in your direction. Or away from it."

"Is that a threat?" asked Mrs. Sparks, bristling.

"It's me expressing what a lot of people want," said Archie. "There were sixty thousand signing petitions against developing the flats, but that public enquiry on it was a farce. It sounds like the deal was already done behind closed doors, and anytime deals get made that way, someone's making money off it 'oo shouldn't."

"Ah, money," said Mrs. Sparks. "We've finally reached the root of your complaint, Mr. Spelling. You're angry because you didn't get your share. Is that it?"

"No, Mrs. Sparks," said Archie. "I'm angry because the kids around 'ere aren't getting theirs."

Patricia returned to collect the soup bowls, then brought in the main course. Iris took a bite of the fish salad.

"This is delicious," she said. "I read about your speech proposing the hostels for the Women's Voluntary Service, Mum. I thought it was good."

"Only good?" replied Mrs. Sparks.

"You know what I mean," said Iris. "You could have gone further."

"You must know, Mr. Spelling, that my daughter has retained many of her tendencies from her experiments in socialism while at university," said Mrs. Sparks. "I can never be progressive enough to please her."

"You still can," said Iris. "Take the hostels. Why not—"

The discussion carried them through the rest of the dinner.

"Help me clear, would you, dear?" asked Mrs. Sparks when they were through.

"Of course," said Iris, collecting dishes and utensils from the table and following her mother to the kitchen, where Patricia was already at the sink, scrubbing out the tureen.

"So, what do you think?" asked Iris when they were out of earshot of the dining room.

"He's a rather charming sociopath," said Mrs. Sparks. "You're frighteningly well matched."

"That may be the most encouraging thing you've ever said about any man I've been with," said Iris. "I'll take it as a positive."

"Don't tell me you aren't dating him simply to throw him in my face," said her mother sharply. "A gangster. For pity's sake, Iris, what were you thinking? Did you ever stop and consider how this might affect me?"

"You do know that not everything I do is done with you in mind, don't you?"

"I don't believe that for a second."

"Why not?" snapped Iris. "You haven't liked any of my boyfriends, so why should this one be different?"

"I liked the tall one," said Mrs. Sparks. "The Italian."

"Sally was a friend, not a boyfriend," said Iris. "Still is."

"Nevertheless, this man, this—spiv. It can't possibly work between you, and you're too smart a girl not to know that."

"Just because you were never capable of making a marriage work doesn't mean I can't."

"So it's marriage now?" asked Mrs. Sparks. "Is that the purpose of all this?"

"Maybe," said Iris, with more assurance than she actually felt.

"Has he proposed?"

"Actually, no."

Mrs. Sparks glanced over at Patricia, who was by this point putting more effort into cleaning the tureen than was needed.

"Do your mother one favour," said Mrs. Sparks.

"What's that?"

"If he does propose, elope," said her mother. "I don't want to be bothered. I've been through enough failed engagements with you already."

"I'll send you a postcard from Brighton," said Iris, turning and starting to walk back.

"Iris," said her mother.

"What?" asked her daughter, turning to face her defiantly.

"Are you taking precautions?"

"Of course," said Iris. "If there's one thing you drilled into my head while we were going around distributing pamphlets, it was that. There are no little Irises running around, Mother."

"I always assumed that you weren't listening to me."

"I've done nothing but listen to you," said Iris. "I'm twenty-eight, Mother. I can listen to myself now."

She walked back to the dining room, pausing for a moment to recompose herself before entering. Her mother followed her a second later.

"No dessert, I'm afraid," she said. "Rationing being what it is."

"That's fine, Mrs. Sparks," said Archie. "It was an excellent dinner and interesting conversation. I see where your daughter gets her brains."

"Very kind of you to say, Mr. Spelling," returned Mrs. Sparks as they walked towards the front door. "Most potential suitors would have tried flattering me by telling me I gave her her good looks."

"Those, too," said Archie affably as he retrieved his hat. "But looks are the least of it, if you don't mind me saying so."

"Good night, Mum," said Iris. "This was fun. We'll have to make it a regular thing."

It was worth saying it to see the momentary recoil in her mother's expression, she thought.

Iris and Archie headed down the front walk. Halfway to the kerb, there was a flash and a pop from down the street. The two of them immediately dove to the ground. An engine revved to life, then a car took off, rounding the next corner, tyres screeching.

Archie got up, then helped Iris to her feet.

"Thought it was a gun for a second there," he said.

"Not a gun," said Iris. "Something worse. A camera."

CHAPTER 4

Which one of us was he after, do you think?" asked Iris.

"Probably me," said Archie. "One of your ex's lads following me around, 'oping to catch me doing something I oughtn't."

"If I'd known it was him, I would have kissed you instead of diving for cover," said Iris.

"Still can," said Archie.

"Still will," said Iris. "But let's get out of here first. I'm spooked enough by the maternal scrutiny looming behind me."

"Where to?" asked Archie, opening the car door for her.

"How about your place?" said Iris as she got in. "The one I never knew about until tonight."

"I thought that might be it," he said, getting behind the wheel. "You've had your suspicious look on ever since it came up at dinner."

"I was wondering why every time I've spent an evening in bed with you, it was in a small flat in Wapping."

"Did you really think that was my 'ome?" he asked. "That I'd been doing what I've been doing all these years, putting myself at risk of life and liberty, just so I could live in a pauper's palace like that?"

"No," said Iris. "That flat seemed like a hidey-hole, a convenient place to bring girls after a night of carousing at Merle's. And I was the latest girl."

"The latest, the one, the only," said Archie as they drove. "Yeah, that's one of my spots, when I'm too drunk to drive 'ere, and Benny's too drunk to drive me."

"So Benny knows about your real home?"

"Benny knows, Reg knows, and now you know," said Archie, reaching into his inside jacket pocket. "The neighbours know I'm there, but not 'oo I am. At least, they don't let on if they do. That's it."

His hand came out with a small, flat box with a ribbon tied around it. He handed it to her.

"Small boxes unnerve me," she said, taking it hesitantly.

"Open it," he said.

She untied the ribbon, then cautiously lifted the lid and peeked. Inside, resting on a bed of cotton, was a bronze key.

"Do I have to become larger or smaller to use it?" she asked.

"Same size you are now," he said. "And 'ere we are."

She looked up to see a white cottage set back twenty feet from a low brick wall.

"This is yours?" she asked.

"This is mine," he replied.

He got out, opened the gate in front of the driveway, then pulled the car in by the side of the cottage. He opened her door to let her out before going back to close the gate.

"Do you garden?" she asked as she looked around at vegetable and flower beds surrounding the cottage.

"I got a gardener," he said. "Local lad. 'E also trims the 'edges and the grass in the back."

"And do you keep house?"

"I got a charwoman, comes in twice a week."

"So no one lives here but you?" she asked as they came to the front door. "No bit on the side or secret wife in the attic?"

"Nope," he said. "But don't go looking in the locked room in the cellar."

She shuddered for a moment, then looked up to see him grinning.

"It's all on the up and up," he said. "Will you do the honours?"

She realised she was clutching the key so tightly that it was leaving an imprint in her palm deep enough to be a mould for a spare. She unclenched her fist, inserted the key into the lock, and turned, then pushed tentatively at the door, which swung open silently.

"Up until this moment, we could have been breaking in for all I knew," she said.

"That might 'ave been fun," he said. "Please come into my 'ouse, Miss Sparks."

She stepped through the doorway into the front hall, avoiding a small pile of letters that were scattered on the carpet. Archie gathered them quickly and dropped them onto a tray resting on an Edwardian hall table to the right, an elegant rosewood piece with turned legs that tapered down to the floor as if they belonged to some large wading bird.

"You haven't been here in a couple of days, I take it," said Iris, nodding at the letters.

"I got caught up in a police investigation yesterday," said Archie. "Made for a late night, so I din't bother coming 'ere."

A collection of framed photographs hung on the walls— holiday snaps; school pictures; men in uniform; and in the centre, in a large oval frame, a young couple standing in front of an altar, the bride in a simple white frock but with a delicate veil clinging to her hair, the groom in his Sunday best, beaming at the camera like he had just won the Derby.

"Your parents," she said, drawn to it.

"That's them," he said. "Abigail and Stanley Spelling. Became man and wife in 1905."

"She was quite lovely," said Iris. "I can see some of her in your face."

"She was beautiful," said Archie. "And if you check out Dad, you can see what my nose woulda looked like if I'd kept it unpunched."

"I like your nose," said Iris. "It has character. It tells a story."

She peered more closely at one of the holiday snaps—the couple in swimsuits, five years older, she with her arms wrapped around a four-year-old girl who was her image, he with a squalling toddler on his shoulders.

"Is that you up there?" exclaimed Iris with delight.

"I was a baby once," said Archie. "I grew out of it. Shall I give you the grand tour?"

"Please."

The sitting room was warm and cosy, with furniture that could have been plucked straight from a style magazine from the early twenties. The dining room was somewhat larger than her mother's, Iris noted. There was only one place setting on the table.

"You don't have many dinner parties, do you?" asked Iris.

"Just me and me thoughts and some takeaway," said Archie. "Usually just the takeaway. I try not to think and eat at the same time. It spoils the meal."

"Why did you choose Hackney, when most of your crew lives in Wapping?"

"Sit, and I'll tell you," he said, pulling out a chair for her.

She sat, and he grabbed a bottle of port and two glasses from the sideboard.

"When Dad was off to war, Mum 'ad to take jobs cleaning 'ouses," he said, pouring her a healthy portion and sliding it over to her. "She couldn't always get someone to watch me and Lily, so she'd drag us along and we'd 'elp as much as we were able. She useter pass by this place coming and going, and she'd always stop and say, 'Ain't it pretty? When Dad comes 'ome, we're gonna get a place like this.' Only we din't. Dad came 'ome, but before 'e gets the bees and 'oney together, 'e gets inter something on the docks, never knew what, and next thing we knew, 'e'd caught someone's knife. And she was gone from the consumption by then."

He took a sip of his port.

"I wasn't even twelve," he continued. "Lily was fifteen. Uncle Ned took us in, and I started in on 'is business, working my way up. And I swore to myself that as soon as I could, I'd buy this place so Mum would know I still remembered what she wanted for us. And I did."

"To your mum," said Iris, holding up her glass.

"To Mum," he said, clinking his against hers.

"So what's this all about?" she asked, holding up the key.

"You introduced me to your mum," he said. "That upped the ante in our little game. So, I see your mum, and I raise you one 'ouse key."

"Are you asking me to move in with you again?"

"You can move in, you can not move in," he said. "But you've got a key now. When you 'ad to go on the run from the rozzers a couple months back, you called me for a place to stay. I 'ad to turn you down, and I felt bad about that. So I am giving you un-restricted access to my 'ome in case you need to do a bunk in the future."

"You could have given me a key to the flat instead."

"Yeah, but that's penny-ante compared to the enormity of you bringing a spiv in to meet your mum. She din't approve of me, in case you 'adn't noticed."

"Join the club," said Iris. "She doesn't approve of me, either. I've given up trying to gain her approval."

"No, you 'aven't," said Archie. "We never give up trying to get our mums smiling at us."

"Even after they're long gone," said Iris, looking around.

"Especially then," said Archie.

"Would your mum have liked me, do you think?"

"She'd be amazed I found someone on your level."

"Stop. I've left a trail of failed romances behind me. On anyone's level, I'm damaged goods."

"Maybe, but you're honest about it. She'd like that."

"Funny thing about that, Arch," she said, smiling ruefully. "I'm only completely honest with you. I think you're the only man I've met strong enough to withstand the full Medusa."

"Which one was she again?"

"A monster who turned men to stone when she looked at them directly," she said, looking at him directly.

He met her gaze unflinchingly.

"Do I pass?" he asked.

"With flying colours," she replied.

"'Ow did Detective Ex 'old up under that petrifying stare?"

"Not nearly as well," she said with a grimace. "How did things go with him today?"

"I think 'e's convinced I don't go in for corpse robbing," said Archie. "Maybe one of the few crimes 'e thinks I 'aven't done."

"Which leaves Reg and Des and whoever else was down there," said Iris. "Who do you think took the ring? Why, for that matter?"

"Dunno, don't particularly want to know," said Archie. "I'd as soon 'ave the 'ole mess go away as quickly as possible. Ain't got nothing to do with me."

He sighed, then tossed back the rest of his port.

"I'm cursed, is what it is," he said. "I should've stuck with the warehouses and the docks, kept things steady, but I took over a club in payment of a debt, and it was fun rubbing elbows with that crowd. So I expanded. This was gonna be my third club. Reg din't want me to buy it. Said we 'ad enough on our plate as it was, but I said, no, it's our chance to go legit, but clubs ain't really legit, everyone knows that. You've got liquor, you've got inspections, and that means bungs thrown everywhere. And then this dead bloke turns up, like he's pointing a finger right at me, saying what do you know about being legit?"

"You'll be fine," said Iris reassuringly. "Mike will be out of your hair in a day or two. He knows what he's doing."

"Yeah, well, I'm sorry it ain't you and Gwen digging into it," said Archie.

"We're trying to stay legit, too," she said. "Murder is not our business."

"Come on, we 'aven't finished the tour," he said, getting to his feet and holding out his hand.

"What's next, the kitchen?" she asked, taking it.

"I was thinking the bedroom."

"Good," she said.

"And I'm raising the stakes again," he said. "Spend the night. You never did that at the flat."

"I don't have an overnight bag," she said. "I hate wearing the same outfit two days in a row."

"I 'ave anticipated that," he said grandly. "You'll find a new outfit waiting for you in the closet."

"Archie! Another trip to the grey market?"

"Oh, this one was as black as coal," he said.

"How did you know my size?"

"Measured you with me 'ands more than a few times, 'aven't I?"

"You scamp! That's all you needed?"

"And I peeked at the labels when you were in the lav once," he confessed.

"Even better," she said. "I don't always trust those hands of yours."

"I bought you something else to wear," he said as he walked behind her up the stairs.

"What's that?"

"You'll see."

Gwen stood inside her walk-in closet, staring at frocks and suits, thinking too much.

It's a first date, she thought. A first date with Walter Prendergast, who has announced his intentions to interrogate me thoroughly to determine if he will choose to fall in love with me.

It sounded like a job interview.

Her eyes turned to her Utility suits, the ones she wore to the office.

She had never worn a suit on a first date. On any date, for that matter, although her previous dating era had been when she was in her teens, long before rationing had made Utility suits de rigueur. By the time she turned twenty, she was already madly in love with Ronnie, forsaking all others.

Since his death, the only real dates she had gone on were with Sally, Iris's chum from her Cambridge days, and those were a small group of tentative, awkward outings, even though she adored him and valued his friendship. She broke it off when it became clear that he wanted Gwen to be something she wasn't.

Prendergast, on the other hand, wanted to find out who she was.

So did she.

Who are you, Gwen? she thought. I don't know yet. I am a businesswoman. I am the co-proprietor of The Right Sort Marriage Bureau by dint of my own enterprise; general partner and principal shareholder of Bainbridge, Ltd., by marriage and inheritance; widowed mother of the ebullient Ronnie the Second, future Lord Bainbridge. And an occasional, if inadvertent, investigator of mysterious crimes.

And I haven't made love to a man in over four years.

A first date with Walter Prendergast would not end in bed, she thought. Which was fine. It wasn't meant to be a seduction for either party. Merely dinner and conversation. An established business-woman such as she would be perfectly justified in wearing a Utility suit on a first date with Walter Prendergast.

But would a Utility suit discourage him from a second date?

I'm out of touch. What do women do nowadays?

It was a disquieting thought for someone who matched couples for a living.

She wanted to call Iris and pick her brain. She was dying to know how the meeting between Archie and Iris's mum had gone. But she suspected that the aftermath of the dinner would be con-tinuing late into the night, either in celebration or consolation for passing that milestone.

It must be nice to have an aftermath, she thought.

She imagined being in bed with Walter Prendergast, then im-mediately banished the image from her mind, shuddering as she did so.

Then she wondered why she suppressed it so quickly. She was no prude (she thought). She had given way to fantasies about other men before, Ronald Colman being a longtime favourite. Lord knows Des had played an active part in her dreams the past few months. Yet the moment she summoned Mr. Prendergast—Walter, damn it! Walter, Walter, Walter!—her reveries snapped back into celibacy.

Why couldn't she give him a chance? There were many admi-rable qualities to Walter. She acknowledged that.

But he never struck her as being fun. And she wanted some fun after all these years of mourning and misery and medication. Dating should be fun. She thought back to her teens, to the ex-citement of being young and in love with a young man, daring to do what they shouldn't, racing through London at high speeds, sneaking into unlicensed clubs, drinking too much and dancing too late, generally behaving with reckless abandon, as if they could see what was coming and needed to cram all of their lives into a few short years.

Now, she was old enough to do all that without permission of parents or courts. The question was, would Walter Prendergast, who was even older, want to do any of it?

And if he didn't, was that sufficient reason to reject him? Or had the time come in her life to give up fun in exchange for—for what, exactly?

There was a knock on her door, a respectful, precisely measured rap that could be produced by none other than Percival, the Bainbridges' butler.

She opened her door, welcoming the interruption to her train of thought before it went hurtling over a collapsed bridge into a ravine.

"I beg your pardon for intruding at this time of night, Mrs. Bainbridge," he said.

"It's only nine o'clock, Percival," she said. "Hardly the wee small hours."

"No, Mrs. Bainbridge," he said. "But I know that your custom is to keep to your room once the boys have been tucked in."

"How boring I sound," she said. "What brings you to my door, Percival?"

"There is a telephone call for you," he said. "A gentleman—well, I am loath to characterise him as such. A man who calls himself Mr. Sticks, which cannot possibly be his actual name. I would have dismissed him, but given your recent contacts with certain denizens of the East End, I thought I had better consult with you before relegating him to the ranks of the disconnected. Is he truly of your acquaintance?"

"I have met him," she confessed. "Although I am perplexed as to why he should be calling me. Did he give you his reason?"

"He did not," said Percival. "Shall I keep the portcullis lowered?"

"No, I'm curious now," said Gwen. "I'll come down."

"Very well, Mrs. Bainbridge."

She descended the stairs and walked quickly to the hallway telephone.

"Hello?" she said.

"Is this Gwen Bainbridge?" came his voice.

"That would be Mrs. Bainbridge to you, I should think."

"You were Gwen when you thrashed me so soundly yesterday," he said. "I should think we're on a first-name basis by now."

"Except that I don't know your actual name," she pointed out.

"River's good enough for now," he said.

"Why are you calling me, River?"

"First, to send you regards from Joe Davis."

"You spoke to Joe about me?"

"I wanted to see if your story was on the level, so I called him up and told him about our little encounter. When he was done laughing, and that took a while, he told me I was lucky not to lose my shirt and suspenders playing you. He said you could've given Margaret Quinn a run for her money had you gone into it full-time."

"I played Margaret a few times privately," said Gwen. "She beat me soundly, then we had ice cream. It was kind of Uncle Joe to say."

"Joe Davis don't puff up anyone who ain't worth it," said River. "Which brings me to my second item. The boys say you come from money, and the fact that you got a butler answering the telephone means they're not wrong. Are you really having dinner with a millionaire on Friday?"

"I'm afraid so."

"Then you're free tomorrow night."

"Free? Free for what?"

"I am challenging you, Gwen," he said. "I underestimated you yesterday, and you justly took me to school. Now I want to see how you and me do going toe to toe. No tricks, no cons, no holding back."

She was glad no one else was in the hallway to see her with her mouth hanging open.

"And what do you propose to wager this time?" she asked.

"Nothing," he said. "No money, no favours. We play for love."

"Love, Mr. Sticks?"

"You know what I mean," he said impatiently.

"Just to clarify," she said. "Is this a date?"

"Bloody hell, woman! Of course it's a date!"

"Then I have a condition," she said.

"I said no wagers, no favours, remember?"

"Nevertheless, I must insist," she said.

"What is it?"

"I won't go anywhere with you unless you tell me your real name."

"Ah, do I have to reveal my darkest secret already?" he asked.

"I'm afraid so."

"Rodman," he said. "Rodman Hilliard. But don't tell anyone. It's too boring."

"Very well, Mr. Hilliard, I accept your challenge."

"Right, I'll pick you up at your office in Mayfair so you won't shock the Kensington crowd."

"You seem to know a great deal about me, Mr. Hilliard."

"You're an object of curiosity in Archie Spelling's world," he said. "All I had to do was ask around the room. Until tomorrow, Gwen."

"Until tomorrow. Rodman."

He hung up.

I'm going on a date with a man I've just met, she thought happily.

Oh, God.

What am I going to wear?

Iris stood in front of the full-length mirror in the entry hall, inspecting her new outfit, a grey and black chicken-foot plaid woolen suit that clung to her curves just right while still projecting a professional demeanour. She had got up early and bathed, then came out to find a robe laid out on the bed with a note reading, "Toast and tea when you're done." They ate in the kitchen together—she smiling shyly at first, then relaxing into the rare experience of breakfasting with a lover when neither of them had to rush somewhere else for propriety's sake.

Now, she waited for him to finish dressing so he could drop her in Mayfair before going off to resume his life.

It felt gloriously ordinary, she thought. As long as she ignored the fact that the life he was resuming was one of crime.

She glanced idly at the photos on the wall, spotting details in both of his parents' faces that had reappeared on his, combining into something entirely new in the process. And there was Stanley in uniform, amidst a group of nine soldiers, grinning reassurance at the camera.

There was another photo directly next to it of Stanley with two men whom she recognised as fellow soldiers from the previous photo. They were in civvies here, suits cut from styles that she remembered from her childhood, which meant from the early twenties. They were seated at a table in a pub, pints raised in salute to the unseen cameraman. The grins were almost the same as in the first photo, but there was something in their eyes, a haunted look that burned through that frozen moment. They were now men who had lived through horrors the men in the first photograph had yet to encounter, and the grins carried no reassurance anymore.

Archie came down the steps while she perused the two photographs, tucking a purple pocket square into the upper pocket of his chalk-stripe suit. He saw which photograph she was looking at.

"That's the last one I 'ave of Dad," he said. "Coupla months before Mum died."

"Looks like a military reunion," she said. "What unit was he in? I don't recognise the insignia on the uniforms in this one."

"He and a bunch of 'is mates from Wapping signed up together.

There was pals' battalions then. Wapping didn't 'ave one, so they joined the West Ham Pals in the Essex Regiment. Only a few of them came back."

"Why does the man to his right in the pub look so familiar?" asked Iris, looking at it closely.

"Ah, you can see the resemblance," said Archie. "You've met 'is boy."

"Des Burton," said Iris in amazement. "Your dad and Des's dad served together."

"They did. Bosom buddies, along with Jenks Emery, the third bloke. All gone now."

"I'm sorry," said Iris. "It must have been terrible to lose him. To lose both your parents."

"I survived," said Archie. "So I'll drop you off at The Right Sort, shall I?"

"How about a few streets away?" suggested Iris.

"Still jumpy about being seen with me?"

"Being seen first thing in the morning, yes," said Iris. "I am running a marriage bureau, after all. I don't want to give our clients the impression that they don't need to get married to have a wonderful time. Don't worry, Archie. I've introduced you to Mum, I've spent the night, and I'm going as your date to Bernie and Tish's wedding on Saturday. All of London will know we are an item. But they don't have to know that this morning."

"Gotcher," said Archie, opening the front door for her. "Your chariot awaits."

He drove her to Mayfair and pulled up on Grosvenor Street, far enough south of The Right Sort to give her cover. He leaned over and kissed her.

"'Ave a nice day at work, dearie," he said.

"You, too, ducks," she said. "Thanks for the invitation."

"Like to come back for seconds?"

"I'll have to," she said. "I left my other suit behind."

She got out of the car and waved as he drove off, then walked to the office, whistling. She stopped in mid-phrase when she saw a man standing in front of the building entrance, smiling at her.

It wasn't a pleasant smile, she thought, but he wasn't a pleasant man. Gareth Pontefract, a reporter from the sleazier echelons of journalism. He was holding a manila folder in his hand.

"You never take the same route two days in a row, do you, Sparks?" he asked as she came up. "Makes a fellow think you were trying to avoid someone."

"At the moment, it's you," said Sparks. "What do you want?"

"I'm investigating a story," he said. "You're part of it."

"Investigating for whom?" she asked. "I heard the *Mirror* gave you the sack. Too hands-on with the female staff even for their low standards."

"I'm freelancing," he said. "Get a good story, sell it to the highest bidder. Think I got one. Shall we talk?"

"Come inside and let's get this over with," she said reluctantly.

"Oh, no, we'll do it right here," he said. "Last time I was in your office, you assaulted me."

"Not that much," she said. "And much less than I could have or than you deserved. It was appalling how easy it was to chase you away."

"I'll stay out here where there's witnesses, if it's all the same to you," he said.

"Fine. Say your piece."

"A picture's worth a thousand words," he said, handing her the manila folder.

She opened it and managed to keep her face expressionless. Inside was a blown-up photograph of her and Archie, coming out of her mother's house.

"So that flash was from you," she said. "Who were you following? Me, Archie, or my mother?"

"Doesn't matter," he said with a leer. "Labour MP's daughter caught consorting with gangster. Clandestine nighttime meeting at politician's home. What corruption is transpiring? I'm sure her constituents would like to know. Care to comment?"

"No corruption took place, and if I wanted to arrange a clandestine meeting, I would make a much better job of it," she said. "Anything else? I could provide you with a menu."

"You could provide me with something much better," he said.

"Like what?"

"This story's fresh. I was up late developing the photo. So I haven't sold it to anyone yet."

"Make your point soon, please. I have a job waiting for me."

"For a reasonable sum, I can make this not happen," he said. "Prints and negative."

"I'm a small businesswoman. We have nothing in the operating budget for blackmail. Go peddle your rotting fish elsewhere."

"I didn't expect it to come from you, Sparks," he said. "You happen to be the common link for the two with the real money. I don't much care who pays me off."

"What makes you think I care about whether this gets published or not?"

"Because you haven't taken a swing at me yet," he said. "And there's no point in getting your gangster boyfriend to threaten me. I've got everything in a safe place, ready to be sent out if I don't check in on a daily basis. I'll take that copy back, if you don't mind. Here's my card."

She exchanged the folder for the card, holding it gingerly by the edge like it was something infectious. He walked away, glancing back to see if she was following. She turned and went inside.

Gwen looked up with concern when she entered their office.

"I saw Pontefract waiting outside when I arrived," she said. "What did he want?"

"Hush money," said Iris. "He caught Archie and me coming out of Mum's house after dinner. He has photographic evidence. Not exactly in flagrante delicto, more in flagrante ambulatorio, but not good."

"How much does he want?"

"He didn't say. He's testing the waters, seeing which way I'll go."

"Which way will you go?"

Iris sat heavily in her chair and kicked back so it tilted her against the wall behind her, her arms folded behind her head.

"How terrible a daughter would I be if I told him to go jump in the river?" she asked.

"That depends," said Gwen.

"On what?"

"On how much you care about your mother and her career," said Gwen.

"Why should it matter to the world if I'm dating Archie?" asked Iris. "The whole point of bringing him to meet Mum was for us to take another step towards daylight."

"You could have taken that step months ago," said Gwen. "You're the one who's been keeping it on the q.t. You wanted to postpone the revelation for the wedding, but that's coming up soon. So what are you worried about?"

"I've been staving off my mother's disapproval, I suppose," said Iris. "What care I what the tabloids think, but one malevolent remark from the Witch of Hackney and I'm reduced to a quivering child again. It would serve her right if I ended up bringing her house crashing down."

"How did the meeting go last night? Did Archie bring enough cheese?"

"He did, and he brought something even better."

"What?"

"An argument. A political discussion, in which he engaged his local MP with intelligence and passion."

"Really? On what topic?"

"The proposed development of the Wanstead Flats. Turns out,

it struck a nerve in him. I'm almost beginning to think his pursuit of my favours was part of a long-term plan to arrange this face-to-face on the topic. And I honestly think she enjoyed it, in her own special emotion-stifling way. But then she told me privately that she thinks I'm dating him to get back at her. And now that that's been planted in my brain, I keep wondering if she's right."

"Sort that out with Dr. Milford," said Gwen. "Now, a more important question: When did you get that suit? I thought we had done all our winter shopping."

"A gift from an admirer," said Iris. "I'd tell you the brand, but it seems to have been acquired before the labels were sewn on."

"It's lovely," said Gwen.

"And you're looking dressier than usual," said Iris.

Gwen had one of her Utility jackets on, but the frock underneath was a soft fawn-coloured sleeveless dress, with ruffles gathered across the front, held on with large, soft buttons.

"Yes, I thought I would mix and match today," said Gwen. "Do you think it works?"

"It does. If I didn't know better, I'd say you were trying it out before your date with Mr. Prendergast," said Iris. "But that's tomorrow, isn't— Why are you blushing?"

"Am I?"

"You blushed the moment I said 'date,'" said Iris. "Why?"

"I, um, have a date tonight," confessed Gwen.

"Did Prendergast move it up after all that formality?" asked Iris. "That's rather last-second of him."

"It's not with Walter," said Gwen.

"You have a date with someone else?" exclaimed Iris. "With whom?"

"His name is Rodman Hilliard," said Gwen.

"And who is he?"

"Someone I met recently," said Gwen. "He called last night to ask me out."

"And you said yes straightaway," said Iris in wonderment. "My goodness, this is a Gwen I have not seen before. What's he like?"

"Brash," said Gwen. "Impetuous."

"Good-looking?"

"Not bad at all," said Gwen, considering. "But it was his directness that I found appealing. Walter has been courting me as if he's been consulting a manual the entire time."

"I can't wait to hear the juicy details tomorrow," said Iris.

"There won't be any juicy details," said Gwen.

"I live in hope."

"Did Archie tell you anything new about the investigation at the White Palace?"

"It sounds like Mike doesn't think he took the ring."

"I wonder how long the police will be puttering around there," said Gwen. "I want the crime solved so the renovations can continue. Do you think they're done examining the scene?"

The intercom buzzed before Iris could answer. She picked up the phone.

"Detective Sergeant Kinsey's calling," said Mrs. Billington.

"Fine, put him through," said Iris.

She mouthed "Mike" to Gwen, who raised an eyebrow in response.

"Good morning, Mike," said Iris. "We were thinking of calling you to see if you were done with the crime scene yet. What's the latest?"

"Funny thing, Sparks," said Kinsey. "I went back there this morning with some of the specialists from the Yard, only someone had beaten us to it. The place was clean as a whistle. No bricks, no plaster."

"Interesting. What do you make of it, and why are you calling me?"

"I want to know if you knew where Spelling was last night."

Iris hesitated, then remembered their previous conversation.

Loyalty to boyfriends has never been a strong suit of yours.

"He was with me," she said.

"For how long?"

"The entire night."

There was silence at the other end of the line.

"When you say the entire night," he said, phrasing it carefully, "were you out in some club? Or were you—"

"In bed," said Iris.

"And can you account for his whereabouts for the entire time you were together?"

"Most of it," said Iris. "We did fall asleep eventually. Would you like details? Comparisons?"

"I know you're together, Sparks," said Kinsey. "But I've been putting the full impact of what that means out of my mind as much as possible. I hate to think you've fallen this low."

"You had your chance, Mike," she said. "Now you have Beryl. Do your job, go home to your wife, and try not to think about me when you take her to bed tonight."

She slammed down the handset, causing the telephone to bounce on the desk.

"What caused all that?" asked Gwen.

"Someone cleaned out the crime scene while everyone was asleep," said Iris. "Or not asleep, in my case. Mike took an opportunity to join my mother in registering disapproval of my relationship. They should form a club and hold weekly meetings."

"I'm sorry," said Gwen. "For what it's worth, you have my support."

"It's worth a great deal," said Iris. "Thank you. In any case, looks like the White Palace can continue with its restoration. Let's get on with planning the details."

They began to discuss possibilities for food, decorations, and music. All the while, Iris thought about her conversation with

Mike. The things she said. But, more important, the detail she had omitted out of loyalty to Archie.

That the three men in the picture from after the Great War were wearing rings that looked like the one stolen from the dead man.

CHAPTER 5

Right, that covers the room, the staff, the security, and the food," said Iris, adding up the figures on her pad while keeping the handset pinioned between her left ear and shoulder.

"You'll want a cash bar," said Archie at the other end. "You'll need two bartenders with that size room."

"That would make sense," said Iris.

"What about champagne?" whispered Gwen, who was peering over Iris's shoulder at the list.

"Gwen wants to know about champagne," said Iris. "Can you get some?"

"Lessee, we're talking about toasts at midnight, not getting sozzled on bubbly throughout," said Archie. "We can squeeze eight toasts out of a bottle. 'Ow many guests?"

"Depends on how many have no better plans," said Iris. "But given that these are our clients, most won't. Let's say a hundred and fifty."

"Call it twenty bottles, then," said Archie. "And you're throwing that in with the price of admission?"

"Of course. It's New Year's Eve."

"I can't guarantee the flutes," said Archie. "People might end up with paper cups."

"Most of them will be getting their first taste of champers since the thirties," said Iris. "They'll drink it out of used coffee mugs if that's all we can forage."

"We can do better than that," said Archie.

"You're quite adept at catering," she said. "I think you may have a future in this business."

"Normally, I would delegate, but seeing as it's you and Gwen, I am taking a personal interest," said Archie. "And it gives us a chance to test out the new club on a liquored-up group, so that's a bonus. All right, here's the moment of truth."

He quoted a price. Iris winced, then scribbled it down and held it up for Gwen to see.

"How much of that would you need in advance?" asked Iris.

"All of it," said Archie. "Items must be procured, and that takes planning and payment."

Gwen tapped Iris on the shoulder. Her partner looked up at her.

"Tell him yes," said Gwen calmly.

"You're certain?"

"I am."

Iris turned back to the telephone.

"Gwen approves," she said. "We'll get you the money this week. Thank you, Archie. I'll see you later."

"You know where I live," said Archie.

"I do now."

She blew a kiss at the mouthpiece, hung up, then turned back to Gwen.

"How are we getting this payment?" she asked. "We can't ask the bank for a loan so we can throw a party."

"We're getting it from me," said Gwen. "I'm in control of my finances now, remember? I have a brand-new chequebook burning a hole in my bag."

"All right," said Iris. "We'll pay you back from the proceeds, of course. Anything over that goes into the kitty. We could actually make some money off this."

"That's the idea," said Gwen, pulling out her chequebook. "Who do I make it out to? Archie Spelling? Or would he prefer cash and no questions asked?"

"Make it out to Spelling Enterprises," said Iris. "We're dealing with his legitimate business for a change. Mostly, anyway."

"Good," said Gwen, entering the name and amount. "That will look better on our books. We have enough questionable entries as it is."

She tore it off and handed it to Iris, who looked at it.

"Cheque number three," she commented. "What were the first two?"

"The Royal Hospital and Home for Incurables, and the Oxford Committee for Famine Relief," replied Gwen. "I thought my re-entry into the world of the sane should begin with charity, especially given the season."

"Very well, it's time to turn Mrs. Billington loose with the invitations," said Iris. "I can't believe we're doing this. It will be quite the coup if we pull it off. We'll have to float some stories to the press."

"Shall I see if Pontefract is still lurking outside?" asked Gwen.

"To any member of the press but him. Oh, don't forget to record this in our expenses."

Gwen pulled out the ledger book for The Right Sort and entered the amount she had fronted in the debits column. She looked over the book after she did.

"You know," she said thoughtfully, "I could repay our loan to the bank now. It would—"

"Don't you dare!" snapped Iris.

Gwen looked up at her partner, startled. Iris's face was livid with anger.

"What did I say?" asked Gwen.

"May I remind you that we are partners," said Iris. "Equal partners. We started this business together, we run it together, and we signed for that loan together."

"I know, but—"

"Maybe coming into your fortune at last has turned this into a hobby rather than a profession, but this is all that I have," said Iris. "And I am damn proud that we are making a go of it. Hell, we're coming to year-end with our ledger firmly in the black, in this economy no less, and how many women can say that?"

"Relatively few, I suspect."

"Exactly. Now, as long as we are paying that loan from our earnings, we continue on an equal footing. But if you repay it without me, then I will owe you my share. I will be in your debt, Gwendolyn Bainbridge, and this will no longer be a real partnership. I will not have that."

"I'm sorry," said Gwen, shaken. "I thought it would help, especially with you trying to get a flat."

"That's my problem, not yours."

"But I can help," insisted Gwen.

"Not like this, you can't."

"Very well," said Gwen. She started to say something else, then hesitated.

"What?" asked Iris irritably.

"The house I was going to look at with you Saturday," said Gwen miserably. "The one in Maida Vale."

"What about it?"

"One of the reasons I wanted you to see it was that it came with an attached flat," said Gwen.

"An attached flat? For me?"

"I thought it could be a possibility."

"And if I took it, to whom would I be paying rent?"

"Well, if I bought the house outright—"

"I see," said Iris. "You would be my landlady. What would

happen if I fell behind on the rent? You can't send Sally to threaten me, he's on my side now."

"I wouldn't do anything like that."

"How exactly was this flat used before?"

"Well—I believe it was meant to be, um, for the housekeeper," said Gwen.

"Servant's quarters," said Iris. "You were going to put me in servant's quarters."

"It's an independent flat," said Gwen. "It could be for anyone."

"Were you going to charge me market price, or subsidise me as another one of your charities?"

"I thought it would be nice to have my best friend close by," said Gwen.

"You're rich again," said Iris. "You'll be making all sorts of new friends, I'm sure."

"That's not fair," said Gwen.

"I suppose it isn't," said Iris. "Forgive me. So much of life isn't fair. I'm going in to speak to Mrs. Billington now."

She walked out.

"Stupid, stupid Gwen," Gwen muttered.

They worked in relative silence for the rest of the day, taking their lunches separately. They walked to their afternoon appointments with Dr. Milford in less than companionable silence. Each spent her session complaining to him about the other, and the good doctor asked them enough questions about their motivations to make them doubt them. The return walk to the office was again silent, but Iris reached out and squeezed Gwen's hand, and the gesture was reciprocated.

As five o'clock approached, Gwen ducked down to the lav, then reappeared with her makeup freshened and a bright shade of red on her lips.

"Too much? Not enough?" she asked.

"Depends on your objectives," said Iris.

"Fun," said Gwen. "Then home to bed."

"But no fun in bed."

"No."

"Then I think you're wearing enough to leave a nice souvenir on a shirt collar," said Iris. "How do you feel?"

"Nervous. Excited."

She glanced at her watch.

"He's probably waiting for me," she said. "Wish me luck."

"Good luck," said Iris.

She gave her partner a head start, then slipped off her shoes and scampered soundlessly down the stairs until she reached the landing overlooking the entrance to the building. She peered out to see none other than River Sticks standing by a powder-blue Riley Merlin. He was wearing a grey demob suit instead of his spiv garb, with a dark blue tie that was muted and narrow rather than garish. His trilby, at a rakish angle, was lifted in salute as Gwen emerged, and he opened the car door for her as a most proper gentleman would do.

Gwen glanced up at the building as she got in, and Iris ducked hastily out of sight. She heard the engine roar into life, and when she risked another look, the Merlin was gone.

"Rodman Hilliard?" she said in wonderment to the empty landing.

"When were you demobbed?" asked Gwen.

"About two months ago," said River. "Then it took me another week to get home."

"From where?"

"Italy. I was a tank driver. Saw the war through a tiny little window. North Africa, Anzio, Italy."

"Was it terrible?" she asked softly.

"I made it through," he said. "Had my tiepin tucked away in my pocket the entire time. Like I said, it's lucky."

"I am so sorry that I asked you to make a wager with it," said Gwen.

"It came back to me, didn't it?" he said. "And now I'm on a date with you, so still lucky."

"Where are we going?"

"A snooker hall over in Battersea."

"Battersea? Not exactly the East End, is it?"

"I got an in with the manager there. He's holding us a table, and they don't kick up a fuss about women playing."

"That's good to know," said Gwen. "It was always frustrating that I couldn't get into some of the better clubs."

"You wanted to play?"

"I wanted to watch. Daddy indulged me up to a point with the lessons, but he would never allow a Brewster girl to sully her reputation in cheap competition. He was the same with my brother when he wanted to race cars."

"Brewster's the maiden name, is it?" asked River, glancing over at her. "I heard about your husband. Sorry for it."

"Thanks," said Gwen.

"Would Mr. Bainbridge have let you into a snooker hall?"

"I'd like to think so," said Gwen. "Certainly when we were young."

"Young?" he said. "You're still young by the looks of it."

"I was young before the war," she said.

He crossed the Thames via the Albert Bridge, then drove into Battersea and parked. He reached behind her to collect a narrow case from the back, then got out.

"The place is on the rough side," he warned her as he came around to open her door. "Don't go wandering off."

There was a pub on the corner, but River led her to a plain metal door on the side with only an eight ball painted in the centre to give any hint of what lay beyond. River opened it. There was a set of steps going up.

"After you," he said.

They emerged at the top to see a large open room with three billiards tables and three snooker tables spread out. A bar ran along the wall by the entrance, with a small group of battered wooden tables and chairs by it at which sat a dishevelled group of men who eyed Gwen suspiciously as if she had come in to lecture them on temperance or hygiene. They relaxed when River appeared by her side.

"Hello, Ralph," he said to the bartender.

"Evening, Rod," said the bartender. "Who's your lady friend?"

"This here is Mabel," said River. "She's come for a lesson."

"Hello, Mabel," said the bartender. "Got a last name?"

"Dodge," said Gwen, trying to match River's accent. "Mabel Dodge. Nice to meetcher."

He smirked, and she realised she hadn't pulled it off.

Fine, she thought. So I'm a posh girl slumming. Won't be the first he's ever seen.

"You wanted table six," said the bartender. "It's ready."

"Thanks," said River. "I'll take a pint. Fancy a drink, Mabel?"

"A pint'll do me fine, thanks," said Gwen.

They carried them over to the far snooker table.

"Cheers," said River, holding his glass up.

"Cheers," she replied, tapping hers against it.

She took a sip. It was flat and watery, but she kept herself from grimacing.

"Yeah, it's pretty horrible," he said quietly. "Grab yourself a cue."

He opened his case, pulled out the two pieces of his cue stick, and screwed them together while she eyed the selection on the rack on the wall. Most were aged and much used, the warping apparent even to casual inspection.

"I could shoot around corners with some of these," she said.

"You don't have your own?" he asked.

"It's somewhere in a closet back in my old home," she said. "And I don't go there much lately."

"I'd recommend that one," he said, pointing at the second from the left.

"My thoughts as well," she said, taking it from the rack.

She examined the tip critically, then gave it a thorough chalking before turning to the table.

It wasn't nearly the quality of the one at Archie Spelling's headquarters, she saw with dismay as he set up the balls. There were cigarette burns in the baize, rips that had been ineptly repaired, some glued down so that there were ridges at the joins, some patches left nearly bald. The cushions weren't even down their lengths, and she had the impression that the entire table may not have been perfectly level.

"I can see why this one was available," she commented. "Are you sure you wouldn't rather play skittles somewhere?"

"You like skittles, too?" he said, pulling out a shilling. "We'll save that for a second date. Heads or tails?"

"Tails."

He flipped it in her direction. She caught it, then slapped it onto the back of her other hand and showed it to him.

"You break," he said, setting up the table.

He rolled the cue ball to her and she set it at the baulk line to the right of the centre ball. Then she bent down to the table, keeping her back elbow bent so that the forearm was perpendicular to the cue, and sighted down the table at the right corner red ball.

She wanted to re-create the same opening shot that she had done the other day, the classic opening that Joe Davis had taught her, but the cue stick felt unwieldy in her hands as she slid it between the knuckles of her left. She tapped the cue ball soundly, but instead of just ticking off the corner ball and finding its way back to her, it struck it solidly, sending a few of the other balls away from the pack and rattling around the corner before coming to a halt at that end of the table.

"You're being nicer to me this time," said River.

"I'm not trying to be," replied Gwen.

"Neither am I," he said.

He quickly knocked in three red balls, following each with the black. On the next shot, the cue ball spun off the cushion and rolled back past the baulk line.

"You didn't leave me much," observed Gwen.

Her cue still felt as if it weren't sliding completely straight, so she adjusted for it, sending the ball gently off the far cushion so it came to rest against the remainder of the pack without dislodging any of them.

"Now we're talking," said River.

He tapped it away from the pack. It bounced off the cushion and came back to much the same spot on the table.

Snooker is a war of attrition, she thought, remembering her early instruction. If you can't pot a ball, put your opponent into an awkward spot, and hope he's the one to make the next mistake.

They traded safeties, each placing the cue ball farther away from the pack. Finally, River left a red ball detached from its fellows. Gwen promptly knocked it in, following it with the black in the opposite corner. The cue ball spun into the pack and broke it up enough to allow her to pass River for the lead before she finally missed a shot, leaving him with a relatively easy angle on one. She stepped back to watch, leaning on her cue.

He surveyed the table, then lined up his shot. To her surprise, he left the easy target on the table, sending the cue ball bouncing back. It knocked against the cushion, then came to rest behind the yellow, just touching it.

"Nasty," said Gwen.

She sent it away from the yellow, bouncing it off the same spot on the cushion, causing it to roll back down to glance off a red without striking any of the intervening colours.

"Nice," he said.

His next shot put the cue ball back at the end of the table, this time behind the brown.

She looked at it, then at him, considering.

"Exactly what sort of game are you playing?" she asked.

"I don't know what you're talking about," he replied.

"It seems to me," she said, "that you are more interested in putting me into difficult positions than you are in scoring points."

"Let's see what you can do with that one," he said.

Instead of reversing the course of his shot, she angled the cue ball off the side cushion. It ticked off a red, then nestled against the top cushion behind the black.

"Good," he said.

"Why good?"

"When you showed me up the other day, the pots you were making were easy ones for the most part," he said. "It was a skillful but simple break."

"That was all I needed for a short game. So what is this about?"

"I wanted to see how you'd do under less ideal conditions, where the positions are difficult, the table is tilted, the baize is shot, and the sticks are rubbish. And where I can get my own game going."

"What's the verdict?"

"You're good, Mrs. Bainbridge. Let's finish the frame."

When the last ball dropped, River had won. But not by much.

"Well done," said Gwen.

"Likewise," he replied. "Let's get a bite, then we'll play another."

"I almost hesitate to ask," said Gwen. "What do they have here?"

"Fish and chips, or fish and chips," he said. "Another pint?"

"Do they have anything better to drink?"

"They do not," he said.

He put in the order with the bartender, who called downstairs, then drew them two more pints, which River carried over to a small table.

"How long since you've played regular?" he asked.

"Summer of forty-five," she said. "They have a table at my in-laws' estate, and I was on my own a great deal. It was therapeutic."

"Who'd you play against?"

"Usually no one," she said. "I divided myself into two players. Good Gwen and Evil Gwen. Good Gwen played by the rules. Evil Gwen did not."

"Which Gwen have I been playing tonight?"

"Good Gwen at the start," she said, eyeing him over her glass. "Evil Gwen has been emerging since I saw what you were doing."

"Evil Gwen is the one I want to play," he said. "Let her start the next frame. In the meantime, I have a proposition for you."

Iris turned her key in the lock at Archie's house, still not quite believing she was doing so. As she entered, she saw a piece of paper on the hall table with her name on top. She picked it up.

Had to take care of something. Should be back by 7:30. A.

She thought about making dinner for the two of them. Having it ready on the table for when he came home.

Is this what a fully domesticated Iris Sparks is like? she wondered.

She went into the kitchen to check on supplies. There was a slab wrapped in butcher's paper in the refrigerator that she opened to reveal a steak the size of which she hadn't seen since before the war.

I wonder if that's for a special occasion, she thought. *Or am I the special occasion? Were Archie's previous lovers considered steak worthy? Or was it being held in reserve for some serious gangster business? Red meat to fuel bloody plans?*

Better not start cooking until I have authorisation.

The oven and range were new, she noticed. Less likely to end one's life by explosion compared to the small one in her kitchen-ette, which leaked gas alarmingly. She wasn't going to miss that place. Too many bad memories for such a short period.

She opened the various cupboards, noting the locations of dishes, tinned vegetables and fruits, canisters of porridge and flour. She pulled out a tin of peas and put it on the counter, then looked back at the gap she had made. There was something hidden in back of the tins. She reached behind them and felt cold steel. She moved a few tins out of the way until she could lift the gun out carefully.

A Browning Hi-Power, a recent acquaintance from her Special Ops training, even though by the time the gun had come into reg-ular issue, she had long blown her chances of going over.

She pulled out the clip. It was fully loaded. She put it back in, then replaced the gun where she had found it and put the tins back.

Well, no surprise when you come right down to it, she thought. The head of the Spelling gang had to anticipate the sudden need to defend himself to the tune of thirteen cartridges. She wondered what other weapons were secreted about this charming little dwell-ing that Mrs. Spelling once thought so dear.

"What've you got to drink in this place?" she asked the empty house.

She went into the dining room to the cabinet where he kept the sherry. There was a selection of liqueurs and dessert wines, but nothing that would go with the steak. She wondered if he kept wine in the cellar.

Then she started wondering what else he kept in the cellar.

Well, she did have the run of the house.

A quick search revealed a door next to the kitchen, which opened to steps going down. She found a light switch and turned it on. A small part of her brain wanted to bring the gun, but she suppressed it. Still, force of suspicious habit led her to creep down as silently as she could, staying ready for anyone who might be lurking.

Lurkers there were none. Wine there was, she was happy to discover. A quite sizable wine rack stood against the wall by the bottom of the steps. She scanned the labels without dislodging the bottles. French dominated, but there was a decent selection of Italians and a surprising number of Germans, given that their recent foes were not exactly exporting to England on a regular basis.

But this was Archie Spelling, the enemy of all things regular, so it was no surprise to see that the cellar matched his ways.

She looked past the wine to see the rest of the cellar. Mostly, she saw stacks of crates and cartons. She went over to the nearest stack. Stencilled on each box was the word "CRACKERS."

What do we have here? she wondered. Biscuits? Grenades?

The top carton wasn't sealed. Someone had checked its contents, but it was too high for her to see inside. She looked around and saw a stepladder propped against a wall by a worktable. She brought it over, then climbed up until she could peer over the top.

Then she laughed. The box was filled with Christmas crackers, awaiting the occasion of their imminent doom.

She climbed back down and replaced the ladder, noticing as she did that there was a door near the other end of the cellar, apparently leading to a room that had been built into it. She went over to it and tried the knob. It was locked.

"What have we here, Mr. Bluebeard?" she muttered.

She tried her house key, but it didn't fit.

She could pick the lock, she thought. Her ever-present set of lock picks were in her bag, which she had left on the kitchen counter. She could dash up and—

"Sparks?" she heard Archie call from upstairs. "Where'd you disappear to?"

"Down here," she called back.

By the time he came down the stairs, she was back at the wine rack, inspecting a pinot noir.

"I was thinking about dinner," she said. "Are we staying in to-night?"

"If you don't mind," he said. "You much of a cook?"

"I do basics," she replied. "I saw a steak in the fridge. Is that available?"

"It is. I saw you found the tins."

"I did. I found something else behind them."

"I 'ope it din't go off," he said. "Bring that bottle with you and we'll figure things out."

She followed him back up. There was a paper bag on the table. He upended it, and a pair of shallots and a head of garlic rolled out. He grabbed a large knife from the counter.

"You like knives, right?" he said, handing it to her with a grin.

"I do. How many weapons have you got stashed around the place?" she asked, taking it.

"A few. I'll give you that tour later if you like."

"Are those here generally, or is there a specific threat I should know about?" she asked as she peeled the shallots and some garlic cloves and placed them on a cutting board.

"We 'ave competitors," he said as he removed the steak and rinsed it in the sink. "Some are more competitive than others."

"Is that why you ducked when that flashbulb went off last night?"

"General practise. If the first bullet misses, don't give 'em a chance to improve their aim."

"Sound policy," she said, chopping away. "Speaking of flash-bulbs, I found out who was behind that."

"Who?"

"Gareth Pontefract. He's a reporter, or something vile posing as one. He got a shot of the two of us coming out of Mum's, then approached me this morning, wanting money to keep it out of the press."

"What did you tell him?"

"I haven't given him a decision yet. It affects you, and it affects Mum."

"What did Mum 'ave to say about it?" said Archie as he patted the steak dry and sprinkled it with salt and pepper.

"I haven't told her yet."

"You told me first," he said. "I'm liking your priorities 'ere. Shall I send some of the lads to 'ave a conversation with 'is kneecaps?"

"No, not at all necessary," she said hastily. "Nor wise. He's expecting threats from that quarter. I've been thinking that come the wedding Saturday, this won't be a news story anymore, so maybe I should stop worrying about what people think."

"It ain't people you're worried about, it's your mum."

"That's true," she said. "On the other hand, I've been talking about this while chopping things, and I haven't cut off any of my fingers, so that's a sign I'm less worried than I thought I would be."

"Better 'and that over before anything 'appens," he said. "I like my steaks bloody, but not like that."

He scraped the minced shallots and garlic into a bowl, then took a jar of beef base from the refrigerator and some olive oil and added some of each.

"If I had known you had olive oil, I would have been your girl much sooner," said Iris, watching as he stirred the marinade.

"I wanted you to love me for meself, not the contents of me kitchen," he said, pouring it over the steak. "Right, we'll let that sit for a while. Let's open up that bottle."

He poured two glasses, and they sat at the kitchen table. Iris opened her bag and pulled out Gwen's cheque.

"To Spelling Enterprises," she said. "For services about to be rendered."

"Look at that," he said. "Our Gwendolyn 'as come into 'er scratch. I'll 'ave the beagle draw up a contract for New Year's Eve."

"Excellent. It's a pleasure doing business with you, Mr. Spelling," she said, holding up her glass.

"Likewise," he said, clinking his against it. "And I look forward to following it with a little pleasure later."

"Likewise."

"Detective Ex told me you vouched for my whereabouts last night, by the way. Thanks. You din't 'ave to put yourself in 'arm's way on my account."

"All I did was tell him the truth."

"A rare and valuable commodity in my world," said Archie. "Now I 'ave to figure 'oo went in there and cleared out the bricks in my newly acquired cellar."

"It wasn't one of your men?" asked Iris.

"Why would you think that?"

"It seemed the most likely explanation," said Iris. "So likely that I wondered if you kept me with you through the night to give yourself deniability while it was happening."

"You 'ave the most suspicious mind," he said. "No, Sparks, my interest in keeping you all night was for exactly what 'appened, and I was an exhausted and 'appy bloke in the morning, thank you very much."

"Likewise," said Iris. "But I still have the sense that you're not telling me everything."

"For example?"

"For example, the dead man's ring."

"We're back to that again?"

"I've seen it since. Or similar ones."

"Where?"

"In the picture of your dad with his mates from the war. They had the same rings, didn't they?"

He took a long sip of wine while he considered his answer.

"Yeah, all right," he said finally. "That was the same ring."

"Did you take it?"

"No."

She wished she had Gwen with her at that moment to apply her cold-reading skills to see if he was telling her the truth. She also wished she wasn't in a position to wish that.

"What's going on, Archie?" she asked. "Who was that bricked up in the cellar?"

"I dunno yet," he said.

"But you're looking into it?"

"It's tricky," he said.

"What do you know about it?"

"I can't tell you, Sparks," he said.

"Because you don't know? Or because you don't want me to know?"

"Whichever you want to believe," he said. "I think that steak's 'ad long enough. Let's light a burner."

"What kind of proposition?" asked Gwen.

"How would you like to help me play a joke on someone?" asked River.

"What kind of joke?"

He paused while the bartender brought their fish and chips over, then continued.

"When I got home, practically the first place I went to was to this snooker hall called Brooke's in Mile End. I was out of practise, snooker tables not generally being available in the theatres of operations I rumbled through. So I pick up a few friendly games just to get my stroke back. There's this bloke, acts the big man of the place, and the other fellers are kowtowing to him. 'Fancy a frame?' he asks, and I, feeling frisky by that point, accept."

"It didn't go well, I'm guessing."

"It did at the start," said River. "My shots were decent, but where I fell short was in the concentration. It was like my ears were still ringing from the six pounder going off over my head, and I kept seeing the lads in the Churchill ahead of me blowing up on a mine. I started missing when things got late in the frame. And that would've been fine, only the bloke sneers at me, 'With aim like that, no wonder it took us so long to win the war.'"

"No!" exclaimed Gwen angrily.

"That didn't sit well with me, to say the least," River continued. "My first impulse was to do something extremely nasty with my cue, but I like this stick, so I held back. Since then I've been practising, working my game up so I can take him on again. But it's not enough to beat him. I want to pay him back for that jab. And that's where you come in."

"Tell me," said Gwen.

"I'm gonna challenge him, whatever stakes he wants. And at some point, I'm going to make a side bet on one shot, get him riled up, then say, 'Tell you what, mate. Not only can I make this shot, I bet my girl can make it, too.' And once he accepts, you step up and knock it in, and we take both his money and his pride at one fell swoop."

"That's a lot of pressure to put on me, coming into a game cold like that. What if I miss?"

"It's a gamble," he said. "But right now, I'm betting on you. What do you say?"

"Let's play another frame," she suggested. "Pick out some shots you want me to take and see how I do."

"Has Evil Gwen had enough of her fish and chips?"

"Actually, I'm rather enjoying them," she confessed. "It's been ages since I've had any."

"Take your time," he said, grinning. "Far be it from me to hurry along anyone's enjoyment."

A few minutes later, her plate was clear and her hands were greasy. Should help me sliding the cue, she thought as she wiped the grease off as well as she could with the inadequately small paper napkin that came with the meal.

They walked over to their table.

"Your break," she said.

"Right, here we go," he said, taking his cue.

"One moment," she said.

She removed her jacket and hung it on a hook by the cue rack, revealing her bare shoulders. Then she took her stick and walked to the end of the table by the triangle of red balls. Slowly, deliberately, she applied the chalk, then pursed her lips and blew the excess dust away. She held the cue in front of her and looked down the table, her eyes fixed on his.

"Go ahead," she purred. "Shoot."

"Evil Gwen has arrived," he said with a laugh. "Think you can disrupt my concentration that easy?"

"Let's find out," she said, her shoulders undulating slightly.

His opening shot was perfection, bouncing the cue ball back past the baulk line. She responded in kind, and they were off.

As the frame continued, she adjusted to the minute flaws in her stick and the balls began to fall. Then she left the cue ball for River near the baulk line, with a red sitting about a foot from the corner at a makeable angle. He studied it, then turned to her.

"This is a shot that I would turn over to you," he said. "Let's see you make it."

She came over by him, studied the table, noting the patches in the baize along her intended route.

"Where do you want me to leave the cue ball?" she asked.

"Keep it down at that end, and try and get it to the other side of the black."

She bent down, bringing her eyeline almost to the level of the baize. Beyond the target ball, she could see other players in the room stopping to watch her with expressions ranging from curiosity to undisguised leers.

There will be more in Mile End, she thought. Ignore them.

She drew back her cue and struck. The ball travelled the length of the table at a medium pace, and knocked the red into the corner pocket. The cue ball continued to the centre of the top cushion, then bounced at an angle, coming to a rest six inches past the black, putting it in line for the next shot.

The other players thumped their cues on the floor in appreciation.

"Perfect," said River.

He retrieved the red from the corner pocket, replaced it on the spot it had recently vacated, then brought the cue ball back and placed it closer to the baulk cushion than it had been previously.

"Let's see you do it twice in a row," he said.

She did, and he looked at her appreciatively.

How nice to be looked at like that for something other than my looks, she thought.

They played on, with more interruptions for her to make increasingly difficult shots, most of which she did. When they were done, he grinned at her.

"You could definitely make this work," he said. "Are you game?"

"I don't want to make a regular habit of it," she said, "but I think it would be fun to do it once."

"Couldn't get away with it more than once," he said. "Word will get out about you."

"Is that why you brought me to a club far away from Mile End?"

"It is," he said, unscrewing his cue and stowing it in its case. "And I think I should get you home now."

She gave him directions once they reached Kensington. He stopped the car a few houses before hers.

"By the way, I haven't forgot," he said.

"Forgot what?" she asked.

"That this is a date," he said, pulling her to him and kissing her. He was gentle at first, letting her get over her initial surprise (but was she surprised? she asked herself. Not really, she answered). She responded with increased fervour, letting herself surrender to the moment.

It went on for a while, then he pulled away and drove the remaining distance to her driveway.

"Was that Good Gwen or Evil Gwen I was kissing?" he asked when they arrived.

"I'm not sure," she said. "They seem to be all mixed up together at the moment."

This time, she initiated the kiss.

"Good Gwen is getting out of the car now," she whispered when she was done. "But Evil Gwen wants you to know that it's with great reluctance."

"Good night to both of you," he said. "I look forward to our next date."

"Will that be at Mile End?"

"I want a date where there's no snooker at all," he said. "I could do worse than to gaze adoringly into those blue eyes for a good long while."

"I'd like that, River."

He got out and opened her door for her, then walked her to the house.

"Are we under observation?" he asked.

"Possibly," she said.

"Then I won't push my luck any further," he said. "Good night, Gwen."

"Good night, River," she said, letting herself in.

She turned and blew him a kiss, then closed the door.

Percival appeared from whatever secret place Percival inhabited at night.

"Good evening, Mrs. Bainbridge," he said, taking her coat. "An enjoyable night out, I hope."

"Thank you, Percival. I had fun."

"I am very glad to hear it, Mrs. Bainbridge," he said. "Fun is a worthwhile objective."

"It is indeed. Good night, Percival."

"Good night, Mrs. Bainbridge."

The boys were fast asleep. She tiptoed into each of their rooms to kiss them lightly on their cheeks, then went to her room, changed for bed, and removed her makeup. As she did, she glanced at Ronnie's picture, smiling back at her.

Would that picture have to be put away if she found someone else? If she remarried?

Not that she considered River a prospect for any of that.

Nevertheless, it was quite some time before she managed to fall asleep that night.

CHAPTER 6

The first thing Iris did when she walked in the next morning was examine Gwen's face.

"What are you looking for?" asked Gwen, pulling back instinctively.

"Evidence," said Iris, sitting behind her desk. "I conclude by the state of your makeup that you slept less than your normal amount last night."

"True," said Gwen. "Nevertheless, I slept alone. So there."

"But a late night before that?"

"No," said Gwen. "I was . . . keyed up. But I resisted the Veronal, which was a triumph of sorts."

"So a date with River left you keyed up," commented Iris. "Interesting."

"Well, it was an unusual— How did you know it was River?"

"I watched out the front window as you left," confessed Iris. "I didn't believe for a moment that you would date someone called Rodman Hilliard."

"Strangely enough, that is his real name," said Gwen.

"How on earth did he manage to wangle a date with you?"

"He asked me," said Gwen. "Actually, he challenged me. We

played snooker. And drank terrible beer and ate some very greasy fish and chips. It was the cheapest date I've gone on since I was twelve and Wendell Hughes took me to a matinee of *Bulldog Drummond* and bought me one small fizzy lemonade after."

"And did you get a kiss afterwards?"

"From Wendell? A quick peck on the cheek, then he turned beet red and was too shy to ask me out again."

"I am going to come over there and shake you. I meant last night."

Gwen tried to control her expression, but the smile came through anyway.

"I conclude that you did," said Iris.

"It was rather glorious, all in all," said Gwen.

"Poor Mr. Prendergast," said Iris. "Sounds like this will be a tough act to follow. And I see you're dressed for business today. Different approach?"

"Tonight's date will be snooker free, and I don't think it's an evening gown sort of occasion," said Gwen.

"Did the jacket come off last night?"

"It's much easier to play snooker when one's shoulders are free."

"I'll bet."

"You, by contrast, look suspiciously well rested this morning."

"I went home after my evening with Archie," said Iris. "I don't want to act too scandalously with my lease running out. I might need a reference from my landlord."

"I'm sorry again about yesterday," said Gwen.

"Forget it."

"I'd still like you to come with me tomorrow when I check out that house in Maida Vale."

"Why?"

"Because I've never done this before, and I value your opinion," Gwen said simply.

"Well, in that case, of course," said Iris, mollified. "But I can't stay long. I have to attend the wedding."

"Right, that's tomorrow. Are you getting nervous?"

"Downright terrified. I'll be meeting Archie's entire family for the first time. At least, meeting those who are not current gang members."

"Odd how it's the noncriminals who scare you," said Gwen. "May I give you some advice?"

"Go ahead."

"It's someone's wedding. The focus of the guests will be, and should be, on the bride and groom. You will be a peripheral curiosity, not the centre of attention."

"Should I dress dowdy and pencil in a moustache, just in case?"

"No, dear. All you need to do is be on your best behaviour and smile."

"I think I can manage that," said Iris.

The intercom buzzed.

"Yes, Mrs. Billington?" answered Gwen.

"There's a Mervyn Stuart on the phone for you."

"Wonderful!" said Gwen. "I'll take the call. Mervyn, darling! When did you get back?"

"A week ago," said Mervyn. "I heard through the grapevine you were looking for a band for New Year's Eve."

"I am indeed," said Gwen. "Are your hands in playable shape? Did you retain all ten fingers?"

"Yes, and yes," he said, laughing. "Picked up some gigs in officers' clubs along the way. I still have about five years of new songs to learn. What's the story?"

"I'm running a marriage bureau with my friend Iris Sparks. We're hosting a New Year's dance."

"Where?"

"They're reopening the White Palace in Mile End. Do you know it?"

"Frankie Reese's old place? Yeah, I played there a few times. They still have that Chappell baby grand?"

"They do," said Gwen. "It's in desperate need of tuning, but otherwise playable. What about a band?"

"If bass and drums are enough, I know some guys," he said. "Might be able to grab Eddie Tremaine on sax if he's not already booked. If you're looking for a larger band, that takes charts and rehearsals."

"A quartet would be lovely," said Gwen. "And don't worry about bringing the new songs. People like to dance to what's in their memories. 'Auld Lang Syne' at midnight, of course."

"Ah, I think I might know that one," he said. "Could I entice you to sing a number or two?"

"Not a chance, Mervyn," she said with a laugh. "I am not the warbler I once was."

"Pity," he said. "Married life has carried away too many song-birds."

She grimaced for a moment.

"Do you think they'd let me practise with the band there?" he asked. "I don't have a piano in my new place yet. I'll even throw in a free tuning."

"I'll give Archie a ring," she said. "As long as you don't mind the renovating going on around you."

"Who's Archie?"

"The new owner. Archie Spelling."

There was a pause on the other end.

"Well, he won't be the first gangster I've ever played for," he said. "Tell you what—give him a ring for the okay and I'll come over with my tuning kit."

"Will do," said Gwen. "I'll join you. I'd like to see how much progress they've made. Let me get your number."

She scribbled it down, then hung up.

"We have a band!" she crowed. "Well, a pianist, anyway."

"Excellent," said Iris.

Gwen met Mervyn outside the Mile End Tube station. He waved with both hands when he saw her, wiggling his fingers.

"I told you I still had them all," he said as she came up. "Wonderful to see you again, Gwen."

He raised her hand to his lips and kissed it, then glanced at the other.

"You're not married anymore?" he asked in surprise.

"Widowed," she said tersely.

"Bloody hell," he said. "Sorry to hear it. You made a handsome couple out on the dance floor. I know there was more to him than that, but that's the musician's perspective on it."

"Thanks," she said. "Shall we?"

He offered his arm, and they walked to the club.

They saw as they entered the main room that the walls were now completely stripped of their old wallpaper. A pair of men were plastering cracks on the end farthest from the bomb damage, while others were applying paint with rollers.

Mervyn immediately went to the piano and removed its cover. He opened the lid and ran his fingers in a chromatic down the keys, wincing when he heard the results.

"Hello, old girl," he said sympathetically. "You've been neglected for too long, haven't you? Don't worry, I'll take good care of you."

He pulled out a tuning fork and hammer from a small leather pouch, struck the tuning fork on his left palm, and held it up to his ear. Then he hit the A above middle C on the piano.

"Almost a quarter tone flat," he said. "It might take more than one session."

He sounds like Dr. Milford, she thought.

"I'll leave you to it," she said. "I'm going to check how things are going."

The walls were being covered in a light cream colour, which she thought worked well. The end that had received the most bomb damage was now sealed from the cold outside air, and some men were installing plasterboard. She watched them with interest, then asked for Archie.

"Headed downstairs, last I saw, ma'am," said one.

"Thanks," she replied.

She felt some trepidation about returning to the cellar, whether it was because of the crime scene or a possible re-encounter with Des. Before she reached the door to the stairs, however, Mike Kinsey emerged, Constable Larkin behind him.

"Mrs. Bainbridge," he said, stopping.

"Detective Sergeant, Constable," she returned. "How goes the investigation?"

"Nearing a dead end, I'm afraid. I came back to see if Frankie Reese had left behind any old work orders or records from when that storeroom was built, but there's nothing much here."

"If you're investigating him, then Mr. Spelling must be in the clear," she said.

"He is on this one," said Kinsey. "Sparks will be pleased about that, I'm sure."

"As am I," she said. "What made up your mind on that point? The age of the body?"

"Correct," he said. "We can't pin it down accurately, but the doc said it's been there at least twenty years, and the cut of the clothes is from the early twenties. No identifiable tailor, unfortunately. This case may be too far gone to solve."

"Is Frankie Reese your principal suspect?" she asked.

"Stands to reason he could have been the culprit," said Kinsey. "Which also reduces the urgency, given that he was summoned to justice by a higher authority than Scotland Yard. I want to speak to his widow, but she rarely came here from all reports. This was his baby to run. She managed another club, and they had a few more besides, but I'll see if she can locate anything useful in their records. I'm about ready to toss this into the unsolved files and move on to ones more solvable."

"I should think you'd still want to find out who the poor man was," said Gwen. "There may be a family out there who are wondering what happened."

"Unfortunately, there are quite a few of those," he said. "People go missing for all sorts of reasons. I've been going through files from the twenties, but I haven't narrowed it down yet; and for all we know, this chap was never even reported."

"I wish you luck," said Gwen. "Did you ever trace the ring?"

"Not yet," he said. "Your picture doesn't match any of the regular regimental or battalion signets that we know of. I'm still wondering why anyone would have taken it."

"You'll figure it out, Detective Sergeant," she said. "I have confidence in you."

"Nice to hear you say after all the times you and Sparks have stepped in and beaten us to the punch," he said. "Good day, Mrs. Bainbridge."

"Good day, Detective Sergeant, Constable."

She passed them and went downstairs. In the distance, at the other end of the hall, she could hear men's voices being raised. She walked in that direction and soon was able to identify them.

"I'm telling you they 'aven't found anything," said Des heatedly.

"It 'as to be there," said Archie. "Why else—"

He stopped as he saw Gwen approaching.

"'Allo, Gwen," he said. "Sorry, renovation squabble. You brought the ivory-tickler?"

"I did," she replied. "His name is Mervyn Stuart. He used to lead a trio before the war. He's upstairs tuning the piano right now, but I wanted to ask if he might use your piano to rehearse with his band while work is still being done."

"Yeah, I don't see why not," said Archie. "As long as there's nothing being done in that immediate vicinity. I'll come up and meet 'im. Shall we?"

"Actually, I was wondering if I might have a brief word with Mr. Burton," she said.

"You don't need me to stick around and chaperone?" he asked. "Last time the two of you were down 'ere together, all 'ell broke loose."

"I'll try not to break anything," she promised. "I won't be long."

"Fine, you're grown-ups," he said. "Talk to you later, Des."

He walked down the hall. Gwen watched until he disappeared up the stairway, then turned to Des, who was looking at her inquisitively.

"What can I do for you, madam?" he asked.

"First, it's Gwen, not 'madam,'" she said. "There's no need for formality given everything that's happened."

"All right, what can I do for you . . . Gwen?" he asked, saying her name as if he had never pronounced those sounds together before.

"I wanted to thank you for saving me the other day," she said. "With all of the confusion at the time, I didn't have a chance."

"It was all reaction," he said. "It wasn't that 'eroic. I wasn't even thinking."

"Nevertheless, your first instinct was for me, and I appreciate that."

"Then you're welcome," he said. "Glad to 'ave done it. Is that it?"

"No," she said. "I also wanted to thank you for saving me before."

"When was that?" he asked.

She gathered her courage.

"When you kissed me," she said softly. "On our walk by the river last summer."

He was silent, but the space between them felt to her like it had been ionised by a bolt of lightning.

"And what was I saving you from?" he asked, his eyes locked on hers.

"From myself," she said. "I hadn't kissed anyone other than my husband for a long time before that, and when I lost him, I went numb. Then you kissed me, and it woke something within me that I thought had died along with him. I realised that I could feel again."

"Not with me, though."

"Maybe with you, maybe not," she said. "I want to be honest with you, Des. I want to be honest with myself. Sometimes the most complicated part of our lives is the timing, both of who we are and where we are. So I have no designs or intentions of disrupting your life, but I wanted to let you know that you meant a great deal to me."

"Meant," he repeated. "Not mean."

"Yes," she said, hoping he believed her. Hoping she believed herself.

"All right, then," he said.

The electricity faded.

"It looks as if you got a lot done here," she observed, looking past him at the remains of the storeroom. "Did you ever find a door in the rubble?"

"No," he said. "Must've been destroyed in the bombing."

"I wonder," she said, looking at the floor. "I don't see any traces of a door where the newer bricks were, just wall all the way around. Whoever built this meant for it to be sealed."

"Why do you care so much?" he asked wearily. "You're worse than that detective."

"Curiosity, I suppose," she said. "Did you take the ring?"

"No, I didn't take the stupid ring," he said in exasperation.

"Look, Gwen, if you're done thanking me, I'll thank you to leave me to finish my work. The sooner I put this place behind me, the 'appier I will be."

"I will leave you to it," she said. "Goodbye, Des."

She walked down the hall towards the stairs, willing herself not to glance back over her shoulder. She sensed without looking that he watched her all the way.

Iris waited until Gwen had left to go to the club, then waited another five minutes. Once she was sure her partner wouldn't be coming back, she dialled a number. A woman answered.

"Mrs. Sparks, please," said Iris. "It's her daughter calling."

"Please wait, Miss Sparks."

Iris gnawed on her lower lip until she heard her mother on the line.

"Well?" said Mrs. Sparks.

"No preliminaries?" asked Iris.

"I'm pressed for time. I can spare you a minute, no more."

"In that case, thank you very much for dinner and did you know Archie and I were photographed coming out of your house afterwards?"

There was a pause.

"More than a minute," said Mrs. Sparks. "What happened?"

"We saw the flash, hit the deck immediately, but it was too late. The next morning, that oozing ball of sleaze Gareth Pontefract showed up at The Right Sort, asking for money to keep it and your name out of the papers."

"How much?"

"He didn't mention the sum, or which one of you should pay for it."

"What sort of deadline are we looking at?"

"Unclear," said Iris. "I say, you're sounding very practical about all of this. I thought you would be upbraiding me for how my choice in men has led us to this."

"I'm saving that for when I have more time," said Mrs. Sparks. "Right now, I am dealing with the problem at hand."

"If it's any reassurance, you should be aware that Archie and I will be considerably more open about our connection as of tomorrow," said Iris.

"Why? What's tomorrow?"

"We're going to a wedding together at Saint Thomas Church in Whitechapel. Archie's nephew is getting married. One of my couples, as it happens. I fixed them up."

"Does Pontefract know about it?"

"No," said Iris. "But if he's looked into Archie and his family, it's something he could find out about. He or anyone else in the press, for that matter."

"Let me think for a moment," said her mother.

Iris waited.

"Connecting a member of Parliament to a known gang leader is never a good thing," said her mother after another precious minute had gone by. "But if it comes out, I shall write off the matter to the unfortunate inclinations of my feckless, ne'er-do-well daughter, with her long history of poor romantic decisions, and my failed attempt to talk some sense into her."

"Yes, that should do very nicely," said Iris, suppressing the bitterness from her voice. "Anything you'd like me to tell Pontefract?"

"Tell him to go and get— No, you should probably paraphrase," said her mother.

"I've got the gist," said Iris. "Goodbye, Mum."

She hung up, then grabbed her bag and pawed through it until she found Pontefract's card. She stared at it, wanting to imbue it with some voodoo-like power that would cause him pain if she tore it to shreds, but nothing happened.

If it were done when 'tis done, then 'twere well it were done quickly, she thought.

She dialled his number and waited until his loathsome voice answered.

"It's Sparks," she said. "We took a vote. It was unanimous. The response is this."

The next words out of her mouth would have shocked her mother and amused Archie, though both would have applauded the sentiment expressed.

"Mrs. Bainbridge?"

Gwen looked up from her glass to see Walter Prendergast looking at her across the table with concern.

"I'm so sorry," she said. "What did you say?"

"I was commenting that you seem preoccupied. And there you were. Preoccupied."

"Forgive me, Walter," she said. "It's been a strenuous week. Various problems have been nagging me, and I'm afraid my mind went elsewhere for a moment."

"You are easy to forgive, Mrs. Bainbridge," he said. "I thought I detected some anguish in your expression. I hope neither I nor the food were contributing to it."

"No, no, you are fine and the food is wonderful," she said. "I haven't been to Kettner's in years."

"I thought it would be a good place to have a conversation," he said. "What is the matter concerning you?"

"Oh, it wouldn't interest you," she said.

"Everything about you interests me."

"I'm about to put the lie to that," she said ruefully. "We are planning a New Year's dance for our clientele. The logistics have proved to be rather complicated."

"A New Year's dance," he repeated, his face falling.

"What's wrong?" she asked.

"I was intending to ask you to a New Year's gathering," he said. "A small but rather influential group will be there."

"I'm afraid I must turn you down. Duty calls."

"I don't suppose you could leave matters to Miss Sparks and join me."

"Walter, this is for our business. How could you even think of suggesting that?"

"No, of course you must attend."

"Attend? I'm running the show," she said. "But here's a thought— would you like to come? I've been so busy planning an event for single people to meet that I've neglected to find a date for myself."

"As I said, the people at the affair I am planning to attend are influential," he said. "I cannot afford to disappoint them."

"Then I guess we must disappoint each other," she said.

"It's a pity," he said. "I was looking forward to dancing with you."

"Do you dance, Walter?" she asked hopefully.

"I've hired an instructor to teach me the basics so I wouldn't embarrass you overmuch. I thought there would be dancing here, but apparently they don't have it anymore."

"You never danced growing up?"

"My family made their fortune first from mills in Pembrokeshire, then from the commodities markets," he said. "My youth was spent learning the complexities of those worlds. There was no call for dancing. It is only recently that I've come to see the role it plays among the wealthier Londoners, so I am taking it up."

"You've never danced on a date before?"

"I haven't had much experience dating, either."

It was interesting, she thought. In a business setting, he could take control of a room with swaggering authority. She had been to his offices on Birchin Lane and the entire staff was both admiring and afraid of him, kowtowing to his wishes in a manner almost medieval in their subservience.

Yet here, sitting across from her, he was anxious, even subdued in his responses, hesitating to put each word out there for fear of its going wrong.

"Sir, you arouse my professional instincts," she said, smiling at him. "I find myself thinking of who would be a good fit for you."

"I don't want to be fixed up, Mrs. Bainbridge," he said. "I want to court you."

"Then you must do three things," she said.

"Name them."

"First, you must start calling me Gwen. Second, we must finish our meal, skip dessert, and pay the bill."

"Very well. And the third?"

"We must go somewhere where there is dancing."

"Was he any good?" asked Iris the next morning as they walked through Maida Vale.

"Not at all," said Gwen. "I had to back lead him half the time, and there isn't a note of musicality in him. My feet took a beating."

"I noticed the limp," said Iris.

"I'll need some time to heal before the next date."

"Aha! There will be a next date."

"You did tell me to give him a chance," said Gwen. "And honestly, it was sweet that he underwent the torture of learning to dance just for me. It wouldn't have been fair to judge him solely on how well he did. Although I would like you to speak to your mother about proposing legislation requiring compulsory dance training for every child at an early age."

"If we ever resume having normal conversation, I shall," said Iris. "Any other impressions of Walter outside his natural habitat?"

"Oddly enough, the best part of the evening was when we discussed business matters, both his and mine. He wanted to know all about my first board meeting as an installed general partner at Bainbridge, Limited. I had to withhold the actual topics because it was inside information, of course, but it was nice to talk about it with someone who is knowledgeable."

"You could talk to me, you know."

"I do, Iris, but he knows the world of finance inside and out, and you and I don't. He had some useful ideas on how to handle Harold's return from convalescence. He was rather engaging during that part of the evening."

"You sound surprised."

"I am," confessed Gwen. "It's unfortunate that he doesn't know how to have fun outside that world."

"Then it's a good thing you've come into his life," said Iris. "You could teach him how to have fun, and that would allow you to have some of your own. Did he kiss you?"

"He did not," said Gwen. "I think at the conclusion of the date he wasn't sure how to proceed."

"He should have read to the end of the manual," said Iris. "The part with the illustrations."

They turned onto a curved street of white stuccoed Italianate houses.

"It should be on the right," said Gwen, consulting her directions. "That must be the agent waiting in front."

A man stood huddling inside a thick woolen overcoat, his hands jammed into the pockets. He removed them hastily as he saw the two women approaching.

"Mrs. Bainbridge, is it?" he called.

"That's me," said Gwen. "Are you Mr. Fortescue?"

"Graham Fortescue, Darby Estate Agents," he said, producing a card from a small silver case and handing it to her.

"This is my friend Miss Iris Sparks," she said, taking it. "I hope we haven't kept you waiting long in this cold."

"Not at all, not at all," he said. "I ducked inside before you arrived to make sure everything was in order. Shall I give you the tour?"

"Please," she said.

He produced a key with a small cardboard tag attached to it and opened the front door. The hallway was devoid of furniture or rugs, the floorboards revealed.

"Main entryway, front parlour to the left," he said. "Previous owners lived here for fifty years, then the wife passed a year ago and he went to live with his daughter out in Surrey."

"Has all of the furniture been sold?"

"I'm afraid so," he said. "Larger sitting room to the right."

"That's a lovely fireplace," she said, coming in to inspect it. "Have the chimneys been maintained since he left?"

"They have, and I can provide records," he said. "Let me show you the kitchen and the back garden."

It may have been the view out the back that clinched it for her, she thought afterwards. A small greenhouse stood to the side, and there was enough lawn to allow an energetic boy to run around and kick a football without leaving the confines of the hedges and the gate at the far end.

Beyond it was a common garden space, with flower beds and benches, the surrounding houses looming over it as friendly guardians. There were hollies with bright red berries, giving it a cheerful aspect even with the grey mid-December skies overhead.

"This is lovely," she said. "One can actually meet one's neighbours."

"If one wants to," said Iris. "You'll all be right on top of each other. You've never lived within eighty feet of anyone else before."

"Maybe I should start," said Gwen. "Could we see the upper floors now?"

He led them up the stairs.

"Four bedrooms, two bathrooms on this floor," he said. "Plus one room that had been a playroom."

"It can be again," said Gwen, looking into it.

"Good light," commented Iris. "Ronnie will be able to continue drawing the adventures of Sir Oswald in here."

"Ronnie would be your son, Mrs. Bainbridge?" asked Fortescue.

"He is," said Gwen.

"How many would be living here?"

"Right now it's him and me, plus his nanny. And I've lined up a housekeeper, but I'm not sure how much larger the live-in staff will be."

"No Mr. Bainbridge?" he asked.

"No," she said.

"Then how do you plan to pay for this, if I may be blunt?"

"I have funds of my own," she said.

"We will need to see documentation of that."

"Of course," she said. "May we see the next floor, please?"

There were smaller bedrooms on that floor. Gwen insisted on seeing the attic space, and she and Iris wandered through it, looking at the roof, holding handkerchiefs to their faces to avoid the dust.

"You need to get someone knowledgeable to inspect the place," whispered Iris.

"A roof guy," said Gwen with a smile.

They came back down.

"You had mentioned a separate apartment," said Gwen to Fortescue.

"Yes. In the basement. You may have noticed the entrance to the side when you came in. It also has a door to the cellar here. Would you care to see?"

"Please," said Gwen.

Iris raised an eyebrow.

"I still want to see it," said Gwen. "Rental income and all that."

It turned out to be a one-bedroom flat with a kitchenette

slightly larger than the one Iris currently had, but the only natural light came from the upper windows by the entrance.

"It wouldn't have worked, would it?" Gwen asked.

"No," said Iris.

They followed Fortescue back into the front hall.

"Any thoughts?" Gwen asked Iris.

"There's no garage," said Iris.

"I hadn't thought about that," said Gwen. "What do people do about cars?"

"There is a garage two streets away," said Fortescue. "Do you actually drive, Mrs. Bainbridge?"

"Not yet," said Gwen. "How long is the leasehold here?"

"Twenty-two years," said Fortescue.

"May I have a moment to speak to Miss Sparks?"

"Of course."

They retreated to the front parlour.

"What do you think?" asked Gwen.

"It's a lot of rooms," said Iris. "Do you plan to take in boarders?"

"The way I see it, there are three possibilities for my life," said Gwen. "I remarry, my mythical husband moves in, and we fill the place with children. Or I remarry, and the mythical husband asks me to move in to his place and fill that with children, so I would sell this place."

She stopped.

"Or you never remarry," finished Iris. "Ronnie inherits the Bainbridge holdings and takes possession of the Kensington house and the estate in the country, and you'll be clattering around this enormous place with just the servants for regular company."

"That sounds bleak but well within the realm of possibility," said Gwen. "If that happens, maybe I'll sell it and move in with the newly minted Lord Bainbridge, if he'll allow it."

"If Ronnie goes ahead with his plan to marry me when he grows up, I'll put in a good word for you," said Iris.

"Thanks awfully."

They rejoined Fortescue.

"I should like to send in someone to inspect the place," said Gwen. "Pending that, I am interested in purchasing it."

She had thought he would be pleased. Instead, he looked hesitant.

"Is something wrong?" she asked.

"My concern is with appearances," he said. "I'm a man of the world, Mrs. Bainbridge. I have seen this sort of thing before."

"What thing?"

"A single, wealthy woman coming to purchase a house with her—friend," he said. "It isn't suitable for our business, if you catch my drift."

"Well, of course she's my friend," said Gwen. "What could you possibly— Oh!"

Iris started to laugh.

"We are not what I think you are implying," said Gwen indignantly. "Miss Sparks is my friend and business partner. There is nothing between us that might otherwise scandalise your reputation."

Apart from the murder investigations, the underworld associations, and the occasional brushes with espionage, thought Iris.

"I'm sorry, Mrs. Bainbridge," he said hastily. "I didn't mean to suggest—"

"You certainly did," said Iris. "I wonder at your sales acumen, insulting a member of the aristocracy like this. You do know who the Bainbridges are, don't you?"

"You mean the munitions people?" he said, turning pale. "You're of that family?"

"I am," said Gwen haughtily. "Would you like me to send you one of our products? Be very careful opening the box if you do."

"My apologies, Mrs. Bainbridge," he said. "I'm sure we could work out something."

"I should think the insult ought to merit a reduction in the asking price," said Gwen. "I shall send in my inspector, and you shall consider the value of your apology. Come, Miss Sparks."

She stormed out of the house, Iris running after her.

"Still shorter than you!" she called.

Gwen slowed her pace so that Iris could catch up.

"The nerve of that man," said Gwen. "First, for assuming that about us. Second, for that to be of any concern whatsoever."

"It does present a fourth possibility," said Iris. "Better than the third, I'd say."

"When I've eliminated the first two, I'll consider it," said Gwen.

"You like the house, though?"

"Very much. More important, the neighbourhood. Do you know the area?"

"Not well. We heard the BBC Symphony Orchestra play at the studio here on a school trip when I was ten. Let's go look at the canal. I've never seen Little Venice."

They walked down to Regent's Canal, which was lined with small narrowboats on both sides, long, squat affairs that were low enough to pass under the bridges should their owners ever wish to travel. Many of them had large flowerpots on the adjacent pavements, the sagging stalks remnants of whatever flowers or vegetables had grown and thrived during the summer. A solitary man in a thick brown coat sat on a chair on the flat roof of one boat, reading a newspaper while a pair of ducks slowly glided by.

"Aren't those clever?" said Iris. "You're right in the middle of the city, yet it's so quiet and peaceful. And you get to look at all of those lovely mansions, knowing full well that they have to look at you in exchange, and that you got the better of the deal on the basis of that alone. Hang on."

There was a small handwritten bill tacked to a green broomstick jammed into one of the flowerpots in front of a boat painted dark green except for white letters spelling "Cecilia" on the bow.

Iris walked up and peered at the bill for a moment, then took out her notebook and scribbled down a telephone number.

"It's for rent," she said as she returned to Gwen.

"You're not thinking of taking it?"

"Why not? I'm running out of time and options. We could be neighbours."

"That would be nice," said Gwen. "You don't anticipate further developments on the Archie front? Oh, I meant to tell you—I ran into Mike Kinsey at the club yesterday. He told me that the Yard considers Archie to be in the clear."

Iris grimaced for a moment.

"What is it?" asked Gwen.

"He isn't in the clear with me," she said.

"Why not?"

"It's hard to pin down exactly, but he knows more than he's letting on about that body. He's been unnerved ever since you found it—"

"I didn't find it."

"Fine, ever since it found you. Then there's the matter of the missing ring, and the fact that Des was there."

"Des? Why does he factor into this?"

She was blushing again, Iris noticed, glancing at her as they walked towards the Tube station.

"I saw a picture of Archie's dad," said Iris. "He was in the army during the Great War. Des's father was in the same battalion. They were friends."

"That's not such a coincidence," said Gwen.

"But there was another picture of them shortly after the war," continued Iris. "And they were wearing rings with military insignia. I couldn't tell if they were the same as that worn by our unknown dead man, but then Archie said they were."

"That might explain—" Gwen began. Then she stopped.

"Explain what?"

"When I went to find Archie yesterday, he was back in the cellar. I could hear him arguing with Des."

"What about?"

"All I heard clearly was Des saying he hadn't found anything."

"What do you think he was looking for?"

"No idea," said Gwen. "But whatever it was, Archie seemed to be in cahoots with him."

"I wonder if— You don't think Archie bought that club just so Des could explore the cellar, do you?"

"That would have been an extravagant gesture. But if he did, I wonder if it's connected to their fathers somehow. We know Archie's was killed in a fight. I wonder if Des's father is still alive. Although he mentioned that it was his uncle who took him into the trade when he was young."

"My, my, you've had some extensive discussions with your Mr. Burton, haven't you?"

"I did talk to him for a moment. I needed to set things straight."

"About?"

"About the two of us, and why it couldn't happen."

"I still don't see— Oh, dear!"

"What is it?" asked Gwen.

Iris was staring at a newsstand. Slowly, she approached it, her hand automatically reaching for a penny in her bag. She came back with a copy of the *Daily Mirror*, transfixed by the front page. Gwen came around to look at it, saw the picture, and winced.

"'Mobster's Moll Is MP's Daughter,'" she read. "'Did Sparks fly?'"

"Looks like Pontefract cashed in," said Sparks glumly. "At least he got my good side."

CHAPTER 7

Iris arrived at the church far too early, her anxiety at being punctual on her first meeting with Archie's family causing her to overplan her route there. She wore her new suit, Archie's gift.

Saint Thomas Church was an outlier in the London parish, one of the easternmost churches before one reached the River Lea. Built in the mid-nineteenth century, it was a modest yellow brick church with bands of red and black bricks for ornamentation, surmounted by a spire containing less than the full complement of chimes compared to some of the older churches. The architect, while no Christopher Wren, had put enough design around the various windows to keep it interesting to the eye, she thought.

And she was noticing bricks a lot more lately.

Not wanting to wait inside for an hour, she wandered over to the church hall next to it, where she spotted a familiar figure among a small group of men unloading wide, shallow boxes from a lorry.

"Hello, Reg," she said as she walked up to him. "What task have you been delegated today?"

"Afternoon, Sparks," he said as he hauled one of the boxes down. "I'm on the decorating committee, looks like. Take a butcher's."

She looked inside. It was filled with small vases of everlasting flowers.

"Lovely," she said. "I'm impressed you could get so many this time of year."

"Oh, I'm a regular Constance Spry, I am," he said, handing the carton over to one of his men. "The Jekylls will do for the regular guests."

"You found some real ones for the bride this late in the year?" she asked.

"Yeah. Long-stem roses, the real thing," he said. "We got a flower guy, keeps a hothouse out in the country."

"Oh, may I take a peek?" she asked eagerly.

"Sorry, Sparks, they were the first ones I took in. They're pricey and I don't want the cold to get at 'em. They're like the wedding gown—bad luck to see them before the main event. And we got some other surprises."

He nodded to some other cartons stacked behind the flowers. She recognised the Christmas crackers from Archie's cellar.

"What fun!" she said. "Do you know where Archie is?"

"In there, avoiding family," said Reg, nodding towards the church hall. "Go make him be sociable. He's driving me batty."

She followed the men into the hall, where tables had been set up around the perimeter leaving a centre square clear for dancing. There was a small stage at one end, an upright piano, a bass fiddle, and a drum kit set up on the right. Archie stood at its centre with his coat off and his shirtsleeves rolled up, barking orders like a quartermaster.

"Come on, get those streamers up," he yelled at two men balanced precariously on the top steps of a pair of ladders. "Vows go off at four, and this place 'ad better be ready for a party at three fifty-nine. Are those the flowers? Two pots at each table."

"May I help?" asked Iris, walking up to him.

"You, Sparks, are my date, and dates don't 'elp set up wedding receptions," he said, winking at her.

"Do dates get introduced to family?" she asked.

"They do," said Archie. "Although they already know you from the papers."

"Yes, I saw our big splash in the *Mirror* this morning," she said. "Any follow-up?"

"Not on my end," he said. "But those inkslingers know better than to tail me if they want to keep their fingers intact. 'Ow'd your mum take it?"

"I don't expect we'll be getting any more dinner invitations in the near future."

"Ah, she'll come around," said Archie. "She's gotta run out of cheese sometime. Right, we'd better get into that church. Nice suit, by the way."

"Thank you, kind sir. A nice gentleman gave it to me. And he'll look even nicer with his jacket on."

Archie rolled down his sleeves and put on his jacket. He was wearing what he called his banker's suit, a light grey three-piece that allowed him to pass for respectable in places that didn't look too closely at his twice-broken nose. He wore a white carnation in his lapel. Not a real one, but still nice, she thought.

"Ready to face the music?" he asked, offering his arm.

"Should be a piece of cake," she said, taking it.

They walked out. The men unloading the lorry looked at his expression and doubled their pace.

"Lily will be on you first and fast," he said as they walked up the steps to the church entrance. "Sister's prerogative. If there's any questions left after she's done with you, the nieces will swarm in. Give us a wave when you need rescuing, and I'll throw you a line. And 'ere's the church."

"There's the steeple," she said. "Open the door and let's walk in like this is normal."

She recognised Lily, Archie's sister, right away. Her face was an older version of the girl from the photographs, with much of her mother's look, had her mother lived to see her early forties.

She was giving orders to a small group of women in the centre of the aisle much as her brother had been doing in the hall, but when she caught sight of the two of them, she stopped and stared, as did the women. Slowly, she raised a white-gloved hand and pointed at Iris.

"You," she said, advancing towards her. "You, you, you."

Iris rapidly ran through defensive maneuvers in her mind, then throttled down the impulse and waited to see what was going to happen.

She did not expect Lily to seize her hand between her own, look at her, then burst into tears.

"God bless you, Iris Sparks," she said, embracing her. "You found our boy a marvellous girl, and I never thought 'e'd find anyone. Thank you, thank you, thank you."

"It was my great pleasure, Mrs. Alderton, and it's an honour to be here at their moment of happiness," said Iris, managing to extricate herself.

"And you've tamed this animal," said Lily, giving Archie an affectionate punch on the biceps that made him wince.

"No one tamed me," he growled.

"Go find that curate, tell him we're on the clock," said Lily to her brother. "I want to talk to this one."

"Yes, Sis," he said, walking away.

"Now, I want to know all about what's going on with the two of you," said Lily, taking Iris's arm in hers and strolling down the aisle. "The stories I 'ear from the boys, you sound like Joan of Arc and Mata Hari rolled into one."

"I can't say I'd want to end up like either of them," said Iris.

"No, of course not," said Lily hastily. "I think they were talking about the parts before. I'm sure they meant it as a compliment."

"Then I will take it as one," said Iris. "I've been looking forward to meeting you as well. I want to hear all the secret embarrassing stories about Archie as a child."

"Oh, we'll 'ave to get together for tea and cakes for those," said Lily. "Archie's a complicated one, to be sure. Felt 'e 'ad to be the man of the family ever since Dad—well, you know what 'appened to 'im."

"Not in great detail," said Iris. "I know your parents died when you were both young. I'm sorry, that must have been devastating."

"It was," said Lily, pulling a handkerchief from her sleeve and dabbing at her eyes. "I 'ave to tell you, I've never seen Archie look 'appier than 'e's been the last few months since you came along, although 'e's been taking to the sadness again lately. 'E's been talking about Dad more this week than 'e's done in years. Must be getting caught up in 'is memories, what with Dad's only grandson tying the knot. Oh, I'm getting all emotional meself."

"Perfectly understandable," said Iris.

I wonder if Mum would cry at my wedding, she thought. And if so, for what reasons?

"None of my children even knew their grandparents," continued Lily. "On my side, anyway. They got my in-laws, and they're nice enough when they're sober, which isn't often, between you and me. But 'ere I am, blabbering on when I'm trying to find out more about you. 'Ow'd you meet my brother?"

Murder investigation, undercover infiltration into his gang, thought Iris.

Better leave those parts out.

"I walked into Merle's one day for a drink with friends," she said. "I'd never been there before. And there he was, holding court in the back room."

"Was it love at first sight?" asked Lily eagerly.

"Actually, someone had told me I could get a pair of stockings from him," said Iris. "I guess he liked my legs. Eventually, he looked up."

"Ah, you can 'old your own with 'im, that's clear enough," said Lily. "Well, you keep doing what you're doing, and we'll be calling each other sister in no time. And if you can somehow persuade 'im back to the straight and narrow, I promise you there'll be a place in 'Eaven for you."

"I'm more likely to end up with Mata Hari than with Joan," said Iris.

"Now, don't be saying that," said Lily sternly. "Not in God's 'ouse. Come talk to me girls. They've been dying to meet you."

Iris was led into a squealing of sisters, one twenty and a pair of seventeen-year-old twins.

"Can you do me next?" asked the older one. "Tish is a brilliant catch!"

"Why 'aven't we met you before?" asked a twin.

"When are you going to marry Uncle Archie?" asked the other.

And so on, until a desperate glance to a grinning Archie brought him into the scrum.

"All right, that's enough," he said. "You got bridesmaid duties. Get on with you."

They dashed away, chattering.

"I've been through police interrogations easier than that," said Iris.

"You can see why I enjoy the peace and quiet of the gang," he said, looking after them fondly.

"They adore you," said Iris.

"You 'ave to admit, I'm adorable," he said. "Shall we take a pew? We're behind Lily."

They sat on the aisle behind the groom's parents and his grandparents. Archie introduced her to Sam Alderton, his brother-in-law, who greeted her warmly. The elder Aldertons nodded at her politely from what she guessed was a drunken fog, having begun their celebration in advance.

The organist sounded a chord, then began playing the processional, "Jesu, Joy of Man's Desiring." The minister emerged to take his place, and Bernie Alderton, resplendent in a vintage tailcoat he must have borrowed from an older relative, came to the front of the congregation along with Harry, his best man. He caught sight of Iris sitting with his uncle and shot them a quick smile. His sisters walked down the aisle more or less in time with the music and took their positions across from him, one of the twins giving him a quick thumbs-up.

The organist segued smoothly into Mendelssohn's Wedding March, and the assembly rose as Miss Letitia Hardiman, former wartime Ack Ack Girl, appeared at the end of the aisle, arm in arm with her father. She wore no bridal gown, shortages being what they were, but a lovely blue crêpe de chine frock with a lace shawl draped over her shoulders, and carried a bouquet of red long-stemmed roses that were at their peak. Well done, Reg's flower guy, thought Iris.

She thought back to her first interview with Miss Hardiman, whose booming ebullience shook the rafters of their building. Now, the imminent bride was beaming like she was going to burst, barely holding back the whoops of sheer joy she wanted to send rocketing into the skies as she saw Bernie waiting for her, his grin matching hers.

And Iris realised with a start that she was holding Archie's hand.

What's all this, then, subconscious? she asked herself. When was this decision made? Who made it? What was the final vote? A surreptitious move while all eyes were elsewhere? Only he was aware that it's happening, you know.

A responding squeeze from Archie confirmed this.

"Love is patient; love is kind; love is not envious or boastful or arrogant or rude," began the minister.

Well, let it be, thought Iris, still clinging to Archie's hand as they sat.

The well-oiled machinery of the service went smoothly. End result: a proclamation, a kiss, cheers, and confetti. Mr. and now Mrs. Alderton practically skipped down the aisle.

"Come on," said Archie. "We'll be needed for photographs."

"Me?" protested Iris. "I've only met most of them this afternoon."

"You are the matchmaker and my date," he said. "Let's 'ave a photograph of us that ain't grist for the tabloids."

They assembled on the church steps, the two of them in back of the main wedding party, behind the nieces. Iris did her best to blend in, smiling away while subsuming her panic and confusion as a well-trained spy should.

The church hall was ready to go with no need for further threats from the Spelling family. The tables were set, the vases of everlasting flowers brightening each. The streamers hung from the rafters and the top of the proscenium. The bassist and drummer were ready at their instruments, and the church organist appeared and joined them at the upright piano. He nodded and they launched into "We'll Gather Lilacs" as people were directed to their seats.

Iris and Archie found themselves at the corner of the long table with the wedding party, the happy couple in the centre, facing the stage. Waiters swarmed through, distributing plates of salad and pouring champagne. She recognised a few of them from the Wapping warehouse.

"Is this another one of your catering ventures?" she asked.

"'E's my nephew," Archie said simply. "I do everything for family. That's why I sent 'im to The Right Sort."

"And you paid his fee with stockings," remembered Iris with a laugh.

"Well, you'll get your marriage bounty in cash, anyways," said Archie with a grin. "'Ow does it feel to see 'appiness and profit come together so neatly?"

"I wasn't thinking about the money at all," said Iris, looking at the happy couple. "I was thinking about how wonderful my job can be at times. Oh, looks like the best man is coming up for the toast."

Everyone turned to the stage as Harry stepped up to a microphone and tapped on it experimentally. It echoed to his satisfaction, and he held up his glass.

"Right," he said. "First, a hearty thank-you to the Hardiman and Alderton families for all of their contributions to these festivities."

"Hear, hear!" shouted several guests.

"Those of us who know Bernie know he's a quiet chap," he continued. "Those of us who now know Tish know that she is anything but. So listening to him speak his vows today may be the last time we ever hear a word out of him."

Tish guffawed loudly and elbowed her husband in the ribs.

"Magnetism is about opposites attracting," said Harry. "I have to say that this is one of the most magnetic couples I have ever seen. Hearing them described, one might think they couldn't be more wrong for each other, but seeing them together, one would know immediately they couldn't be more right. Raise your glasses, ladies and gentlemen. I give you the magnetic miracles. To Tish and Bernie!"

"Tish and Bernie!" chorused the room.

"And now we have a special surprise, courtesy of Bernie's uncle Archie," said Harry. "In honour of the Christmas season—we have crackers!"

The waiters re-emerged with trays of Christmas crackers, which they quickly distributed to all of the guests.

"Not yet! Wait for it," instructed Harry. "We want to make as much noise as possible."

"I got a special one for us," said Archie, pulling one from inside his jacket pocket.

"Special?" said Iris, turning to him. "How so?"

"Grab the other end and you'll find out," he said.

"Is everyone ready?" called Harry. "On the count of three. One! Two! Three! Happy Christmas!"

Iris pulled. There was a small pop, joined by other pops from around the room, along with cries of "Happy Christmas!" and squeals of delight and joy as the prizes were revealed.

A small black box tumbled out of her cracker.

"I told you small boxes unnerve me," she said, reaching for it as the cacophony continued around the room.

Then Archie slammed back against his chair, toppling it, a look of surprise and pain on his face as he hit the floor, blood welling across his shirtfront.

"Archie!" screamed Iris, kicking her chair away and kneeling beside him.

His chest heaved convulsively, a bubbling noise coming from his throat.

"I need a doctor!" she shouted. "We need an ambulance! Now! He's been shot!"

There were screams, crashes of chairs as people ran either to help or to flee in panic.

"Where'd it come from?" shouted a man.

"Who shot 'im?"

"I've got to get out!" screamed a woman.

Time seemed to slow around Iris as she tore his shirt open to reveal the hole in his chest.

"Clear a space!" shouted Benny as he ran up. "Gary, get over here. Move, Sparks, he was a medic."

She felt strong arms pull her away, then one of the gang kneeled next to Archie. He placed his ear against his chest, then grabbed a cloth napkin from the table and pressed it against the wound.

"He's still breathing, but he's coughing up blood," he said. "We need an ambulance fast."

"No time," said Reg, joining them. "Benny, get the lorry backed up. London Hospital is five minutes away."

"Thirty seconds," yelled Benny, running out the door.

"You lot, grab something to put him on," ordered Reg.

A table was cleared and the legs folded underneath as dishes flew in every direction. Gary kept pressure on the wound while two other men moved Archie onto the improvised litter. Then more joined them and lifted it up, carrying it towards the door.

"You three go look for a shooter," said Reg. "Did anyone 'ear where it came from?"

"It was all crackers popping and screaming," said one. "Didn't 'ear no shots in all that."

"Right, I'm riding with 'im in the lorry," said Reg. "Danny, you're in charge 'ere."

"What about the police?" cried someone.

Had to be from the bride's side, Iris thought dully. That would be the last thing any of Archie's men would have suggested.

"Yeah, someone should call them, I suppose," said Reg, moving to the door.

Then he was gone.

The room had cleared out except for those of Archie's men who were searching the stage and the kitchen areas. The wreckage of the celebration was strewn across the floor—streamers, fake flowers in shattered vases, the remains of the crackers, gaily coloured and torn apart, their prizes and mottos scattered every-where.

Iris sat numbly in her seat, unable to take in what had happened. Then she saw the small black box lying on the floor by her left foot. She reached down and grabbed it, then sat up and opened the lid.

Inside was a gold ring with a diamond set in it.

"Oh, you stupid, stupid man," she whispered.

Then she slammed it shut, shoved the box into her coat pocket, and started to run, not stopping until she reached the emergency department at London Hospital.

She went through the entrance on Whitechapel Road. The receptionist took one look at her and immediately ran towards her, her face filled with concern.

"What happened, dear?" she said. "Where were you wounded?"

"Not me," said Iris.

"But the blood," said the receptionist, staring at her hands.

Iris looked down. Her hands were covered in blood, more splattered across her sleeves and skirt. She reached up to her face and felt the dried spatters.

"I'm all right," she said. "It isn't mine. My—my friend was shot. They brought him here not long ago."

"Oh, you're with Mr. Spelling," said the receptionist. "I believe he's already in surgery. The family and friends are in the waiting hall. Let me take you."

"Thank you," said Iris.

The wedding party and a large number of spivs were seated on rows of worn wooden benches in a vast central hall under a steel-framed roof, the linoleum floors scuffed from years of racing trolley wheels and pacing feet. Everyone looked up as she came in, many in shock at her appearance. Reg and Lily immediately came up to her.

"Sorry, Sparks, I didn't think about getting you a ride 'ere," said Reg.

"Don't be ridiculous," said Iris. "I wasn't a priority. What's the story?"

"Still alive when we got 'ere," said Reg. "They took 'im straight in. No telling 'ow long it'll take."

"You come sit with us," said Lily, taking her arm. "You look a fright. They're bringing tea around."

Iris sat with the Aldertons, thinking how incongruously well-dressed everyone was for the setting. The newlyweds sat close together, clutching each other's hands tightly.

As she had been clutching Archie's not thirty minutes before.

"You two," said Lily to Bernie and Tish. "You're married. You 'ave to go and be married."

"Archie's my family now," said Tish. "We're staying."

"God bless you," said Lily, and the two of them embraced.

Reg was speaking to the other spivs.

"The coppers will be coming as soon as they're done with the scene," he said. "You tell them what you saw and 'eard, no more. There will be no speculating as to 'oo might 'ave done this. I don't want you starting any rumours that will start any wars. But we will find out. The moment we're done, you get on to every source you got. I want to know before the Yard does, and I want to know yesterday. And we don't know what else is coming, so warn everyone to man the barricades. Understood?"

The others nodded without speaking, several going over to make calls at a bank of telephone boxes.

One shot, thought Iris. Didn't see where it came from, didn't notice when it happened, thanks to the noise. And the shooter got away.

Very professionally done.

We 'ave competitors, Archie had said.

The minute hand on the clock on the wall moved at an agonising speed. Every time the doors to the room opened, they looked up in hope and fear, but no one emerged for them.

It was another thirty minutes before the police arrived. A pair of detectives and a handful of constables came in. The detectives looked familiar to Iris. One was a balding, thickset man in his fifties, already looking like he was done for the day. The other, younger, thinner, jumpier, glanced at the spivs with a slight sneer on his lips, which was studiously ignored in response. The two took a look around the room, then focused on Iris.

The blood, of course, she thought. But it turned out to be more than that.

"You're Iris Sparks," said the older one, coming up to her.

"Yes," she said.

"I'm Detective Inspector Gilbert Florey, Homicide and Serious Crime Command," he said. "This is my partner, Detective Sergeant Conrad. We'd like to speak with you."

"Where's Mike Kinsey?" she asked. "He should be investigating this."

"It's my case, Miss Sparks," he said. "Come with me. There's an office we can use here."

They led her past the waiting group, Lily watching her anxiously, Reg lighting a cigarette and trying to look nonchalant.

"You're next," Florey said to Reg as they passed him.

"Glad to be of assistance," replied Reg.

They came to a door marked "For Police Use."

"You get enough business here to have your own office," said Iris.

"A desk, a telephone, and a few chairs," he said, opening the door. "Have a seat."

He sat behind the desk as she took the seat in front of it. Conrad took a chair by the door, making sure no one was listening from the hallway.

"We haven't met," said Florey. "I know about you, of course. You and Mrs. Bainbridge were instrumental in clearing up a case of mine last month. I dealt with her on that one."

"I remember your name," said Iris. "Why isn't Mike Kinsey handling this one?"

"Why should he be?"

"Because he's investigating a murder from a club Archie—Mr. Spelling—owns."

"That old body from the twenties? Why do you think that's connected?"

"Proximity. Timing. It can't be a coincidence. Why isn't Mike handling this?"

"Because you're involved, Miss Sparks," said Florey bluntly.

"I see," she said. "A conflict of interest."

"Obviously," said Florey. "You were engaged. You broke it off."

"He broke it off."

"Don't care, doesn't matter," said Florey. "He's conflicted. Cavendish was next up, but Detective Superintendent Parham decided given your recent experience with him—"

"When I was interrogated in a padded room for hours while handcuffed to a wall? That experience?"

"That you and the Yard would be better off with a fresh set of eyes," he finished, ignoring the interruption.

They don't look so fresh, she thought, looking at the bags under them.

"Ask your questions," she said.

"What is your relationship with Archie Spelling?"

She hesitated, the small black box suddenly taking on weight inside her pocket.

"Girlfriend," she said.

"That's it?" asked Florey.

Fiancée! the box seemed to scream at her.

No, she replied to it. *Not yet. I haven't given him an answer.*

"Lover," she said reluctantly. "If you wish to be more precise."

"How long?"

"We started dating this past summer. Late June."

"How did you meet?"

"We were—"

"Who is 'we'?"

"Mrs. Bainbridge and I were investigating the Tillie La Salle murder. She turned out to be linked to Mr. Spelling. When that matter was resolved, he called me up and asked me out."

"A spiv asked you for a date out of the blue, and you said yes, just like that?" asked Florey.

"It seemed like a lark at the time," said Iris. "Then it ascended."

"If you were my daughter—"

"I'm not, so skip the lecture," said Iris evenly.

"How much did he talk to you about his criminal activities?"

"Very little," she replied.

"He thought you were better off not knowing?"

"Are you married, Detective Inspector?"

"I am," he said.

"Do you discuss the details of your investigations with your wife?"

"As a matter of fact, I do," he said. "I find her feminine perspective to be quite illuminating at times. I fully expect to talk to her about you tonight. Has Mr. Spelling expressed any particular concerns about his personal safety to you?"

"Nothing specific," she said. "He mentioned competitors."

"Did you ever see him commit any act of violence or carry a weapon?"

"Neither," she said.

He never carried the gun, she thought.

"Any specific competitors' names come up?"

"I don't know of anyone that you wouldn't already know, I'm sure. Manfred Willoughby operates in a territory adjacent to his."

"You know Willoughby?"

"I know of him," said Iris. "Only by name and reputation."

"I wonder if you do know his reputation, Miss Sparks," said

Florey. "One of the most dangerous men in London, as far as we're concerned. He's entirely capable of making a move like this."

"Is that your working theory?" she asked.

"I work from the most probable theory on down," he said. "It's a system that's done well for me in my career."

"But you'll talk to Mike about his case, won't you?"

"Has Mr. Spelling said anything to you about this old case from his club that made you think there was a connection to his—to this attempt on his life?"

He was going to say murder, she thought. Not yet.

And there was the matter of the missing ring and the photograph of his dad wearing one. The same one? Do I bring it up this time?

She looked back and forth at the two detectives. Florey's expression was skeptical. Conrad's bordered on contempt.

Well, if they've made up their minds already . . .

"Only that it spooked him," she said.

"That doesn't seem like much to go on," commented Conrad.

"Anything you noticed about the actual shooting?" asked Florey. "You were right next to him. Did you hear the shot? See a flash?"

"No," she said. "I was distracted. We were pulling a Christmas cracker. Everyone was. Then I saw him—"

She stopped, thinking.

"Yes, Miss Sparks?" Florey prompted her.

"We were seated facing the stage," she said. "He was shot in the chest. The bullet had to come from that direction."

"Who was on the stage, if you remember?"

"The best man was up by the microphone," she remembered. "And the band. Three musicians. The piano player was the church organist. But they would have been seen easily if any of them had suddenly produced a weapon, and it would have taken a hell of a good shot to hit him with a handgun from that distance."

Florey looked over at Conrad and nodded to him. Conrad immediately got up and left, closing the door behind him. Iris, left alone with the senior detective, looked at him curiously as he leaned across the desk and lowered his voice.

"Detective Superintendent Parham mentioned a few things about you in confidence," he said. "That your experience may encompass more than you let on."

"I have no idea what you're talking about," she said.

"Which is exactly what I would expect you to say," he said. "You're right about the bullet coming from the stage. There's a catwalk running along above the back of it, with a clear angle from the rear corner to where Spelling and you were seated. We found a rifle there."

"What kind?" she asked immediately.

"You know about rifles?" he asked.

"What kind?" she repeated.

"A Lee-Metford Mark Two," he said. "Familiar with it?"

"Old British army sniper rifle, used up through the Great War," she said. "Quite accurate at that range. But it would have made a noise. The best man, the musicians would have heard something."

"There was some form of silencer used," said Florey. "It was left there. The band was playing, the crackers were popping, the guests were screaming and cheering. The shooter timed it for the noise, then left the rifle there. There's a storage area with a back exit to the street behind the stage. He could have slipped out easily in all the pandemonium. This was a professional at work. So, how does that comport with your theory that it's connected to Kinsey's case?"

"It doesn't," she said.

"No, it doesn't," he agreed. "I will work from the most probable theory, Miss Sparks, that this is one gang preying upon another."

"Which means when a gangster dies in London, you don't consider that to be a loss or a priority," she said bitterly.

"I work every case I am assigned the same for everyone, Miss Sparks," he said. "Good people or bad. Do you know why?"

"Why?"

"Because I am also a professional," he said. "If the shooter can be found, I will find him. Now, if you can't think of anything else to assist us, I will let you return to the waiting hall. I hope for Mr. Spelling's sake that he survives this."

"Thank you," she said.

"And I hope for your sake that you do better for yourself," he added. "You're above this lot."

"People keep telling me that, yet here I am," she said defiantly.

"There you are," he agreed. "With Spelling's blood splattered all over that nice new suit."

He got up and opened the door.

"Conrad?" he called. "Come take Miss Sparks back to the waiting hall and bring Reg Townley in here."

"Will do. Come with me, miss," said Conrad, beckoning to Iris.

She sensed the younger detective's scorn as they walked back to the waiting hall. His contempt spread across the room to encompass the crowd of spivs and family, judging them all alike, when all they were doing was hoping Archie would survive the night, regardless of who he was or what he had done.

This lot.

She separated from Conrad, who motioned to Reg to join him. Reg sauntered up, raising an eyebrow at Iris as he did. She nodded slightly, and he nodded back, sending his approval. He walked away with Conrad.

One of the nieces—Iris still hadn't sorted out which—silently came up to her with a cup of tea and handed it to her.

It was still hot.

This lot.

Who had embraced her immediately and accepted her, family

and spivs. And there was a ring in a small black box in her pocket inviting her in even further.

This lot.

She wasn't above this lot.

They were hers and she was theirs.

And right then she vowed that she was going to find whoever had brought them harm.

CHAPTER 8

I ris sat on the bench as the time stretched into hours. Every fifteen minutes or so, Conrad would reappear and bring away another man for questioning. The ones he released immediately went to Reg for hushed recapitulations. So far, Reg seemed satisfied with what he heard.

She was the only woman Florey had spoken with. He hadn't bothered with the family or the wedding party yet, besides Harry, the best man, who went in for longer than most, then returned without anything enlightening to tell the assembly.

He went straight to Bernie and Tish, avoiding the spivs, she noticed.

She stared disconsolately into the dregs of her tea. There had been a girl back at boarding school who had claimed she could read their fortunes in the tea leaves. The girls would gather clandestinely after lights out, lighting a single candle while heating up the kettle on a smuggled hot plate, snatching it away at the first faint whistle, suppressing their giggles. The purported seer wrapped herself in shawls and veils and seated herself in some vague asana posture, then proceeded to terrify them over their futures. Iris, the resident atheist and skeptic of the group, would have none of it.

She wished she could believe in it now, she thought. She very much needed to know what the future held.

She sensed his presence looming first, then the old reassuring voice uttered the single word, "Sparks." Then she was clinging to Sally hard, sobbing for the first time, mashing her face into the thick worsted wool lapel of his overcoat.

He simply held her until she finished crying it out, only then relaxing his hold so she could peer up at his face, so she could see the compassion shining down, a compassion tinged by losses of his own.

Salvatore Danielli, the Cambridge Titan. Her best friend. Sally.

"You're here," she whispered.

"I'm here," he said. "For whatever you need, Sparks, I'm here."

"How did you know?"

"Gwen called me."

"Gwen? How did she know?"

"Benny called me," said Gwen.

Iris peered around Sally to see Gwen standing a short distance away, her eyes brimming. She came forward and gave Iris a quick embrace.

"I will return to you right away," she whispered. "I must make the rounds."

They watched as she went first to the newlyweds and bent towards them, taking the hand of each and pressing them between her own.

"It's a terrible thing to have this happen on your wedding day," she said. "It would be a terrible thing to say congratulations, but you have each other now. You are being tested from the start as no couple ever should be tested, but it would be so much worse if you didn't have each other. So be with each other, and remember this."

"We will, Mrs. Bainbridge," said Bernie. "Thank you."

"Now, please introduce me to your parents."

They led her to the rest of the family, who goggled at the tall, elegant figure approaching them.

"How does she do that so easily?" marvelled Iris.

"A little touch of Gwendolyn in the night," said Sally.

Gwen shook each parent's hand in turn, holding on to Lily's the longest.

"Your brother has helped me in ways you don't know and I may never talk about, Mrs. Alderton," she said to her. "I want you to know that he is in my heart and will be first in my prayers."

"Thank you," said Lily. "I can't believe you came."

"I hope you don't mind," said Gwen. "I will wait until there is word. Bless you all."

She returned to Iris and Sally. Reg and Benny came up to greet her.

"Thank you for letting me know," Gwen said to Benny.

"I thought Sparks could use a friend or two," said Benny.

"I find myself with quite a few more than that," said Iris.

"We know who you are, Danielli," said Reg. "We met that time in the warehouse. You probably don't remember us. I'm Reg, this is Benny."

"I never forget a face, but you were wearing ski masks that night," said Sally, shaking their hands. "Pleased to meet you. Call me Sally. I was—"

"There's the doc," said Reg, interrupting him.

The surgeon, a slender, greying man in his early fifties whose hands looked too large for his wrists, walked into the room, looking around.

"Family for Spelling?" he asked.

More than twenty hands went up.

"My word," he said. "I am Dr. Solomon Benzimri, the treating surgeon. We have completed the initial surgery, and Mr. Spelling has come through it alive."

There was a shriek of joy from the nieces. Dr. Benzimri held up his hand.

"He is by no means out of the woods," he continued. "The bullet missed the heart and major arteries. It did not miss the lung. We've managed to drain it and resection the damaged tissue, then reinflate it, but this will be the first of what I anticipate to be several procedures. He's lost a great deal of blood, and that will have cascading effects on other organs. The greatest dangers over the next twenty-four hours besides that are shock and sepsis. We've stabilised him with drains, and will go back in tomorrow if he's strong enough to withstand another surgery."

"He'll be strong enough," said Benny confidently.

"He is a tough one," agreed Benzimri.

"What are the odds?" asked Reg.

"Better now," said Benzimri. "They will improve dramatically after twenty-four hours. Does he have immediate family here? Is there a wife?"

Most of them glanced at Iris, who tentatively raised her hand.

"I'm his girlfriend," she said. "Is that enough?"

Fiancée! screamed the ring.

"I'm sorry, but not at this point," said Benzimri.

"Sister," said Lily, approaching him. "I'm the closest family 'e's got. Mrs. Lillian Alderton."

"Very well, Mrs. Alderton. He's in recovery. I'll have a nurse—"

"Wait," said Reg. "What kind of security do you 'ave on 'im?"

"The hospital has security at every entrance."

"Not good enough," said Reg. "We take care of our own."

"I don't believe—"

"You!" said Reg, looking over his shoulder at one of the police constables. "Get your boss in 'ere."

"My boss is at the precinct," said the constable.

"I meant Florey."

"He's with a different command," said the constable. "So not my boss."

"'E's the highest-ranking officer on the scene, inne?"

"Well, yes, but—"

"Then bloody get 'im 'ere!" shouted Reg.

He turned back to Benzimri as the constable walked off, looking back at Reg resentfully.

"Pardon me for shouting, Doc," Reg said. "I appreciate what you done for Archie, and I realise security ain't your responsibility. So 'oo should I talk to in either Security or Administration right now to arrange things?"

"On a Saturday night?" replied the surgeon, glancing at a hospital guard who had tentatively made his presence known.

"Mr. Armbruster is night manager," said the guard.

"Then would you be so kind as to summon him here," said Benzimri.

"This may take some time," Gwen whispered to Iris. "Come with me to the ladies' and I'll get you cleaned up."

Iris allowed herself to be led to the ladies' room to the left of the dispensary.

"Don't look in the mirror," Gwen advised her as they entered.

Iris immediately looked in the mirror. The spatters she expected. The long smear of dried blood across her jawline and chin was an unwelcome surprise. She looked down at her hands.

"I was trying to stop the bleeding," she said. "I must have rubbed my face after. I look like a vampire. I probably scared the hell out of all of them when I appeared."

"Wash your hands first, then I'll take care of your face," directed Gwen.

Iris turned on the taps and held her hands under. The hot water wasn't running well, and the cold was a shock. She reached under the soap dispenser for the powder, which felt harsh and abrasive on her palms. She rubbed them together hard, craving the small stings of contact against her nerve endings before the powder dissolved. Gradually, the blood came off, swirling down the drain in front of her.

Gwen wet her handkerchief under the tap, then took Iris in hand, working gently on the large smear, then dabbing at the spatters.

"How much makeup do you have with you?" she asked.

"Not much," said Iris.

"I took the liberty of bringing a few items," said Gwen, reaching into her bag. "Enough to make you presentable again."

Iris stood motionless as her face regained some colour by artificial means.

Gwen paused to contemplate her handiwork.

"Promise me you're not going to go after them yourself," she said quietly.

"Stop reading my mind," said Iris.

"I don't need to," said Gwen. "I saw it in your face the moment we came in."

"They shot Archie. He almost died. He may still die."

"I know," said Gwen. "But the police are on it—"

"I don't trust them."

"Florey's all right," said Gwen. "Methodical, thorough. He'll get the job done. And if he doesn't—well, I'm sure Reg and the lads are well ahead of the Yard by now. My point is that forces on both sides of the law are marshalling troops who are hell-bent on catching whoever did this, and there is no need for you to get caught in the cross fire."

"You want me to sit here and wait for Archie to die."

"I want you to sit and wait," said Gwen. "I know you don't pray. I'll handle that part."

"What if it were Ronnie in there?" asked Iris. "What if you were me? Would you sit and wait for Ronnie to die and do nothing?"

"I did exactly that for four and a half years," said Gwen. "The moment he left to fight, I knew that every single day could be his last. I kept my chin up, and prayed, and cried, and put on a good face for the world and wrote cheerful letters to the front and steeled myself for the possibility that it might happen. Then it did happen, and you know the rest. For all my preparations and self-deceptions, I still fell apart like a cheap card table the moment I learned he was dead."

"We're not the same," said Iris.

"No, we're not," agreed Gwen. "That's what scares me. You scare me. You scare me because you're stronger than I am, far stronger than I will ever be. And you will take action precisely because you are stronger than me. But that doesn't mean it won't go horribly wrong in the end. And I don't want to lose you."

"Then help me," said Iris. "Help me go after them."

Gwen looked at her partner's face, then pulled out her hand-kerchief.

"I missed a spot," she said, wiping off a speck of blood from Iris's neck. "You'll have to get this suit cleaned professionally, I think."

"Will you help me or not?" asked Iris.

"I think it would be best if neither of us made any decisions right now in a hospital ladies' room," said Gwen. "You need to eat something. You need sleep. Promise me that you won't do anything rash tonight."

"In exchange for what?"

"I will go to church in the morning with my family and pray for guidance," said Gwen. "I will come back to the hospital after lunch to get an update on Archie. Meet me here at two, and we will figure things out. Maybe the assassin will already have been caught by then by the people who are good at this sort of thing."

"We are good at it," argued Iris.

"We are," said Gwen. "But we aren't good at it right now. Two o'clock in the waiting room, Iris, and you don't go off on your own before then. Promise?"

Iris gripped Gwen's hands hard, then leaned into her, closing her eyes.

"I have no right to ask you this," she said.

"You have every right," said Gwen. "Let's rejoin the group, shall we?"

They returned to find Reg, Florey, and a weary gentleman from the hospital, presumably Mr. Armbruster, arguing while everyone else looked on with expressions ranging from the appalled to the downright murderous. Bernie and Tish were no longer there, which was a relief to both the matchmakers.

"You can't have armed spivs in the hospital, Townley," said Florey.

"Who said armed?" asked Reg.

"Are you saying they won't be?"

"I'm saying that someone put a bullet in our friend, and when 'oever did it finds out it didn't do the trick, the old men at the doorways 'ere ain't gonna 'ave no more stopping power than a 'andful of tissues. So unless you're prepared to station a bobby at 'is door—"

"I am not."

"Then we're gonna protect our own, and you can kindly look the other way until 'e's out of danger."

"Which may not be for weeks."

"It may not be," said Reg. "But 'is security is my job, got it?"

"You haven't demonstrated much competence at it today, have you, Townley?" said Florey.

Reg turned dark red, and spivs and bobbies edged nearer, eyeing each other fiercely.

"Gentlemen, may I offer an alternative?" said Armbruster.

"By all means," said Florey. "What do you propose?"

"This is not the first such patient we've had recuperating here," said Armbruster. "I can recommend a private security firm. Licensed, of course. Run by a man named Troulan."

"Anyone know them?" Reg barked over his shoulder.

"Yeah, Reg," said Benny. "We've used them before. For that—that thing in East Ham."

"That was them?"

"Yeah. They're okay."

Reg looked back at Florey.

"We stay until these blokes arrive," he said.

"Very well," said Florey, pulling a card from his pocket. "I've got all I need here. My card, in case anything else comes to you."

"You'll be the first person I call," said Reg, taking it.

"Of course," said Florey. "Come, gentlemen. Mrs. Alderton, I hope the best for your brother."

"I'm sure," said Lily. "Thanks."

Florey and the rest of the policemen left. Reg watched until the doors closed behind them, then crumpled the card in his fist and tossed it onto a bench.

"Well, that was unnecessarily exciting," said Sally. "What now, ladies? I've got the Hornet, which means I can only drive one of you home, unfortunately."

"Take Iris," said Gwen. "I'll get a cab. Thanks for the lift here."

"Good night, Gwen," said Sally. "Thanks for alerting me. Give my regards to Ronnie and John."

"Good night, Sally," she said, coming over to kiss him on the cheek. "It was good to see you again."

"Likewise."

Gwen made her last round of goodbyes, then vanished.

Sally watched her longingly, then turned to Iris, his expression immediately becoming one of concern.

"You look done in," he said. "Let me take you home."

Iris reluctantly joined him, first surrendering to one last smothering embrace from Lily.

"The Good Samaritan is open, should you require immediate liquid reinforcement," said Sally as he guided her outside. "Or we could dine. Whatever you need, I will conjure it."

"You are my genie," said Iris. "Let's find your car and sit for a moment. Amidst all the other shocks of the day was seeing you and Gwen show up together just when I needed you the most. Are you two— What exactly are you two? How did this happen?"

"She called me," said Sally. "First time since—well, since things ended, or didn't end, but came to a halt. Needless to say, I was surprised to hear her voice, but once I knew the reason . . ."

"I hope it wasn't too painful a reunion. I never heard the full story of why you broke up. From either of you."

"I don't know if you can call it a breakup when we were never quite together," he said. "Call it recognition of the failure of the attempt. I wasn't what she wanted."

"Did she say that? In those words?"

"Basically, she wanted me to be myself," said Sally. "And I didn't want to be myself. Don't like him, never have."

"Give him a chance," said Iris.

"Tell me," said Sally. "Is she seeing anyone else?"

"She's gone out on some dates," said Iris. "I cannot tell you more."

"No," said Sally. "No need for anything more."

She reached over and squeezed his hand.

They walked in silence to where he had parked. The air was cold and damp, the fog that had covered the city during the day only starting to clear. Sally opened the door for her, then went around to the driver's seat and folded himself in.

"Where to?" he asked. "A place of sustenance, or straight back to Marylebone?"

"Drive me to Hackney," she said.

"Hackney?" he repeated in surprise. "You're not actually planning to show up on your mum's doorstep after all this, are you?"

"Archie's house is in Hackney."

"Ah. You're on the prowl. Planning to break in and get a start on the police?"

"I have a key."

"Do you?"

"I do."

"That's something you haven't shared with me," he said, starting the car. "I would have thought I'd be the first one you'd call about something like that. Are we not the keepers of each other's secrets?"

"We are," she said. "It's a recent development. I've been remiss. I'm sorry."

"Forgiven," he said.

"Here's another," she said, pulling the box from her pocket. "Happened at the reception."

He glanced over, and his eyes grew wide when she opened it.

"I didn't know they made atom bombs that small," he said. "When did he propose?"

"He didn't get the chance," said Iris. "There was a bullet from the gods."

"A proposal does seem implied by the nature of the ring," he said.

"My very thought."

"Did you know your answer? Do you now?"

She didn't respond.

"Unfair question, I withdraw it," he said. "What terrible timing. You're frozen in the moment twixt one romantic state and another, and all of this horror comes flooding into this limbo."

"Something like that," said Iris. "Distract me. What have you been up to recently?"

"I've started writing another play," he said.

"Have you? Are you done with *The Margate Affair*?"

"Never, but I've put it aside for the moment. There's—"

He stopped for a moment, shaking his head.

"There's too much of her in it," he said. "I can't set myself apart enough to rewrite. I can't think about love right now, so I'm writing a war play finally. Plenty of helpful, accessible demons perched on my shoulders chittering in my ears for that. It feels good to get it out of my system. Assuming it does get out of my system. Maybe once I put the horrors on paper, they'll be easier to face."

"You will read the scenes to me when you finish them?"

"If you're willing," said Sally. "You're already three behind."

"Call me when this—just call me, Sally."

She directed him to Archie's house. He pulled up in front and cut the engine.

"Nice place," he commented. "Not at all what I would have thought someone like Archie would have."

"What did you expect?"

"Something more, I don't know, baronial. Fortified. Do you want me to come in?"

"No, Sally. Thank you."

"Why here, Sparks?" he asked. "Why do you want to be in here of all places, given everything that's happened?"

"Good night, Sally," she said, kissing him on the cheek.

"Call me tomorrow," he said. "Whatever happens, I'll be there in a heartbeat."

"I will," she promised.

He got out, opened the door for her, and watched as she walked up to the front door. She made a display of taking out her key and unlocking it, then turned and waved as she opened it. Sally waved back, then got into the Hornet and drove off.

She turned and faced the threshold.

Why do I want to be here, Sally?

Because I want to sleep with the scent of him in my bed before it fades away forever.

She went inside, locking the door behind her. She scooped up the letters and placed them on the table. There was a little light coming in from the outside, enough for her to see the stairs and the hallway going back. Enough to illumine the shapes of the figures in the photographs—those long gone and those still alive, with Archie hovering on the border.

She shook off that thought.

She was hungry, she suddenly realised. By this point, she should have been dancing the night away, filled with whatever meal Spelling Enterprises had cooked up for the evening.

All that food, wasted. She hoped that the church had stepped in and procured it for some poorhouse.

Have to eat. Gwen said so, and Gwen was always right.

She wondered if there was anything left of the steak she and Archie had shared two nights before. She went through the house to the kitchen, turned on the light, and opened the refrigerator. Then she stepped back in dismay.

A bottle of champagne waited inside, a silver ribbon tied around its neck, curled to produce a festive, celebratory knot.

I guess he knew my answer, she thought. Even if I still don't.

There was some steak on a plate to the side. She reached in gingerly to grab it, avoiding the champagne like it was booby-trapped.

Should be enough, she thought. Maybe open a can of peas.

What was that line from *Hamlet*? "The funeral baked meats did coldly furnish forth the marriage tables." But this was the opposite—

No. There will be no funeral, Archie. Not this time. Not until I hear it out loud that you want me to be your wife. Otherwise—

Why the hell did you plan to do it today? she thought angrily.

To steal the spotlight at your own nephew's wedding. I hope you had the courtesy to ask them in advance.

I'll bet he did ask them. Maybe all the happy family members there were in on it, the band ready with the appropriate fanfare, everyone waiting for the astonishing sight of Archie Spelling publicly renouncing his bachelor ways, on sacred ground, no less, or at least in a community space adjoining sacred ground. She wasn't sure how far the consecrated borders extended.

She needed a drink.

Anything but champagne. That cork will not be popped until—

Anyhow.

Wine. There was wine in the cellar.

She went down the steps to the cellar, looked over the selection, then paused.

It's one thing to finish a man's leftover steak, she thought. But opening a bottle of his wine, no matter how much you're sharing his life, is stealing.

Declare yourself! cried the ring, whose voice had now taken up permanent residency inside her head. *Say you're his fiancée, and the wine is yours!*

She looked at the bottles longingly, then stepped away.

The cellar was much less cluttered than it had been on her previous visit. The boxes with the crackers were gone, of course, but there must have been other party supplies she hadn't noticed, for other boxes were missing as well, although some more were still stacked against the walls. She could see all the way across to the locked room.

The one he had jokingly warned her from opening.

She reached inside her bag and retrieved the small case in which she kept her lock picks, then walked over to the door and went to work. She had it open in twenty seconds.

All right, Mr. Bluebeard, let's see if I'm really your first.

Whatever lurid flights of fancy her mind had taken in expectation were dashed. She stepped into a small office holding a desk, a chair, a standing lamp, an old brown filing cabinet, and some more photographs on the walls. There were three items on the desktop, however, that immediately caught her eye.

A .38 revolver. A thick scrapbook. And on top of the latter, acting as a crude but effective paperweight, a brick.

She sat at the desk, turned on the lamp, then started with the gun, first checking the cylinder. Fully loaded.

He did say there were other weapons in the house, she remembered, putting it down gently. This must have been the cellar's last line of defense.

On the wall directly ahead of her was a shadow box containing a number of items. A small photograph of his father in uniform. A patch with the insignia of his battalion. A small, green octagon, attached by a cord to a small red disc. Both, she knew, made of vulcanised asbestos fibre. His military identification tags, designed to withstand even a conflagration.

And a ring, mounted with the insignia facing outwards. The martial sparrows, just as Gwen had described them.

She picked up the brick next. Was it from the collapsed wall in the cellar of the White Palace? The colour seemed right. She wondered why Archie would have brought it here.

She turned it over in her hands, then squinted as she noticed something. There was a manufacturer's mark that must have been pressed into the clay before firing. "M. Fletcher & Co."

Did that mean anything? She'd have to find out.

Or, assuming that she did the responsible thing, turn it over to Mike, if he hadn't already taken one from the scene. Or she could give it to Florey.

She wasn't feeling particularly responsible at the moment.

She set aside the brick and turned to the scrapbook, the item that had spiked her curiosity the most. It wasn't new, certainly. The spine was supple and cracked in a few spots, and the paper inside had yellowed on the edges. There was no dust on it. No dust anywhere, she noted approvingly. This room was in frequent use.

She took a deep breath, and opened it.

On the first page was taped a picture of Archie's dad, the same one from the front hall, flanked by his two mates from the war. Only there was something written in pencil below each smiling figure.

Ted Burton. Shot. December 17, 1922.
Stanley Spelling. Stabbed. November 28, 1922.

And under the last: *Jenks Emery.* Next to it, traced over several times to thicken the lines, was a large question mark.

She riffled through the pages, saw that they were filled with newspaper clippings and other scraps of paper.

Looks like I have something to read at the kitchen table, she thought.

She picked it up, turned off the lamp, and carried it out of the office, making sure to lock the door behind her.

She went back up to the kitchen and placed the scrapbook on the table, then opened a can of peas and heated them up on the stove, her moral quandaries over the wine rack not extending to items she could replace more easily. When the peas were done, she drained them, spooned out a helping next to the steak, poured herself a glass of water, then sat down at the table and opened the scrapbook, turning past the photograph to the next page.

"Dockworker Stabbed to Death" read the first clipping she saw.

Dockworker Stanley Spelling, 37, was found dead near the Royal Docks last night. According to the police, he had suffered multiple stab wounds to the chest and neck. Reports of shouts from the vicinity drew the attentions of the night watchman who discovered the body but did not see the perpetrator. Police are making enquiries and requesting that anyone with knowledge of this affair call . . .

There were articles from other dailies, carrying the same information. The press lost interest quickly as the investigation petered out. One article drew her attention: "Reward Offered for Information on Spelling Death."

A reward of one hundred pounds sterling has been posted by the Docks Group of the Transport and General Workers' Union for information leading to the identification of the killer of Stanley Spelling, who was a member in good standing and a longtime member of the DWRGLU prior to the merger. The reward was announced by Ned Spelling, vice president of the Docks Group and elder brother of the deceased. A collection has also been started for the benefit of the Spelling children, left orphans after the death of their father.

So that's who Uncle Ned was, she thought. A powerful man in a lucrative area. He was the one who took Archie under his wing. He must have passed on as well at some point. He wasn't in charge of the Spelling gang anymore as far as she knew.

There were no more articles about Stanley's death. She assumed it remained unsolved. She turned a page: "Man Found Floating in Thames Was Shot, Say Police."

Ted Burton, Des's father, coming to a bad end a month after Stanley. She read through the articles. He was a carpenter, in business with his brother. No one knew of any enemies.

No connection was made to Stanley Spelling's death.

Why would there be? she thought. Different methods used, different precincts investigating. Nothing about Burton being tied in with the dockworkers. No one would think of putting the two events together.

Except for Archie.

How long had he been keeping this scrapbook? she wondered. From the start, as a twelve-year-old, or years later, when he was old enough to start putting the pieces together?

She wished he had shown her this before.

She finished her meal and washed the dishes, then brought the scrapbook up to the master bedroom. The scandalously short, sheer nightie she had worn on her inaugural first night in the house was on a hanger in the closet next to her new robe. She didn't want to wear the nightie. That was for him and him alone. She dug through his bureau drawers instead, locating a pair of flannel pyjamas that were absurdly large on her when she changed into them.

She brushed her teeth, then climbed under the covers, pausing to bury her face in his pillow and inhale deeply.

She propped the pillows against the headboard and pulled the scrapbook onto her lap. She expected when she finished the articles about Burton and his unsolved murder that the next page would begin the saga of Jenks Emery and how he merited that thickly drawn question mark.

To her surprise, the next group of articles were from 1921 starting in October. "Brazen Trio Robs City Jewellery Store," shouted the first.

Murnau's Jewellery on Shaftesbury Avenue fell victim to a daring daylight robbery yesterday at two in the afternoon. Three men entered, scarves pulled up over their lower faces, with pistols at the ready. Two herded the customers and employees into the rear while the third emptied the registers and two display cases containing diamonds and other precious stones. The three men then fled in a waiting car. Police arrived on the scene moments after the incident and obtained descriptions, but have little to go on. . . .

Interesting, she thought. Why is this here?

Were the three men Spelling, Burton, and Emery?

Each clipping detailed another robbery. There was no geographical pattern that she could discern, nor did they favour particular categories of victims. There were no jewellery stores after that first. They were sticking to cash hauls. No banks, she noticed as she turned the page, but upscale restaurants, high-end retail clothing stores, some swanky nightclubs, places where the cash registers filled fast and could be emptied just as quickly. The getaway cars were never the same, and frequently stolen themselves not long before the heists. The faces of the men were never seen, but more than one witness remarked on the near-military precision of the execution.

Then they stopped. The last clipping told of a club hit in Mile End in the middle of November 1922.

A chill hit her as she saw the White Palace named as the latest to fall victim.

Less than two weeks later, Stanley Spelling was killed, and there were no more robberies committed by the anonymous three.

Seemed like cause and effect there. Only who caused the effect?

Let's see what Archie learned about that.

No clippings about the sudden death of Jenks Emery. One mentioned his disappearance, with the police asking the public for any information. It didn't say why they were looking for him. Was there family worried about him? Or had the police connected him to the robberies?

The first item after that was a photograph of a steamship, the S.S. *Fowler,* with people waving from the decks. One man, his face partially obscured, was circled. Above it, in Archie's handwriting, was the word "Emery?"

There was a copy of the passenger list. No one by that name on it. It was dated January 18, 1923. The *Fowler* was bound for Argentina.

She turned the page. More lists of passengers bound for everywhere far away, with some names circled, then crossed out. A small page of lined loose-leaf paper had a list marked "Relatives." Several were named Emery, with addresses scribbled by them. Most had a large check mark next to them, with a date added. The dates started in the late twenties and extended into the late thirties.

Archie was trying to find Jenks Emery all that time, she thought. Then he gave up the quest. Nothing to indicate whether Emery was dead or alive. If he had betrayed and killed his partners, then fled the country with the loot, it may be that Archie had given up.

Only he wasn't the type to give up, she thought.

And this was all speculation, of course. Maybe—

She froze. There was a noise downstairs. A door opening, then shutting.

She turned off her light immediately, then carefully got out of bed, listening. She hadn't checked the bedroom for any weapons. She had been sure enough about her safety at the wedding to leave her knife and metal knuckles behind, but her faith in that safety had clearly been misplaced. She quickly rolled up the legs of her pyjamas past her knees, freeing her legs, then thought about anything there she could use as a weapon. She could defend herself in unarmed combat more than proficiently, but she preferred to have something she could swing for the first blow. There was a clock with a thick marble base on the bureau. She felt for it carefully, then hefted it.

It would do.

She listened. Footsteps, but not heading up to this floor. Heading to the kitchen.

Maybe it was only a hungry burglar, she thought.

Then she heard another door open, and steps receding down.

He was going to the cellar.

Right, she thought. That gives me a chance.

She replaced the clock, then opened the bedroom door and made her way silently down the stairs, then back to the kitchen.

She opened the cabinet door, reached behind the cans, and found what she was looking for. She pulled out the Browning, cocked it, then grabbed a torch that she had spotted by the knife rack.

The door to the cellar was open. Whoever was down there was carefully nearing the bottom of the steps, using a torch of his own. Iris tried to remember if any of the steps creaked, then threw caution to the wind and simply walked down, flicking on the torch when she was halfway to the bottom. The man started to turn.

"Freeze," she said. "I've got a gun. Hands up where I can see them."

The man raised his hands, his torch pointing at the ceiling. The other was empty.

"Turn around slowly," she said.

He turned, his eyes squinting as his face came into the torch beam.

"Jesus, Sparks," said Reg. "You nearly gave me an 'eart attack."

CHAPTER 9

W ould you mind lowering the gun?" asked Reg.

"That depends," said Iris. "Are you armed?"

"Someone put a bullet in my boss today, and I'm second-in-command and next in line," said Reg. "Damn right I'm armed."

"Come up the stairs slowly and with your hands raised," she said.

She backed up carefully, keeping both her torch and gun aimed at him. He followed her, making sure to keep his hands in position. She flicked on the light to the stairs when she reached the top, then turned off her torch and placed it on a counter, her eyes never leaving his.

"Take your gun out, forefinger and thumb on the butt," she said.

He reached into his jacket and produced a Webley revolver.

"Hold it in front of you at arm's length, then walk towards me until I can reach it," she said.

He complied, bringing it to her. She grabbed it by the barrel, and he released his grasp.

"Come into the kitchen," she said. "Then sit."

He moved after her as she backed towards the rear door, then sat compliantly at the table. She put his gun on the counter.

"Feel like talking now?" she asked.

"I was ready to talk from the start," he said. "You're the one pointing a gun. How about lowering it now?"

"Fine," she said, dropping her arm to her side.

"You 'ave to uncock it," he added helpfully.

"I know," she said, doing it. "I've made it unready to shoot, and now I am ready to listen. What's going on? Why are you here?"

"Because, Sparks, I'm second-in-command, and business don't stop when the boss goes down," said Reg. "And the coppers don't stop, neither, which means sooner or later, Florey's gonna get it in 'is sweet plodding 'ead to come poking around Archie's 'ouse, and there are a few boxes in that cellar that contain things that are not exactly party favours, if you take my meaning. So I wanted to re-move them as quickly and as quietly as possible to places Florey don't know about so that Archie won't wake up 'andcuffed to 'is bed rails."

"You have a key to this place?"

"I do," said Reg. "So do you, which was news to me. Sorry if I frightened you, but Lord knows you evened that score."

"Why the torch if you've got a key to the place?"

"Because Archie's made the BBC news already, and I din't know if 'is neighbours would be wondering about lights going on in the 'ouse."

"I've lit them tonight without anyone knocking on the door," said Iris. "How long will you need here?"

"Four trips down and up should do it," he said.

"I could help you and make it two."

"Then you would be abetting a crime, Sparks," he said. "I don't want you in jeopardy."

"It wouldn't be my first crime, Reg," she said. "Not even my first with you."

"I appreciate the offer, but no thanks."

"Then how about I make you a cup of tea while you're loading the car? I don't think that would constitute any great criminality."

"That would be greatly welcomed," he said. "It's been a day and an 'alf, all right. Oh, and mind if I take my gun with me? It ain't like there still ain't a target on my back."

She handed it over and he tucked it back inside his jacket.

"You can roll them pyjama legs back down," he said as he got up. "Don't want you catching cold on top of all this."

"Thanks," she said. "I'm going to run up and put a robe on. Meet you back here when you're done."

They headed to their respective stairways. She came down, robed and wearing a pair of Archie's woolen socks on her feet, just as Reg was passing through the hall carrying a large crate. She ran to the front door and held it open for him. He nodded his thanks as he went out, then she ran back to the kitchen and started the kettle.

By the time he had carried out the last box, the tea was ready, and she had located a tin of biscuits, which she set out on the table.

"Milk?" she asked as he sat down.

"No thanks," he said.

She poured two cups, then sat across from him.

"Any word?" she asked quietly.

"Still the same," he said. "They got 'im pretty heavily sedated. The private guard showed up about an hour after you left. There were some reporters trying to poke around, but we scared them off for now."

"How did they get onto it?"

"Either the 'ospital or the cops tipped 'em. Bound to 'appen. That 'eadline can write itself. 'Gangland shooting at church wedding 'all.' Read all about it."

He practically spat the last words out.

"Sorry," he said, taking a biscuit. "I'm on edge. And I can't imagine what it's been like for you. 'Ow are you 'olding up? And why are you 'olding up in 'ere instead of your flat?"

"I needed to be here," she said. "Being where he lives. Protecting his house."

"Doing a damn good job of it, too," he said. "Better job of protecting 'im than I did today. That crack from Florey about failing at it, that 'it 'ome, it did. I always figure events like this were safe. There's a code of sorts. And there weren't any chatter about this being in the offing. We 'ad all been getting along lately."

"Florey seemed to think Manfred Willoughby was most likely to be behind it," said Iris. "What do you think?"

"He's closest to us," said Reg. "And 'as a bigger territory and the manpower to go with it. I din't think 'e'd been out to make any moves, but 'e's as good a bet as any."

"Who else?"

"Why do you want to know, Sparks? This ain't your fight."

"I'm as good a soldier as anyone you've got, Reg," she said. "And I'm angrier than all of them."

"Which may be why you shouldn't be barging in," said Reg. "You don't know the territory like we do."

"I'm a quick study. I can get in places your men can't."

"No, Sparks," he said gently. "I won't let you."

"Why?"

"Because I work for Archie Spelling, and what 'e'd want more than anything else right now is for you to be safe."

"What about what I want?"

"I'd think you want to be safe, too."

"If I wanted safety, would I be with Archie?"

"Maybe not," he replied. "But that's my decision."

"Am I in any danger at the moment?"

"Can't rule it out," he said. "But you might be safer 'ere, come to think of it. If Willoughby or anyone else decided to come after you, they'd most likely be looking for you at your flat."

"So I'm safe for the night."

"I'd say so. Although I'm gonna want to take that gun with

me. Don't want Florey arresting you for anything, neither. Do you know if there are any others lying about?"

"I found one in the cellar," she said. "I'll go get it."

She ran up to the bedroom and fetched her bag, then returned to the kitchen.

"Back in a tick," she said. "Have some more tea."

She returned to the cellar. Picking the lock to his office now that she knew the feel of it took her only seconds this time. She retrieved the revolver and searched the desk drawers and file cabinet, looking for other weapons. There were none, but she found two boxes of cartridges, one calibre for each of the guns she knew about. She emptied the revolver's cylinder into the box of .38s, then left the office, again locking the door.

"This is all I've found," she said when she came back.

She placed the revolver and boxes on the table, then reluctantly added the Browning to the collection.

"Yeah, I can see why you'd like to keep one by the bedside," he said, standing and stuffing the guns and boxes into his coat. "But best not get caught with anything."

She pulled the two biggest kitchen knives from the rack.

"I'll be fine," she said.

"What time do you want to come to the hospital?" he asked. "I'll send Benny to pick you up."

"Gwen said she'd meet me there at two. She wants to sit with everyone."

"The Duchess is really something, God bless 'er," said Reg. "All right, I'll tell Benny to swing by 'ere at one thirty. Thanks for the tea, Sparks. And for not shooting me in the back."

"You're welcome. The next time you're planning on sneaking in, call first."

"Will do."

She walked him to the door, then made sure to lock it after him.

She still had the knives in her hand. She carried them up to the bedroom with her.

She couldn't sleep after that unwanted extra excitement, so she placed the knives under her pillow and picked up the scrapbook. As she opened it, she noticed that there was something thicker than paper stuffed in it towards the back.

Shouldn't turn to the last page in a mystery, Sparks, she admonished herself.

But she did it anyway.

There was the missing signet ring, taped to the middle of the page. Underneath it was written the date the dead man had turned up in the cellar.

Underneath that was the word "Emery," followed by several question marks.

And the last thing written in the scrapbook after that: "Des on bricks."

Gwen's cab pulled into the driveway. Percival, the butler for the Bainbridges, had the front door open before she had finished paying the fare.

"Good evening, Mrs. Bainbridge," he said, taking her coat, scarf, and gloves. "How is Mr. Spelling?"

"Alive, but in bad shape, I'm afraid," she said, unpinning her hat. "I'm going back after lunch tomorrow to check in on him."

"And Miss Sparks?"

"I may need to check in on her even more."

"I'll have Nigel ready to take you."

"No, Percival, we can't waste the petrol. It's only the East End. I'll take the Tube."

"Very well, Mrs. Bainbridge."

"Who's still up and about?"

"The boys have gone to sleep," he said. "Lord Bainbridge has retired for the evening. Lady Bainbridge is in the library. If you would like to join her, I could bring you something."

"If she's still having sherry, I'll have one with her," said Gwen. "If she's moved on to whisky—hell, I could use a stiff one myself. I can pour my own, Percival. You go ahead and lock up."

"Very well, Mrs. Bainbridge. Oh, and Mr. Daile is with her."

"Simon got in from Royal Ag already? Wonderful! We weren't expecting him until tomorrow."

She walked down to the library to find her mother-in-law and Simon Daile, John's uncle, sitting together in the armchairs by the fireplace. Simon held a small glass of sherry, more for etiquette's sake, she thought, as it had barely been touched, and was doing his best to preserve an expression of polite interest as Carolyne regaled him, an empty sherry glass on the side table and a half-full tumbler in her hand.

"Gwendolyn, at last," exclaimed Simon, rising to his feet with a look of relief. "How is Mr. Spelling? We've been quite concerned."

"I haven't," declared Carolyne. "The man is as indestructible as a cockroach."

"He isn't bulletproof, Carolyne," said Gwen, coming over to kiss Simon on the cheek. "Still in danger, I'm afraid. I'll be going back tomorrow after lunch. Hello, Simon, it's so good to see you. How was first term?"

"Ten weeks down, two more terms to go," he said. "We have considered the lilies in the field, we have harvested wheat and barley and oats, we have gleaned, we have processed, and we have learned. The next ten weeks will be spent in hothouses, which I am greatly looking forward to. But tell us about Archie. I only met him once under unusual circumstances, to put it mildly, but I know how much he means to you and Miss Sparks. If there is anything I can do to help, name it."

"All we can do is pray at this point," said Gwen. "Although since I have you both here, perhaps I could consult you on one point?"

"Of course," said Simon.

"Long or short consultation?" asked Carolyne. "I might need my glass refreshed. And you don't have one yet. Whisky or sherry?"

"It's become a whisky sort of night," said Gwen. "Don't get up, dear. I'll fetch my own."

Simon raised an eyebrow slightly as she poured a generous amount, then ceded the armchair to her and pulled a wooden chair away from the wall for himself.

"It's not at all certain that Archie will survive this," she said sombrely as she sat.

"I am sorry, Gwen," said Simon.

"As am I," said Carolyne. "Unfortunately, it is an occupational hazard in his milieu."

"I'm afraid it is," said Gwen. "But the one I'm concerned about now is Iris. She's hell-bent on retribution, and I'm not sure I can stop her."

"Why would you want to?" asked Carolyne.

"Carolyne, I'm surprised," said Gwen. "With all that's happened to you this year, you've been, if not a model of forbearance, at least setting a decent example of turning the other cheek."

"That's because there are children in the house," said Carolyne. "One is forced to behave better. But if someone had killed the man I loved—"

She stopped, considering.

"At least, at a time when I loved him," she concluded. "If it had happened then, I would have sent for the Farquharson from the gun room and gone stalking."

"But not now," said Simon.

"No," said Carolyne. "Not now."

Interesting, thought Gwen, looking at the man from Nyasaland and the woman from the Empire that had colonised it. They were nothing alike, but they were allied by their shared hatred of the man who had betrayed them both, under whose roof they all lived and pretended to the best of behaviour.

Which they had to do for the sake of the children, Ronnie and John.

"How willing is she to listen to reason?" asked Simon.

"This is Iris we're talking about," said Gwen. "I could see the steam building up the entire time I was there."

"Does she want justice or revenge?"

"Whichever one will allow her to use her bare hands."

"That's what you're worried about," said Simon. "Not that she will hunt for this man. You're worried about what will happen when she catches him."

"Yes," said Gwen. "Even with Scotland Yard and the Spelling gang in full pursuit, it won't be enough. She wants to find him herself."

"Can you stop her?"

"I don't think so," said Gwen.

"Then the answer is clear," said Simon. "If you wish to prevent her coming to harm or harming another, you have to be there when she tries."

Gwen looked at him, then sighed.

"That's it, isn't it?" she said. "The only way I can intervene at the right moment is to help her track down her quarry."

"Would you like me to send for the Farquharson?" offered Carolyne. "I could have it here by tomorrow evening."

"Very kind of you, but no thanks," said Gwen.

Carolyne leaned forward, glass raised, her teeth bared in a terrifying grimace. Gwen held up her tumbler, and Carolyne tapped it gleefully.

"Tally-ho!" she whispered.

Carolyne, as was her habit, fell asleep in her armchair, snoring lustily. Gwen and Simon immediately pressed the button summoning those servants with the unenviable task of maneuvering her to her rooms upstairs, then made a break for the front parlour.

"Has she been horrible?" asked Gwen.

"No more than normal," he replied. "Told me scandalous stories of people I've never heard of and am unlikely to meet, and I laughed when she reached what she thought might be a punch line. She's trying, Gwen, and I respect her for that. But if it weren't for John—well, I have to figure what's next in my life, I suppose."

"Do you have another date with Miss Sedgewick?"

"I do," he said. "Dinner Wednesday evening. Some part of London where nobody will recognise her or tell her parents she's seeing me. And you, Gwendolyn—apart from the current tragedy, how are you? Are you happy?"

She got up, peered down the hallway to make sure no one was within earshot, then came back and sat next to him.

"I think I found a house!" she said conspiratorially. "In Maida Vale."

"Is that nearby?"

"Close enough to keep Ronnie in the same school and for him and John to visit easily."

"Ah, good," he said. "That was my greatest worry. John has so few playmates. If only there were a way to carry him off with you."

"I know," she said. "But I can only save one child from this place, unfortunately."

"Does Ronnie know yet?"

"No," said Gwen. "I haven't even told him about regaining custody yet. He won't be happy about moving. This is all the life he's ever known."

"He can learn a new one," said Simon. "It won't exactly be one of deprivation, will it?"

"He will have everything that I can give him," said Gwen.

Simon grimaced for a moment.

"What?" asked Gwen.

"It's so easy for you to say that now," he replied. "Lord knows you've suffered enough. But don't spoil the future lord. Let him build some real character before he's forced back into the servitude of the Bainbridges."

"I may need your help for that," said Gwen. "You have a permanent invitation to visit us whenever you please. And a place to stay, should you feel you need a respite from Carolyne's anecdotes."

"It's only been a few hours," he said. "I've survived so far. I understand there is a family outing next Saturday."

"Yes," said Gwen. "She got us all tickets for *Peter Pan* at the Scala Theatre. I hope it's a decent production. Alastair Sim is Hook—he's done it a few times before, and I hear he's marvellous."

"This will be my first time in a London theatre," said Simon.

"Carolyne picked the show with your nephew in mind," said Gwen. "He read the book and fell in love with it. Maybe piracy is in his future."

"Given his paternal heritage, more than likely," said Simon drily.

Iris woke to the sound of church bells tolling somewhere in the area. She lay in bed, trying to regain her bearings. Then her hand came into contact with the scrapbook, still open beside her.

Right, she thought. I'm in Archie's bed. Without him.

She got up, washed, and dressed, then made the bed, placing the scrapbook on the bureau next to the clock.

She didn't want to lug the scrapbook to the hospital, but she felt uneasy about restoring it to Archie's office in the cellar if the police were coming by to search. She wasn't ready to turn it over to them until she had a better idea of what it meant and what to do with it, and she needed Gwen for that.

So, what to do with a gangster's secret scrapbook inside a gangster's secret hideaway?

There has to be a place, she thought. This was Archie, after all.

It took her the better part of the morning to find it. A false panel in the attic concealed a space with a few thick packages wrapped in waxed paper that were the shape and size of banknotes. She didn't want to open them and find out.

Not enough here to be the proceeds of those robberies, she thought. Best not to wonder where they came from.

There were no more weapons, fortunately, but there was enough room for her to stash the scrapbook. Then she replaced the panel and repositioned everything that had been carefully stacked in front of it.

If it took her that long to find, she doubted that the police would stumble upon it, she thought. For now, at least.

At one thirty, she was in the front parlour, peering out from behind the curtains. Benny pulled up. He got out, looked around carefully, one hand staying inside the car. Then he looked at the house and nodded.

She came out, pausing to wedge a tiny piece of scrap paper in the base of the front door after she closed it, then walked briskly to the car and jumped into the front seat. He had the car moving before she had finished closing the door.

"Get any sleep?" she asked.

"Nobody 'as," he replied. "Except for Archie. I'll 'ave to get a dose of whatever they're giving 'im when this is done so I can catch up. And you might want to take a butcher's at the paper there."

A copy of the Sunday *Pictorial* sat by her feet. She picked it up. Under the lurid headline "Mobster Marriage Murder Attempt!" were two side-by-side photos. One was of Archie being carried out of the social hall on the makeshift litter.

Next to it was a photo of Iris, running from the church in a state of disarray. Even in black and white, the blood was visible on her face.

The photo credits were to Gareth Pontefract, as was the byline.

"How did he know about the wedding?" she asked.

"Dunno," said Benny. "But there's a crowd of them at the 'ospital now. I'm taking you through a different entrance."

"Thanks," she said.

The trip to the hospital was quick. Perhaps too quick. There were moments of havoc passing through intersections that could have been choreographed by Mack Sennett as Benny glided through traffic with inches to spare.

"Is this how you always drive, or are you showing off?" asked Iris.

"Sorry," said Benny, marginally slowing down. "Driving relaxes me. I've noticed it sometimes 'as the opposite effect on anyone with me."

"Gwen said the Yard thinks you were a getaway driver when you were rising through the ranks."

"Now, why would you even bring something like that up, Sparks?" asked Benny. "What's past is past, I always say. Nothing good ever showed up in a rearview mirror."

"Sorry, didn't mean to offend," she said. "I'm grateful for the lift. And the company. Did the Aldertons get any sleep?"

"They went 'ome once the security bloke showed up. They were planning on church this morning to put in a good word before coming in. We've quietly put a few extra lads in the hospital without mentioning it to anyone. Can't 'urt to have some backup at a time like this."

"No question," said Iris. "Any thoughts on who did this?"

"Too many," said Benny. "Narrowing them down is the problem."

He pulled up to an entrance on the other side of the hospital.

"You've met my cousin, Chip," he said. "'E's inside that black door. Knock three times, then two more, and 'e'll let you in and direct you to the waiting area. I'm going to park, then I'll meetcher there."

"Thanks, Benny."

She got out and knocked as directed. A second later, she was striding through the corridors until she reached the waiting hall.

There was a passel of press cordoned off in one corner. They immediately shouted her name when she entered, but she ignored them and went over to Lily, who was back on her same bench with various family members gathered about. Flashbulbs popped as they embraced.

"Anything?" asked Iris.

"They're going back in," said Lily tearfully. "Said there was too much bleeding going on. It's the same surgeon as yesterday. 'E's come in on a Sunday— Isn't that amazing?"

"More impressive he was in on a Saturday, come to think of it," said Iris. "All right. May I get you anything?"

"No, I've got me girls with me," said Lily, grasping as many of her daughters' hands as she could. "Oh, and there's a detective waiting to speak with you. 'E's over there."

"Florey again?" asked Iris, looking around in exasperation. "I thought he'd be—oh."

Mike Kinsey was standing inside the corridor that led to the police office, making sure he was out of the line of sight of the reporters. He nodded at her, then turned and walked towards the office.

"Be right back," said Iris.

She followed him inside, then sat in front of the desk.

"Hi," he said, sitting behind it.

"Hi," she replied. "How may I help you, Detective Sergeant Kinsey?"

"I wanted to see how you were, Sparks," he said. "I called your flat, but you weren't answering. And I called your mum—"

"You called Mum?"

"I did."

"Why on earth did you do that?"

"Because I was concerned for you," he said. "I still am. So I came here. The family said you were coming in, so I waited."

"You've done all that?" she asked. "For me?"

"Of course."

"Does Beryl know you're here?"

"No," he said. "She thinks I'm working on a case. How are you doing?"

"I'm barely holding things together, since you asked, but I am. All I can do is wait at this point, but there are people to wait with. Family, and Gwen's been an absolute rock."

"So I've heard. Was that where you spent the night? At the Bainbridges'?"

"No," she said. "I stayed at— Heard from whom?"

"What?"

"When I said Gwen's been a rock, you said, 'So I've heard.' Who told you about Gwen?"

"I mean generally, in my encounters with her."

"Ah," said Iris, leaning back. "You've come here to be nice to me. What did you say to me the other day? 'You suddenly turning nice would catapult you to the top of my suspect list.'"

"Sparks, it isn't like that."

"'Were you not sent for?'" she said, her voice rising. "'Is it your own inclining? Is it a free visitation? Come, come, deal justly with me.'"

"You always brought out the *Hamlet* quotes when you were peeved at me," he said. "Fine. I spoke to Florey last night. He asked if I could speak with you informally. He knew we were once—close."

"And now he's using you to get at me."

"Sparks, there may be a gang war about to erupt, and there'll be enough blood in the Thames to make its own tide if that happens. The Yard is going on full alert. Anything you know or can find out to forestall this might save lives. Is there anything?"

"What's going on with your investigation on the White Palace murder?"

"That has most emphatically been put aside until the current crisis is over," he said. "Why are you even mentioning it?"

"Curiosity," she said.

"Florey told me you thought it was tied to Spelling's shooting," said Kinsey. "He didn't see any connection. Neither do I, quite frankly. Have you found one?"

"Nothing other than the timing," she said.

"Then forgive me if I put current matters ahead of those from the twenties. Is there anything else you've learned that could further this investigation?"

"Yes. I've learned that you've put your job ahead of whatever had remained of any feelings between us. That makes it much easier for me to get up and walk out right now. Goodbye, Mike."

"Sparks!" he called after her, but she ignored him and walked back to the waiting area.

Gwen had arrived and was sitting with the family. She got up when she saw Iris come over, glancing past her.

"I do believe I see the heels of Detective Ex receding into the distance," she said. "Is everything all right?"

"Wonderful. He went out of his way to irritate me on his day off. Speaking of Sundays, how was church? Any insights? Advice? Revelations from on high?"

"I don't think you should pursue this, Iris," said Gwen.

"I know," said Iris, her shoulders sagging.

"But if you do, I'm with you, of course," continued Gwen. "Every step of the way."

"Well, then good," said Iris, brightening. "Because I may have some leads."

"Already? I thought you weren't going to do anything until we talked."

"I didn't. Archie did. I'll have to show you what I've found."

"Found where?"

"Archie's house. Will you come back there with me when we're done here?"

"Are we breaking in?"

"I have a key," said Iris. "He gave me one the other day."

"My goodness. You mean— Hang on, looks like Reg wants a word with you."

Reg had just come into the room, surveying it until he saw the two ladies together. He immediately went up to them.

"There's been a development," he said. "We got a note 'and delivered this morning from Manfred Willoughby."

"A note?" asked Sparks. "Saying what?"

"'E wants to meet with someone representing us at a neutral location so we can clear the air," said Reg.

"Sounds like a setup," said Iris.

"Yeah, I 'ad that exact thought, only there's something more. Willoughby doesn't want to meet with me or Benny or any other man from the gang."

"Who, then?" asked Iris.

"Mrs. Bainbridge," said Reg.

"Me?" exclaimed Gwen, turning pale.

"You. 'E wants to see you, Duchess."

CHAPTER 10

"How did I get dragged into all this?" asked Gwen.

"First, Willoughby knows you," said Reg. "From your sit-down with 'im and Archie after—"

He stopped, glancing around the room. Some of the press were eyeing the three of them.

"After your little incident," he concluded, dropping his voice to a murmur. "You impressed 'im as a negotiator."

"Ridiculous," said Gwen.

"More important, word 'as gotten out about you and your abilities."

"My what?"

"I don't believe in psychics or seers or any of that nonsense," said Reg. "But you 'ave a knack for cold reading equal to any music 'all act I've ever seen, and I know lads who can spot a tic at an 'undred yards who can't pick up on people like you do."

"Willoughby knows about that? How did he find out?"

"That night we all went out to celebrate after the warehouse? The drinks were flowing, and towards the end of the night, we were all pulling out our party tricks, remember?"

"Oh, God," said Gwen. "We did, didn't we?"

"I did some knife throwing," recalled Iris.

"You did," said Reg. "And the Duchess got competitive and bet she could tell if each one of us was lying or telling the truth on one statement each. And she got every one of 'em right. That got around, and you and Sparks being objects of curiosity in our crooked corner of the world, Willoughby 'eard about it. So the end of the tale is that 'e 'as something to say to us, but 'e wants to say it to someone 'oo can tell if 'e's lying or not and 'oo won't be coming in with guns blazing."

"What do you think, Reg?" asked Gwen.

"I think it's crazy enough to try," he said. "It's worth it if we can avoid any more blood being shed, and I don't think 'e'd pull any stunts with you, Duchess."

"Why wouldn't he?" asked Iris.

"Because she's not one of us," said Reg. "So 'er value as, say, an 'ostage is low as far as we're concerned."

"There goes my self-esteem," said Gwen. "I have increased in value recently."

"Yeah, but that was the point of your negotiation before, wasn't it?" Reg pointed out. "Willoughby agreed that 'is lads would leave your family alone. That was binding."

"And if he reneges, what do I do? Sue him for damages?"

"No, Duchess," said Reg grimly. "The Spelling gang goes to war on your be'alf. That was Archie's part of the agreement, and that binds all of us."

"Oh," said Gwen. "That does make me feel a wee bit more confident. How would this work?"

"You can't be serious," protested Iris.

"If it can ease hostilities, I think I'm honour bound to try," said Gwen. "Where would we meet? I don't want to go into his place of business."

"We use the zoo for these meetings," said Reg. "It's public, it's outdoors, and you can talk privately. I'll set it up for lunchtime tomorrow, if that's all right with you. I'm trying to figure out if there's any of my boys I can plant there 'e doesn't know, just in case."

"There's a simpler solution," said Iris. "I'll go with her."

"But Willoughby said—"

"That no men from the gang can be there. I'm not in the gang, and I'm definitely not a man, Reg."

"No," he said with a tired smile. "You are definitely not, and I'm giving up arguing with you. I'll tell Willoughby that the Duchess'll 'ave another woman with 'er. After all, we can't 'ave a proper lady wandering around the zoo unescorted, can we? Where shall I call you with the details?"

"At The Right Sort," said Gwen.

"Thank you for this," he said, shaking her hand. "It's above and beyond, for certain. I feel like I oughter be bowing or something."

"Don't, please," said Gwen. "It's for Archie. For all of you."

He left for the phone boxes.

"When did you turn into me?" asked Iris. "What happened to the 'we-shouldn't-be-doing-this-it's-too-risky' girl I once knew?"

"She came under the influence of a much braver woman," said Gwen.

"Who is telling you we shouldn't be doing this."

"I haven't been to the zoo in years," said Gwen wistfully. "Maybe we could see the new panda after we're done negotiating gang wars. There's Dr. Benzimri."

A flashbulb went off from behind the cordon as the surgeon came out, and he immediately fixed a glare on the group so fierce that the rest of the photographers involuntarily lowered their cameras.

The family, Iris and Gwen, and the few gang members who were on hand gathered around him.

"Mr. Spelling is still alive," he said. "We've stopped the bleeding this time. That's the good news. However, we are still dealing with the various related traumas from the initial injury. The immediate danger continues to be infection. We're treating him with tyrothricin for that. It's been effective in the battlefield, so we're hoping it will help here. The other danger—the hemorrhaging did affect other organs, possibly including his brain."

Iris immediately felt for Gwen's hand, gripping it hard.

"He hasn't regained consciousness yet," Benzimri continued. "His pupils are responsive, so there is still neural activity, but it's going to be a long slog. All we can do is treat him for what we can, and hope that Nature will take a beneficial course."

"May I see him?" asked Iris.

"I'm sorry," said Benzimri. "Given the risk of infection, we're still restricting access to his immediate family for now."

"I will get you that visit," promised Lily. "Archie needs you."

"Thank you, Lily," said Iris.

The surgeon answered questions with patience for people who knew nothing about medical matters, then excused himself.

"Let's go," said Iris.

They located Benny, who led them out through a maze of corridors that he had already mastered, avoiding the press.

"Back to your flat?" he asked once they were in the car.

"Actually, back to Archie's house, if you don't mind," said Iris. "I left some things there."

"Shall I wait?"

"No, we'll be fine. We can walk to Hackney Downs and take the trolleybus."

"All right," said Benny. "But I ain't leaving until you give me the all clear."

"Of course," said Iris. "Thank you, Benny."

He drove more sedately this time, Iris noticed. Whether it was due to her prior comments or the presence of Gwen in the car, she didn't know, but she was grateful.

"Isn't this pretty!" exclaimed Gwen as they pulled up to the house. "I never would have expected it."

Benny scanned the area, then got out and opened the rear door, his right hand never straying far from his pocket.

"Sure you don't want me to go in first?" he asked Iris.

"I'm sure," she said.

She pulled out her key, then walked confidently to the front door, Gwen following. Iris examined the lock and the doorframe. The scrap paper she had wedged in the bottom was undisturbed.

"So far, so good," she said, pointing it out to Gwen.

"Unless our imaginary attacker went in through the rear," said Gwen.

"Fine," said Iris. "You stay in the front hall, and I'll do a quick sweep of the perimeter before we send Benny away."

She opened the door and turned on the hall light, then walked quickly into the parlour, re-emerging with a poker from the fireplace.

"Be right back," she said.

The rear door to the kitchen was secure, as were all the ground floor windows. She came back, leaned out the front door, and waved to Benny. He waved back, then drove away.

Gwen was looking at the pictures on the wall.

"Iris," she said, pointing to the one of the surviving pals. "That's the ring I saw. All three of them are wearing it. And their faces—that's Archie's father, of course, but am I right in thinking that that one looks like Des Burton?"

"You are," said Iris. "Come sit in the kitchen while I go fetch what I've found."

She ran upstairs to the attic and retrieved the scrapbook from its hiding place, then came back and handed it to Gwen. She started the teakettle as Gwen opened the front cover.

"I'm going to pack my things," said Iris. "I'll be back by the time the water boils."

She ran up to the bedroom, found a small valise in the closet, and threw her suit and smalls into it. She debated over the robe and nightie, then decided to leave them there for luck.

The kettle was beginning to steam when she returned. Gwen was engrossed in the scrapbook, jotting down notes in a small notebook from her bag as she turned the pages. Iris poured the tea and pulled out the remainder of the biscuits, which Gwen munched on absently as she read.

When she got to the last page and saw the ring, she looked up at Iris sharply.

"When did you find this?" she asked.

"Yesterday evening," said Iris. "I spent the night here."

"And you haven't told Mike about it?"

"No. Or at least, not yet."

"Why not?"

"Because he's not taking seriously the idea that Archie's shooting was connected to this," said Iris. "And because I'm mad at him."

"I see," said Gwen. "I suppose you think that justifies concealing evidence. It does answer the question of who took the ring. As for the connection—I'm sorry, Iris. I don't see it, either."

"Blast," said Iris disconsolately.

"But that doesn't mean there isn't one," said Gwen. "So let's stop looking for it, assume it exists, and move on from there."

"All right," said Iris. "How does that help us?"

"What strikes me about Archie's quest to find this Emery fellow is that it ended in 1937, based on the entries," said Gwen, consulting her notes. "He had looked into all of Emery's family and friends, even hired a private investigator to follow up on some of them. And then he gave up."

"So?"

"So the next entry is the ring. Nine years have gone by, then the dead man turns up and Archie is back on the prowl for his father's killer, the difference being he had thought Emery was his quarry before. Now, he believes it's someone else, because he thinks the dead man in the cellar is Emery. And if Archie's back on the hunt, then he's become a threat."

"A threat to the man who killed Jenks and walled up his body," said Iris. "Archie was never a threat before because he was going after the wrong man."

"And the discovery of the body in the White Palace was not exactly a secret," said Gwen. "The police know, the workmen know, the gang knows. Word gets around quickly in those circles. It could have reached the original killer, who struck first before Archie could find him. That could be how the two matters are linked."

"Why couldn't I see this?" Iris asked in chagrin.

"Because you're too close to it," said Gwen. "Iris, you have to tell Mike. There must be a way they can tell if that body was Emery. Maybe there are dental records, some means of identifying him. Something that would ease his family's uncertainty."

"Right now, Mike is off with the rest of the police gearing up to stop a gang war," said Iris. "He doesn't give a damn about Jenks Emery, or whoever that was."

"He will once hostilities settle down," said Gwen. "If things work out with Willoughby tomorrow, then they may settle down before there's a chance of unsettling."

"Then I'll let Mike know on Tuesday. Fair enough?"

"There's nothing fair about any of this," said Gwen.

She tapped on the last entry.

"Archie and Des," she said. "They must have been in on this together."

"I think so, too. One of the reasons I wanted you to see this was to help me find Des and learn what he knows."

Gwen pulled her address book out. There was a telephone on the counter. She carried it back to the table, then dialled a number.

There was no answer. She hung up, then dialled another with the same result.

"No luck, either at home or at his shop," she said, hanging up. "I expect he's spending Sunday with Fanny like a good fiancé should."

"You have both of those numbers? Not just his shop?"

"I do. Don't make any more of it than you should."

"We might be able to find him at the White Palace tomorrow," said Iris. "But people will wonder why we're looking. And there's no working telephone there."

"Hang on, I've an idea," said Gwen.

She flipped through her address book, then dialled another number. A man answered.

"Hello, Mervyn? It's Gwen Bainbridge."

"Hello, Gwen. To what do I owe the pleasure?"

"I was wondering if you were going back to the White Palace tomorrow."

"As a matter of fact, I am. I need to give that beast of a piano another tuning, then thought I'd practise for a while. I need to run through my repertory, find out if it's still in my fingers."

"Excellent. Might I ask you a favour?"

"Certainly."

"There's a carpenter working there, name of Des Burton. I may have a job for him, and I want him to give me a call. Could you pop down the cellar and see if he's about while you're there?"

"No problem at all. Should I have him call you at your office?"

"I think that would be the best place to reach me. Thank you, Mervyn."

"Glad to be of assistance. I'll throw in a check on the renovations as well. Good night, Gwen."

"Good night."

She hung up, then glanced out the window.

"It is getting dark out," she said. "I've lost track of the hour. Shall we grab a bite somewhere before we go?"

"All right," said Iris. "But before we do, one more surprise."

She pulled the black box from her bag and placed it on the table. Gwen looked at it, then at Iris.

"May I?" she asked.

"Go ahead."

Gwen opened the box, then held it up so that the diamond could catch the light.

"Good cut, good colour, good clarity," she pronounced. "From Archie?"

"Yes."

"When?"

"At the reception."

"Did a proposal come with it?"

"I suspect one was about to," said Iris.

"Oh, Iris," said Gwen, taking her hand. "That makes things so much worse. Did you have any idea this was in the works?"

"None," said Iris. "There were jokes that in retrospect I now realise were attempts to sound me out, and I would joke back in kind, not rising to the bait. I threatened Mum with the idea, but that was more to torment her than because I actually thought it was coming. Two failed engagements have made me gun-shy on the topic. I've been channelling all the matrimonial instincts I have into work."

"Were you going to accept?"

"I don't know," said Iris. "I can't separate the shock of the proposal from the shock of the blood. They're all jumbled up together, and I can't find my feelings in any of this anymore, other than rage and revenge."

"Have you tried it on yet?" asked Gwen, handing the box back.

"I'm afraid to," confessed Iris. "If I try it on, then all of this becomes real."

"It's real," said Gwen. "You're going to have to make a decision."

"I can't," said Iris. "Not now. Not while— I just can't."

She put the box in her bag, then picked up the scrapbook.

"Would you keep this safe for me?" she asked. "I don't want to leave it here, and I don't have anywhere good to hide it in my flat."

"You're asking me to conceal evidence? Doesn't that make me your accomplice?"

"Every step of the way," Iris reminded her.

"I was in church this morning," Gwen said with a glance upwards. "All right. There's a space behind a loose panel on the right side of my closet, in case you need to retrieve it."

"Good to know. Next flat I get should come with a secret compartment. Let's go."

Gwen arrived at the office at eight thirty the next morning. Iris came in an hour later, looking haggard from stress and lack of sleep.

"Sorry," she said as she hung up her coat. "I stopped by the hospital first."

"No apologies necessary," said Gwen. "How is Archie?"

"No change," said Iris. "He still hasn't woken up."

"He will," said Gwen. "He's made it this far. The worst of it has to be over."

They went through their normal business distractedly, starting each time the telephone rang, staring at it apprehensively until Mrs. Billington either connected them to the call or more often than not handled it herself.

Mervyn called after ten, asking for Gwen.

"Your carpenter didn't come in today," he reported. "No one knows why. He wasn't part of the regular crew, so he didn't have to sign in with the foreman."

"Thanks for trying," said Gwen. "How are the renovations going?"

"Coming along nicely, I must say, although there was some concern about whether they were going to be paid on time, what with Mr. Spelling being at death's door. You didn't tell me he had been shot, by the way."

"Sorry. I didn't want to scare you away from the party. Was much said about it?"

"An executive from Spelling Enterprises showed up, a fellow named Townley. He assured everyone that it was business as usual. And when I say 'assured,' I mean he said they'd better have the place ready in time or Spelling would most likely rise up from his hospital bed and come down to beat the living daylights out of any man who wasn't pulling his weight."

"My goodness!"

"Quite inspirational, he was. Reminded me of a sergeant I had during the recent festivities. I felt like I should have been playing some patriotic medley underneath it, but I held off."

"I think that was wise."

"But I've finally whipped this piano into playing shape. I'm going to be their very own *Music While You Work* now. Oh, and I lined up Eddie Tremaine for New Year's, so the quartet is complete."

"Wonderful, Mervyn. Thanks for doing all this."

"A pleasure, Gwen."

She hung up, then pulled out her address book and dialled Des's shop, then his home. There was no answer.

"No luck with Des," she said as she hung up.

"Maybe we could swing by his shop after our zoological expedition," suggested Iris.

"But if he isn't there—"

"We won't know that until we try," said Iris. "And if he isn't, we could still poke around and see what we can find."

"No panda for Gwen, then?"

"No panda for Gwen, sorry. We'll go see it when this is over. I promise."

"Suddenly I'm six again," said Gwen.

"Six-year-olds don't have clandestine meetings with gang bosses."

"Given the behaviour of some six-year-olds I've seen, that's lucky for the gang bosses."

The call from Reg came at eleven thirty. Gwen took it.

"The Mappin Café, one hour from now," he said. "You'll be meeting them outside on the terrace."

"Them? Not just Willoughby?"

"Gus Clement's gonna be with him," said Reg. "Ever 'eard of 'im?"

"I'm afraid not."

"What Willoughby is east of the Lea, Clement is south of the Thames, from Surrey on."

"What does he want?"

"Same thing as Willoughby. Maybe you should open a booth and charge a shilling a read."

"When the weather gets warm, I'll think about it. Won't we all stand out? It's in the teens outside. The zoo isn't likely to be having many visitors."

"True, but there won't be many coppers wandering about, and the ones that are will be visible for miles."

"Very well. We'll call you after."

"If I don't 'ear from you by two, I'm sending in a rescue party. Good luck."

He hung up.

"Well?" demanded Iris.

"The Mappin Pavilion, outside the restaurant, twelve thirty," replied Gwen. "Do you know of a Gus Clement?"

"Archie mentioned him. He said he runs his territory by brute force, but isn't much in the way of a brain. Is he going to be there?"

"I'm afraid so."

"Then it's a good thing I'm going with you," said Iris, getting up and grabbing her coat and scarf. "If things turn nasty, he's mine."

There had been a light dusting of snow during the night, the first of the season. They entered through the North Gate, paying their fees at the lone open booth. There were no school groups touring, given the time of year, and no mothers or nannies were foolish or cruel enough to be pushing prams around in the frigid temperatures. Only the most dedicated animal enthusiasts were out and about, mostly elderly people who seemed to have nodding acquaintances with whichever creatures were willing to meet their admirers outside.

"Can you read people when they're shivering violently?" asked Iris, her hands stuffed as far into her coat pockets as she could get them, one clutching a knife she had taken from Archie's kitchen.

"I suspect that the location signifies having the meeting inside the restaurant," said Gwen. "I do hope the gentlemen will be buying."

"Send our bill to Spelling Enterprises if not," said Iris. "This is their business we're doing."

"We're early," said Gwen. "Could we at least stop by and visit the coypu?"

"Why the coypu?"

"We adopted it during the war," said Gwen as they crossed the canal. "Sponsored its diet during rationing. They eat grass, so we'd send bags of clippings from the estate, along with acorns for the other animals. Ronnie loved collecting acorns when he was a toddler. He'd run around, yelling, 'Zoo! Zoo!' when he picked them up. I think 'zoo' was his fifteenth word."

"You collected his words?"

"Of course," said Gwen. "Oh, good! It's outside."

They paused by the cage, where a massive rodent with frighteningly large orange incisors was munching on some dried stalks of hay.

"Glad to see you, Ernest," called Gwen. "I'll bring the boys by in the spring. I should tell you Ronnie is obsessed with narwhals now, so it will probably be a quick visit."

The coypu looked up momentarily as it heard her voice, then went back to its meal.

"How do you know his name is Ernest?" asked Iris as they continued down the path, the Regent's Canal to their right, a few of the hardier mammals out on both sides, sniffing the cold air curiously.

"He sent us a thank-you note," said Gwen. "Or one was sent on his behalf."

"That might not be the same coypu," said Iris.

"In which case, he was very polite in not pointing out my error," said Gwen.

They passed through a tunnel under the Outer Circle, emerging by the War Memorial. Iris immediately shifted into high alert, scanning everyone she saw, looking for those she couldn't see, catching any flicker of movement that might be someone watching from any possible means of concealment.

The Mappin Café was a brick building by the Regent's Park border of the zoo, with a rounded terrace overlooking three artificial hills, a pond, and a small grassy area. The café itself was rounded on this side, with pairs of white columns supporting a red pantiled roof projecting over white-framed glass doors and floor-to-ceiling windows that allowed patrons to eat with a full view of the man-made environment. A few desultory bears roamed one of the hills, indifferent to the cold, and several people watched them from the safety of the terrace. Two men did not, however, marking the arrival of the two women with interest beyond that of men on the prowl for women who came to the zoo unescorted. One, a dapper gentleman in his fifties, carried a silver-handled walking stick and wore a sumptuous fur-trimmed overcoat that would have made the bears anxious. His eyes met Gwen's, and he doffed his derby in recognition.

"Gus, our dates have arrived," he said to the other, a thickset but powerful-looking man who appeared ready to charge any animal who challenged him. "Mrs. Bainbridge, how good of you to find time in your busy schedule to accommodate us. And is that Miss Sparks with you?"

"It is," said Mrs. Bainbridge, coming forward to shake his hand. "Miss Iris Sparks, may I present Mr. Manfred Willoughby?"

"Charmed, Miss Sparks," said Willoughby, shaking her hand in turn. "May I introduce you both to my colleague Augustus Clement."

"Niceter meecher," muttered Clement. "The short one's the spy?"

"According to my information," said Willoughby.

"'Ow many of my men 'ave you spotted?" asked Clement.

"Well, I can't say who is working for whom," said Sparks, "but I count five men and one woman."

"A woman?" Willoughby asked in surprise. "Which one?"

"The one with the binoculars pretending to be consulting her guide," said Sparks, nodding slightly in that direction.

"Flossie?" said Willoughby to Clement. "You brought Flossie? For a meeting with two women?"

"No, I brought Flossie in case you tried anything with me," returned Clement.

"Reasonable," conceded Willoughby. "May I suggest that we retire to the café for some refreshments?"

"Please," said Mrs. Bainbridge.

Willoughby offered his arm. She took it after a moment's hesitation, and he led her in.

"I guess you're with me, then," Clement said to Sparks, offering his arm to her.

"If you don't mind, I'd like to keep my hands free," said Sparks.

"Gotcher," said Clement. "Same goes for me."

The café was about a third full with visitors escaping the elements. A hostess seated the foursome at a round table covered with a white tablecloth. Sparks took a seat by the window, noticing four of the six bodyguards casually drift in and take seats with direct lines of sight. The woman called Flossie was the farthest away, allowing her a view both of their table as well as of Willoughby's men. One of her hands remained hidden under the tablecloth. She nodded affably as she saw Sparks look her way.

"If there's to be any gunplay, do us the courtesy of warning us first so that we can dive under the table," said Sparks.

"Of course," said Willoughby. "Let's get a pot of tea and place our orders before we begin. That will give us time to conduct our business without interruption."

A waitress came over, distributed menus, and placed a teapot on a trivet. They scanned the menus while watching one another.

"May I suggest sandwiches?" said Willoughby. "That way Miss Sparks will still have one hand free for combat."

"I can manage with neither hand free," said Sparks.

"I'm sure of it," said Willoughby. "I doubt that any of this posturing is necessary. I would like to extend my sympathies for Archie's plight, if I may. This must be a terrible time for you right now."

"Same 'ere," said Clement.

"I refuse all sympathies until my partner has vetted them for their sincerity," said Sparks.

"Of course," said Willoughby. "Here is our waitress."

They placed their orders.

"I'll pour," said Mrs. Bainbridge. "How do you take your tea, gentlemen?"

"Milk, please," said Willoughby.

"Milk, two sugars," said Clement.

She poured four cups, then they all took a sip, grateful as it removed some of the chill.

"Now, how is this accomplished?" asked Willoughby. "Do we each make our statement and be done?"

"What makes this challenging is that you both came here seeking my judgment," said Mrs. Bainbridge. "You want this to work for whatever reasons. But you are suspicious of me, both for my ability and for my closeness to Mr. Spelling."

"She's got that right," said Clement.

"Your natural inclination is to put me to the test," she continued. "Plus you both have very large masculine egos that seek to challenge any woman who dares to confront them."

"My word," said Willoughby, laughing. "You have anticipated my reactions quite accurately. How do we overcome these obstacles?"

She pulled her notebook and a pencil from her bag.

"I am going to ask each of you three questions," she said. "You may answer them truthfully or not. I will write down my response to each, and that will give me a better idea of how to read you. Are you ready?"

"Who goes first?" asked Clement.

"The braver man," said Mrs. Bainbridge.

"Neatly done, Mrs. Bainbridge," said Willoughby. "You have placed our large masculine egos in competition. Gus, what do you say to a coin flip?"

"Long as it's my coin," said Clement.

He reached into his pocket, holding up his other hand to forestall any reaction to the movement from the bodyguards, and pulled out a shilling.

"Call it," he said as he flipped it.

"Heads," said Willoughby.

Clement caught it and slapped it on the back of his hand.

"Tails," said Clement, showing it to him. "Do your worst, Madame Blavatsky."

"What is your mother's first name?" asked Mrs. Bainbridge.

"Laura," he said with a smirk.

"Your middle name?"

"Tiberias."

"Why?"

"Me dad liked to read about Roman emperors," he said. "Then 'e took it out on me. Was that the third question?"

"It will do," said Mrs. Bainbridge, scribbling in her notebook. "Mr. Willoughby, it's your turn."

"Fire away," said Willoughby, looking at her steadily.

"What did your grandmothers call you when you were a child?"

"I only knew the one," he replied. "She called me Manny."

"How old are you?"

"Fifty-three."

"What was the name of the first girl you ever kissed?"

"Ida," he said, slightly startled by the question. "Ida Jensen. I was fourteen. Good Lord, I haven't thought about her in ages."

She placed her notebook face down on the table.

"Just for fun, I would like each of you to tell me the total number of lies you just told," she said.

"Ain't that cheating?" asked Clement.

"Humour me," she said.

"All right. I told you one."

"Mr. Willoughby?"

"Also one."

"And that makes one more lie for each of you," she said, turning over the notebook.

Under "Clement," she had written: 1. True. 2. True. 3. True.

Under "Willoughby": 1. False—false. 2. False. 3. True.

"Mr. Clement told the truth throughout," she said. "Then he tried to trick me when I asked how many lies he told. Mr. Willoughby only told the truth about his first kiss."

"Why did you write 'false' twice on the first one?" asked Willoughby.

"Because you lied twice in your response," she said. "First, as to having known only one of your grandmothers. The second, as to the name she called you. I can't say whether you knew both or neither, but it wasn't the truth."

"Wow," said Clement.

"Mrs. Bainbridge, I am prepared to offer you a job starting immediately," said Willoughby.

"Me, too," said Clement. "At double whatever 'e's gonna pay you."

"I appreciate the offers, gentlemen," she said. "But I am quite happy with my current situation. Shall we get on to the main reason we are here? Mr. Willoughby, you may go first this time."

"Very well," he said. "I did not shoot Archie Spelling, nor was it done at my behest."

"Mr. Clement?"

"Same 'ere."

"Please say it fully."

"I din't shoot Spelling, nor— What does 'be'est' mean?"

"At your command," said Willoughby wearily.

"Right," said Clement. "I din't order it done, neither."

"Did you have any prior knowledge of it?" asked Mrs. Bainbridge.

"I did not," said Willoughby.

"Me, neither," said Clement.

"Do you have any knowledge of who did it?"

"I do not."

"Nope."

She looked at Sparks, who had been watching them closely.

"They're telling the truth," said Mrs. Bainbridge.

"You're sure?"

"I am."

"Then I accept your sympathies," said Sparks. "Thank you."

"I hope that he recovers," said Willoughby.

"That was a lie," said Mrs. Bainbridge.

His eyes flashed angrily for a moment, then subsided.

"I won't deny that there will be certain advantages if he does not," he said. "Tell Mr. Townley that there will be discussions, but in light of the present situation, we won't meet until after the New Year. Well, this was a fascinating experience, I must say. Now—"

"I have a question," said Sparks.

"Yes, Miss Sparks?" replied Willoughby.

"What do you know about the death of Archie's father?"

CHAPTER 11

"Archie's father?" repeated Willoughby, looking bewildered for the first time.

"Stanley Spelling," said Sparks. "Stabbed to death in November, 1922, near the Royal Docks."

"What's that got to do with anything?"

"I'm researching the family history," said Sparks. "Looking for a reason someone might take a shot at Archie."

"Why ask me?"

"The Royal Docks are east of the Lea," said Sparks. "Your territory."

"My territory now," said Willoughby. "Not twenty-three years ago."

"But you were around then, weren't you?" Sparks persisted. "You're fifty-whatever now, so thirty-whatever then, clawing your way up the ranks. Stanley Spelling was Ned Spelling's younger brother, Ned was running the Docks Group, so the murder had to have made quite the impact in those circles."

"Ancient history," said Willoughby. "Stan Spelling's name hasn't come up in decades. And there are some things that should stay buried."

"Then maybe people ought to do a better job of burying them," said Sparks.

"This is about that body in the cellar of the White Palace, isn't it?" Willoughby asked.

"You know about that."

"Of course I know about it."

"How did you hear about it?"

"From Archie. That evening, after he was done talking to the police."

"Archie called you?" exclaimed Sparks.

"You and Archie had an arrangement of some sort, didn't you?" guessed Mrs. Bainbridge.

"Yes, Archie and I had an arrangement for the White Palace," admitted Willoughby. "We invested in it together. So what? We've had arrangements before."

"I want to know about his father," said Sparks. "Tell me."

"Why should I?"

"Because you owe us now," she snapped. "You owe us for coming here with your goons and goonette ready to pump us full of lead at the slightest signal. You owe us for brokering a peace with the Spelling family, who are angry and fully prepared to go to war on anyone they think had something to do with shooting Archie. And the angriest one of them is me."

"You're not a Spelling," said Willoughby.

"Your intelligence is out of date," she replied. "I'm sure you saw my picture in the *Pictorial* yesterday. That was Archie's blood anointing my face. I'm as much a Spelling now as if I'd been born to it."

"You said I owe you," he said. "If I owe anyone, it's Mrs. Bainbridge, not you."

"We're a team," said Mrs. Bainbridge. "I'll cede my favour to her."

"What do you think, Gus?" asked Willoughby.

"I'm out of this conversation," said Clement.

"I'm asking your opinion."

"That's a first," said Clement. "In that case, you ain't giving up much. It's ancient 'istory, like you said. I don't see much 'arm in it."

"Apart from discussing our years of criminality with two civilians," Willoughby reminded him.

"Yeah, but if they were the types to be spilling secrets to the rozzers, they wouldn't be 'ere now, would they?"

"True enough," said Willoughby. "Very well, Miss Sparks. In the early twenties, Ned Spelling ran the docks on both sides of the Thames. Those territories were divided up into their current portions ten years ago when he fell ill. He wanted to get out while things were peaceful."

"Not always peaceful," said Clement.

"Relatively peaceful," amended Willoughby. "They weren't so peaceful north of our territory back in the twenties. Different gangs were constantly moving in, being driven out, what have you. Protection was a service offered, and occasionally the protectors required a demonstration as to why it was necessary. Stan may have been a dockworker and a Spelling, but he was known to, shall we say, work on commission outside our jurisdiction."

"Doing what?"

"Doing what he did best. Brute force. He could walk into a spieler, drop a shilling on black, then put five men in hospital before the wheel stopped spinning."

"Not the best way to make friends," commented Sparks. "Who was he working for when he hit the gambling clubs?"

"The Reeses, most of the time," said Willoughby. "They ran the majority of the clubs and billiard halls. Jack Reese was the emperor of the north back then. He didn't tolerate having any competition."

"Reese," said Mrs. Bainbridge. "Someone named Reese owned the White Palace."

"Frankie Reese. He was Jack's nephew."

"How often were Stan Spelling's . . . commissions?" asked Sparks.

"I couldn't give you a number. Word would get back to Ned. He called Stan on the carpet a few times, but Stan would bring up his sick wife and his kids and Ned would go soft on him every time."

"I would imagine that put people's backs up," said Sparks.

"Certainly, but people were scared of Ned because of who he was and Stan because of what he could do."

"What line did Stan cross that led to his death?"

"It didn't come from us," said Willoughby. "Rumour had it that Spelling got too cocksure. He went rogue in the wrong establishments."

"The robberies," said Sparks.

"You know about them? How?"

"Research."

"Remarkably quick work," said Willoughby, his eyes narrowing. "You must have spent your entire weekend in the library."

"A Cambridge education is good for some things."

"I wouldn't know."

"Did Ned know about the robberies?"

"He found out fairly late. He was furious. He was trying to expand on the quiet, and he didn't need any attention coming to the Spellings. I heard that he and Stan had it out one day. Stan stormed out of the office, and Ned came out later with a bruise the size of a double guinea on his jaw."

"The robberies stopped after Stanley's death," said Sparks. "Who caught up with him? Was it the Reeses after the White Palace was hit?"

"I can't say I have any direct knowledge as to that," said Willoughby carefully.

"I'll settle for indirect knowledge," said Sparks.

"The White Palace job was a big score, by all reports," said Willoughby. "The club was a front for funnelling funds from all over Reese's holdings, and the robbery hit right when the collections had come in. That put a major crimp in Reese's operation. He went berserk, sent out every man he had to shake down anyone and everyone for who had done it and where the money got to. Word was there was a falling-out among Stanley and his crew when they realised how much trouble they were in."

"So was Stanley killed by one of Reese's men or one of his crew?"

"He was stabbed to death," said Willoughby. "Think about that for a moment. He was on the docks and on the lookout for any of Reese's men who might be looking to do him dirty, yet he let someone on his home turf get close enough to use a knife."

"Someone he knew," said Sparks. "Someone he trusted."

"That's what we thought," said Willoughby. "Ned put out word that he wanted whoever killed him, so there were two gangs out looking for the crew now. One of the crew turned up in the Thames a few weeks later, probably thanks to Reese. And the brains of the group flat-out disappeared."

"Jenks Emery," said Sparks. "Did you think he got away?"

"I did," said Willoughby. "We didn't hear anything otherwise, and Jack Reese kept looking for that money until the day he died."

"Would it surprise you to learn that Jenks Emery was the body in the White Palace cellar?"

"No," said Willoughby. "That wouldn't surprise me at all."

"Reese never recovered the stolen money?" asked Sparks.

"Never did," said Willoughby. "That was the beginning of the end for him. He missed paying his men and lost credibility in the community. Once that happens, you become vulnerable. Ned made his move, and the empire of the north fell, piece by piece."

"Whose idea was it to buy the White Palace?" asked Mrs. Bainbridge.

"Archie called me about it a few months ago," said Willoughby. "He'd been getting into nightclubs more and more. He was short liquid capital and needed help if he was going to fix it up properly."

"Did he say anything about any of this? About his father and the Reeses?"

"No."

"Did you?"

Willoughby hesitated slightly.

"I may have mentioned something about it," he said.

"What?" asked Sparks.

"I said Jack and Frankie would be rolling in their graves if they knew Stan's boy was running one of their places."

"What did Archie say to that?"

"He laughed and said it served them right."

"You bought it from Frankie's widow?" asked Mrs. Bainbridge.

"Right. Vanessa Reese."

"Now, she was a looker back in the day," said Clement fondly. "High point of a night at Brooke's was when she'd make her entrance and sashay around the room. Every game stopped on the spot for gawking."

"I hear she still likes to make an entrance there, but the games tend to continue on uninterrupted, now," said Willoughby. "She clings to the last remnant of the once-mighty Reese empire like a limpet. And that's all I know about it. Are we square, ladies?"

The two women glanced at each other. Mrs. Bainbridge nodded.

"We're square," said Sparks. "Thank you for indulging us."

"It was an intriguing line of questioning," said Willoughby. "I'll be interested to know if it leads anywhere."

"For the moment, it leads us out of here," said Sparks.

"Thank you for lunch," added Mrs. Bainbridge.

"Gus, that is our cue to assist the ladies with their coats," said Willoughby, rising to his feet.

"I knew that," grumbled Clement. "I remember manners."

"Shall I tell the two men outside to come in and get some tea?" asked Sparks. "They must be frozen to the marrow by now."

"That's their job," said Clement.

"We should call Reg and let him know we survived," said Gwen as they walked away.

"There're some telephone boxes by the shop," said Iris. "You call. I'll keep watch."

"Do you think they're following us?"

"I would in their place."

Gwen dialled the number for the warehouse.

"Hello, is this Eggy?" she asked. "So nice to finally speak to you. It's Mrs. Bainbridge, Miss Sparks's partner. Yes, the Duchess, if you prefer. Is Reg available? Thank you."

She poked her head out.

"Eggy sounds just like I imagined," she said.

Reg came on the line.

"'Ow'd it go?" he asked.

"Safely," replied Gwen. "Which was a good thing, as we were considerably outgunned. Are you familiar with a woman named Flossie?"

"Clement brought Flossie? 'E was taking this seriously. So what's your verdict?"

"Neither of them had anything to do with shooting Archie."

"You're certain?"

"I am, although I don't claim to be infallible. Also, Willoughby told me to tell you that there will be discussions after the New Year."

"Nice of 'im to give us that long," said Reg. "Nice of 'im to give us notice, for that matter. Mrs. Bainbridge, I can't thank you enough."

"Any news about Archie?"

"Still the same. Still alive, or still not dead, 'owever you want to look at it."

"I will put the best possible light on it. Goodbye, Reg."

She hung up and emerged to where Iris stood, shivering miserably.

"That tea wore off quickly," said Iris.

"I'll bet the panda enclosure is nice and warm," said Gwen. "I'll even trade you for a visit to the Insect House, and you know how much I loathe them."

"Tempting," said Iris. "But I don't want to lose our chance to speak to Des, and it will take us an hour to get there with all the changes we have to make."

"It will take us forty minutes by cab," said Gwen. "A nice, comfortable cab where we can huddle together in the back and keep warm, and not have to walk a mile in the frigid cold because Benson Quay is nowhere near the Underground."

"Cabs cost more," said Iris. "I don't mind the walk."

"I am invoking my powers as a wealthy woman to override your frugal, socialistic tendencies," said Gwen. "Not only will we take a cab, we will pay the cabbie to wait for us outside so that we can take it back to Mayfair."

"Fine," said Iris. "There're usually some by the main entrance."

There was exactly one cab waiting, and the driver looked puzzled when Gwen told him their destination.

"Benson Quay, ma'am?" he asked.

"London Docks, off Garnet Street."

"In Wapping, I know. But why are a couple of proper ladies like you going there?"

"We're stowing away on a freighter," said Gwen. "Drive, please."

"Right you are," he said, putting it in gear. "There's a blanket on the back deck if you need it."

"Excellent," said Gwen, unfolding it. "Come here, darling."

Iris allowed herself to be bundled into her partner, who draped one arm over her shoulders and covered as much of their bodies as she could with the blanket.

"You're still shivering," said Gwen softly. "It isn't just the cold making you do that, is it?"

"No," said Iris. "It's all of it. I have to keep moving, to keep pushing forward on this. If I stop, then I see his face right in front of me. Right after—"

She stopped as the trembling increased. Gwen squeezed her tight, and it subsided somewhat.

"I haven't thanked you for everything you've done," said Iris. "Especially for bringing Sally along Saturday. That couldn't have been easy for you."

"It was remarkably easy," said Gwen. "I rang him up and said, 'Iris needs us,' and that was all I needed to say."

"Was it awkward seeing him?"

"I think we both suppressed whatever we felt about seeing each other in the interest of the greater good of being with you. No, that's too harsh. We didn't part on bad terms, so it wasn't terrible seeing him again."

"It was difficult for me when you were together," Iris confessed. "And it's a different sort of difficult now that you're apart. I want there to be times when the three of us are doing things together. Or—"

"Or what?" asked Gwen.

"We never went out as a foursome. You, me, Sally, Archie. The only times when we were all in the same place were when something hideously criminal was happening."

"I'll tell you what," said Gwen. "When Archie is well enough to dine out again, we'll go out to celebrate together. Just the four of us."

"That would be nice," said Iris. "Speaking of double dates, what would you have done today if you thought either of our luncheon companions was lying to us?"

"I would have found some way of withholding my conclusions."

"How would you have done that if they asked you for the results?"

"I would have told them that they both passed, thanked them for their time, and hoped that they believed me. Then I would have been looking over my shoulder until we got to safety."

"We're in a safe place now. Is that what happened?"

"No," said Gwen. "They were both telling the truth. Were you hoping otherwise?"

"It would have made things simpler," said Iris. "It's difficult to find out what's going on when so much of it is buried so far in the past. Even the gun dates from the previous war."

"Did anything you learned today surprise you? Or spur you on to any further ideas?"

"I've been wondering if it would be worth speaking to Vanessa Reese. Maybe she knows something."

"I may have a way of getting in there without arousing too much suspicion."

"How?"

"It's a snooker hall."

"The new boyfriend?"

"He's not a boyfriend. He's a diversion."

"From whom or what do you wish to be diverted?"

"From everyone and everything," said Gwen. "From myself, most of all."

"Do you like him?"

"It was one date."

"But you had fun."

"Loads. I almost hate to spoil it by dragging him into this, but it would give me a chance to scout the terrain before we make our move."

"Our move," repeated Iris. "I like the sound of that. How do you think we should approach Des?"

"Tell him that we know about his father and Stanley Spelling," said Gwen. "Tell him we know that he and Archie were looking into their deaths together, and that we want to know what he knows."

"That's rather direct, don't you think?"

"There is nothing subtle about us showing up unexpectedly at his shop," said Gwen. "We may as well be up front about it."

Iris was silent.

"What?" asked Gwen.

"I just had a nasty thought," said Iris. "What if this was about the missing money?"

"How so?"

"What if the two sons of the original robbers both realised that they had turned up the third member of the gang, a man they thought had gone on the lam when they were boys? What if somehow the two of them figured out where the money was?"

"And?"

"What if Des shot Archie? You said you heard them arguing. Maybe Des got onto it first, and was worried Archie might come after him?"

"He wouldn't do that," said Gwen.

"Are you sure? You barely know him. You've fantasised about him, but you really don't know him."

"He's led an honest existence as a carpenter," said Gwen. "He could have gone into the Spelling gang, but he chose another path."

"Nevertheless, he was working in the cellar of the White Palace," pointed out Iris.

"He needed the work. It's a slow time of year."

"It was a lot of money. That creates temptations, especially for someone who needs work."

"I still don't think he would stoop so low."

"Will you promise me something?" asked Iris.

"What?"

"Will you keep your internal polygraph turned on when we talk to him? If you rule him out, then I will accept it and we can go on to the next suspect."

"Do we have a next suspect?"

"Not at the moment," said Iris. "So I am grasping at any straw that presents itself. Including Des."

"I hate this," said Gwen with a sigh.

"I know."

"Very well. I'll watch him."

The taxi turned off the highway onto Garnet Street, which ran between the Shadwell New Basin and the Eastern Docks.

Warehouses lined it on both sides, with lorries backed into loading docks, ready to take whatever cargo the ships had unloaded.

"It's just past the drawbridge," Gwen told the driver. "That group of buildings on the left."

"Very good, miss," he said.

"Would you be able to wait for us and keep the meter running?"

"I'm sorry, miss," he said regretfully. "I'm at the end of my shift. I have to take the cab back to the garage. But here's a card for the fleet. Call when you need to go, and they'll have someone pick you up in ten minutes, I promise."

"All right," she said, taking it and paying the fare.

"Stay warm, ladies," he said as they got out.

"Not likely," muttered Iris as he drove away.

There was a collection of shops facing the basin from the south, providing various skills or equipment needed for maritime repairs. Burton's Carpentry was on the corner, right off the street.

"There's a light on," observed Gwen. "That's a hopeful sign."

"I hope he has heat," said Iris.

Gwen glanced in the window but didn't see any activity inside. She turned the knob on the door and went in, setting off a bell dangling from the ceiling.

"Hello, is anyone about?" she called.

There was no answer.

They looked around. Boards of various lengths and thicknesses were propped against one wall, their sizes printed neatly on small wooden slabs nailed to the posts holding them. Various electrical saws and sanders stood in mute formation to the right, awaiting their calls to action.

"Hello?" Gwen called again. "Des, are you about?"

"It's drafty in here," complained Iris.

"Maybe he's out back," said Gwen.

"What's out back?"

"No idea. But I don't think he would have left the shop unlocked and unattended. Iris, look!"

Iris looked where her partner was pointing. Hanging on the wall, amidst a small group of framed photographs, was the same picture of the three survivors of the West Ham Pals that hung in Archie's front hallway. Gwen went up to take a closer look.

"Eerie, now that we know what happened to all of them," she commented. "I wonder if—oof!"

The last was forced out of her as Iris threw herself across the space between them into Gwen's midriff, bringing them both down to the floor.

"Stay down!" Iris hissed. "Don't move!"

"Wha—" Gwen started, but Iris clapped her hand over her mouth, then pointed up and to her left.

"I found where that draft is coming from," whispered Iris.

Gwen looked up at a window facing the street.

There was a small, round hole in the centre of it.

"Iris?" she said, almost whimpering.

"Stay here," said Iris. "Do not move from this spot. I'm going to make sure it's safe."

"But—"

"Stay here, Gwen. I mean it."

The window overlooked an open office section of the shop, where a desk and a pair of short counters enclosed a small rectangular space. There was a telephone on the desk next to an open ledger. Iris crawled under the counter to a spot beneath the window, resolutely avoiding looking to her left. She pulled her compact from her bag and opened it, then sat directly beneath the window, keeping her eyes on the small, round mirror. Only the mirror, not letting her gaze drift over its perimeters to the view beyond, refusing to look at what she knew had to be there.

Slowly, she raised the mirror, angling it so she could see what the world presented outside the window. There were some other shops across Garnet Street. She didn't care if they were open or not. She wanted to see if anyone was still on the rooftops, silhouetted against the setting sun, with a gun still pointing at this window, waiting for any sign of movement.

But she saw no one, which meant she finally had to look at the desk, or, more to the point, the area behind it.

"What is it?" called Gwen. "Are we safe?"

"Stay there, Gwen," said Iris numbly.

"But are we safe or not?"

"We're safe," said Iris. "But stay there anyway. You don't want to see this."

"See . . . is it Des?" asked Gwen, her voice faltering.

"Yes," said Iris.

"I'm coming over," said Gwen.

"I said stay there!" shouted Iris. "Please, Gwen, stay there. You shouldn't have to see this. I've already seen it. Seen him. There's no reason for both of us to. We can't do anything for him, Gwen, not now, so don't come over."

"But he might still be—"

"No," said Iris. "He's dead."

"But are you sure? Did you check for a pulse?"

"There is no possibility he could have one."

"Please, Iris," Gwen begged her, sitting against the wall and starting to sob. "It's Des."

Iris closed her eyes for a moment, then crawled towards him, keeping her gaze on the floor below her. When one boot came into view, she took her glove off, reached forward, and felt under his pants cuff.

"No pulse," she said. "He's cold to the touch. I'm sorry, Gwen. He's been dead for hours at least."

She started to inch back, then something caught her eye. A small, light reddish rectangular shape, lying under the desk, not far from where one outstretched hand lay.

A brick.

She took a deep breath, then reached forward and snatched it away, turning her head from the gruesome aspect before her as soon as she could. She emerged from behind the office area, brushing herself off, then came over and plopped down next to Gwen.

"Now you're trembling," she said.

"What did you expect?" said Gwen, her breath coming in short gasps.

"I found this," said Iris, holding up the brick.

"What's a brick doing in a carpentry shop?" Gwen wondered aloud.

Iris turned it over. "M. Fletcher & Co." was legible on one face.

"Archie had one just like it on his desk at home," said Iris. "The last thing he wrote in his scrapbook was 'Des on bricks,' remember?"

"Do you think that's what he was doing?"

"He had the brick when he was shot."

Gwen stood up unsteadily.

"What are you doing?" demanded Iris. "I told you not to look."

"I'm not," said Gwen. "I won't. But there's an open ledger on his desk, and there's a pencil on the floor over there. He was writing when he—when it happened."

"I don't want to be the one responsible for you relapsing," said Iris, getting up. "You stay here."

"What about you?" asked Gwen.

"The damage is done," said Iris. "I'll add it to the list. Maybe Dr. Milford will give me something fun for the nightmares."

"Look, I'll close my eyes and walk over there," said Gwen. "You can guide me if I'm about to trip over anything."

"You can resist your morbid curiosity enough to do that?" asked Iris.

"If I can't, it's my own fault," said Gwen, facing the desk and closing her eyes. "Right, here I go. It should be about ten paces."

She walked slowly forward, her hands out in front of her.

"Stop," said Iris. "You're veering off to the left. Turn slightly. Good. Four more steps and you're there. Three, two, one—stop. Good, it's right in front of you."

I don't want to look, I don't want to look, Gwen thought over and over as she felt for the ledger. She picked it up, then turned away. She opened her eyes to see Iris watching her with apprehension.

"My sanity prevailed," said Gwen, walking back.

She sat down with the ledger propped against her bent legs. Iris sat next to her.

"Oh, God," whispered Gwen.

Drops of blood were splattered across the two broad pages.

"There," said Iris. "The final entry. 'Fletcher. Shipment of two pallets to White Palace, Maplin Street, Mile End, January sixteen, 1923.'"

"After the first two were killed," said Gwen. "Wasn't the date the *Fowler* set sail for South America the eighteenth of that month?"

"I guess Emery missed the boat," said Iris.

"Why stab him, then go to the elaborate trouble of walling up the body instead of dumping him somewhere?" asked Gwen.

"The money," said Iris. "He wasn't stabbed first. They kept him there and started walling him up to get him to talk. Then they stabbed him and completed the job."

"How horrible," said Gwen.

"I'll put the ledger and the brick back, then we'll get out of here," said Iris, getting to her feet and brushing herself off.

"What do you mean?" asked Gwen, looking at her in shock. "We have to call the police."

"We'll get safely away, then ring them up anonymously."

"We can't do that," said Gwen.

"Why not? We've done it once before."

"That was someone we didn't know," said Gwen. "And we were in danger."

"We may be in danger now."

"This is Des!" cried Gwen angrily. "We know him. We know

his fiancée. We can't just leave him. I won't. There is a telephone
on that desk, and if you don't want me seeing anything then you'd
damn well better go over there and use it."

Iris didn't move. Gwen glared down at her, then got up and
started towards the desk.

"Wait," said Iris, getting to her feet. "Give me the ledger. I'll do it."

She took the ledger, then went back to the desk and put it in
the position she remembered it. She took a deep breath, then went
back under the counter and quickly replaced the brick. Then she
came back out, grabbed the telephone, and dialled a number.

"Hello, I need to speak to Detective Sergeant Kinsey," she said.
"It's urgent. Yes, it's Miss Iris Sparks. I don't care what he told you,
put him on. There's been a murder."

She waited, looking at Gwen.

"Mike, it's me," she said. "We're at Des Burton's shop by Shadwell
New Basin. He's been shot, possibly by the same sniper who shot
Archie, so you'd better bring Florey along. The we? Gwen's with me.
No, we won't touch anything, I promise."

Gwen looked at her sharply. Iris shrugged in response.

"Right. See you soon."

She hung up.

"Satisfied?" she asked.

"You lied to him," said Gwen. "We touched things. We disturbed
the scene."

"We put them back where we found them," said Iris. "The trouble
I'm in is far greater than that."

"The trouble we're in, you mean. How much do you plan to
share with them?"

"Nothing about our meeting with Archie's counterparts," she
said. "That's not relevant."

"Everything else, though?" asked Gwen. "Everything we've
learned? Because if you don't tell them, I will."

"Including the ring sitting in your closet hidey-hole? Shall we all get arrested for concealing evidence? They'll have to handcuff Archie to a bed rail until he regains consciousness."

"Damn you," said Gwen. "I suppose that we don't know for certain that the ring in the scrapbook is the same one from the body. We never saw him remove it. I'll keep quiet about the scrapbook."

"And by said legal quibble, our consciences and our necks are preserved," said Iris. "There's a police car pulling up."

Two constables emerged from the car and came into the shop.

"Who called it in?" asked one.

"I did," said Iris.

"You're Miss Sparks?"

She nodded.

"I'm Police Constable Richards. This is my partner, Mallory. We're from the Wapping Station. We got the call from Serious Crime to come secure the scene. Where is the victim?"

"Behind the desk," she replied.

"And who are you, miss?" he asked, turning to Gwen.

"I'm Mrs. Gwendolyn Bainbridge," she said.

"You were with Miss Sparks when she found the body?"

"Yes."

He went over to the desk, leaned across it, and peered down.

"Blimey, that's a mess," he said. "Have you touched anything?"

"No," said Iris. "Well, I checked for a pulse."

"Not much point in that, was there?" observed Richards, straightening.

He looked over at the hole in the window, then back at the body.

"I'd say he was sitting behind the desk when the bullet hit," he said. "Looks like it went through, then he toppled over to the left. The bullet's probably over there somewhere."

"Oh, dear," said Gwen, sagging against the wall.

"Could we hold off the more gruesome parts of the discussion?" asked Iris, coming over to support her partner.

"Sorry, miss, but I need to know what we're securing," replied Richards.

"Found it," reported Mallory, who had gone past the desk to inspect the stacks of lumber on the other side of the shop. He pointed to a hole bored into a board.

"Good, leave it for the crime scene lads," said Richards. "Either of you know the name of the deceased?"

"Des Burton," said Iris. "He's the owner of the shop."

"Know his home number? Any relatives?"

"I have his home number," said Gwen, reaching for her address book. "I don't think his parents are alive. He has—had a fiancée named Fanny. I don't know her last name, and the number I had doesn't work anymore."

"They may know it over at Merle's," offered Iris.

"Yeah, we'll try more private means before we go there," said Richards. "Rather she hear it from us than a bartender. Ladies, I'm going to ask you to step over to that corner away from everything. It's about to get crowded in here."

They could hear sirens in the distance, getting louder by the second. Then a pair of black Wolseley police cars roared up, followed by a pair of patrol cars. Iris took a deep breath as she saw both Kinsey and Florey get out, followed by Conrad and another officer they recognised as Police Constable Godfrey, who was carrying a camera case and his forensics kit. Other constables stood at the ready, awaiting orders.

The first four entered, glanced over at the two women, then nodded at the constables.

"I'm Florey," said the detective inspector. "I'll be picking this one up."

"PC Richards. My partner, PC Mallory. Wapping Station."

"Good to meet you," said Florey. "Behind the desk?"

"Yes, sir."

The constables parted as the detectives came forward and peered over the desk.

"You've met him before," Florey said to Kinsey. "Is that him?"

"Yes," said Kinsey. "That's Burton."

"Start with photographs," Florey said to Godfrey. "I doubt we'll need prints, but give the area around him a going-over, just in case someone was looking for something. Mrs. Bainbridge, Miss Sparks, I see you are both wearing gloves. Have you had them on the entire time?"

"I took one off to feel for a pulse," said Iris.

"Where did you touch him?"

"His left leg, above his boot."

"Very well, we won't bother with exemplars from the two of you."

He put a pair of rubber gloves on from the kit, then lifted the hinged countertop and stepped gingerly into the office space.

"Anyone find the bullet?" he asked.

"Over here, sir," said Mallory, standing by the hole.

Florey looked back and forth between the two holes.

"Not much drop from one to the next," he said. "It wasn't fired from the rooftop. From a vehicle, most likely. Conrad, go ask around those shops, see if anyone noticed a lorry stop for any unusual interval."

"Yes, sir," said Conrad.

"Godfrey, when you're done, see if you can extract the bullet without damaging it. If you need to take an entire board, do so."

"I will bet you dinner that the bullet is a .303 fired from a Lee-Metford Mark Two," said Iris.

The policemen turned to look at her.

"I am here because of that very possibility, Miss Sparks," said Florey. "You should have called me, not Kinsey."

"I called Mike because your cases are connected," said Iris. "It's about time you two started listening to me."

Kinsey walked over to their corner and stood in front of her, his arms folded.

"I'm listening," he said. "Now, talk."

CHAPTER 12

That picture," Iris began, pointing to the photograph. "Look at it. Tell me what you notice."

Kinsey and Florey went over and peered at it.

"That's Stan Spelling, Archie's dad," said Florey, jabbing a finger at him. "I remember him from when I was starting out. He was a holy terror from all reports, but nobody could make anything stick. Then he bought it out on the docks somewhere."

"Near the Royal Docks," said Iris. "The end of November 1922."

"Who are the other two?" asked Kinsey.

"The first is Ted Burton, Des's father," said Iris. "Killed in December 1922."

"Same method?" asked Florey.

"Spelling was stabbed, Burton was shot," said Iris.

"The rings," said Kinsey, leaning forward. "They're all wearing the same military rings."

"They were in the West Ham Pals together during the Great War," said Iris.

"Archie told you that?"

"Yes."

"Do you think the third man did in his mates?" asked Kinsey.

"That's one possibility," said Iris.

"Did Archie happen to mention his name?"

"Jenks Emery."

"You think he's out there now with a couple of rifles, coming after the next generation twenty years later?" asked Florey skeptically.

"No," said Iris. "I think he's the man from the White Palace cellar."

"Jenks Emery was a name on one of the missing persons reports from 1923," said Kinsey. "Fine, say the body is him. What then, Detective Sparks?"

"The three of them may have robbed the White Palace," said Iris. "Their deaths may have been payback."

"How did you know about the robbery?" asked Kinsey. "Archie again?"

"Yes," said Iris. "And I heard something about it from another source."

"Care to give me his name?"

"No," said Iris. "The source wasn't an eyewitness to anything, merely a supplier of rumours. But that would put Frankie Reese into the picture."

"It would," agreed Kinsey. "Which is why I talked to his widow about it the other day."

"You did? You never told me about that."

"Why would I tell you anything?" asked Kinsey. "You're not a member of the force. What makes you think you're entitled to information about an ongoing investigation?"

"I just thought—"

"Thought what? That you have privileges where I'm concerned? Did it ever occur to you that the last person with whom I would share information is a gangster's girlfriend? You've been compromised, Sparks, and you know it. But I will tell you this for free. The first line of enquiry I pursued was the Reese gang, not only because of the location but because I found the robbery file from

1922. The trouble, of course, is that there is no Reese gang any-more. They got kicked out or absorbed into other gangs, primarily your boyfriend's, and Frankie, the last of the Reese family, died years ago. So, yes, I did my job with the body from the cellar and I tracked down anyone from the gang who might have known any-thing, which was fruitless, and I talked to Vanessa Reese, Frankie's widow."

"Did she tell you anything useful?"

"She mumbled about marital privilege, but I told her the spouse in question was dead and beyond prosecution. She then very re-luctantly told me about the aftermath of the robbery and how the Reeses searched under every rock in London for the men who did it. Then, maybe two months later, Frankie told her that they got the man who was the brains of the operation. She asked Frankie what happened, and he smiled and said not to worry her pretty little head about it because he wasn't going to give them any more trouble. She knew better than to ask any questions."

"So you've closed the case," said Iris.

"As far as I'm concerned, that body was there because Frankie Reese put him there, and Frankie is dead and beyond the reach of earthly justice. I appreciate your finding a name for the deceased. I'll see if there are any records from that period that will confirm it, but that case is otherwise finished."

"Only it isn't," said Iris. "There are two men shot who are con-nected to it."

"How, Sparks?" demanded Kinsey.

"I'm still working on that."

"Are you? How jolly for all of us, which leads me to the main question: Why the hell are you here? How did you two wind up in the London Docks with a dead body?"

"We wanted to ask Mr. Burton what he knew about all this. And about the bricks."

"The bricks? You mean from the cellar?"

"Yes."

"Why did you think he knew anything about anything? Especially the bricks?"

"Archie had mentioned something about them," said Iris. "That Des was going to look into them. Des had some contacts in construction."

"And you came here just in time to find him dead."

"I don't know how long he's been here," said Iris. "It's Monday afternoon. He didn't come into the White Palace for work this morning."

"How do you know that?"

"Because I tried to reach him there," said Gwen. "He hadn't shown up. That's why we came here."

"Did you call here?" asked Kinsey.

"Yes," said Gwen. "There was no answer."

"When was that?"

"Sometime after ten."

"And you waited until this afternoon to come pay him a visit?"

"Yes."

"Why wait, if the two of you are so hot on the trail?"

"We had other things to do," said Iris.

"Couples to match, a dance to arrange, then back to crime solving," he said, scoffing.

"It's been a long day," said Iris.

"And you came all this way to find out about some bricks," he said.

"It was a lead."

"Which I followed already," he said, pulling out his notebook and flipping it open. "'M. Fletcher, shipment of two pallets of bricks to the White Palace in January 1923,' which corresponds roughly with the age of the body and helped narrow down the time of death. Give me some credit for knowing what I'm about, Sparks. You were only four days behind me."

"So it seems," she replied. "Would you like a blue ribbon?"

"I would like you to stay out of police business!" he shouted. "I would like you to stay out of my business, whether it's professional or personal. I would like never to see your face again, if you could manage that."

"I would be happy to," she said. "The problem is someone put a bullet in my lover the other day, and now I am forced to deal with you lot."

Florey winced at the phrase.

"I'm done listening," said Kinsey. "I'm going to dig up some dental records, match Emery to the body, then file this. I've got cases with some actual urgency that need my attention. I'm not wasting any more time on this, or on you."

He stormed out. A few seconds later, they heard his Wolseley roar to life and pull away.

"I'm going to need a ride back," said Godfrey from behind the desk.

"You can get one with the doc when he gets here," said Florey.

Conrad returned.

"No luck across the way," he said. "I was told quite pointedly that they don't get paid to look out the window."

"Check with the shops on this side, then the warehouses on the other side of the bridge," said Florey. "Take Richards and Mallory with you. Then see what you can do about locating next of kin. Call in every hour."

"Yes, sir," said Conrad.

"Ladies, I am going to bring you back to the Yard," said Florey. "This is not the proper place to carry on a conversation."

"Oh, we're calling them conversations now?" said Iris.

"If you'd rather stay here, we could."

"Iris, let's get away from here," Gwen begged her.

"Fine," said Iris. "Take us back."

No one said anything on the ride to Victoria Embankment.

The Wolseley turned through the arched entrance to New Scotland Yard and stopped in front of the building where Homicide and Serious Crime Command was located. Florey got out and opened the door for them, then led them inside. He took them upstairs rather than down, Iris noted with relief, remembering her night in a subterranean interrogation room some months previous.

"I'll take you one at a time, if you don't mind," said Florey when they reached his office. "Mrs. Bainbridge, please wait here. I'm sorry we don't have anything more accommodating at the moment."

"I'll be fine," said Gwen, sitting on a chair in the hall.

"Miss Sparks, please come with me," he said.

She entered his office and sat on a chair by a desk that must have belonged to another detective, if the family photos were any indication. Florey closed the door, then took off his coat and hung it on a hook.

"Kinsey was out of line back there," he said as he was sitting down. "As I said, he's too emotionally involved when it comes to you."

"Compromised."

"Lacking in objectivity, certainly. You should have called me first on this one."

"But you don't trust me," said Iris.

"Not entirely," admitted Florey. "You've gone over to the other side in your loyalties, that much is clear."

"Then why are we talking?"

"Miss Sparks, I've spent a great deal of my career investigating organised crime in London," he said. "I've been forced to resort to working with informants of the slipperiest variety on more than one occasion. While I understand your sympathies, quite frankly I don't care about them one way or another. I need to know what you know, and I need to know it now."

"Why should I trust you? You're hell-bent on making a case against Willoughby or someone like him."

"I was," he said.

"No longer?"

"I am not so hidebound in my thinking that I cannot change direction when new information comes in," he said. "As I said, I know the underworld quite well. Des Burton's name has never come up as part of it before. Not once. And his death by similar means to the attempt on Spelling has moved my thinking closer to your theories. But if they're incorrect, and we truly have a war about to break out between the various factions, then we have to do everything within our power to prevent it. Have you heard anything that will help us determine our course of action?"

"Nothing is going to happen between Willoughby and the Spellings," said Iris. "At least, not imminently. And you can include Clement's people in that."

"And you base that opinion on what?"

"A source," said Iris.

"The same source who provided you with the story of the White Palace robbery?"

"Yes."

"When you say not imminently, could there be violence in the future?"

"I believe that negotiations will be taking place after the New Year."

"I see. How high up is this source of yours?"

"High enough to back his words with actions," said Iris. "Or for now, no actions. Call it a Christmas truce."

"God bless us, every one," said Florey. "I've read Kinsey's case file on the body in the White Palace, incidentally. Who took the ring?"

"Can't tell you," said Iris. "I wasn't there when it went missing."

"That doesn't mean you don't know who did it."

"It doesn't matter much now, does it?"

"Perhaps not," he said.

His telephone rang. He answered it.

"Florey here. Yes? It was. No surprise there, although we should get confirmation from someone at Ballistics. Right, keep at it."

He hung up.

"Godfrey retrieved the bullet," he said. "Looks like you were right. It's from a .303."

"You owe me dinner."

"I never took the bet, Miss Sparks," he said. "Now, don't go rushing out to investigate any more of your ideas. I don't want the next person at the receiving end of the rifle to be you or Mrs. Bainbridge."

"What's your plan of action?"

"No, Miss Sparks, this is not an even exchange of information. If you ever return to the side of the angels, perhaps we'll be able to have a real conversation."

"Didn't Mike tell you?" she replied as she got up. "I'm an atheist. There are no angels."

"There are still devils, Miss Sparks," he said as he opened the door for her. "Stay out of their sight."

Gwen stood as Iris came out.

"Mrs. Bainbridge, please come in," said Florey.

She entered and took the same seat Iris had used.

"Do you need a moment?" asked Florey, noticing the streaks in her makeup. "I could have someone take you to the ladies' if you need it."

"After," said Gwen. "Let's get this over with. It's been a wretched day."

"It's a terrible thing, finding a man dead like that," said Florey sympathetically. "Even a stranger—"

"He wasn't a stranger," said Gwen.

"That's right, Kinsey had mentioned in his reports that you knew him," remembered Florey. "What was the nature of your relationship?"

"There was never a relationship," said Gwen quickly.

"I meant, how did you meet?"

"At a viewing, then at a wake," she said. "We were—Iris and I, I mean—we were looking into the Tillie La Salle murder. Des was Miss La Salle's cousin. I was pretending to be someone I wasn't, looking for information about her, and there was a brief flirtation. After that matter was resolved, I saw him again."

"You dated him?"

"It wasn't a date," she said. "I went to apologise for deceiving him, and to tell him that it wasn't possible for me to date him. We walked along the Thames together, and talked, and—"

"And?"

"And he kissed me," she concluded, the tears running freely again.

"That has all the hallmarks of a date," he said. "When was the next time you saw him?"

"When we went with Archie to see the White Palace last week," said Gwen.

"Burton was with you when the body was discovered."

"Yes."

"Was that the last time you saw him?"

"No. I was at the club on Friday, checking on the renovations, and we spoke again."

"Did any of it concern the body?"

"I did ask him about the ring," said Gwen. "He denied taking it. The rest of the conversation was personal."

"Then I won't pry. Was there anything else?"

"He and Archie were arguing when I went down there," said Gwen reluctantly.

"What was the argument about?"

"Des was saying there was nothing there. Archie seemed surprised."

"Interesting," said Florey. "Maybe they were hunting the money that was stolen."

"Then why would they be looking in the place it was stolen from?"

"I wonder," said Florey.

"Maybe there wasn't a robbery," said Gwen.

"What?"

"This is an odd idea, but what if the robbery was staged?" she asked. "Maybe Frankie Reese collaborated with the robbers to steal from his family's gang, then eliminated the men who knew about it after? All that time, the Reese gang was searching for the money, and he had it hidden in the last place they'd look, his own club."

"Fascinating idea," said Florey. "Impossible to prove or disprove at this point. So, Miss Sparks told me she spoke to Willoughby and Clement about all of this. Is that true?"

"What's your mother's maiden name?" asked Gwen, looking at him closely.

"Southwell," he said in surprise. "Louise Southwell."

"Iris said nothing of the kind," said Gwen. "Please don't treat me like a suspect."

"My apologies. And my sympathies for the loss of your friend. It must have been a tremendous shock to see him like that, given your affection for him."

"I didn't see him," said Gwen. "Iris wouldn't let me."

"Then she did you a kindness," said Florey. "Let me show you out."

They shared a cab again. Iris didn't protest at the expense this time. Once inside, she immediately leaned against Gwen, closing her eyes. Then she sat up again, shuddering.

"Sorry," she said. "Too many terrible pictures flashing across my mind."

"I know," said Gwen. "Thank you for shielding me from this one."

"How are you feeling? I'm wrecked, and supposedly I'm the strong one."

"It's horrible. I feel like I've caused it somehow, that I set a chain of disasters in motion when I went down in that cellar and saw Des there."

"These things would have happened even if you hadn't," said Iris. "The wall was being demolished, the body would have been found."

"But maybe Archie would have dealt with it in some other way if we weren't there forcing his hand," said Gwen. "Without bringing in the police, or putting the assassin on alert. Now Des is dead, and I'll never know if— Do you know, I've only spoken to him five times? I counted, Iris. Three in June when we met, twice this past week. Yet he's been a constant fantasy, and what made it powerful was that even though I knew I probably wouldn't let go of myself and go for him, as long as he was alive and nearby, there was still a chance that I might. Now that's died with him, and I'm mourning something that might have been. I have no one else in my life with that powerful a hold on me. Not Walter, not River."

"Not Sally?"

Gwen sighed.

"I wish it could be Sally sometimes," she said. "There were moments with him, but they came with—this is going to sound terrible."

"Tell me."

"The times I wanted him the most came at times when I had been in danger."

"You wanted him to rescue you?"

"Not that, so much," said Gwen. "Well, maybe in part. But I saw him in action, fully himself, and that was an impressive man to behold. If he could be that man more often—but that's the person he wants to leave behind."

"He's afraid of that man," said Iris. "Of what will happen if he loses control. What he might do."

"Sometimes I think control is overrated."

"You lost control once before," said Iris. "It didn't go well."

"I know," said Gwen.

They were quiet until they reached Iris's building on Welbeck Street.

"What's the plan for tomorrow?" asked Gwen.

"There is no more plan," said Iris. "I'm done with this. I've seen enough. I'll let Florey do his job. See what he turns up."

"Good," said Gwen, giving her a quick hug. "Get some sleep. I'll see you back at The Right Sort in the morning. The world must be peopled."

"The world must be peopled," Iris echoed wearily.

She got out of the cab. Gwen watched her until she was safely inside, giving her one last wave, then gave the cabbie her address in Kensington.

The world must be peopled, they both thought. Especially now that there was one fewer worthwhile man in it.

Iris unlocked her door and went into her flat. It had been two long, arduous days since she had been there, and she looked around like it was an old museum exhibit she had wandered into that had been mothballed for years. Every stick of furniture seemed strange to her now. It wasn't until she saw her knife and metal knuckles in the dish on the hall table where she usually kept her keys that a sense of ownership returned to her. She slipped the knuckles onto her fingers, then slammed them into the palm of her left hand, welcoming the jolt of pain. She slipped them into her bag, then picked up her knife and flicked it open, wanting to hurl it into something.

Into someone.

She felt better holding it, even though there was no one else present to threaten her. She was finally ready to defend herself after two days of feeling helpless.

Although a knife was useless against a Lee-Metford in the hands of an expert.

She folded the knife and added it to her personal arsenal, then opened her refrigerator, half-expecting to see clumps of wild mould and fungi filling it, but it was still the same as when she had left it. The half-filled bottle of milk was still good, and there were sufficient meals in tins in her cupboard to carry her through without going out to shop again.

Ownership, she thought. That was a sad joke under the circumstances. Her lease had two weeks of life left, and she was no closer to finding a new place. Archie had given her unrestricted access to his cottage, but she didn't feel right squatting there for any great length of time, not while things were in a state of chaos. She didn't want to take up Gwen's offer to live in that dreadful cellar apartment. In fact, she was feeling generally inclined to avoid all cellars for the near future, given the curse that one had recently cast upon their lives.

She lit a burner and started boiling water, then went into her bedroom and peeled off her suit and blouse, throwing on her pyjamas and wrapping her robe around her before plodding back into the kitchen.

Her telephone rang as she was pouring her tea. Archie, she thought, trying to avoid scalding herself as she raced to answer it. But it was a different voice, one she had hoped not to hear for some time.

"I've been calling since Saturday evening," said her mother.

"I was staying somewhere else," she replied.

"Clearly," said her mother. "Are you all right? I've been worried."

"I'm not all right, but I'm coping," said Iris. "Thank you for worrying."

"Don't be snippy, Iris. I heard about Mr. Spelling on the radio and I've been trying to contact you ever since."

"You could have come to the hospital," said Iris.

"After that dreadful newspaper article, I couldn't afford to be connected to him more than I already was."

"So your desire to comfort your only daughter was not your first priority."

"Iris, please show some sense," said her mother. "Think who I am and what I represent, then look who he was."

"*Is*, Mother. He's still alive."

"Of course, but you and I both know something like this was bound to happen someday. Or if not this, arrest and imprisonment. Nobody lives that life untouched."

"No one lives any life untouched," said Iris. "Not even you."

"Yes, I've been touched," said her mother. "But I held to my path. You, on the other hand—"

"Let's not go any further with this line of conversation, shall we?" Iris pleaded.

"All I'm saying is that this might be for the best in the long run," said her mother. "You don't see that now, but I do. And you will someday."

"You're happy about this," Iris said. "You're actually happy that this happened to him."

"No, of course not, but—"

"Do you know what puzzles me, Mother? I mean, many things do, but how was it that Gareth Pontefract happened to be lurking outside your house that night?"

"I am in the public eye, you know."

"No, not really. You're a minor backbencher of not much interest or scandal, so why was Pontefract there? That night, of all nights? How did he know Archie would be coming to dinner?"

"Maybe he was following Mr. Spelling," suggested her mother.

"Nobody follows Archie without Archie noticing," said Iris. "It's one of the many things we have in common."

"Are you suggesting that I tipped off Pontefract? Why would I do that?"

"To drive a wedge between Archie and me," said Iris.

"Really," huffed her mother. "The next thing we know, you'll be suggesting I arranged to have him shot."

"To be honest, I hadn't ruled you out until the second shooting."

"What second shooting?"

"Sorry, I guess it hasn't made the news yet. Gwen and I have been investigating. A man we wanted to talk to was shot with the same calibre rifle that Archie was. We found the body. There, I've shared today's horror, and you don't have to call me to tell me how worried you are again."

"Who was he?"

"Not a constituent of yours, so don't fret. He's not your problem."

"Is he yours?"

"No," said Iris. "I've given up. I've finally left it to the police. I doubt that I'll show up in any of the news coverage, so your reputation should stay untroubled."

"Iris, please stop directing your anger at me," said her mother. "I do care, you know. Tell me what I can do to help."

"Can't come up with a single thing," said Iris. "Well, come to think of it, there is one."

"What?"

"Change your vote on the Wanstead Flats. Keep them from developing there. Only you and I would know it came from Archie, but I would like to know that you had come to agreement about one thing, at least."

"I will consider it," said her mother. "In exchange, will you consider doing something more sensible with your life?"

"I may not have any other choice, the way things are going," said Iris. "I'm going to turn in now, if you don't mind. I'm exhausted."

"I hope he recovers, Iris. I mean that."

"It's good of you to say. I'll take it on face value for now."

"That may be the best we can do, dear. Sleep well."

"Good night, Mother."

She hung up, then padded back into the kitchen to find that her tea had gone cold.

Met with some gang bosses, stumbled upon a murder scene, and still got home in time for dinner, thought Gwen later on as she sat at her dressing table and removed her makeup. How does one behave as if nothing seriously abnormal had happened during the day? How does one make conversation without running screaming from the table?

Because the children are there, of course, and we pretend that the world isn't frightening for their sake.

She had made it through the evening somehow. She even managed to read the boys a story at bedtime, though afterwards she could not for the life of her recall what it was about. Then she pleaded a headache and fled the evening nightcap with Carolyne and Simon, the latter shooting her a look of concern that she left unanswered as she dashed up the grand staircase.

The strain of maintaining appearances was evident when she looked at her reflection. The burden of keeping it all in. It was one thing to talk to Carolyne and Simon about going off on an investigation with Iris as if it were a mad picnic, but it was very much another to come home to report that another murder had crossed her path. She couldn't bring herself to incur either Carolyne's lurid interest or Simon's gentle concern.

She wanted very much to talk about it to someone, but there were only three people in her life who had shared this aspect of it. She didn't want to call Iris, of course. The last thing she wanted to do was set her friend back on the hunt when she was finally willing to let the police do their job.

And there was Sally, who had been with them through each of these insane adventures. He would listen. He would understand.

Or would he now? After their parting of the ways, would he complacently accept listening to her rattle off about another murder? Of the death of an object of desire who wasn't him?

Which left Dr. Milford, and it was three days until her next appointment. Would this qualify as an emergency? She thought it might. But it was too late in the evening to call him.

Let's see if you can get through the night without nightmares, Gwennie, then find out how you are in the morning.

She felt restless. She didn't want to read any novels when reality was so overwhelming. She walked into her closet to hang up her suit and change into her pyjamas, then glanced down at the panel that concealed her secret trove.

Well, if I can't take my mind off it, might as well drown myself in it, she thought.

She opened the panel and retrieved Archie's scrapbook, then went back to her bed and climbed in. She opened the book, looking first at the ring.

We'll have to find some way of returning it for the burial, she thought. If there's a way of doing that without being arrested.

She flipped through the pages, reading about the robberies again with Willoughby's information filling in some of the gaps from her previous pass through. She pictured the three men hitting each location, pulling their masks up as they entered, fanning out with their guns drawn as women screamed, moving through quickly and even brutally before vanishing into the night, maybe outrunning the police in some high-speed chase.

Vanishing . . .

She sat bolt upright, turning the pages furiously, tapping each yellowed clipping as she sped through it. When she was done, she closed the cover and leaned back against her pillows.

What do I do? she thought. Do I tell Iris? Set her off again? Or go directly to the police, and endure her lasting resentment when she finds out I went behind her back?

There was only one right answer to that.

She fell asleep, clutching the scrapbook to her breast.

Iris came into work the next morning to find Gwen already there, sitting behind her desk, looking at her expectantly.

"What?" asked Iris.

Then she saw the scrapbook open on Gwen's desk. Gwen had moved Iris's chair next to her own. She patted it.

"Take off your coat and sit next to me," she said.

Iris dutifully obeyed.

"I was reading some unpleasant bedtime stories last night," said Gwen, sliding the scrapbook to where Iris could read the clippings.

"The first robbery was at the jewellery store," continued Gwen, pointing to it. "Three-man job. Two handled the people there, the other grabbed the loot."

"Yes. So?"

"Then they fled in a waiting car," said Gwen. "Here's the next one. Same thing. Over and over. Three men go in, and every time there's a car waiting outside for them, ready to roll. Every time."

"Oh, my goodness," Iris said softly.

"They had a driver, Iris," said Gwen. "It was a four-man gang, not three. And I'll bet he's still out there somewhere."

CHAPTER 13

Benny!" said Iris.

"He would have been eight years old then," said Gwen. "As talented a driver as he is, I doubt that he was that much of a prodigy."

"No, of course not," said Iris. "I forgot to factor in the lapse of time."

"It would have to be someone the three of them knew who also had a reputation as a getaway driver," said Gwen.

"And a sniper," said Iris. "I keep coming back to that rifle and the Great War. It had to be a man that the three of them trusted implicitly who had those skills."

"Someone they knew in the war," suggested Gwen. "Maybe from the same battalion."

"The West Ham Pals," said Iris. "That would make sense. So I need to contact someone from the Records Department, find out who was in the unit with them then who's still alive now, with sniper training— What?"

Gwen was shaking her head.

"This is something that would be better done by Florey," she said.

"But I have contacts—"

"So does he. Official ones who will take his request more seriously and with more speed than you with your clandestine network of connections and favours."

"But—"

"But you want to do this yourself," Gwen finished. "I understand entirely. Let me ask you something. Say you found a possibility. What would you do then?"

"I'd go looking for him," Iris said immediately.

"And when you found him?"

Iris didn't answer.

"What if there was more than one candidate?" Gwen continued. "There must have been several men in the battalion with sniper training. And they tended to stay in position rather than go over the top charging into no-man's-land, so their survival rate would have been higher."

"How do you know that?"

"Father was in the army," she said. "He served during that war. He talked about it, especially at dinner parties. I probably knew more about battlefield tactics than most girls knew about fashion growing up. My point, Iris, is that there might be many men to look into. If we want this man caught quickly, the best way to do that is to pass this theory on to Florey. He has the resources and the manpower."

"I don't want him caught," said Iris. "I want him dead."

"The Crown will take care of that, not us," said Gwen. "Temper vengeance with prudence. I don't want you following whoever he is into oblivion."

Iris drummed her fingers on the scrapbook for a few seconds.

"You win," she said finally. "I'll call him."

"Thank you, Iris," said Gwen. "It's the right decision."

Iris slid her chair back to her desk, then dialled Florey.

"It's Iris Sparks," she said when he answered.

"Yes, Miss Sparks?"

"Mrs. Bainbridge and I have been putting our heads together, and have some further thoughts to share."

"Go ahead."

"There was a driver on the robberies," she said. "A fourth man waiting in a car with the motor running while three went in. Archie—Mr. Spelling—never picked up on that, or if he did, he didn't find out anything about what happened to him."

"How did Mr. Spelling communicate this information to you, Miss Sparks? Did you discuss this case before Saturday?"

"No," said Iris reluctantly. "I found a scrapbook he'd been keeping on the circumstances of his father's murder. That's how I learned about the robberies."

"I see," said Florey. "I'm glad you've finally come clean about that. Was there anything else of interest in the scrapbook?"

"He had been chasing down Emery for years, then finally gave up," said Iris. "There are records of that. Passenger lists, addresses of Emery's relatives, and so forth. Mrs. Bainbridge and I think Mr. Spelling and Des Burton resumed the chase after Emery's body turned up, and that may be what got them shot."

"By the onetime driver."

"Yes. And given the use of a Lee-Metford, it was probably someone who served in the Great War, maybe in the same unit with them. So you might want to look into the West Ham Pals and see if any of their snipers is still kicking around. Someone with superior driving skills as well, although that wouldn't have come from the army."

"That sounds like a promising direction," said Florey. "Where is the scrapbook now?"

"I have it at The Right Sort."

"I'm sending a man over to collect it."

"Must you?" asked Iris, her voice faltering. "It's only speculation based on clippings."

"It's evidence, Miss Sparks," said Florey. "You should be grateful that I'm not charging you with concealing it from us. I might have done so were you not so forthcoming."

"I am grateful," said Iris, swallowing her anger. "I await your messenger."

"Thank you, Miss Sparks," he said. "The Yard appreciates your co-operation and your assistance. Good day."

He hung up.

"He's sending someone for Archie's scrapbook," said Iris.

"All right," said Gwen. "Are we in trouble because of it? I noticed you bending over backward not to implicate me."

"You're not in trouble," said Iris. "My trouble has been suspended. Florey will probably use it as leverage some day down the line."

"What about Emery's ring?" asked Gwen. "You didn't mention that, either. As you said, that puts Archie in jeopardy."

"What do you propose we do?"

"We could remove it and send it to Emery's next of kin," said Gwen. "That would give them something to remember him by and protect Archie at the same time."

"I don't want to endanger your immortal soul more than I already have," said Iris. "We'll leave the ring and let Florey sort everything out. It's just that I hate giving up the scrapbook. It's the only keepsake I have of Archie's, bizarre as that may sound."

"It's not the only one," said Gwen. "There's the engagement ring."

"Which I possess, but which does not yet possess me," said Iris. "It doesn't have his handwriting, or his thoughts, or his scent. It is a glittering rock on a shiny piece of metal in a box, and I have not succumbed to its allure."

"You have to decide before he wakes," said Gwen. "It will be the first thing he'll ask about, don't you think?"

"I have until then to think about it," said Iris. "Let's see if we can get some work done, shall we? I could use the distraction."

A police constable came by half an hour later, and Iris turned over the scrapbook without a fuss. The Right Sort was getting enthusiastic responses to the ball, and Mrs. Billington was besieged with telephone calls as a result. Iris and Gwen struggled to focus on their regular work, but managed to come up with several possible matches.

"If nothing else, they can have their first dates at the ball," said Gwen as she addressed an envelope to a prospective suitor. "An extra helping of romantic atmosphere to speed things along."

"I'm worried that everyone will postpone their weddings until June," said Iris. "That's one of the problems with our business plan. The big money comes in seasonally."

"There's always Valentine's Day," said Gwen. "People like to get married then."

"People like to propose then," said Iris. "They get married in June. Ah, I hear footsteps coming up the stairs. Hopefully a walk-in with five pounds ready to turn over."

Walter Prendergast appeared in the doorway.

"Oh! Walter!" exclaimed Gwen. "I wasn't expecting you. You should have called."

"May I speak with you privately?" he asked, looking at her portentously.

"Privately?" replied Gwen. "We don't have a spare office."

"Perhaps Miss Sparks could absent herself momentarily," suggested Prendergast.

"I am working," said Iris irritably. "This is my office, this is my desk. I don't go barging into Prendergast Enterprises, or whatever it's called, and ask you to vacate the premises, do I?"

"It's Prendergast and Company," he said huffily. "Mrs. Bainbridge, I must insist."

"We can go to the third floor hallway," she said. "It's still vacant. No one will disturb us."

"I suppose that will have to do," he replied. "Shall we?"

"I'll be back shortly," Gwen said to Iris as she got up.

"Take whatever time you need," said Iris.

Prendergast stepped aside for Gwen to go through the door. As she did, she shot a look of desperation over her shoulder at Iris, who could offer only a sympathetic shrug in response.

Gwen led Prendergast down to the third floor, still unoccupied since the Blitz. She glanced at the landing below to make sure no one was about, then turned to him.

"It must be something quite serious for you to show up unannounced, Walter," she said. "What has happened?"

"Mrs. Bainbridge—"

"Gwen, please."

"Gwen," he began hesitantly. "When I first approached you on a romantic basis, there was a certain amount of turmoil in your life."

"That's putting it mildly," she said.

"I found your ability to overcome the obstacles that cropped up in front of you to be one of your most admirable qualities," he continued. "My own life has been one of assessing risks and calculating in advance how to avoid them. It is a very ordered and measured existence, so there was a certain illicit thrill in being drawn into the pandemonium that surrounded you. It was unlike anything I had known before. But after you asked me to back you at the Court of Lunacy last month, I thought: Finally, she'll have a chance to settle down and renounce all this. Finally, she'll be able to rejoin my world."

"I thought we lived in the same world, Walter," said Gwen.

"Only the same physical world, Gwen. But there are circles within that world, tightly bounded, and travel within those circles requires orderliness if one wishes to succeed. I am a man who wishes to succeed."

"Have I somehow been preventing you from doing that?" she asked.

He reached into his pocket and pulled out a piece of newspaper. It had been clipped quite neatly from the *Mirror*.

"A man was shot and killed yesterday," he said, handing it to her. "Not the sort of story I would peruse, normally, but I have my clipping service keep an eye out for any mention of you."

"Do you?" she said as she glanced over it. "Ah, there I am. 'The discovery of the body was by two women, Mrs. Gwendolyn Bainbridge and Miss Iris Sparks. Detective Inspector Florey would not comment upon what business the two had with the deceased.' Is that why you're here, Walter?"

"I wanted to ask you what you think you were doing getting involved with something like this," he said.

"I was helping Iris," said Gwen.

"Your partner. Who is the lover of a gang leader who was similarly shot this past weekend."

"His name is Archie Spelling," said Gwen. "He is a friend of mine as well."

"You see, there's the rub of it," said Prendergast. "Despite escaping the oversight of the Master of Lunacy, you continue to maintain contacts with these undesirables, and you continue to throw yourself into situations which are quite unsavoury."

"I've been dragged in more than I've thrown myself in," she said.

"Yet that's because you have these associations. Gangsters and forgers and whatnot."

"How did you know about the forgers?"

"I've looked into your background, of course."

"You what?" she exclaimed indignantly. "How? By hiring some tawdry private investigator to dig into my past?"

"On the contrary, I used a most reputable firm used to handling these matters for the upper classes."

"That makes it so much better," she said. "Why did you do that, Walter?"

"Because I am a person of wealth and position," he said. "Because men in my circumstances must be careful with whom they choose to spend their lives. If you and I are to continue on this journey, then I can't have any scandal. It may make for amusing anecdotes at dinner parties, but the peccadillos of one's youth must be set aside at a certain point, particularly for one of your sex."

"Should I have you investigated as well?" she asked. "I am also a person of wealth and position."

"I assure you that you'll find nothing of interest," he said.

"I'm starting to wish that I would," she said. "Well, you'll be glad to know that our involvement in this particular matter has ended. We have turned over the rest of the pursuit to the police."

"I'm relieved to hear it," he said. "But your associations with this sordid group must come to an end. I cannot show up at any gathering of influence with you on my arm if they continue."

"Is that how I matter to you?" she asked. "As something decorative?"

"No, of course not," he said hastily. "I apologise. I am still disappointed that you're not coming with me on New Year's Eve."

"I'm disappointed that you're not coming with me," she said. "My plans were in place, and they do involve my commercial enterprise, which I would think you of all people would understand."

"All that work to turn a profit of, what, not even a hundred pounds if you're fortunate?"

"That, and the publicity, goodwill, and future profit that it will bring."

"If you forego this venture, I could cover your company's losses easily."

"You shall do nothing of the kind," she said. "I will not disappoint our clientele who we have invested so much time recruiting.

The party goes on, and I will continue to work towards organising it. Which has been fun, Walter."

He took the article from her hand and held it up.

"You regard this as fun?" he asked.

"No, of course not. But that was not a consequence, or in any case a foreseen consequence—"

"You walked into a disreputable club owned by gangsters and failed to see that something dubious might come of that?"

"Also part of the fun," she said. "It's what you miss when you don't take risks. You took a risk when you backed me in Lunacy Court, for which I owe you my undying gratitude. You took an even larger one when you asked me out after that, despite my less than stellar past as a madwoman who prowls the dark corners of London investigating the unseemly side of existence. That uncharacteristic risk that you took was why I agreed to go out with you, and if you are going to retreat back into the safety of your previous life, so be it. But you cannot force me to retreat as well. I don't look for these situations, Walter, but I won't shy away from them, either. If you cannot accept that about me, then end this."

"That was not my purpose in coming here," he protested, looking stricken. "I was hoping to persuade you to change your mind about New Year's Eve."

"I'm busy that night," she said. "If you wish to impress me, cancel your plans with your influential friends, then show up at this disreputable club and dance with me."

"I can't," he said.

"Go back to work, Walter," she said wearily. "I need to get back to mine."

He took a step towards the stairwell, then stopped.

"I should have kissed you at the end of our date," he said.

"You should have," she agreed. "Why didn't you?"

"I didn't know what to do," he said disconsolately. "I lack experience."

"Dear God, forgive me," she said, then she stepped forward and kissed him.

He struggled for a moment, then thought better of it and acceded. She released him a few seconds later.

"It's like that, but with passion and feeling," she said. "Now you have experience. Do better with the next woman. Go back to work, Mr. Prendergast."

She turned and walked up the stairs. He watched as she turned the corners on the landing, then disappeared. Her footsteps receded into the upper floor. He heard a door open and close. Then there was silence.

He stood in place for a good long while, his hand slowly rising to his lips to see if they felt any different. Then he began the long descent back to the streets of London.

"Didn't go well, I take it," said Iris as Gwen collapsed into her chair.

"He disapproves of my chosen companions, my occupation, and my extracurricular activities," said Gwen. "My wildness was what attracted him, but now he wants to tame me so I can be properly presented at whatever boring financial functions he attends. He's thinking of me as an accessory."

"Funny, that's how the police think of me," said Iris.

"He actually had the nerve to suggest that I cancel the ball so I would be available New Year's Eve," said Gwen. "He offered to pay for our losses, can you believe it? And, yes, I am conscious of the irony of complaining about a wealthy person trying to buy his way into my affections when I've done similar things with you."

"I wasn't going to say anything," said Iris.

"You don't have to," said Gwen. "This is the universe providing me with some moral comeuppance. Forgive me again, and let's make this ball a smashing success so we can show everyone we were right."

"Done. And you're forgiven. Again."

"Thank you. Let's get back to work."

"I hadn't stopped working," said Iris. "You're the one who had the unannounced visitation from a possible boyfriend."

"No longer possible," said Gwen. "I kissed him goodbye and sent him out of my life."

"Good," said Iris, turning back to her index cards.

A minute later, a disturbing thought struck her. She turned to face Gwen.

"You didn't literally kiss him, did you?" she asked.

"Um, yes, I did," said Gwen shamefacedly. "I thought he should know what it was like."

"Always leave them wanting more," said Iris. "Are you keeping the door open in case he mends his ways?"

"No," said Gwen. "He wants too much."

"Right," said Iris. "Goodbye, Walter."

They returned to their work.

"Too much," Gwen muttered.

"Too much what?" asked Iris.

"Too much control in my life, not enough fun," said Gwen. "Hand me the telephone, would you?"

Iris passed it across, wondering who her partner was calling. Gwen consulted her address book, then dialled a number.

"Hello, River, is that you?" she asked. "It's Gwen. Are you free tonight?"

Iris's eyes grew wide in astonishment.

"Good," said Gwen. "Pick me up at five and take me somewhere with a better table so I can practise. Then we'll go to Brooke's and give this scheme a go. Shall we?"

She listened for a moment.

"Fine," she said. "I'll be in front of the office."

She hung up.

"You're going to Brooke's?" asked Iris. "With River?"

"Yes," said Gwen.

"But I thought we weren't going to continue investigating," said Iris.

"I'm not going to be investigating," said Gwen. "I'm going there to have some fun. Maybe lose control with someone for a change."

"Playing snooker?"

"Yes."

"What is this scheme you mentioned?"

"I'll tell you all about it tomorrow," said Gwen.

Iris's curiosity over Gwen's evening grew steadily over the course of the day, but her partner gave her no further details of her intentions. Around four thirty, Lily Alderton rang from the hospital.

"What's the latest?" asked Iris.

"He hasn't woken up yet, I'm sorry to say," said Lily, "but they're moving him out of critical care."

"They are? That has to be a good sign, doesn't it?"

"I don't know," said Lily. "The doctor said they had him stabilised, but they can't say when he'll wake up, or if he'll wake up, or what he'll be like if he wakes up. What if he stays like this? What if his brain was damaged?"

"All we can do is hope for the best," said Iris. "The doctors have got him this far, so that's good."

"I suppose it is," said Lily. "Oh, and I finally got them to put you on the visitors' list. You'll have to show your ident at the front desk, and again to the security fellow guarding his room."

"Wonderful! Thank you for doing that. I'll come by after work tonight. Will you still be there?"

"I'll be here until they throw me out," said Lily.

"Then I'll be landing next to you," said Iris. "I'll see you there." She hung up.

"Good news, I hope," said Gwen.

"They're moving him to a regular room," said Iris. "I'm going to be able to see him at last, even if he doesn't know I'm there."

"He'll know," said Gwen. "And it will help him."

"I wish I had your belief in higher powers," said Iris.

"I hope the higher powers cast a blind eye on me tonight," said Gwen.

"Isn't there a line about punishment for snooker somewhere in Gilbert and Sullivan? Something about elliptical billiard balls?"

"It's in *Mikado,* and it's for a billiard sharp, not us poor, innocent snookerists," said Gwen, getting up from her chair. "Anyhow, I'm off. Give my regards to Lily and a kiss to Archie. I'm so glad you're finally getting to see him."

"Thank you," said Iris. "And thank you for talking me through everything today."

"Talking is easy," said Gwen. "Thank you for listening. I'll see you tomorrow."

She put on her coat, hat, and scarf, then left with one final wave.

She had to wait only a few minutes before River pulled up in his Riley Merlin. He got out to open the door for her.

"Evil Gwen reporting for duty," she said as she got in.

"That's the one I want," he said as he slid behind the wheel.

"I think we should practise at a place where the baize is decent this time," she said. "I would imagine Brooke's keeps their tables in good shape."

"They do," he said. "And I'm going to let you use my stick so you can get the feel of it."

"I am honoured," she said.

He drove north this time, taking her into Spitalfields where he parked on Wilkes Street, the smokestack of the Black Eagle Brewery looming ahead of them.

"I'm guessing the beer will be better at this place," she said.

"It is, but don't overindulge," he warned her. "I need you sober tonight."

"I won't get potted before potting," she said. "But you'd better buy me a decent drink afterwards if we pull this off."

"I will, Evil Gwen," he said.

The tables here were much better. Rather than playing a full game, he started placing balls at various points on the table, then handed her his cue stick.

"The two most likely side bets come from long pots or escaping snookers," he said. "We'll practise both. How's the cue feel?"

"Fine," she said. "It's a Peradon. That's what we had at home."

He started her with some unobstructed long shots, then started putting other balls near the lines of approach. After a while, she was making a good percentage of them.

"Nicely done," he said. "Now let's see how good you are at wriggling out of trouble."

She shimmied for a second, and he grinned in response. Then he took the cue ball and placed it behind the brown so there was no direct path to the reds at the other end of the table. She struck the cue ball away from the brown, bouncing it off the cushions at the corner. It rolled past the blue, narrowly missing it before bouncing off the cushions at the corner at the other end, slowly coming to a halt resting against one of the reds in the pack.

"Absolutely beautiful," he said.

He was looking at her, not the table, she noticed. She didn't mind that at all.

"Let's make it more difficult," he said.

This time, he set up the cue ball in front of the corner pocket and placed the yellow in front of it. She studied them for a minute. She had to get the cue ball out from behind the yellow without touching it, and still get enough power behind the shot to strike one of the reds. There was a narrow margin to one side of the yellow. She positioned the tip of the stick to strike the cue ball high and off-centre. It sneaked past the yellow, spinning madly, then ricocheted crazily off the cushion. The spin took over, sending it down the table to collide with a red ball.

"I think you're ready," he said. "It's a half-hour drive to Brooke's from here. The bloke I'm looking for usually strolls in around seven. Oh, and I have something for you in the car."

"What?" she asked.

"You'll see."

When they reached the car, he opened the boot and pulled out a hatbox.

"You bought me a hat?" she asked, laughing.

"Not quite," he said, opening it to reveal a brunette wig. "There could be a fellow or two there from Spelling's warehouse who might recognise you. But not as a brunette."

"What fun!" she said.

They got into the car and she put on the wig, using the rearview mirror as a guide while she poked errant strands of her blond hair under until she was satisfied.

"If I had known I was going to be a brunette, I would have worn a different outfit," she said. "What do you think?"

"You're equally gorgeous as a brunette," he said.

She threw her arms around his neck and kissed him.

"Let's go get him," she whispered fervently.

"Kiss me like that again, and I'll skip the snooker and take you straight back to my place," he said.

"After," she said.

"Yeah? You mean it?"

"I mean it. Let's go teach him a lesson."

"Duty calls," he said with an exaggerated sigh as he started the car. "Right, so the mark's name is Oscar Holliday. He'll be strutting around, wearing his waistcoat unbuttoned, usually with some floozy in tow. I'm going to challenge him to a two-out-of-three match for ten quid. The side bet could come at any point, so pay attention. My signal for a possibility will be to look at you while I'm holding my stick with my middle finger crossed over my index finger, like this."

He demonstrated with his left hand on the steering wheel.

"Got it?" he asked.

"Got it," she said.

"Now, if you think you can make the shot, hold your right hand so your middle finger is touching the index. If you don't, have it touching the ring finger instead. Let me see you do each."

"If I can," she said, holding up her hand with her fingers in the first position. Then she changed them. "And if I can't."

"Perfect," he said.

"It's subtle. I like it."

"That's the point," he said. "Now, if you have any doubt at all about making the shot, don't give me the positive sign. We'll have only one chance for this, and I want it to work."

"How much are you wagering on the side bet?"

"Fifty quid."

Gwen whistled appreciatively.

"Do you think he'll take a bet that size?"

"Trust me, I'll have him ready, willing, and able."

River parked a hundred feet from their destination, the nose of the car pointed away from the entrance.

"Might have to make a quick exit after I've taken his money," he explained. "In fact, if things get noisy, you slip out ahead of me and I'll meet you by the car."

"What if you don't make it out?"

"You're an optimistic one, aren't you? In that case, the Mile End station is the closest one."

Brooke's Snooker Club, unlike the others she had been to with River, wasn't shy about advertising its whereabouts. The name was emblazoned in red neon letters over a double door painted the same shade of green as the baize of a snooker table. A formidable-looking bouncer stood in front, blowing on his hands in the cold.

"Evening, Hector," said River affably as they strolled up. "Good pickings tonight?"

"If there's anyone to be picked, they've probably been cleaned out already," said the bouncer. "You know the drill."

"Of course," said River, holding out his arms.

Hector patted him down quickly, then looked inside his case.

"You're good," he said.

"Ta," said River as Hector opened the door.

They went in, Gwen glancing around the room. It was larger than most halls, accommodating twenty tables, only half of which were in use. There was a long bar at one side with four-legged wooden stools with squared seats that looked like they could be wielded quickly in a brawl. Coats hung on a double row of hooks set in the wall to their right. There were three rows of bleachers against the wall opposite the bar, allowing spectators a view of the action. Photographs of players past hung on every available space.

"Let me get your coat, Mabel," said River.

"Thanks, love," said Gwen as she removed it.

He hung it on a hook in the middle of the row of coats, then hung his next to it.

"The loudmouth holding forth at the end of the bar," he muttered. "He's got a blonde with him."

"Are you going straight at him, or are you planning to work your way up?"

"I figure he's already seen me," said River. "No time like the present. Let's go."

He took Gwen's arm, then walked boldly up to where Holliday stood. The latter watched him approach, his grin broadening.

"Well, well, look who's come back for another beating," said Holliday. "Brought your mum along for protection, didjer?"

"You know, if it came to actual blows, I bet she'd clean your clock quite handily," said River, looking at Gwen appreciatively. "Given how you've never had to fight anyone for real in your life. Or did you take on the Nazis from in here, you half-pint hero?"

"Listen to the soldier boy trying to impress his girl," Holliday said to the blonde. "Think it's working on her?"

"Doubt it," said the blonde. "It wouldn't work on me."

"It's a shame, that," said Holliday to River. "Maybe once I show her what you really are, she can join us for a proper party after. What do you say, Toots?"

"The name's Mabel," said Gwen. "Call me Toots again and I'll show you what manners are like where I'm from."

Did a better job with the accent this time, she thought. Nobody gave her any odd looks.

"Enough small talk," said River. "I'm here to win my money back."

"You think you're worth my time?" scoffed Holliday.

"I'm doubling the bet," said River. "Ten quid. Two out of three."

"Ten, is it?" said Holliday. "Tell you what. Ten it is and a kiss from your bride-to-be to make it interesting."

"What do you say to that?" River asked Gwen.

"It wouldn't be that interesting," she replied, looking at Holliday with disdain. "But it won't happen, so sure, throw that in."

"Do I get to kiss him, then?" asked the blonde hopefully.

"I'll pass, thanks," said River. "I wouldn't want to set you up for a life of disappointment after."

"Oh, ha bloody ha," she said.

"I'm taking my usual table, Fred," Holliday called to the bartender, who took a piece of chalk and put a check mark in a box next to the number eight.

That's going to be a table whose imperfections are known to him, guessed Gwen. Where every untrue bounce will work against River. And me.

River took his stick from his case and screwed the two pieces together, then took a coin out of his pocket.

"Heads," said Holliday.

River flipped it.

"Tails," he said.

He chalked the tip, then turned to Gwen with a mischievous glint in his eyes.

"How about a kiss for luck?" he said.

"Cheeky boy," she replied, coming up to him.

She kissed him softly as men hooted from around the room, then blew the dust from the tip of the cue as he held it up in front of her.

He played carefully the first game, learning the table as he did, making no attempts at the side bet. Holliday, with his better familiarity, went ahead with his second break, but a poorly played safety allowed River to pull within a few points. Nevertheless, he missed a crucial long shot on the last red, leaving Holliday to pot it and the remaining colours for the win.

"You've been practising, I see," said Holliday as River reset the table.

"I have."

"You needed it," said Holliday.

"Shut up and break," said River.

This time, River knocked in a long pot and kept the cue ball around the black, allowing him to knock in one ball after another, stalking the table like a panther. By the time he missed one, the game was his. Holliday didn't even bother to leave his seat. He wasn't smiling anymore.

The blonde had sidled over to where Gwen was standing, watching the match intently.

"Your lad's pretty good," she muttered. "He should be careful."

"What do you mean?" asked Gwen.

"You don't want to show up the local hero," she said, nodding her head slightly towards the bar, where a number of men had gathered, watching the game unfold with interest.

"Your man never lost before?" asked Gwen.

"He loses. He doesn't like it much, especially when it's to a younger man. Word to the wise."

She ambled back over to Holliday, patting him on the shoulder.

"Rubber match," said River as he reset the table. "Exciting, isn't it? Playing with me breathing down your neck. You're not used to that, are you, mate?"

"I'm not your mate, boy," said Holliday. "Tell your girl to freshen up her lipstick."

This will be the frame, thought Gwen, leaning forward to watch the path of each ball, noting a scratch in the baize on the left side, an odd bounce off the baulk rail at one spot. The two players were eyeing each other after every shot, River with an insolent smirk, spinning his cue cockily when he put the pink in the left centre pocket, then following with a safety that put the cue ball far from the reds scattered about at unmakeable spots on the table.

"Oh, dear, did I leave you with nothing?" he said. "So sorry, mate."

Holliday studied the table carefully, then sighted along his cue and struck.

"When you've got nothing," he said, "give your opponent less than nothing."

The cue ball ticked off a red, bounced off the far cushion, then travelled all the way back to bounce off the baulk cushion, coming in just behind the brown, which blocked all direct access to the reds. The men watching from the bar gave a raucous cheer.

"Let's see you get out of that one—mate," said Holliday with a sneer.

There was a way, Gwen saw. Not only to escape the snooker but to keep the break going. Two of the reds were touching in a way where if one was hit at just the right angle, the other would cannon into the corner pocket. But to get the angle, River would not only have to bounce it off two cushions, but thread the needle between two of the coloured balls without touching either.

Makeable, she thought. Does he see it?

River looked at the table, then glanced at Gwen.

His fingers were crossed on the hand holding the cue stick. Her hands were down at her sides, the middle finger on her right touching the index.

"Tell you what," said River. "I'll bet you twenty-five quid that I get out of that jam and pot a red into the bargain."

"The cannon into the corner?" replied Holliday. "Not a chance. You're not that good."

"Then it's free money for you, isn't it?" said River. "Or are you afraid maybe I am that good?"

"Your mouth is larger than your talents, boy," said Holliday.

"Oh, I don't know," said River. "It's not that hard a pot. In fact, I bet even my girl could make it."

"Her? That piece of—"

"Careful now," warned River. "She's got a temper."

"You're saying twenty-five quid on her making that pot?"

"If it's her taking the shot, I'll bet you fifty quid," said River. "One chance. On my girl."

Holliday turned to stare at Gwen, then walked over until his face was inches from hers.

"Who are you, then?" he asked. "Joe Davis in drag?"

"I'm the woman you'll never get to kiss," said Gwen calmly.

Holliday looked at her, then back at River.

"Tell you what," he said. "Let's make it a hundred quid, only my girl takes this shot. If she makes it, I get to pick one of mine for your girl to take later, and that one will be for the money. How about that, my lad?"

For the first time since they came in, River's swagger faded slightly.

"Let us have a moment," he said.

"Take your time," said Holliday.

River motioned Gwen over to the wall by the end of the bleacher seats.

"Wasn't expecting that," he said softly. "But this could still work."

"It could," agreed Gwen.

"The problem is if it doesn't, I don't have a hundred quid to my name," said River. "I'll need you to back me on this. All right?"

Gwen glanced back at Holliday and his girl, who were watching them avidly.

"No," said Gwen. "Not all right."

"What?"

"Count me out," said Gwen. "The game is over."

"What do you mean?" asked River, puzzled. "There's still a frame to finish."

"I mean your game, River," said Gwen. "It's done. And so are we."

CHAPTER 14

W hat're you talking about?" asked River.

"What's she talking about?" Holliday asked his girl.

"Shut up and maybe we'll find out," she replied.

"I'm usually good at knowing when people are lying to me," Gwen said to River. "But you've been a special case. You've been lying to me so much that it's been difficult to know when you're telling the truth."

"What makes you—" he began.

"Stop," she said wearily. "When I studied with Uncle Joe, he didn't just teach me about the game of snooker. He also taught me about the games around the game. One of his lessons was if someone asks you to join a con, the odds are good that the mark is really you."

"So this was a scam," said Holliday angrily. "I knew it!"

"Of course you knew it," said Gwen. "You were part of it. More important, so was she."

"Me?" protested the blonde.

"Blackpool, 1932," said Gwen.

The blonde blinked.

"We were there for summer holiday," continued Gwen. "The casino was holding a ladies' tournament as a publicity stunt. I was fourteen and obsessed with the game, so I begged my father to take me. Since they made the women play in bathing suits and high heels, he had no objection at all to going. The outfits may have been ludicrous, but the players were top-notch. The final was between Ellen Sealy and Daisy Pinkins, and they played to a draw. Pinkins won the toss, and knocked in the black on her first shot for the win. It was a marvellous game, Miss Sealy."

"Thanks," said the blonde, whose expression had changed from indignation to a sad, resigned smile during the course of Gwen's reminiscence. "Glad you caught me in my prime."

"I'm sure you're still quite good," said Gwen. "That was the plan, wasn't it, River? Rope me into your righteous scheme as a ringer, get me to back you for a large bet you couldn't afford, then bring in a better ringer to make sure we lose and I end up covering the hundred pounds when it turns out you didn't have the scratch yourself. Unfortunately, I recognised Miss Sealy. Does that sound about right?"

"When did you make me?" asked Sealy.

"Early on," said Gwen. "I was waiting to see how River was going to play it after that. I must say, Mr. Holliday, you did show me what he really was. I don't think I'll be joining your party, though. Thanks for the invitation."

She turned and walked away. River followed her.

"Gwen," he began.

"Not another word," she said, her fury rising. "This was supposed to be fun tonight, and you destroyed it. I guess you were getting back at me for showing you up at Archie's. I could have been yours tonight, River. I was ready to throw caution to the wind for the first time in years, but now you've lost both me and the hundred pounds. Well played. Now, go finish the frame. Maybe you can actually beat him without me. I really don't care much at this point."

"But—"

"That was another word," she said. "Were you not listening? Get away from me."

She turned her back on him, staring moodily at the photos on the wall. She sensed him standing there for a few seconds more, then he walked back to the table.

Not wanting to give anyone the satisfaction of seeing her face, she focused on the pictures. This section was devoted not to players, but to a gorgeous young woman, first seen striking amateurish dance poses in a series of chorus girl outfits, some of which were little more than some strategically placed ostrich plumes. Then there was a wedding photo with her next to a man who had to be thirty years her senior, followed by the two of them standing with their arms spread in welcome in front of Brooke's, with bunting overhead proclaiming "Grand Opening!" On the margin at the bottom, someone had written "June 12, 1912."

"I was quite the beaut once, wasn't I?" remarked someone standing behind her.

Gwen turned to see a woman wearing a deep red gown covered with sequins, a few of which were missing, and a matching jacket. She was thicker about the waist and the bust, and her hair colour now had assistance, but there was no mistaking the face of the woman from the photographs.

"I would say you're more beautiful now," said Gwen.

"Ah, they raised you proper polite at home," said the woman.

"You're Mrs. Reese, I take it."

"Vanessa, please," she said. "And who might you be? You're a new face around here."

"I'm Mabel Dodge," said Gwen. "You're right, it's my first time."

"Welcome to my club, Mabel," said Reese. "I just heard about what they tried to pull on you. I hope you don't hold that against us. It's a fine place if you like to play, and I take it you do."

"Yes, I do," said Gwen. "I'd come back, but I don't like going to clubs unescorted, and I'm not going anywhere with that bloke anytime soon."

"Are you any good?" Reese asked curiously.

"Pretty good," said Gwen.

"What's your highest break?"

"Alone, or in front of people?"

"Ah, everyone shoots the maximum when no one's looking," said Reese with a laugh. "Against a flesh and blood opponent in front of a crowd, of course."

"Eighty-three," said Gwen. "It was at a party, and some gent was spouting off about how no woman could ever take on a man in snooker. So naturally, I did."

"Naturally," said Reese. "He mistook you for a sweet young thing."

"Oh, but I was," said Gwen, her voice high and breathy. "He didn't learn the truth until I had his money."

"Hah! I love it!" said Reese. "Tell you what, dearie. I've been thinking of starting a ladies' night here on Wednesdays. Half off at the tables, and once a month we'll stage a tournament. You interested?"

"I am," said Gwen.

"We'd want the girls dressed to, you know, show off a little," continued Reese. "Get the gentlemen coming in to watch. I think you could do very well if you can play."

"Oh, I don't know if I'm the type the gents will come to see," said Gwen.

"Come off it," said Reese. "You could get in as a Windmill Girl with your figger."

"I'd rather stick to snooker, thanks," said Gwen. "When are you starting this?"

"I want to see you play first," said Reese. "Up for an audition?"

"I don't want to play anywhere near them, if you don't mind," said Gwen, nodding in the direction of her three would-be scammers.

"Perfectly understandable," said Reese. "Come with me. I'll open up the VIP lounge. It will be just the two of us with no prying eyes."

Gwen followed her to a pair of doors with a mahogany plaque

with brass letters over them jauntily labelling the room beyond as the VIP lounge. Reese pulled a key from somewhere inside her jacket and unlocked them.

The mahogany theme continued in the interior, on recessed panels on the walls and a small bar whose shelves held a better selection than the one available to the general public. There was a card table in a corner and thick, plush-cushioned sofas along the walls. The photographs here were nicely framed, each an annual club champion holding up a cheap-looking trophy. The last three were of Holliday, she noticed.

The snooker table was in the dead centre of the room, the balls already laid out for play.

"Grab a stick and warm up," said Reese. "I have to let my manager know I'm using the room. I'll be right back."

"All right," said Gwen.

Reese left, closing the doors behind her. Gwen hefted the available cue sticks until she found one that suited her. She took some practise shots using the three colours on the baulk line so she wouldn't disturb the racked balls at the other end. There were chalks on a sideboard by the wall of champions. She went over and grabbed one, glancing over the photos, all of which included Vanessa and Frankie Reese on either side of that year's champion, until the last few years where it was only Vanessa. You could see the Reeses aging, she thought as she perused them. Or getting younger, depending which direction you chose. Some of the champions she recognised. Her mentor, Joe Davis, had won a few in the early thirties, probably paid to participate by the Reeses. She went back to the twenties, then stopped as something caught her eye.

In the crowd to the side, saluting the 1921 champion with an upraised pint . . . wasn't that Stanley Spelling?

It was, she thought, as she looked more closely. And Des's dad next to him, with someone who could have been Jenks, his face partially obscured.

Could the fourth crew member have been someone in that crowd? she wondered. Maybe she could ask Mrs. Reese when she came back. Or whoever was the champion that year, if she could find him. She glanced over to where their names were engraved on thin brass plates, following them back to that year. She nearly jumped when she came to it.

She turned back to examine the photo, leaning in to see his hands. As she did, she heard the door open behind her. She turned, expecting to see Mrs. Reese. She was there, smiling.

But she wasn't alone.

River, Holliday, and Sealy were standing behind her, none of them looking happy about it. The source of their unhappiness was evident. Hector, the bouncer from the front, and two other impressively large, muscular men were standing behind them, gripping their hands behind their backs.

"Hello again," said Mrs. Reese. "Time we all had a little chat."

There were two bus lines that ran along Oxford Street and on through the city to the East End. It was rush hour, and Iris had to let three go by before she could cram into one. She paid for a one-way ticket to Whitechapel. The clippie punched it, and she wedged her way in between businessmen in suits, workmen in coveralls, and secretaries and switchboard operators trying to fend off all of them. She grabbed onto the top of a seat to steady herself as the bus lurched forward.

She was tired and frustrated. Without the tunnel vision of the investigation to drive her, she had nothing left to ward off the horrors of the last few days. Even the constant grinding of the bus's gears and the squealing of its brakes failed to drown out her internal soundtrack of Christmas crackers going off, the image of Archie's expectant grin changing to a grimace of pain as the bullet struck.

She wondered how much further Florey had got since she spoke with him. Military records from the Great War would not be as easily accessible as those from the current one, which required constant updating with demobilisation going on. And then to follow up with each possibility—

Gwen had been right about ceding this to the police, she realised with chagrin. It was her own desire for revenge and, she was forced to admit, to be the heroine of her own story that blinded her to that. As smart as she was, as successful as she had been on these adventures, she was still only one woman. Or two, when Gwen worked with her. But it was time to be sensible about things.

She hated being sensible about things.

And Gwen, having been a pillar of Virtue and Moderation in the last few days, had done a bunk the moment things came to a close, abandoning her best friend to go off and have fun with some lowlife sharp.

The best friend who was now taking the slow bus to see the lowlife's boss. Her lover. So who was she to judge?

Don't begrudge Gwen her fun tonight, she thought. There is so little to be had, and life, as has been demonstrated far too often lately, is short. You've been on the shelf for years, Gwen, so have yourself a fling or two. We're still young. Youngish. Under thirty. Plenty of time to settle down later.

Or sooner, she thought, remembering the ring, still in its box, burrowing into the depths of her bag.

Crackers went off in her head again. She saw the small box toppling out of the one connecting her to Archie, and somewhere above the rear of the stage must have been a pop slightly louder than all the rest of them.

Atrocious timing, that. The assailant should have had the decency to wait for the proposal to be made, the acceptance given. Assuming she would have accepted.

Back to that again.

Maybe the assailant saved her from making the biggest mistake of her life.

Whichever way she would have decided.

Damn it.

The memory of the shooting replayed in her mind for the entire trip, and by the time she got off in front of the Whitechapel Road Market, she was skittish and exhausted. A backfire from a passing lorry nearly sent her diving for cover, but she got hold of her nerves and made it across the thoroughfare to the hospital.

Why can't I let it go? she thought as she went inside. I'm doing no one any good by obsessing over it at this point. There's too much noise going on in my brain. Although maybe the crackers are drowning out even worse thoughts I haven't dredged up yet.

The shooter was lucky he had the crackers covering for him, she thought.

Then she stopped dead in her tracks for a moment, following that idea.

The receptionist looked up as she approached, pulling her ident from her bag.

"Archie Spelling," Iris said, showing it to her. "I'm Iris Sparks. I should be on the visitors' list."

"Right, you are," said the receptionist, consulting a clipboard. "He's in three oh seven. It's in the rear."

Iris took the lift up to Archie's floor, then followed the corridors to the southeastern corner of the building. Archie's room was easy to spot. It was the one with a very alert man standing by the door. He was wearing a brown suit that bulged slightly by the left lapel of his jacket.

He looked at her suspiciously as she walked up, then relaxed when she showed him her ident.

"They told me you were on the list," he said. "Go on in. Mrs. Alderton is with him."

Iris took a deep breath, then walked into the room.

He seemed smaller, was her first thought. Archie lay on the

bed, an IV running fluid into his arm from a bottle hung on a metal post next to him, rubber tubes coming out of his chest dripping into a metal container hanging on the lower bar of the bed rail. His breathing was torturous, a wet rasp that frightened her the moment she heard it.

But he was still breathing.

Lily looked up from a chair next to the bed when Iris came in, and immediately got up to hug her. Iris allowed it, welcomed it, in fact, and the two of them stood like that for a minute, rocking gently.

"It's terrible what they did to 'im," said Lily when they finally let go. "I keep seeing 'im when 'e was a little one, before everything went so 'orribly wrong. I remember 'ow 'e'd smile at Mum when she gave 'im a sweet, 'ow 'e'd shriek when Dad picked 'im up and tossed 'im in the air and caught 'im again. I want someone to catch 'im now."

Iris sat on the edge of Archie's bed, stroking his hair back from his forehead, then leaned down to put her lips by his ear.

"I'm here, Archie," she whispered. "I'm with you again. I've missed you so much."

There was no noticeable reaction from him.

"I've been talking to 'im," said Lily. "I know 'e can 'ear us. I'm sure of it. I'm so glad they moved 'im in 'ere. They were going to put him in a large room with others, but Reg kicked up a fuss, told them to put 'im in one of the single rooms or there'd be 'ell to pay. You can't really see it now, but there's a bit of a view out the window. It'll be nice for him to have the sunlight coming in."

"Yes, it will," said Iris, glancing out the window at the other side of the bed. "I'm going to go use the lav. I'll be back in a few minutes."

"All right, dear," said Lily.

Iris left the room and approached the security guard.

"I need you to do something," she said. "And I need you to do it now."

"A chat about what?" asked Gwen.

She was gripping the cue stick tightly. Hector saw it, she realised as she glanced back and forth at the group. He shook his head slightly, and she loosened her grip.

You can't take on all three of them, she thought. Find out what this is about, then talk your way out of it.

"You three, on the couch," directed Reese.

River, Holliday, and Sealy sat down as two of the men took positions on either side. Hector closed the doors and locked them, then turned to face the room, his arms folded across his chest.

Reese went behind the bar, took down a bottle of scotch, and poured herself two fingers. She didn't offer anyone else a drink. She took a sip, closed her eyes in appreciation for a moment, then looked up at Gwen.

"Something you should know about my club," she said. "It's all I have now. It's my livelihood, my home, my life. So anything that threatens the club threatens me, understand, girlie?"

"Of course, Mrs. Reese," said Gwen.

"Now, if you intend to play here, there are rules to be followed," continued Reese. "One is that if any cons get run, I get ten percent."

"That's fair," said Gwen.

"And if I find out that one is being run without word to me, there's a penalty," she said. "Two penalties, in fact. Oscar, tell her what they are."

"Vanessa, I swear we were going to cut you in," he said, looking sick.

"Another rule is when I tell you to do something in my club, you do it," said Reese. "Tell her, Oscar."

"You get banished from the club," said Holliday.

"And?" she prompted him. "Before that?"

"You get a finger broke," he said glumly.

"That's the other one," said Vanessa.

"Look, they didn't get anything from me," said Gwen. "There's no need for this."

"Listen to her, trying to save them after what they done," Reese commented. "This isn't about you, dearie. This is about them. And me. The rules are rules, and my decree is final. Now, we still have to talk about you."

"Me?" gulped Gwen.

"You came in here to con someone," said Reese. "That was the idea, wasn't it?"

Gwen didn't respond. Reese's smile vanished.

"I asked you a direct question," she said.

"Yes," said Gwen. "Yes, I did."

"Now, it's your first time here, and you didn't know the rules, so I'm going to give you a pass. But only this once."

"Thank you, Mrs. Reese."

"But you're going to watch while we execute the sentences," said Reese.

Gwen looked at the three conspirators' faces. Holliday was turning paler by the second. Sealy had tears running down her cheeks. River looked at her steadily, then mouthed, "I'm sorry."

"Is this truly necessary?" Gwen asked desperately. "Is there no other way of resolving this?"

"I'm afraid not, dearie," said Reese, motioning to the two men by the couch.

"I'll play you for them," said Gwen.

"Mabel, don't!" River said immediately.

Reese looked at her, trying to read her expression.

"Why should I agree to that?" she asked.

"You wanted to see how I play under pressure," said Gwen. "This is pressure beyond any money on the table. If I win, they leave unharmed."

"And if you lose?" asked Reese. "What then? Is it double or nothing? Do I break two of their fingers?"

"No, of course not," said Gwen.

"It's really not pressure if you don't have anything of your own at stake," said Reese. "I admire your pluck, Mabel, I really do, but you have to come up with something better than that to make it interesting."

"Your ten percent if they had taken me."

"That's ten pounds, dearie. My principles are worth more than that. Tell you what, how about another broken finger?"

"I don't think they should be—"

"I mean one of yours," said Reese.

Gwen automatically glanced down at her hands, then slowly looked back up at Reese.

"It's a bet," she said. "You and me, one frame."

"Oh, I'm not taking these off for the likes of you," said Reese, holding up her hands, which boasted rings on eight of her fingers. "I'll pick someone from out there."

"That wasn't the bet."

"Start with Oscar," said Reese, and the two men moved in on him.

"Wait!" cried Gwen.

They stopped.

"Fine," said Gwen. "Choose your champion."

"You're lucky, girl," said Reese. "The best player here is sitting on the couch waiting to get his finger broke, so you'll have to play against the runner-up. Hector, who's the second-best player in the house tonight?"

"Keef came in a little while ago."

"Perfect," said Reese. "We'll have this little exhibition in the main room while the rest of you stay put. I don't want anyone in here to give him the nod."

"Let her use my stick," said River.

"Is that what you want?" Reese asked Gwen.

"Yes, actually," replied Gwen.

"Very well," said Reese.

"Could I say something to her?" asked River.

"She's got your stick. That's all she needs from you," said Reese.

"I want to apologise to her," said River. "Shake her hand good-bye while I can still use it."

"Go ahead," said Reese.

Gwen reluctantly went over to River.

"You don't need to do this," he said. "I'll heal."

"So will I, if it comes down to it," said Gwen. "Goodbye."

"Good luck," he said, taking her hand between his and pressing something into it.

He released her. Hector opened the door, and she walked into the main room, Reese following her closely. Gwen glanced down at the object in her hand.

It was River's lucky stickpin.

She pinned it to her frock over her heart, then went over to the table where their evening had first begun. She set up the balls, then picked up River's cue.

"I'm ready," she said.

Hector was speaking to a man at the bar who glanced over at Gwen and grinned wolfishly. He picked up his case and came over.

"Hello, Mrs. Reese," he said, taking her hand and kissing it. "You're looking ravishing as usual."

"Cut the flattery," said Reese. "This is Mabel. She thinks she can play snooker."

"With looks like that, she doesn't need to," he said with a leer. "Hello, Mabel. What are we playing for?"

"Mabel already has a bet going with me," said Reese. "You're playing to keep me happy. One frame."

"At your command," said Keef. "Where's Oscar? This is his table. Isn't that his stick?"

"It is," said Hector, taking it. "I'll bring it to him."

"He doesn't like me playing this table when he's not here," said Keef.

"That won't be a problem," said Reese. "Get on with it."

Keef shrugged, then produced a shilling from his waistcoat pocket.

"Heads," said Gwen.

He flipped it. It was tails.

"Here we go, then," he said, placing the cue ball between the yellow and brown.

He used a standard break, the cue ticking off the right corner of the rack before bouncing back past its point of origin. Two reds separated from the pack, one on each side, both coming to rest against the rails.

"Let's see what you got," he said to Gwen.

He doesn't normally use this table, she thought. And I've had nearly an hour to study it.

Use that, Gwen.

She glanced at the scratch on the baize on the left side. If she could lure him into thinking he could make a long pot, and he missed, then she would be in good position for that end of the table. She wanted to get as far ahead as early in the game as she could.

Right, she thought, sighting down her cue at the left side of the remaining pack. She struck the cue ball. It bounced off the pack, freeing more of the red balls. The cue ball bounced off the far end of the table, then came back to rest to the left of the green. One of the reds stopped eight inches from the corner.

"Great, Mabel," she muttered in chagrin. "You gave him a gift."

At some point in every game, one has to chance potting a long shot, and she had just given him that chance. Only the scratch in the baize lay between him and the target ball.

He saw it, of course, but the overall clumsy appearance of her shot encouraged him.

"Looks like this will be a quick one," he said as he took his shot.

He sent the cue ball down the length of the table, its path taking it over the scratch, which caused it to deviate by a fraction of an inch from its intended destination. It was enough to cause the red to rattle between the jaws of the corner pocket and stop short of the precipice.

Keef looked at it irritably.

"I gave you an easy one," he grumbled.

"Very kind of you," she said.

She used the bridge to knock it in, gently bouncing the cue ball off the far rail to line up the black for the opposite corner.

Then she went to work.

Remember to breathe, girl, came Joe Davis's voice in her mind. *Keep your head as low to the table as you can.*

"Black, right corner," she said.

In it went. Keef replaced it.

Methodically, easily, she cleared the freed reds below the pack, adding the black each time. On the last one, she sent the ball up to the middle of the table to pick off the blue, then one errant red that thought it could escape in that direction. By the time she missed a shot, she had accumulated fifty-three points.

"She's got a decent short game," commented Keef as they switched places. "All low-hanging fruit so far. Should be enough left on the table for me."

There were eight remaining reds for him to work with. He potted seven, adding six blacks and a pink to pull ahead of her by two. He finished with a safety that left the last red two inches from the far cushion and equidistant from the corners, with the cue ball at the other end of the table.

She had no choice but to play a safety shot. She tried to think of what she could do to inconvenience him, what other faults in the table were available.

There was that spot on the baulk cushion that had the odd bounce to it. If she could force him to use that and miss the red, she could pick up four points on the foul.

She was going to need speed and the right angle. And a great deal of luck.

She reached up and touched River's stickpin for a moment, then settled behind the cue ball.

Breathe.

Stay low.

Strike.

The cue sped down the table, glanced off the red, then banged off the corner rails. It rolled back to Gwen as if it had free will and self-control, bounced in front of her, and came to a stop. The yellow ball, which had sat in its spot doing absolutely nothing, was now in a direct line between the cue ball and the surviving red.

Keef looked at the alignment, then over at Reese.

"Now, that was a very good shot," he said.

"It was," agreed Reese, glaring at Gwen. "How come I've never heard of you before, Mabel Dodge?"

"It's been a lamp-under-a-bushel sort of existence for me," said Gwen.

"More like a wig than a bushel, if you ask me," said Reese. "Get out from behind there, Keef, and finish her off."

"Said like someone who doesn't play the game," said Keef, examining the table. "But where there's a rail, there's a way."

He stood by the corner, aiming at the baulk cushion, intending to bank the cue between the green and brown to tap the red. But when he struck, the cue ball hit the defective spot and clicked off the green ball for a foul. He leaned forward in dismay, catching himself with his hands on the rail, then looked up at Gwen. She came over to the table and slowly slid four counters over to her side with the cue.

"Fifty-seven and my shot, I believe," she said.

She potted the last red in the side pocket, then sent the blue into the other side, spinning the cue ball towards the baulk line.

"Looks like you've got it," said Keef.

"Don't count your chickens before they hatch," she said. "Aesop, I think, but good advice in snooker."

She took a breath, then potted the yellow, the green, and the brown for nine more points, bringing her to seventy-two. She had a seventeen-point lead with eighteen points left on the table.

Don't get overexcited, she thought. Don't overthink it, either.

She tapped the cue ball softly. It connected with the blue, which matter-of-factly hit the middle of the side pocket and dropped from sight.

"I concede," said Keef.

"I won't bother with the last two," she said. "Thanks for the game, Keef."

"Give us your number," he said immediately.

"Sorry," she said. "I've given up dating snooker players. Did I pass the audition, Mrs. Reese?"

Reese turned to Hector and nodded. He went over to the doors to the VIP lounge, stuck his head inside, and said something. She turned back to Gwen and waved, her rings glittering in the bright overhead light.

"Get your coat and get out of here," said Reese. "Don't come back."

"I wasn't planning to," said Gwen.

She unscrewed River's cue and packed it. Then she grabbed her coat, hat, and scarf and walked out. Hector held the door for her and gave her a quick, surreptitious nod of approval as she passed him.

She stood across the street and waited until River, Holliday, and Sealy came out. Holliday immediately walked away to the east. Sealy gave her a long, sad look, then followed. River stood stock-still.

She held up the case with his cue stick and beckoned to him.

He crossed to join her. She handed over the case, then held up his stickpin.

"Keep it," he said. "You already won it, and it's worked better for you than it has for me tonight. I take it you won."

"I did," she said. "I didn't hear any screaming or loud cracking noises, so I take it she honoured the bet."

"That part of it," he said. "We're still banned from Brooke's."

"Serves you right," she said.

"I didn't deserve to be helped by you," he said.

"No, you didn't," she said.

"Why did you, then? It was a hell of a risk to take."

"I couldn't leave you like that," said Gwen. "There were higher powers watching me."

"Tell them to keep watching," he said. "So I guess this is it."

"Not quite," she said. "I need a ride to London Hospital. Rather quickly."

"It's not far," he said. "Are you ill?"

"No," she said. "Iris is there. I need to find her."

"What's the emergency?" he asked as they walked to his car.

"I recognised something on an old photograph in there," she said. "A ring someone used to wear when he played here."

"Why isn't he wearing it anymore?"

"Because Vanessa Reese is wearing it now."

CHAPTER 15

He stepped outside, propping the access door open with a brick that someone had left there for that very purpose. He kept his gloves on for the moment as the cold wind whipped around the roof of the Medical College. There was a low, flat parapet running around the edge, perfect for his purposes. He pulled one glove off so he could check his watch. It was eight thirty. Visiting hours ended at nine, and they'd start clearing them out of the rooms before then. The nurse had already come in to check Archie's vitals and change the bag on the IV. He could see Lily still sitting with him from this vantage point, but she'd be leaving soon.

Once the room had cleared and no one was at his bedside to sound the alarm, he would put Archie out of his misery.

He set the flower box down, then opened it and patted the rifle resting inside. No one suspects a man with a flower box in a hospital. Or in a medical school, as it turned out. No security worth a damn here. He had come in through the loading dock, didn't even have to jimmy the door to get in. Then he was just a bloke with a flower box, walking up the stairs until he reached the roof.

He wanted to smoke, but he couldn't risk being seen from across the divide between the two buildings. Like it was thirty years ago and he was back in the trenches again. Light a match, and a German sniper would blow it out for you, along with half your brains. He saw it happen more than once. He had done it himself to more than a few careless Jerries smoking whatever passed for cigarettes on their side. He had promised himself back then that if he made it out of the war alive, he'd light up every time the sun went down, just to show the world he could.

Eight fifty. Better get set up. He took out a Lee-Metford and attached the silencer and the tripod. Then he loaded it with a single .303 cartridge. He had left the tripod home when he was at the social hall. If he had had it then, he probably would have done the job cleanly the first time, although Archie was a tough old bird. Almost as tough as his dad.

He knelt and rested the tripod on the parapet, then took a quick look down the sights.

"Freeze," said a woman behind him. "I've got a gun."

"Sparks?" he exclaimed, starting to turn.

"I said 'freeze,' didn't I, Reg?" said Iris.

He stopped moving.

"I thought I took away all your guns," said Reg.

"Someone should have taken away all of yours," she said. "Put the rifle back in the box. Oh, and unload it while you're at it. Slowly. I have no compunction about shooting you in the back this time."

River pulled up in front of the hospital entrance. Gwen dashed out of the car without saying anything.

The receptionist looked up at her with concern as she ran towards her, then came skidding to a halt.

"Archie Spelling," said Gwen, gasping. "I need to see him. It's an emergency."

"Name?" asked the receptionist.

"Gwen Bainbridge. Look, you won't find me on the list, but this is urgent."

"I'm sorry, Miss Bainbridge, but if you're not on the list—"

"Could you call the nurses' station then?" asked Gwen. "Ask them to get Iris Sparks to the telephone."

"Oh, if it's her you want to speak to, she's gone," said the receptionist.

"Gone? Are you certain? It's still visiting hours."

"Short, brunette, hyperactive?"

"That sounds like her."

"She ran out a few minutes ago," said the receptionist.

"Ran?"

"Ran."

"Do you know where she went?" asked Gwen.

"I'm afraid not."

Gwen glanced out the door. River's car was gone.

"Listen," she said, turning back to the receptionist. "I know I can't go up, but tell me Mr. Spelling's room number. I'd like to send some flowers."

"That I can do," said the receptionist. "He's in three oh seven."

"Which side of the hospital is that?"

"Which side?" asked the receptionist, taken aback.

"I like to know that they'll be getting enough sunlight," said Gwen. "The flowers. Sorry, I'm obsessive about these details."

"It's in the back on the right," said the receptionist, pointing vaguely behind her. "Should be some sun in the—ma'am?"

Gwen disappeared on the run through the front doors.

Fragments of conversation surfaced in her mind as she turned the corner.

Useter be one of me dad's regular watering 'oles, wasn't it, Reg?

Oh, yeah. Your dad would 'old forth long past closing, 'im and 'is mates, and if anyone said otherwise, 'e'd counter with 'is fists. Saw some beauties of a brawl back then.

Look for higher ground with a good view, she thought, scouting the area.

You ever come 'ere, Reg?

Nah, I was usually playing snooker over at Brooke's. . . .

"'Ow'd you know it was me, Sparks?" asked Reg.

"You were in charge of security at the reception," said Iris. "You're too good at what you do to have slipped up that badly."

"That was it?"

"That wasn't it," said Iris. "The sniper picked the perfect moment for the shot: when the crackers were going off, which gave him enough noise and confusion to get away from his position without people noticing where the sound came from. Only, to do that, he had to know in advance about the crackers, and they were a surprise from Archie. But you knew about them. You knew about Archie's secret cottage, and what he had stored in the cellar. Hell, you brought them to the reception yourself! They were in the lorry along with the flowers. And the rifle, I suppose. I'm guessing you smuggled that in the box with the long-stemmed roses for the bride."

"You got a good memory, Sparks," said Reg. "How'd you know I'd be up here?"

"You made them move Archie to a private room facing the Medical College," she said. "I thought about it from a sniper's perspective. Up here for position, and wait for visitors' hours to end for the timing."

"You 'ad some sniper training, I take it."

"Some," she said. "I never got the chance to put it to use. By the way, you wouldn't have killed Archie."

"Is that so? It's a clean shot from 'ere."

"Because that isn't Archie lying there anymore. We switched in a medical training dummy they have. With the sheet up, easy to mistake at this distance. Poor Lily's been sitting next to the dummy this entire time, absolutely terrified, poor woman, but we needed to keep up appearances."

"You figured things out nicely."

"What I haven't figured out is why you shot Archie," said Iris. "You could've run. I'm sure you've got enough stashed away to make a clean escape. Archie trusted you. He depended on you for everything. I think he loved you like the father he lost. The father that you took away from him. Why shoot him when you'd been looking after him for so long?"

"Because he was protecting someone else," said Gwen, standing in the doorway. "Someone he loved. Weren't you, Reg?"

"When did she show up?" he asked.

"No idea," said Iris. "How'd you know we'd be here?"

"Higher ground, best angle, of course," said Gwen.

"Another sniper," muttered Reg.

"Hunter," said Gwen. "Grouse, rabbits, deer, that sort of thing."

"Did Sparks tell you it was me?"

"No, I came to tell her that," said Gwen. "I was at Brooke's this evening. You played there back when you were young and fresh out of the war. You even won the club championship in twenty-one and twenty-two. There are photographs of you in the VIP lounge. You were a good-looking young man back then, Reg. And Vanessa Reese was quite the head turner, wasn't she?"

"Still is," said Reg. "Will be to her dying day, I expect."

"In those pictures, you wore the same signet ring as Stanley Spelling and the other two. You can see them off to the side in one of them, toasting your victory. You were together during the war, weren't you?"

"The West 'Am Pals, God bless 'em all," he said. "We 'ad those rings made up after we got out, just for the four of us."

"You were the driver for the robberies?" asked Sparks.

Reg didn't answer.

"You were in the Reese gang then, not the Spelling," said Gwen. "So it would have been a death sentence for you had you been exposed. Then along came the robbery at the White Palace. Frankie

Reese's club. You hit them on the perfect date, after the collections had come in. You had inside information about that, didn't you? From your lover. From Vanessa, who's wearing your ring now. How long were you together by then?"

"She married Frankie too young," he said. "'E plucked 'er from the chorus when she was seventeen and 'e was almost fifty, and by the time I started coming there, 'e 'ad moved on to 'is pick of the showgirls at the White Palace, leaving 'er 'igh and dry. She wanted a divorce, but Frankie wouldn't give 'er one. So she gave us the tip. We were gonna run off together.

"The other three wanted to keep it going. They said if I didn't, they'd pass the word on to Frankie that I was part of it and Vanessa gave us the tip, and they 'eld on to my share of the loot. I went to talk to Stan, to ask 'im if 'e could talk the others into letting me out. And 'e sucker punched me, and I panicked. You never saw a more violent man with 'is fists. I thought 'e was gonna kill me. But I 'ad a knife, and that was that."

"What about the other two?" asked Iris.

"Once I done Stan, I knew the others would suspect me. I caught up with Ted, tried to make 'im tell me where the money was, but that didn't work out. Then Frankie Reese caught up with Jenks."

He shook his head at the memory.

"The Palace was closed down for renovations. Frankie put Jenks in the cellar, started building the wall around 'im over a couple of days, brick by brick. Said 'e'd let 'im starve in there if 'e didn't give up the money, but Jenks 'eld out. I was standing right there watching it with the rest of Frankie's boys, wondering if I was gonna 'ave to shoot my way out. Frankie needed someone to stand guard at night in case Jenks changed 'is mind or talked in 'is sleep. I volunteered. The moment we were alone, Jenks begged me to let 'im out, said 'e would tell Frankie about me and Vanessa if I didn't. I told 'im I would if 'e told me where the money was first. 'E did. Then I stabbed 'im."

"How did you manage to explain that to Frankie?" asked Gwen.

"I told 'im Jenks grabbed me when I was grilling 'im about the money, and I 'ad no choice. Frankie bought the story, lucky for me. 'E decided it was safer to finish bricking up Jenks where 'e was than to sneak the body out."

"Did Vanessa know about that?"

"I kept 'er out of it. When I jumped over to the Spellings, I took Archie under my wing. I 'ad found out 'e was looking for 'is dad's killer, and I kept steering 'im away from Vanessa and me. I told 'im Frankie knew it was Jenks, but 'e 'ad got out of the country. Eventually, Archie gave up, and I thought I was safe. But I stayed with 'im ever since, just to make sure that idea stayed in 'is 'ead."

"You really do play the long game, don't you, Reg?" said Iris. "You kept both Archie and Vanessa in the dark all this time."

"Which was a mistake, because she ended up selling the club to Archie before I knew about it. If she 'ad known . . . well, things would've gone different, and we wouldn't be up on this roof in the cold."

"You tried to talk him out of buying the club," Iris remembered.

"Yeah. Once Archie saw the ring on Jenks's finger, I knew it was only a matter of time before 'e figured out why I kept feeding 'im that story. 'E said 'e was thinking about cornering Vanessa. I 'ad to keep 'er safe. So I did."

He stopped and jerked his head up as a siren sounded in the distance. Then another. They were getting louder.

"Coming for me, I expect," he said.

"I'm afraid so," said Gwen. "I contacted them before I came up here."

"Yeah, well, here's the problem," said Reg, standing up. "I think Sparks is bluffing about 'aving a gun."

He turned to face her. Iris was standing six feet away, her knife in her right hand.

"No gun," she said. "Still dangerous."

"I'm still dangerous, too," he said. "I 'ave an automatic in my coat. Think you're good enough to stop me from getting it?"

"It will be a genuine pleasure to find out," said Iris.

"Iris, no!" cried Gwen, coming out from the doorway.

"Stay back, Gwen," warned Iris. "I don't want you mixed up in this."

"Every step of the way, remember?" said Gwen as she approached them. "But there's something you should know first."

"What's that?"

"He's lying about having a gun," said Gwen. "Aren't you, Reg?"

He looked at her forlornly.

"Ah, Duchess," he said. "Why'd you 'ave to show up?"

He took a step backward onto the parapet.

"Don't, Reg!" pleaded Gwen. "It isn't worth it."

"Oh, it's worth it," he said. "You should've seen 'er back then."

Then he took another step backward.

Iris started forward, but Gwen grabbed her arm.

"No," she said. "No more bad pictures. My turn to shield you."

She went to the parapet, put her hands on the edge, then carefully leaned over and looked down. She remained there for a long moment, then straightened up and returned to Iris.

"Right," said Gwen. "We had better go speak with the police now. Put your knife away. It doesn't set the proper tone."

They walked back into the building. Iris kicked the brick away, and the door slammed shut behind them.

"That's everything he told you?" asked Florey as they sat in his office the next morning.

The two women nodded.

"You should have contacted us before going up there, Miss Sparks," he said.

"I didn't know for sure I was right until I saw him," said Iris. "I didn't want to waste your valuable resources on a hunch."

"The next time you get a hunch, ring me first," said Florey. "I think you've earned my trust in them."

"I don't want there to be a next time," she said.

"I wonder if the money is still out there somewhere," he said.

"If he did get the money, he probably shared it with Vanessa to help her keep Brooke's going," said Gwen.

"We'll be looking quite closely at Mrs. Reese and her finances," said Florey. "Tell me, Mrs. Bainbridge, would you consider assisting Scotland Yard on a regular basis? Helping with interrogations and such?"

"Sorry," said Gwen. "I already have a job. And we have a New Year's ball to throw in two weeks. I need to get back to that."

"In that case, my very best wishes for the holidays to you both."

The two women walked out of New Scotland Yard, then turned north towards Mayfair.

"Why do you think Reg told us so much at the end?" asked Iris.

"I think he was still protecting Vanessa," said Gwen. "Maybe she was more involved than we knew. Maybe she persuaded him to kill the others once they threatened to expose her."

"Couldn't you tell if he was lying?"

"He had his back to me, Iris. I need to see a person's face for that to work."

"Well, I couldn't tell him to turn around, because I was bluffing about the gun," said Iris. "We were working at cross-purposes. It seems we have discovered your Achilles' heel. I shall make a point of turning away from you whenever I want to lie about anything."

Gwen suddenly grabbed her and pulled her into a fierce hug.

"Don't you ever turn away from me, Iris Sparks," she said. "I need you in my life."

The police raided Vanessa Reese's residence over Brooke's that afternoon, only to find that she had cleared out. The only thing she left behind, perched on a pillow in her opulent bedroom, was Reg's signet ring. Next to it was a note saying "Bury it with him."

The expedition to see *Peter Pan* was a tremendous success. The family returned from the theatre with the two boys chattering away, collapsing into giggles as they competed with their Captain Hook imitations. They dashed up the stairs the moment they returned, seeking their toy swords for immediate reenactment.

"A successful show, I gather," said Percival as he took Gwen's coat and accoutrements.

"Wonderful," said Gwen. "The boys will be pirates for the remainder of the holidays, I should imagine."

"A gentleman stopped by with a package for you," said Percival. "I have placed it by the tree."

"Who?" she asked.

"He didn't give his name," he said. "An admirer, I would guess."

Her curiosity was immediately piqued. She walked into the drawing room, where the tree stood proudly in one corner, covered with ornaments and some tinsel that had been packed away in the attic for years. Underneath it, amidst the packages wrapped in whatever paper could be reused for that purpose, was a long, thin box with an envelope marked "For Gwen" taped to the middle.

It isn't Christmas yet, she thought, but I'm a grown-up, so I can do as I damn well please. At least as far as the envelope goes. She plucked it carefully from the box and opened it.

It was from River.

Dear Gwen,

I got the stickpin back, thanks very much. If I keep giving it to you, will you eventually accept it?

You told me you didn't want to take my luck away. You didn't. My luck was meeting you. And true to form, I screwed it up, for which I apologise once more. You don't have to forgive me, but if the spirit of the season moves you, I would be grateful.

I don't want to be the man who took your fun away. You should play, whether as Good Gwen or Evil Gwen or Mabel Dodge or whatever name suits you, but you should play. And anyone worth her salt should have her own stick, so now you are worth yours.

My other present is this: Ellen Sealy would like to play you. For real, this time. She's thinking about picking up the ball that Vanessa dropped so abruptly and starting a ladies' league. I am enclosing her number.

I don't know what the future holds for me. The world is chaotic, but sometimes I can get it to do what I want on a smooth, green table. Keep playing, and maybe our paths will cross again someday. If they do, give us a wink, and that will be enough.

Happy Christmas,
Rodman Hilliard

Gwen reread it, a smile slowly coming to her face. Then she copied Ellen Sealy's number into her address book.

On Christmas Day, Iris curled up in bed with a murder mystery, resolutely avoiding the radio, the happy throngs, the bells ringing everywhere outside. It was a bell ringing inside that brought her out from under her quilt, padding over to answer the telephone in her sitting room, book still in hand, one finger stuck inside to keep her place.

She thought it would be Gwen, but it was her mother instead.

"Calling to wish your atheist daughter Happy Christmas?" Iris asked.

"No, I learned that lesson years ago," said Florence. "How are you holding up?"

"I have tea and crumpets and the latest Christianna Brand mystery," said Iris. "I'm as close to Heaven as a nonbeliever can get."

"Have you figured out where you're going to be living after the New Year?"

"Lily said I could stay at Archie's for a while. It would be good to have someone there to keep the pipes from freezing."

"Do you have any idea of what to do with frozen pipes?"

"None, but I'll learn."

"You could stay with me," suggested her mother.

"We both know how that would work out, but I appreciate the offer."

"How is Archie doing?"

"Still in a coma," said Iris. "I left today for Lily and his family to spend with him. I'll go over tomorrow after work. How are you?"

"Things are rather untidy at home," said Florence. "I gave Patricia her notice."

"Really? Why?"

"I found out she was the one who let that horrible reporter know about Archie coming to dinner."

"I thought that might have been the case," said Iris.

"You did? Why didn't you tell me?"

"I always assumed that you weren't listening to me," said Iris. "I won't say I'm sorry to hear she's gone. I never liked that woman. Who is doing the cooking for you now?"

"I'm doing it for myself," said Florence. "Would you like to come over for dinner?"

"You promise not to poison me?"

"Not intentionally, but you never know with my cooking."

"All right," said Iris. "This wouldn't be a sneaky way to give me a Christmas present, would it?"

"I won't, I promise. I'm not a Christmasy sort, either. But is there anything I can give you, just as a random, nonseasonal gesture of maternal goodwill?"

"As a matter of fact, there is," Iris said thoughtfully.

Six days later, the White Palace opened its doors to the throng waiting outside.

"Come in, come in out of the cold, bless you," called Mrs. Billington at the front desk. "Happy New Year! The coatroom's over there, then come check in with me. Hello, Mr. Scarborough, so glad you made it. Miss Greenleigh, how lovely you look!"

The clients of The Right Sort came through the doors of the White Palace, some eagerly, some with looks of trepidation. They presented their tickets to Mrs. Billington, who greeted each by name, checked them off her list, then directed them through the red velvet curtains, which had only been hung that afternoon, to the main room.

The paint guy had come through, as had the lumber guy, the chandelier guy, the parquet tile guy, all the guys who were at the beck and call of Spelling Enterprises for favours owed or threats made. Benny's ghost lady had swept through the building that morning, muttering incantations and scattering sachets of dried herbs, paying special attention to the final resting place of Jenks Emery, now just a blank brick wall with some shelves. The White Palace had been not only restored but revived and transformed from its original splendour. The walls were cream coloured, covered with patterns of crimson roses bursting from winding green tendrils. Fluted glass sconces glowed from the sides, and dangling from the centre of the ceiling was the massive chandelier, each crystal gleaming and the broken ones replaced. The parquet floor gleamed with fresh polish, and the stage was dominated by the grand piano, with Mervyn Stuart seated at the keys, he and the rest of his quartet resplendent in tailcoats. Servers and cigarette girls roamed the room, while bartenders stood at the ready on both ends.

At eight fifteen, the crowd was abuzz and expectant. They burst into applause as their hostesses for the evening, the co-proprietors of The Right Sort, walked up to the microphone, Gwen wearing a crêpe de chine Molyneux evening gown the colour of sea-foam, rescued from a cedar chest, unworn since before the war, and Iris, despite the cold weather, in a short black frock that showed her legs to good effect.

"Welcome to the first annual Right Sort Hopeful Hearts New Year's Ball!" cried Gwen. "My goodness, that's a lot of words put together, isn't it? It has been a tumultuous year for all of us, but the world is at peace now and things can only get better."

"It is also the first New Year for our little venture," said Iris. "I am happy to say that we are making a go of it, and that is thanks to all of you. It seems to be working! We had fifteen marriages this year, and as many engaged couples! Many of them are here tonight. I see the Farnhams, the Perrys, and, my goodness, the Cornwalls! And let's give a rousing round of applause for our latest married couple, the Aldertons, Tish and Bernie!"

Tish and Bernie waved and blew kisses to the stage.

"We would like to thank Spelling Enterprises for the yeoman's work they have done getting this place ready in time," said Gwen. "Let us all take a moment for a brief prayer for the recovery of Mr. Spelling, who is in hospital."

There was a moment of silence, and looks of gratitude on Tish's and Bernie's faces.

"Now, let the festivities commence!" said Gwen. "Mix, mingle, meet, drink, dance, and discover. But I have a mission for you all. I happen to know that the numbers of single men and single women here are exactly the same. In less than four hours, we will start a new year, so by the stroke of midnight, I want all of you to find someone to kiss!"

There were cries of shock and delight from the assemblage.

"It doesn't have to go anywhere beyond that," she continued. "It may be only for a moment, but it could be the beginning of a lifetime. The important thing is that whatever else happens in 1947, you are starting it with a kiss."

"Leave the engaged and married couples out of it!" Iris warned them sternly.

"We will have party games to help you along," said Gwen. "And at eleven forty-five I will summon those who haven't made a connection yet to the dance floor and match you according to my whim. No one leaves this room unkissed tonight!"

There were cheers at that.

"Ladies and gentlemen, let me introduce an old friend and a marvellous musician, Mr. Mervyn Stuart!"

Mervyn counted off, the drummer launched into a Latin beat on a pair of bongos, and the song "Coax Me a Little Bit" filled the room.

The two women divided the hostessing chores. Iris scurried around the kitchen and monitored the staff while Gwen roamed through the ballroom, making sure everyone was having a good time. Mervyn provided a good mix of standards and new songs, and even got the crowd behind his efforts to persuade Gwen to come to the microphone for one number. She chose "We'll Meet Again," which she delivered with grace, bringing everyone in for the final chorus, conducting them with outstretched arms.

She even let herself be brought onto the dance floor, although she didn't want to take up too many spots with eligible bachelors. She saved one dance for Simon, who was there with Bitsy Sedgewick.

"This makes your fourth date together," she said as they waltzed about. "Going well?"

"I think she likes me," said Simon. "It is still too early to say. She was very excited about coming here tonight. She wanted to see the spot where the body was found right away."

"She knew about that?" Gwen exclaimed with dismay.

"Oh, I think everyone knows about it by now," he said with a grin. "It's helped make the party a hit."

"How perverse," said Gwen. "Well, if anyone asks me about it, I am merely going to look mysterious and say nothing."

"You still haven't told me everything about it," said Simon.

"No. And I'd rather not revisit it."

"Then I will not press you further," he said as the music slowed to a finish.

He gave her one last twirl, then released her and went back to his date.

At eleven thirty, Iris came up to her, coat in hand, and they stood together for a moment, watching the crowd whirling about.

"You were right," said Iris. "This was a wonderful idea."

"Thank you," said Gwen. "I think we're going to come out ahead financially after all is said and done. There's Benny at the door."

"That's my ride," said Iris. "Are you sure you can manage without me?"

"Go," commanded Gwen. "Happy New Year!"

"Happy New Year," said Iris, giving her a quick hug. "See you in 1947."

She slipped through the crowd into the foyer. Benny helped her on with her coat, then the two of them went outside to where his car was waiting.

"Thank you for doing this," she said as she sat in the passenger seat.

"It's my honour, Sparks," he replied as he sat behind the wheel and started the engine.

"How are things on Wapping Wall?"

"We've been running things by committee, more or less," he said as he drove. "There was never any third-in-command after Archie and Reg. The fellers are eyeing each other, waiting to see 'oo makes a move first."

"You don't have any interest in the job?"

"'Ell, no!" he said. "I do what I do. I keep track of where everyone is, and I drive."

"You drive very well," she said.

"I should. Reg taught me."

"I never knew that," said Iris. "This must be hard for you."

"Life is 'ard," he said. "But sometimes there's dancing."

"I'll try to remember that."

"Funny thing," he said. "Some of us were chatting the other day about 'oo would be the best candidate to run the gang, and someone brought your name up."

"That must have got a laugh out of everyone."

"I won't lie, there was a lot of guys in favour of it," he said, grinning at her. "Shall I put you up for the job?"

"I'll pass, thanks," said Iris. "It's been complicated enough being a gangster's girl."

It was a short trip to the hospital. When he pulled up, she leaned over and kissed him on the cheek.

"Happy New Year, Benny," she said.

"You, too, Sparks," he said. "Tell Archie 'ello from me."

Visiting hours were long past, but the woman at the front desk wasn't surprised to see her.

"You must be Miss Sparks," she said. "Mr. Spelling's girlfriend."

"Fiancée," said Iris, holding up her hand so the other woman could see the ring.

"Fiancée, of course. One minute while I ring Mr. Armbruster."

She picked up her phone and dialled an extension. A few minutes later, Mr. Armbruster, the night manager, came to the desk.

"I'll bring you up, Miss Sparks," he said.

"Thank you. It's good of you to do this on New Year's Eve."

"Just another Tuesday night at the hospital," he said as he brought her to the lift. "Having a visitor this late is against the rules of course, but when a member of Parliament asks us to make an exception, we accommodate her. It's good to have friends in high places."

"Yes," said Iris. "Sometimes it is."

Gwen quickly sorted the remaining unmatched into couples. When she got to the last two, she paused.

"Lest everyone think Miss Buckley and Mr. Baugh are the final ones picked, you should all know that I was planning to match them up before tonight," she announced. "The Fates have decreed it! Everyone go get a glass of champagne! It's almost midnight!"

The crowd queued up, two by two, at both ends where the bartenders had poured bubbly into wineglasses, which were the best the glassware guy could do.

Not as good as flutes, but better than paper cups, thought Gwen as she took the stage.

A radio was wheeled out.

"Hush, everybody!" she said as she turned it on.

The countdown began. Gwen joined it on the microphone, and it was quickly picked up by the entire crowd, guests and workers alike.

". . . three, two, one! Happy New Year!" she cried.

The room erupted in cheers, which were quickly muffled as each couple swept into a kiss, some awkwardly with quick pecks, many giggling through it, others seizing the moment and putting everything they had into it.

Mervyn played a fanfare, then the quartet began "Auld Lang Syne."

Gwen stood to the side of the stage, absorbing it all, letting the waves of happiness sweep through her as the tears ran freely down her cheeks.

"Gwen," came a voice from behind her, one she knew well.

She turned to see Sally standing in the wings, dressed impeccably in his dinner jacket.

"How did you sneak in here unnoticed?" she demanded.

"Parachuted from ten thousand feet through the searchlights onto the roof, rappelled down into an open window, chloroformed a few guards, and here I am," he said blithely. "You know, the usual."

"Liar. You sweet-talked Mrs. Billington into letting you in," said Gwen.

"She does adore me," he confessed. "I happened to notice that while you have taken care of all of your vast number of clients, you neglected to arrange for a kiss for yourself. I've decided that I am the man for the job."

"Are you?"

"I am," he said. "I know it may only be for a moment, as you said earlier, but you should have that moment, at least. I would like there to be many more such moments. I know that I made mistakes in my first clumsy forays with you. I have spent a large part of my life trying to be someone I'm not and I wanted you to be someone who would match that person. No more of that. Let's not make each other into anything, but find out who we are instead. I warn you that it may be a terrifying journey in my case."

She walked up to him and put her arms around him.

"That's what makes it fun," she said softly.

From his vantage point on the floor by the front of the stage, Walter Prendergast watched them kiss, a bouquet of flowers clutched in his hands. Then he turned and started away, bumping into a woman who was staggering tipsily from the dance floor.

"Sorry," he said, then he shoved the flowers at her. "Here."

"Gosh, thanks," she said, putting them to her face and sniffing them. "Did you get your kiss all right? I've got more to spare if you haven't."

"I'm fine," he said.

"How about a dance then?" she asked hopefully.

"I'm not much of a dancer," he said. "Sorry."

"Happy New Year!" she called after him as he walked out of the ballroom.

He collected his coat, then disappeared out into the night.

Iris listened to the church bells ring in the New Year as she lay next to Archie on his hospital bed.

"Can you hear them, Archie?" she asked. "You made it to 1947 against all odds. Well done! Now, pay attention."

She took his hand and pressed it on top of her left.

"Do you feel that, Archie?" she asked. "That's the ring you gave me. My answer to your unasked question is yes. I am wearing your ring, and I will marry you and love you for the rest of our lives. I will live with you in your house, and we will have brilliant, mischievous children who will break all the rules and go on to do wonderful and terrible things in the world. I will marry you, Archie Spelling. But you have to wake up for that to happen, do you hear me? You have to wake up."

She nestled into him, wrapping her arm carefully around his chest, and pressed her face against his cheek. Then she kissed him gently and clung to him, inhaling his scent into her nostrils, holding it for as long as she could, refusing to let it go.

ACKNOWLEDGMENTS

In addition to sources cited in previous books, the author would like to acknowledge the following:

For the contemporaneous methods of treating gunshot wounds, "Gunshot Wounds of the Chest: A Review of Two Hundred and Eighty Cases," Harry G. Hardt Jr., M.D., and Lindon Seed, M.D. *Archives of Surgery*, v. 44, no. 5, May 1942.

Zoo-related questions were answered by Natasha Wakely, archivist for the Zoological Society of London.

Brick-related questions were answered by Michael Hammett, enquiries secretary for the British Brick Society. Yes, there is one!

Faithful fan and friend Lesley Keech read and commented on early attempts at writing snooker scenes. The author has also spent much too much time watching videos of Ronnie O'Sullivan, who is to snooker what Pelé was to football.

This would be a most appropriate time to thank my editor, Keith Kahla, without whom this series would never have come into existence. I would also like to thank everyone else at St. Martin's Minotaur, whether in editorial, design, production, or marketing, with particular thanks to Martha Schwartz, the copyeditor for most of the series, who has pulled me from the fire or held my feet over it on too many occasions to list. Any errors left over from her scrutiny belong to me and me alone.

And finally, as always, to my spouse, who put up with me in a small, confined space as I wrote this, and who came up with the title after all other attempts had failed.

ABOUT THE AUTHOR

ALLISON MONTCLAIR grew up devouring hand-me-down Agatha Christie paperbacks and James Bond movies. As a result of this deplorable upbringing, Montclair became addicted to tales of crime, intrigue, and espionage. Montclair now spends their spare time poking through the corners, nooks, and crannies of history, searching for the odd mysterious bits and transforming them into novels of their own.